The Priest's Tale

The Ottoman Cycle Book Two

Revised edition

by S. J. A. Turney

For Prue

I would like to thank everyone who has been instrumental in this book seeing the light of day in its final form, as well as all those people who have continually supported me during its creation: Robin, Alun, Barry, Nick, David, Miriam and of course Jenny and Tracey and once again my little imps Marcus and Callie who interrupted me at the most opportune moments, driving me to wonderful distraction. Also, the fabulous members of the Historical Writers' Association, who are supportive and helpful as ever.

Cover image by J Caleb Designs.
Cover design by Dave Slaney.
Revised Ed. editing courtesy of Canelo.
Many thanks to all concerned.

Also by S. J. A. Turney:

The Marius' Mules Series

Marius' Mules I: The Invasion of Gaul (2009)
Marius' Mules II: The Belgae (2010)
Marius' Mules III: Gallia Invicta (2011)
Marius' Mules IV: Conspiracy of Eagles (2012)
Marius' Mules V: Hades' Gate (2013)
Marius' Mules VI: Caesar's Vow (2014)
Marius' Mules: Prelude to War (2014)
Marius' Mules VII: The Great Revolt (2014)
Marius' Mules VIII: Sons of Taranis (2015)
Marius' Mules IX: Pax Gallica (2016)
Marius' Mules X: Fields of Mars (2017)

The Praetorian Series

The Great Game (2015)
The Price of Treason (2015)
Eagles of Dacia (Autumn 2017)

The Ottoman Cycle

The Thief's Tale (2013)
The Priest's Tale (2013)
The Assassin's Tale (2014)
The Pasha's Tale (2015)

Tales of the Empire

Interregnum (2009)
Ironroot (2010)
Dark Empress (2011)
Insurgency (2016)
Invasion (2017)

Roman Adventures (Children's Roman fiction with Dave Slaney)

Crocodile Legion (2016)
Pirate Legion (Summer 2017)

Short story compilations & contributions:

Tales of Ancient Rome vol. 1 - S.J.A. Turney (2011)
Tortured Hearts vol 1 - Various (2012)
Tortured Hearts vol 2 - Various (2012)
Temporal Tales - Various (2013)
A Year of Ravens - Various (2015)
A Song of War – Various (Oct 2016)

For more information visit http://www.sjaturney.co.uk/
or http://www.facebook.com/SJATurney
or follow Simon on Twitter @SJATurney

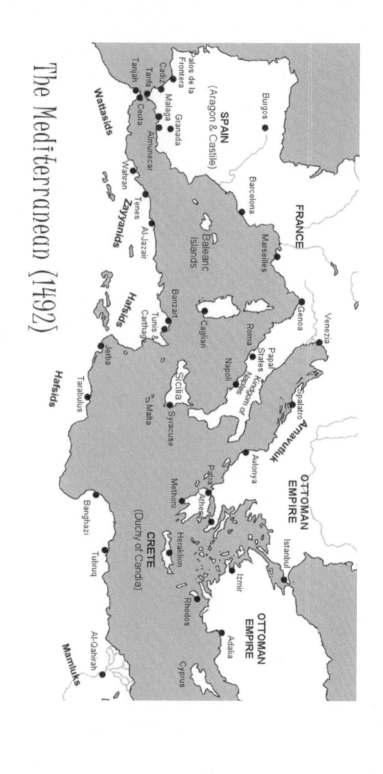

The Mediterranean (1492)

SPAIN
(Aragon & Castile)

Burgos

Barcelona

FRANCE

Marseilles

Genoa

Venezia

Spalatro

Palos de la
Frontera
Cadiz
Malaga
Granada
Tarifa
Tanjah
Ceuta
Almunecar
Wahran
Tenes
Al-Jazair

Wattasids

Zayyanids

Balearic
Islands

Cagliari

Roma
**Papal
States**
**Kingdom of
Naples**
Napoli

Banzart
Tunis &
Carthage
Hafsids

Jerba

Tarabulus

Hafsids

Sicilia
Syracuse
Malta

Banghazi

Tubruq

CRETE
(Duchy of Candia)

Heraklion

Al-Qahirah

Mamluks

Anavulluk

Avlonya
Patras
Athens
Methoni

Istanbul

Izmir

Rhodos

Adalia

Cyprus

**OTTOMAN
EMPIRE**

**OTTOMAN
EMPIRE**

Prologos

Winter, early 1492. Bay of Al-Jazair (Algiers)

Ahmed Kemaleddin, the Reis – captain – of the Ottoman Iberian expedition, leaned on the rail of his *kadirga* galley, basking in the glow of the sun reflected off the turquoise waters. The awning that covered the aft section of the ship provided blessed relief from the sun's blasting rays and, combined with the sea breeze, provided most relaxing and pleasant conditions.

Kemal Reis – for such was he known – felt neither relaxed, nor pleasant.

For five years he had sailed the waters of the western sea between the cursed land of Spain, the semi-hostile coast of Africa, and the dangerous shores of Italia. Since being dispatched from Istanbul with a fleet of twenty-two ships and a sizeable force of soldiers to help the beleaguered Emir of Granada defend his lands from the brutal expansionism of the Christian rulers of Aragon and Castile, he had watched the Arab world in the west crumble and fail beneath the iron-shod boot of the hated Fernando and Isabella.

But the loss of Granada and the end of Muslim rule in the peninsula was not what soured Kemal's mood.

1

For three more years he had fought on in the desperate hope that something could be saved from the failure of the western campaigns. He had landed troops in areas with small Christian garrisons and sacked coastal towns that had until recently been staunch Muslim strongholds. And yet nothing had arrested the decline. The Iberian Peninsula remained Christian and its new despots set about the removal of all that offended their Christian noses. In the end, Kemal had admitted defeat and sent the bulk of the fleet east, back to Istanbul and the Sultan, himself remaining behind with a small flotilla of three ships to carry out the last tasks of an unsuccessful expedition.

But the failure of his attempts and the disbanding of his forces were not what soured Kemal's mood.

For the past two years Kemal Reis and his subordinate captains, Etci Hassan and Salih Bin Abdullah, had forged routes through the increasingly hostile waters of the western sea, finding desperate Muslim refugees forced out of their homes after seven centuries of peaceful life, and ferrying them to the ports of sympathetic rulers, along with Jews who were being systematically eradicated in the 'New Spain' and who saw more of a hopeful future with Muslim rulers than with their new Jesuit-driven Christian overlords. And even this brought endless difficulties for Kemal, the Hafsid, Zayyanid, Wattasid and Mamluk dynasties who controlled the entire southern boundary of the sea bearing no love for the Ottoman Empire.

But the difficulties of trying to save the last of the old world in the face of the unnecessary hostility of the new were not what soured Kemal's mood.

No.

What soured Kemal's mood on such a glorious morning was the man standing four feet along the rail, seething with a resentment and barely controlled rage: Etci Hassan. One of his two remaining subordinates and the captain of the kadirga *Yarim Ay*.

The half dozen ships' boats were returning across the clear waters from the great port of Al-Jazair, having delivered the last of the Muslim refugees rescued from the Balearic Islands, after which the diminished fleet of the Ottoman force could move on.

The question was: where to?

Kemal had discussed the matter at length the previous evening with his subordinate Salih, and they were of a mind that it was worth continuing on their current path for the foreseeable future. So long as good Muslims – and well-paying Jews – languished in distress, it was Kemal's duty to ferry them to safety despite his original objective of saving Granada having long evaporated. Then, and only then, when the last of the displaced exiles were seen to safety, would the three ships sail east and return to the Sultan for a new assignment. It was what any honourable officer of the Ottoman navy would do. Salih, always a friend as much as a colleague, had been wholeheartedly supportive.

Yet despite the fact that Kemal solidly outranked his fellow captains, he had spent a night in discomfort, dreading the conversation with Hassan this morning. And with good reason.

Etci Hassan had listened sullenly as his commander had explained his intentions and the plan for the next season's campaigning. More of the same, in effect. Kemal had watched the irritation slowly building in the other captain's disconcerting eyes, his mouth taking on a grim set, his eyelid twitching and flickering.

Now, for the past half-minute, the pair had lapsed into an uncomfortable silence. Kemal could feel Hassan standing like a taut siege weapon, waiting to unleash his barbed tongue upon his senior, but unwilling to break etiquette by speaking without being bidden.

Kemal Reis took a deep breath, savouring the fresh sea air.

'Speak.'

As though the dam of his rage had been breached, Etci Hassan turned and raised his hands, his voice a low, dangerous hiss, his perturbing cold gaze intense.

'In a lesser captain I would say the decision was foolish in the extreme, and even cowardly.'

A carefully worded attack. Hassan was no fool.

'Explain.' There was no real need. Kemal knew his subordinate's mind well, but the man would hopefully lose some of his excess rage and bile if he could voice it openly.

'The west is lost. What we do now is the job of the defeated, of failures. We are warriors – officers in the Ottoman navy, not ferrymen. Our place is behind the bow and the sword and the gun, bringing death to the infidel and the light of Allah and the blessed Sultan to the dogs who would quash our culture.'

Despite the bile in the words, Kemal had to admire the eloquence of the rhetoric. Hassan's words would sway many a good Turk.

'I have no love for the Christian scourge, Hassan, and you know that. We have fought them all we can, but we are far from our world and all but surrounded by theirs. We are but three kadirga and the very idea of making war against the Christians now is beyond foolish. I was granted the position of defender of the Granada Emirate and my duty is clear: to see the last survivors of that land to safety before I move on.'

3

'The Granada Emirate is *gone*, my Lord Reis. The blessed crescents are torn down and melted for their cannon, replaced with their ridiculous crosses. The mosques are ruined, the mihrabs smashed and filled with statues of their blasphemous 'Maria'. You cling to a world that has died, master. Bury it in the hatred it deserves and turn your eyes to the glory or war, I beg of you.'

'Have a care, Hassan. You overstep.'

Still vibrating slightly with coiled anger, Hassan bowed respectfully, his teeth clenched.

'My apologies, Lord. You know how I feel.'

'I do. And I sympathise, in truth. But the task here is not yet complete and I will not abandon my position, no matter how untenable, until the job is done. Then and only then will we return east and see what the glorious Bayezid, may Allah bless his line for a thousand years, has in mind for us next. Would you have us return with an incomplete mission? Do you think the great Sultan will favour us then?'

'Respectfully, Lord Reis, I believe the Sultan will condemn us for our failure no matter when we do so. Returning east is as much accepting failure as continuing to playing ferryman to the lost here. What we should do is sack the ports of the Christian dogs and sink their ships. We should attack their transports and take their goods. We should enslave the infidels and sell them to the Mamluks to whip to death. We have an opportunity to bring a true fear of the Empire to our enemies, along with the word of the Prophet – may the peace and blessings of Allah be upon him – while making ourselves ever richer and more powerful.'

Kemal felt his blood chill as the fire of jihad danced in his subordinate's ordinarily cold eyes.

'Then,' Hassan continued, the spittle of the fanatic wetting his lips, 'when we have treasures beyond imagining and captured ships and gold and the heads of the great lords of the west rotting on spears, we can return to the Sultan in glory and he will laud our success, rather than breaking us on the hooks for our failure. Do you not see?'

Kemal turned slowly.

'I see that you advocate piracy and slavery in the name of the glorious Sultan.'

'It is not piracy if we are at war, Lord.'

It was a convincing argument, Kemal had to acknowledge. Many an Ottoman captain would be swayed by it, and the political situation here in the west was vague enough and hostile enough that a clever captain would be able to officially justify almost any level of depraved behaviour. But Kemal had accepted a commission, and he would not turn to the ways of the pirate until the Sultan himself gave him leave. His duty was clear.

'My mind is made up, Hassan. We will tarry here a year or more yet, to see our work done. Then, and only then, will we return to Istanbul and the Sultan. We will have no small amount of coin from the saving of the Jews, and he will be pleased with this. Once we return, you may seek a position with another commander if our next duty is not to your liking, but until we stand before the blessed Bayezid you are my subordinate and will obey my word.'

Hassan's eyelid flickered slightly faster as he lowered his head respectfully.

'Yes, my Lord Reis.'

Once more, Kemal turned to the beautiful turquoise waters of the bay and the boats crossing back to their ships. The discipline and chain of command of the Ottoman navy forced the other captain's acceptance, and Hassan would do as he was bidden, but beyond that, Kemal would sooner trust a Popish bishop than his own subordinate. Now would be an excellent time to part ways temporarily, until the man had calmed enough to accept his duty. Fortunately, Kemal had a task of some urgency that would keep the man away for some time.

'Our supplies are low, Hassan.'

With such a diminished fleet, the captains were no longer powerful enough to sack villages and towns for the requisite goods, and the nearest friendly port for resupply was far to the east. The lords of the African lands would be unlikely to help and, even if they did, their prices would be extortionate.

'They are, my Lord Reis.'

'Salih and I will run the coast of Spain once more for refugees. To save you such a bitter duty, I would have you sail east to Avlonya and collect fresh supplies for our campaign.'

'You would turn me into a merchant, my Lord Reis? A beast of burden?'

'Would you rather be a ferryman of the Jews?'

Kemal watched the turmoil in his subordinate's expression. For three heartbeats, Hassan wrestled with the choice between two duties he considered equally onerous. Finally, something seemed to change in his uncanny eyes, and he nodded his head respectfully.

'Of course, Reis. I will travel to Avlonya and bring back as many supplies as my kadirga will hold. I will require some of the 'Jew-saving'

5

money, of course. And the journey will be long and dangerous, passing the Hafsid coast and the land of the Popes, so I may be some time.'

Kemal wondered for a moment whether allowing Hassan to slip the leash might be a poor decision, but the benefits of his absence likely outweighed the burdens. Something about the man had changed so instantly. Etci Hassan seemed almost *eager*.

'Return before Ramadan and you will find us at our usual rally point in the Bab el Zakat.'

Hassan nodded once more and turned without further acknowledgement, marching away purposefully towards the small skiff that would ferry him back to his own ship. Kemal Reis watched him go, hardly daring to breathe until the man was aboard the small boat and bouncing across the waves towards the kadirga anchored nearby.

'That went well then?'

Kemal turned at the soft spoken words. Salih Bin Abdullah had remained out of sight close by throughout the exchange and had waited patiently until his counterpart had left before returning to the open deck. It was unusual – and certainly disrespectful – to address the Reis with no honorific, though Kemal had granted his friend such permission whenever they were alone.

Salih was smiling at the expression on his commander's face, and Kemal realised that he must look as though he had chewed a lemon.

'It could have been better, Salih.'

'He is going to be trouble, that one. He lusts after command. He would see himself in your place, Kemal Reis.'

'He would not dare defy his commander, Salih. If word of it reached the Sultan, Hassan would be split in two for mutiny.' Kemal nodded to himself, though in truth he was not so sure. 'Anyway, I have arranged for him to be blessedly absent for a few months, fetching our supplies from Arnavutluk. What harm can he do on a simple supply mission?'

Salih raised an eyebrow as he turned and watched the small skiff rising and dipping as it approached the twin-masted, black-and-red-painted kadirga of Etci 'The Butcher' Hassan.

'What harm indeed.'

Chapter One - Of changes wrought in tranquillity

May 1492. Heraklion, Duchy of Candia (Venetian Crete).

The sun beat down mercilessly on the small whitewashed courtyard as Skiouros staggered backwards, dust and gravel kicked up into the sizzling air and momentarily obscuring the man facing him across the dusty gravelled flags. The young Greek narrowed his eyes, partially from the glare of the reflected rays bouncing off the dazzling white walls and partially from puzzlement as to how the man had managed to throw him off balance yet again.

Don Diego de Teba stood calm and composed, his elegant black and silver doublet and hose untouched by the endless white dust, his neat beard and coiled black hair glistening in the sun, the only sign of their activity a fine film of grey dust on the lower half of his high, black leather boots. His beautiful sword carved arcs and circles in the air languidly as he waited for Skiouros to recover.

The Greek looked down at his own dishevelled figure and noted with dismay that he had two new rents in the shirt that had cost him so much half a year earlier – more stitching required – but the thing that irritated him most was the fact that he was as dirty and dishevelled as Don Diego was neat and clean. The dust and grit was so ingrained in his clothes it seemed to form part of the very fabric. He looked like the poorer cousin of one of the peasants who worked the fields outside the walls. Poking a finger into one of the neat cuts in his shirt he had to grudgingly admire the man's abilities. In the preceding weeks, Don Diego had slashed, poked and rent Skiouros' shirts, doublet, breeches and even his boots and had managed to draw blood only once, even that a bare scratch that was now long gone.

'Your right high guard is still very open and unstable. You are fast and accurate to thrust from it, but you are unable to hold the guard or move into any other defensive position without making yourself a big fat target.'

Skiouros glowered at his teacher, glancing around the colonnade and the gates that sealed in the courtyard to make sure that no one was witnessing his latest admonishment. As usual the dusty grey figure of the Romani beggar lurked at the outside gate like a vulture waiting for his pickings. Worse than simply being upbraided was the fact that Skiouros' grasp of the flouncy Italian tongue was still new and troubled, and Don Diego – not a native speaker himself – made sure to speak slowly and to clearly enunciate each word so that his pupil understood. That, of course, meant that any passer-by had plenty of time to listen to detailed accounts of what a clumsy, oat-brained oaf he was with a sword.

Skiouros sighed as he brushed the worst of the dust from his formerly expensive clothes. For more than a year now he had been taking lessons with the sword, and yet every day brought some fresh humiliation. The early lessons had been brutal and hard, but were at least basic and had been formed of the bulk of standard moves a man with a blade needed to know, beyond which end to stick in the enemy. Iannis had been a tough but likeable teacher, having been pensioned out of his military service for the Duke of Candia following a harrowing illness that had almost claimed his life. A resurgence in that sickness had laid him low again almost two months ago and he had been forced to relinquish his position as Skiouros' teacher. Briefly, the young Greek had paid a local hoodlum instead, but Draco had proved to be more handy with the seedier side of fighting than the use of a blade, and so finally Skiouros had come to retain Don Diego and accept his teachings. Despite that, he still saw Draco once a week for a little less noble instruction – it was always worth knowing a few extra unexpected tricks.

'My right high guard,' Skiouros replied, wrapping his tongue with some effort around the strange language, 'is somewhat hampered by the fact that you have me wielding a sword that appears to weigh the same as a pregnant cow. My arm shakes when I try to hold it aloft.'

Don Diego gave his customary sneering smile as he carved figure eights in the air, twisting the ends of his moustaches with his free hand.

'Your Greek swords are lighter, but they are also shorter and less protective.' Don Diego paused in his endless whirling of steel to indicate the gleaming blade that his pupil would be willing to wager cost more money than Skiouros had ever held. 'The Spanish rapier,' the Don went on, 'is a more elegant sword with a longer reach, a more flexible blade and side rings for extra finger protection and grip. It is becoming the norm for the gentry of Spain and presents a good, effective and graceful weapon when compared with the glorified meat cleaver developed here in the east.'

'I don't need to look elegant. I just need to be able to fight.'

'There is no point, young Greek, in learning to do something poorly. Learn correctly or decide not to learn at all.'

Skiouros swished saliva around his mouth for a moment and spat the dusty dryness out onto the floor, causing the Spaniard to roll his eyes in disapproval.

'Come on, then. Let's try again.'

Skiouros stepped forward and raised the heavy, gleaming Spanish blade so that he gripped the hilt close to his chin, left foot extended forward for stability and the sword point slightly inclined down towards Don Diego's groin.

'Up! Up!'

Mumbling curses in his native Greek, Skiouros raised the tip.

'The whole blade, boy. Not just the tip. Hold it by your ear!'

With more grumbles and muttering, Skiouros lifted the blade, feeling his muscles complaining at the weight. A distant carillon from the bells of Saints Petros and Paulos told him that the day's lesson was almost over and he felt an overwhelming sensation of relief.

A shimmering line of gleaming sunlight sliced a neat line through his shirt close to the waist. Skiouros' mind drew back from the impending end of the lesson to realise that he'd been struck as his mind drifted. Damn the Spaniard!

'What was that?' he snapped.

'That was a reminder that I am here, costing you money,' Don Diego laughed, 'and that daydreaming is a good way to get yourself killed in a fight. Concentrate!'

Skiouros glared at the man, noting with irritation how the tip of his own sword wavered and dropped slightly in front of him as he seethed.

'I am going to come in from the left,' the Spaniard announced, 'and fast. Show me how quickly you can bring the blade down to block.'

Skiouros narrowed his eyes. There was something about the Spaniard's stance and his manner that suggested a lie. Skiouros had always been good at recognising lies – it was a prime requisite of the professional liar.

A strange silence descended, broken only by the song of a contented bird in one of the trees just beyond the wall, the dying echo of the church bells and the constant chirring of the cicadas that hummed and buzzed across the whole island. The sun continued to sizzle in the cloudless sapphire sky, causing the ground to shimmer in the heat.

And Don Diego de Teba lunged, uncoiling so fast that he blurred, moving with the grace and speed of a hunting bird. His blade flashed out, coming round not from the left as he'd said, but from the right. Though he'd not the time to smile, somewhere inside Skiouros congratulated himself on his powers of observation as his rapier dropped in the path of the Spaniard's strike. The swords met in a loud ring of steel and then a rasp as the blades grated along one another before they came away once more.

Why he did what he did next, Skiouros wasn't entirely sure, other than the fact that the ever-superior Spaniard had just pissed him off a little too much today, or possibly that he felt the need to show his ability in some way other than badly.

As Don Diego swept his blade away, spinning in order to present himself for the next move, Skiouros ignored the standard instruction to come straight back up into a guard position as the Spaniard would always have it and, instead, took a heavy step forward, following closely the retreating master and bringing his heavy boot heel down upon the man's foot, causing him to stumble and lose his cool. With a smooth motion, Skiouros lunged out with his loosely-held rapier and flicked Don Diego's own blade from his grasp as the man staggered.

The Spaniard lurched to a halt and brought himself up straight, one eyebrow arched in a supercilious manner. Skiouros dipped to the floor and retrieved the teacher's blade from the dust, swishing it a few times before reversing the sword and offering the hilt back to the man.

'What, may I ask, was that?' Don Diego enquired in a low voice, and considerably faster than his usual slow, deliberate instructive tone.

'That,' Skiouros spat with a malicious grin, 'was a move that my *other* instructor gifted me.'

The Spaniard took his blade and examined it for damage from the gravel, noting with relief that the beautiful silvered hilt was still gleaming and unmarked.

'That was the act of a street brute. No gentleman of Spain would stoop to such base thuggery.'

Skiouros rolled his shoulders.

'If I were feeling malevolent I might be tempted to ask what such a fine Spanish gentleman as yourself was doing so far from home trading his skills as a sellsword?'

'Some stones are best left unturned, young Greek. Leave it at that.'

'Don Diego, since I require only the ability to defend myself and fight off would-be attackers, I fail to see the need to learn the etiquette of gentlemanly swordsmanship. I will never move in such circles and I have no need to ever visit your homeland, my sights being set on closer goals than Spain. Perhaps you could concentrate more on the practical than the elegant?'

'Perhaps the time has come to sever our arrangement, if you feel you are not learning what you need, young man?'

Don Diego stepped back into the shade of the colonnade, wiping his blade on a linen square and then sheathing it at his waist. Skiouros stood for a long moment, sword in his hand, until the strange spell was broken by the bells of the great Saint Titus Cathedral picking up the ringing of the hour from the dying echoes of the Church of Saints Petros and Paulos, which was always two minutes early. As the fresh clanging filled the air, Skiouros nodded.

'I fear my time for lessons may be coming to an end anyway, Don Diego, through no fault or failing of yours. Time presses and a long-set-aside task looms in the coming days. If I find that I have the time and funding to continue I will seek you out, if that is acceptable.'

The Spaniard pursed his lips and gave a curt nod. 'Unless my services have been fully retained elsewhere I am still amenable to our arrangement.'

As Don Diego sketched an elegant bow and stepped away into the darkness of the colonnade and the doors it concealed, Skiouros sheathed his own blade and wiped the patina of sweat from his brow – a futile move that simply made room for the next wave of perspiration that broke

11

across his hairline. It really was remarkable what a difference in weather he had experienced since leaving Istanbul almost a year and a half ago and travelling down here to this ancient island that formed the southern arc of the Greek world, albeit under Italian mastery these days.

The winters were temperate, lacking the snow that occasionally cursed the new Ottoman capital, providing only regular – even warm – rain. The summers seemed to present an endless sky of bright, deep blue and a searing heat that blanched the world and sapped the energy of its inhabitants. Crete seemed to suffer a sun-inspired languor that would be abhorrent to the busy world of Istanbul.

He would be sad to leave, but leave he must – and soon too.

Walking across to the horse trough at the side of the courtyard, Skiouros bent double and dipped his head in, straightening and throwing it back so that the tangled, unkempt hair – too long to be fashionable and too short to be seen as exotic – sprayed a diamond stream of droplets through the air – droplets that hissed into steam almost as soon as they hit the ground. Blinking away the water, Skiouros rubbed his face with sun-tanned hands and straightened before collecting his doublet from the stone bench and making for the gate, noting with some satisfaction that the ragged Romani had disappeared.

Should he visit Lykaion?

Time was not an issue – he could easily spare five minutes to dip into the great church of Saint Titus and spend a moment in deep conversation with the ornate yet featureless casket that held his brother's mortal remains. The priests and monks at the church had become more than used to his daily visits over the past year and a half, expressing their admiration at the diligence with which the young man paid reverence to the hallowed relic. They would piss their cassocks if they knew the truth: that the head of Saint Theodoros – which sat in blessed state close by the sacred and powerful head of Saint Titus – was in fact the head of Lykaion, son of Nikos the farmer, a former Janissary in the Ottoman army. What they did not know could not hurt them.

Perhaps he would visit later.

His ever-growing understanding of the world of the Catholic church and its denizens, gleaned over a year and a half of daily visits, reminded him that the great feast of Annunciation fell on the morrow, and the church would be in a state of organised chaos in preparation.

With his almost special relationship to the church of Saint Titus – he was on name terms with many of the priests – there was a good chance he would be roped into some role for the festival if he poked his face into the cathedral.

No. He'd seen Lykaion after breaking his fast, while the sun had still been mercifully cool, and his brother was going nowhere. He could wait 'til the morning now. Once the festival had begun, most of the activity would take place in the streets and the church itself would be a haven of peace among the madness until the time came for the services to draw the population back in.

For now there were other matters upon which to ponder – matters on which he was unsure of Lykaion's ability to help.

Matters of the future.

Running his hands through his tangled hair to wring the bulk of the moisture from it, Skiouros opened the iron catch and swung the gate wide, stepping out into the narrow street, bounded on both sides by pale stone buildings, many whitewashed against the heat. The road was of old, flattened and smooth cobbles, interspersed with fragments of horse dung that had remained trapped in the grooves so long that it had lost all moisture and smell and become little more than straw and dust.

The narrow road led down a gentle slope towards the centre of town, with its churches and monuments, the great marble palaces of Venetian power, the bustling markets and the numerous inns, including the modest yet respectable one that had become his home more than a year gone.

He was not bound for the centre now. In fact, as he walked, greeting the passers-by in a friendly manner and pausing to scratch between the ears of the vast population of stray dogs, he moved in a circuitous route, edging round the centre of the town, keeping to the smaller, quieter streets until he finally emerged, blinking and sweaty, into the Via Porta, which ran from the larger markets and the mercantile quarter down to the great harbour. Here were taverns that provided anonymity and peace. Though filled with off-duty sailors carousing and with endless revelry, a man could sit in these houses of Bacchus and sup, keeping his own company without being scrutinised by the other occupants.

Such care was, of course, unnecessary.

He was a legitimate inhabitant of the city. He had arrived moderately well-off and had stayed within the aegis of the law his entire time on the island. He had been a model citizen and a regular church-goer (even if only to visit Lykaion). But old habits, as they said, died hard. A decade of hiding from the authorities and watching his tracks back home was not a practice that could be broken in a year and, despite his newfound legitimacy, he was still more comfortable keeping to himself wherever possible.

Skipping lightly around a small group of sailors rolling barrels down the street towards the docks, Skiouros made for the Taverna di San Marco, one of the better establishments on the street, and one that had the thoughtfulness to provide a set of benches on the street front, shaded by a canvas canopy. Passing the wooden railing and dropping with relief onto a bench out of the sun, Skiouros watched with no small amusement as a barrel suddenly escaped one of the passing sailors' inexpert grasp and careened away down the street, causing shrieks of alarm and a scattering of the populace. Half a dozen of the men from the same ship – including two seated in this very tavern – suddenly burst into life, chasing down the rolling barrel. A futile gesture. They could hardly hope to catch it. Shame… it was probably the sweet hot Candian wine or Tsikoudia brandy bound for the markets of Venice, worth more than any dozen sailors. Those men would be living frugally for years to pay off the loss of that barrel.

For just a moment Skiouros flinched, his memory furnishing him with an image of the massed ranks of barrels filled with black powder in the explosive store of the abandoned church back in Istanbul. If *these* barrels were of gunpowder then Skiouros could only pity the people gathered wherever the container came to an abrupt halt. With the heat of some of the stones and glass in this sunlight, gunpowder was a menace just in the open sunlight, without the need of a naked flame to ignite it.

Still, nothing came of the barrel's descent, barring a great deal of arguing some half a thousand yards down the hill, and Skiouros felt himself relax once more. A serving girl appeared through the doorway and spotted the new arrival. Rhea was a pleasant enough young woman, though her complexion spoke of a childhood run-in with the pox. Glancing in his direction, she gestured simply – a drinking motion. Skiouros nodded. An economy of communication. Rhea knew what he would want and would make sure he got the better wine and not the cat's piss the owner tended to dole out to the sailors when they started to become too inebriated to notice.

As he waited for the drink to arrive, Skiouros glanced around the street at the general hubbub of the city and, satisfied that no one seemed to care who he was, opened up his doublet and slid out a leather folder, dropping it onto the table with a slap.

14

The folder was of fine calfskin, elegantly stitched and branded with the mark of the Medici, whose tentacles reached into every corner of the mercantile world, extracting their fees for managing the finances of the great and the good – and sometimes even the poor and forgotten.

Slipping the thong aside, Skiouros opened the container and perused the records within.

It was a less than thrilling sight.

Sliding the upper vellum sheet down, he examined the records on the next – earlier – one. Why, he had no real idea... it was hardly a surprise. If he looked back over all fourteen of them that went back to his arrival on the island, all they would show would be a steady dwindling of his funds to the latest depressing evaluation.

He scratched his head and concentrated, hoping that perhaps he was misinterpreting the figures. His understanding of Italian as a *spoken* language was still a little slow, but his grasp of their *written* word was very tenuous. Indeed, if he went back to the early sheets, he could find the serious dent in the finances where he had withdrawn enough money to pay the tutor the exorbitant fees he had demanded to teach the written word in both Greek and Italian and the spoken in the latter. As a bonus, the man had thrown in some rudimentary Latin lessons, claiming that their understanding would aid in the learning of Italian. It hadn't – not to Skiouros' mind, anyway.

But no matter how unfamiliar the alphabet and how much he hoped that what he saw was the result of his struggling, the plain facts were there before his eyes, penned in black and red ink on the sheets of the local Medici banker.

He would last another month or two at most. Less if he lived well or continued his sword lessons.

His time was almost up.

He paused and hurriedly folded the leather case as Rhea arrived with a tankard of good imported Piedmont wine, plonking it down before him with a friendly smile before turning and hopping away into the gloomy interior. As soon as he was alone once more, he reopened the folder and sighed once again at the figures that stared back at him,

He had known this moment would come, even all those months ago when he'd first arrived on Crete. And yet, now that it was upon him, he found himself strangely reluctant to commit. There remained an unfinished task on the ledger of his life, many leagues away to the northwest, and everything he had done here in this past year had, theoretically, merely been steps in readiness for that task's undertaking.

15

So many things achieved, really, in such a short time.

He had learned his letters and a passing grasp of Italian from an expensive tutor. The latter had been made a great deal easier, admittedly, by regular contact in port with Captain Parmenio of the *Isabella* and his purser, Nicolo, who had become the closest friends he had ever achieved. Possibly the only friends he had ever achieved? Parmenio had been experiencing a run of ill luck with trade and commissions and had found that for the past year all he could manage were small, moderately profitable runs to Santorini, Athens or Rhodos, or occasionally distant Cyprus. Despite bidding for big contracts to Venezia or Napoli or further afield, he had found himself in somewhat limited circumstances – a fact that had brought him and Skiouros into an ever closer understanding.

And still, despite that closeness, Skiouros had revealed nothing of his true past or his end goal to the good captain – some things were meant to stay private. But without Parmenio's aid and friendship, the past year would have been considerably more difficult.

Then there was the fencing. His skills with the blade and even fist fighting had come on leaps and bounds in the past year and a half. Oh, he was no warrior – never would be – but at least now he felt that, should he ever find himself in the same sort of circumstances that had forced him away from Istanbul in the first place, he would at least be confident that he could hold his own.

And around his language skills and his martial training, he had devoted whatever free time he could find to a study of the Catholic church of the Italian Pope, and to maps of the Italian peninsula and its surroundings and even the spider's web that was the politics of the Italian city-states. After all, it was worth knowing everything one could about a dog before placing one's hand in its mouth.

And that dog was likely to be deadly, because where Skiouros was bound there was danger of a level and intensity he could scarce imagine. The Mamluk assassins and the Janissary traitors of his home city would be as nothing compared to what he would face when he left here.

Not for the first time, Skiouros wondered whether there was an alternative open to him. Perhaps he could take on a job? He was skilled enough now to make a decent wage. Then he could retain his rooms and continue to live in this balmy land, improving himself.

But no.

Such thoughts, as always, led down ever more shadowy passages until he found himself picturing Prince Cem Sultan – the failed usurper of the Ottoman throne, exiled these past ten years and imprisoned first by the Knights of Saint John, and then in France by their grand master. Skiouros had never laid eyes upon the pretender lord and knew him to be held captive somewhere impregnable and unattainable at the bidding of that strange shadowy Italian priest-king – the Pope. But with the traitor Hamza Bin Murad and his co-conspirator the Mamluk Qaashiq exploded and buried in the rubble of their own plotting, and the three assassins they had brought sent to their God, only the would-be-sultan Cem remained as an instigator of the disaster that had torn Lykaion from this world.

No matter how difficult the task might be or how long it took, Cem had to answer for the evil he had wrought. Only then would Lykaion go to heaven and stop talking to Skiouros in the silence of the night and the privacy of his head. Only then could Skiouros take his brother home to Istanbul in the knowledge that the Sultan Bayezid the Just ruled solely and benignly over them.

Only then would it end.

No, there could be no ordinary life – no settling down into a mundane job – while Cem Sultan breathed God's air, whichever God that might be.

And there again was the sudden reminder that his spell here was up. Crete was already passing away from him in the endless current of time, as had Hadrianople, then Istanbul – and with it his brother. And it was now time to move on to his goal: on to the fragmented states of Italia and his destiny, whether it be the divinely-ordained death of the Ottoman pretender or – more likely – his own tortured demise in the dungeons of the Pope's castles.

A few more days was all; then gone.

Skiouros took a deep pull of the rich, flavoursome wine and folded closed the ledger, tying it with the thong before slipping it into his doublet and leaning back against the bench, sighing with mixed relief and regret in the warm air beneath the shade of the canopy.

How long he spent with comfortably blank thoughts, enjoying the temperature, he couldn't say. There was the faint possibility that he even drifted off to sleep briefly – the sun tended to have that effect after a morning of exertions.

Skiouros opened his eyes with a start, his heart lurching as it does when one suddenly becomes aware that one is being watched intently.

As he came bolt upright, his eyes hurriedly refocused on the figure sitting on the bench opposite, arms folded on the table.

'What in the name of damnation do *you* want?'

The Romani beggar rubbed his knee as though soothing a pain, the plaited bones in the strands that gleamed white in his tousled and dusty black hair clattering together as his head moved. The sun-darkened and weather-worn face tilted up towards him and the white, inquisitive eyes narrowed slightly.

'Be off with you,' Skiouros snapped. 'I came here for a little solitude and peace. Since you seem to be my self-appointed shadow, you must know that's why I chose this place.'

The Romani simply smiled and cradled his hands on the table.

'If I buy you some wine will you go away?'

It was a pointless tactic and he knew it. The old Romani beggar had been an uninvited and oft-unwelcome fixture in his life for a year and a half and he knew well enough that the old man only left when he felt like it.

To some extent, Skiouros had brought it all on himself. That first day as he'd left the harbour and walked inland, the beggar had offered his services as a guide for a pittance and Skiouros had, after looking him up and down, somewhat reluctantly accepted. He had been in a new land and totally lost, and the Romani woman in Istanbul still sometimes occupied his thoughts with her apparent prescience and understanding. And the old beggar had proved a very useful guide in those early days.

But then, after a month, when he had become thoroughly familiar with the city and even some other parts of the island, Skiouros had terminated the man's employment, leaving him with a more than generous severance payment. But the damage was already done. The old Romani was something of a limpet, attaching himself permanently and irremovably to Skiouros' life and cropping up regularly – mostly when his presence was most disruptive.

'Look, I just want to sit in peace and contemplate a few things. I don't want to seem selfish...'

The Romani frowned, though his slightly deranged smile remained locked in place, displaying his crooked and sparse teeth.

'But you *is*.'

'What?' Skiouros asked, taken aback by being spoken to in such a manner. The old man had always shown a certain grudging deference before.

18

'You is,' the man repeated. 'Selfish,' he explained, as though educating a child.

Skiouros felt confusion and anger battling for dominance in his mind. As he tried to decide how best to rid himself of the unwanted beggar, he reached for the wine and took a pull, only to find the cup empty. Had the damn Romani even stooped to stealing his wine now? He'd only had one long sip himself.

'I am going to grant you that one free insult. You're a mad old man and I'm not a belligerent fellow. Consider my wine that you've clearly already drunk a parting gift and be on your way before I have to start taking offence.'

'You can be what you wants to be, sure-en, sure-en. But yous bin a thief and a cheat and that sticks to a man's soul like wet shit, so t'does. Selfish's in the bone, even if'n you doesn't want it like that.'

'Look, I'm getting a little irritated by this.'

The Romani shrugged.

'Where's you bound?' he said as if the younger man's agitation was of no import.

Skiouros narrowed his eyes. This particular tack of questioning was getting close to something that he really did not want to discuss, particularly with a mad beggar and certainly not in the open street.

'I have tasks in other lands. Now kindly leave me alone.'

'To Rome, eh?'

'Shut up,' Skiouros snapped, panic suddenly overwhelming his surprise. His eyes strayed across the other patrons and those folk in the street, but no one had been paying them any attention. A few heads turned at his sharp retort and he paused only long enough to watch them lose interest and go back to their drinks and games.

'*Shut up*,' he repeated, his tone now lower and more conspiratorial. How had this man heard such a thing? Rome? It was hardly something he discussed in the open – or indeed even in private, with the exception of consulting Lykaion's ghost in the church of Saint Titus. Lykaion had become – in a strange way – his confessor.

'I didn't think you'd followed me into the church. I thought they tried to keep the Romani out – especially beggars. Whatever you've overheard, you would do well to forget it.'

His hand slipped to the pommel of the sword at his side – the expensive Spanish rapier that had made such a dent in his bank account, but which Don Diego had insisted he needed. He knew he would not draw it to fight here, as he'd end up incarcerated at the pleasure of the

19

Duke of Candia – besides he had only learned to fight to defend himself and he knew damn well there was every likelihood that he lacked the conviction to attack a man in cold blood.

Except Cem, of course. He would not falter there when the time came.

'Rome, oh yes,' smiled the Romani as though picking the thoughts out of Skiouros' mind. 'After 'e traitor prince, none less, eh?'

Panic gripped Skiouros once more.

'*Shut up, shut up, shut up,*' he hissed.

'Selfish,' declared the old beggar once more.

'What?'

The man simply smiled with irritating smugness.

Glancing around again to make sure they were not being too carefully observed, and removing his hand from the sword pommel with deliberate slowness, Skiouros lowered his voice and leaned forward across the table.

'*What* is selfish?' he hissed.

'Revenge,' the man said quietly. 'Revenge be allus selfish.'

Trying not to dwell too deeply on just how much this beggar seemed to know, or wonder whether the man really could just see into his head, Skiouros concentrated instead on the argument at hand.

'How can it be selfish to put myself at great risk in order to avenge my brother? Even to avenge a whole empire and protect it from the potential danger of a usurper war? How is *that* selfish?'

''venge *be* selfish. Self-indulgy-hent.'

'What?'

'You b'lieve ye brother de head care if'n sultan man dead?'

Again, the panic rose and Skiouros had to clamp down on the urge to shout at the old man, his eyes straying around the tavern and the street to be sure they were not being scrutinised.

'Listen to me, old beggar man. My motivations are not a matter for discussion with anyone, least of all you. I can see now that perhaps this is your new plan to dredge money out of me? To learn my secrets and hold me to ransom over them? Well you're in for a tough time, as I've only a little more money than *you* now, and as soon as I can arrange passage on a ship, that'll see an end of my finances all together. Find someone else to prey upon.'

The old Romani simply smiled and leaned back.

'Ye passage be n'ready fated and first sign comen e'en now. Think on't, theh, yon Greek, fer time comen it be put'n to test. Selfishness. Tarnish thar soul.'

Skiouros prepared his retort but held it behind clenched teeth as the man rose, accompanied by a variety of clicks and groans and turned, limping away from the table and out of the tavern.

'I will be well rid of you,' Skiouros hissed as the man passed close by on the other side of the wooden railing.

'Ye will,' the man agreed, pausing. 'But na yet. I's 'nother meet fer ye yet.'

With a conspiratorial tap of the side of his nose, the old Romani limped off up the street.

Skiouros stared after him, anger and surprise spinning like a maelstrom within. What if someone had heard? What if they went... Foolish. Who would care what happened to an Ottoman usurper here, of all places? Besides, no one had even stirred or looked up.

His eyes refocused as the old man disappeared and Skiouros frowned at the sight that greeted him out in the sloping street.

Nicolo!

The purser of the *Isabella* and right hand man of Captain Parmenio was walking slowly down the street towards the docks, a dozen sailors around him leading pack mules and carts of stores and supplies. Skiouros' frown slowly cracked and opened up into a smile.

A sign from God if ever there was one. He tried not to think of Romani prescience and granted such providence to the Lord instead.

Here was he, contemplating what to do about the future, and the Lord had provided. There were far too many supplies there in that convoy for the short jaunts Parmenio had been lumbered with this past year. This was no trip to Santorini or even Cyprus. This was Nicolo stocking up the ship for a proper voyage, perhaps to Venezia, or even west past the Italian peninsula altogether.

Serendipity.

Nicolo had barely advanced any further down the street before Skiouros was out of the Tavern and hurrying after, leaving a few remaining coins on the table to pay for his drink.

Chapter Two - Of decisions and plans

Parmenio scratched his beard as he peered down over the *Isabella*'s bow, watching his men struggling to direct a collection of disobedient and irritable Cretan donkeys that dragged carts full of barrels and crates along the jetty. It was one of the joys of sole ownership and captaincy not to have to involve oneself in the day-to-day manual labour of the sea-trader's life.

It was perhaps an even deeper joy to be able to land the task heavily on the shoulders of Nicolo, particularly after the previous evening's games of *Trionfini* in which the purser – may his head shrivel and fall off – seemed to have an almost magnetic attraction to that fickle bitch the Queen of Swords. Parmenio's purse had been worryingly lighter this morning.

The big surprise was not the speed and efficiency with which Nicolo had purchased and transported the requisite supplies – the purser was endlessly competent and had been the supporting pillar of Parmenio's business for many a year. No, the big surprise was the figure trolling along in his wake, sword slung at his side and a three-day growth on his chin, peering around at the folk in the port as though each and every one were spying on him for some unknown reason.

The young Greek permanently sported a look of the hunted man – it seemed to be an unchangeable facet of his character.

'Well, well, well. Look what crawled out of his pit. Don't you have a fencing lesson or a book to read?'

Skiouros grinned up at the captain at the rail.

'Nicolo informs me that you're bound for western climes?'

'Does he indeed? His mouth is as big as his damn purse, then.'

'You've a good commission?'

Parmenio looked left and right as though expecting conspiratorial listeners to eavesdrop on their conversation, almost a mirror of the young Greek's general demeanour. The port bustled and thrived as usual, but no one was paying particular attention to them.

'Get up here before you start shouting my business.'

Skiouros frowned and followed Nicolo up the bowing, rickety plank ahead of the rest of the sailors, who began to unload the carts and heft the goods aboard between them, bearing boxes and bags on their back and crates and barrels in pairs, their hearts in their mouths as they tried to manoeuvre them up the narrow boarding ramp.

As he stepped onto the deck, noting with surprise its almost-new look, scrubbed clean and freshly waxed, Skiouros followed Parmenio's beckoning finger to the shade of the doorway into the stern compartment and its navigation room, galley and officers' cabins. Skiouros was still frowning as he stepped out of the searing sunlight and into the gloom, blinking to adjust as he did so. The smell of fresh tar, oil, wax and canvas was almost overpowering.

'Have you no wits, Skiouros, you brainless son of a Greek goat?'

'What?'

'I have secured a very agreeable pair of concurrent commissions,' the captain hissed, holding up his hand to cup his mouth in a manner that was so conspiratorial it was almost comical to Skiouros. 'The two commissions could move me up from my current rut and into the big time, but nothing is ever set in this world until everything is on board and we've cast off. You go shouting your mouth off about my good fortune and the next thing I know I'll have *lost* said commissions because some other captain at a nearby jetty with unusually large ears has undercut me. You get my drift, boy?'

Skiouros frowned. It seemed exceedingly unlikely to him that anyone else nearby had stood even the faintest chance of learning anything useful from their exchange. Moreover, what was a life-changing commission to Parmenio was probably the standard fare to most of the captains in port, who seemed to enjoy a steadier run of luck than the *Isabella*'s owner-operator.

Still, Parmenio was a friend and the business was his livelihood, after all. Skiouros lowered his voice and leaned closer.

'Where are you bound?' Skiouros tried – and failed – to keep a certain tense excitement from his voice.

'Why?'

23

'Because the time has come for me to leave Candia.'

Parmenio narrowed his eyes.

'Why do I get the feeling that there's either some young woman knocking around the city with a growing bump on her front or that some nobleman's wondering where his best silver's gone?'

'Nothing like that,' Skiouros answered with a smile. In truth, the very idea of thievery had become almost utterly alien to him over the past eighteen months and he had not contemplated swiping even the easiest of hauls for over a year. As to the likelihood of a romantic liaison... well, Skiouros would be forced to admit to himself that while he was finding it easier these days to form friendships with people – such as Nicolo and the captain – he was a long way from opening up and trusting someone in a more intimate way. Such vulnerability was anathema to him. The habits of his formative years would be many more in the breaking.

'You're not in a hurry? Why me and now, then?'

'Because with that level of supplies you have to be on a long trip west, and not just island-hopping; and because you're a friend,' Skiouros said, trying to interject a level of dismay into his voice at the very idea of his motives being questioned.

Parmenio simply pursed his lips and waited.

'Because you might sell me passage cheap,' Skiouros admitted with a sigh. 'I'm fast running out of money.'

'That sounds a little more genuine. How cheap are we talking?'

'I can spare maybe twelve ducats without leaving myself to starve when I arrive.'

Parmenio huffed and folded his arms. 'For twelve ducats I might consider passage for one of your legs!'

Skiouros grinned. 'Let's haggle.'

Nicolo, leaning across from behind where he was busy marking a list as goods were ferried aboard, snorted. 'You think you'd be better with an arm *and* a leg sailing west, eh? What about the rest of you?'

'I think the boy means to fleece me in the same manner as my purser,' Parmenio grinned. 'I've seen him haggle in the market, and he's become something of a master this past year. He could get the undergarments off a nun with just his tongue.'

'I've known men who could do that too,' grinned Nicolo, causing the captain to explode in a fit of laughter. Taking a deep breath and still smiling, Parmenio straightened and fixed Skiouros with a straight look.

'In the long run I'd be better accepting the twelve ducats for full passage now, rather than having to give him the shirt off my back too.'

Skiouros grinned.

'I'm no shirker, captain. I'll work my passage to pay off the shortfall in my funding.'

'That you will, boy. That you will.'

'You haven't told me where you're bound yet other than 'west'?'

'You haven't told us where you're going,' Parmenio replied archly.

Skiouros paused for a moment. His ultimate goal was still shrouded in as much secrecy as he could manage. In all his time on Crete, only in whispered conversations with the head of his brother had he even mentioned the Italian peninsula or Prince Cem Sultan. Still, how could the captain expect to give him passage without at least knowing his destination?

'I'm bound for the Papal States. Rome, specifically.'

'Rome? Then you're in reasonable luck, lad. We're sailing for Napoli and on to Genoa – curse their black Sforza hearts and harbour taxes – and Marseilles. So, while we're not putting in for Rome, Napoli's only a little over thirty leagues from there and it's easy enough to cross the border from the Kingdom of Napoli to the Papal region. You could easily find passage from that port and for a good low price. Are you planning on returning to Crete?'

Again the defensive walls came up in Skiouros' mind, shielding his plans and aspirations from the ears of others.

'Why?' he asked guardedly.

Parmenio narrowed his eyes again in suspicion. 'Let me rephrase the question: am I taking just you, or you and all your worldly goods?'

'Everything,' Skiouros replied with a slow exhale. 'I'm taking everything and leaving Candia behind. Not that everything is very much, in truth.'

'Good, since space will be at a premium on this trip and I cannot afford to pass up possible income in order to store your motley collection of clutter.'

Skiouros nodded. 'It will only take me a few hours to organise everything. I'll have to withdraw the rest of my money from the Medici house in the city, pay off my landlord and then gather my things.'

'You've plenty of time,' Nicolo interjected again from his list checking. 'We don't sail until the morning tide two days from now.'

Skiouros smiled and reached out to clasp the captain's hand. 'I'll return at dawn before you sail, then, captain.'

'I'm sure you will,' Parmenio replied, sharing a look with Nicolo.

With a last look at the two men, Skiouros strode off down the boarding plank and to the jetty, turning and making his way back into town. 'A few hours' had been something of an exaggeration. Skiouros was well aware of the pitiful ties and possessions he could call his own and it would take no time at all to clear up matters in the city and prepare to sail.

He tried to stifle his irritation as he reached the end of the jetty and spotted the gaunt, dusty black figure of the old Romani beggar man standing with a cup held out for coins, leaning on an old cracked barrel and entreating passers-by to save him from abject poverty with the transfer of just a simple copper coin. The beggar gave Skiouros a look that was altogether too penetrative and knowing for the young Greek's liking and he repaid it with a scowl before scurrying past the man and off across the dock, past the sailors, the merchants, the dockers and teamsters and the endless pack animals and carts of goods, towards the Via Porta.

He had plenty of time, of course. By his estimate, within two hours he could be back at the *Isabella*'s boarding plank with everything he possessed crammed together in a sack, waiting to sail. But if the events in Istanbul that had driven Skiouros and his disembodied sibling to Crete in the first place had taught him anything it was that to be unprepared was to risk utter failure. He would never be caught out again without prior planning. The ship sailed the day after tomorrow, but he would have everything prepared and stowed tomorrow and his room paid up until that final morning in advance, so that all he had to do was stroll down to the jetty and board.

He eyed the taverns up and down the wide street with some wistfulness. Once he passed up that boarding ramp in a day and a half's time, he knew he'd seen the last of such relaxed social emporia for the duration of the voyage: at least a fortnight. Two weeks of living off whatever tight rations Nicolo had requisitioned and drinking only the cheap, watered muck generally kept onboard. At least, unlike the trip from Istanbul, he would not have to feign illness this time and could actually enjoy the journey.

Besides, he reminded himself as he dragged his eyes from the tavern fronts and set his gaze determinedly on the street ahead, his meagre remaining funds would hardly facilitate an afternoon of drinking.

That thought settled his first port of call. Striding away up the street, he turned right onto another wide boulevard that still displayed the remnants of the once crucial Byzantine walls – a strange echoing ghostly reminder of Skiouros' homeland. Past one of the crumbling towers with its familiar stone, brick and tile construction, he approached the ornate, arcaded and balustraded white marble façade of the Medici house, the graceful carved architecture and leaded windows almost glowing in the late afternoon sun. The door stood open. The Medici were always willing to receive prospective clients.

He had been led to believe that in their native peninsula the banking houses of the powerful Medici family seethed with activity like the great spice markets of Istanbul. The house in Candia was considerably quieter. Skiouros had never seen more than one or two other clients at a time and despite its size and grandeur, the bank was staffed by only a half dozen personnel.

The large hall that occupied most of the ground floor was dominated by a central desk that ran in a square with a solid oak frontage which stated quite clearly: clients outside, staff within. Inside that defensive square of desk stood cupboards and chests of drawers, numerous sets of scales of different sizes, baskets of empty money bags, inkpots and quills and all the paraphernalia of the banking world. The banker himself – along with his assistant – perused a heavy book, while a clerk scribbled indecipherable marks in a ledger.

Off to the left stood the doors to the three consulting rooms where clients could speak to their banker in secluded privacy, while to the right was the ornate curving, graceful staircase that led to the upper floor where the real work of the banking house went on.

Where the money was kept.

Giovanni Bagnara affixed his most welcoming smile as he realised someone had stridden into the building, their soft footsteps clicking on the marble. The warm – if fake – smile quickly slid away to be replaced by a resigned frown as he realised which particular client this was.

In the grand style of bankers everywhere, Bagnara was the soul of grace and attention for a new client – or a rich one – and had been at Skiouros' beck and call in the early months on the island. But as time went on and it became painfully obvious to the Medici official that there would be no fresh injection of coin into the young Greek's account and that he was simply winding down towards poverty, Bagnara had made consistently less effort, saving his most genuine smiles and his greatest assistance for those whose account had a future.

27

'Master Skiouros Nikopoulos. How can I be of assistance?'

Skiouros felt a flare of minor annoyance at the endless categorisation and bureaucracy that seemed to go hand in glove with banking. Bagnara had been flummoxed when presented with an account in the name 'Skiouros' or even 'Son of Nikos'. In his world, such nomenclature simply did not exist, and he had worked hard with his clerk to contort the appellation into a very Italian 'fore-name, last-name' format that fitted his records better.

'I fear it's time to close my account, Giovanni.'

Bagnara threw him a look of deepest sympathy and regret that had taken only a fraction of a second to rivet to his emotion-free face.

'We shall be sorry to lose your business, Master Nikopoulos.' His eyes suggested otherwise, despite the smile. Skiouros resisted the urge to point out that, regardless of the fact that his account had done nothing but decline, the Medici had made a tidy sum from managing that slide into poverty, and they really had nothing to complain about.

'And I shall be sorry to leave, but I am bound for distant climes. May I enquire as to the final balance of my account?'

He braced himself. His leather folder contained last month's balance and he had a reasonable mental note of his spending since then, but one should always be prepared for the news to be worse that one expects – since it almost always is – and the Medici had yet to extract their fees for the final month and the inevitable costs of account closure.

Bagnara crooked a finger to the clerk, who had already – with typical efficiency – replaced his quill, closed his ledger and opened another from some hidden place beneath the desk. Wordlessly, he dropped the ribbon down to mark the page and passed the open book to Bagnara. The banker frowned at the pages and then dropped the book to the desk, turning it to face Skiouros.

'Twenty-one ducats plus two lira and sundry copper.'

Skiouros tried not to show his disappointment. Lower than he expected. As his eyes ran down the figures, he felt his spirits sink once more as he noted that the last mark was almost a week earlier, meaning that the final deductions had yet to be taken.

'After the closure and final monthly fees...' Bagnara muttered, 'Bernardo?'

The clerk leaned across and peered at the figures, running calculations in his head before adding a final mark to the ledger and scribbling *Chiusura* beside it – a word unfamiliar to Skiouros, yet clearly indicative of the account being closed.

'Eighteen ducats and three lira,' Skiouros read with a deflated sigh. And he had yet to pay off his final week's lodgings, too. When he reached the Italian peninsula, he was going to be very hungry. He would probably be walking from Napoli to Rome, as well.

He ran through his mind a variety of wheedling phrases he might be able to use on Parmenio to lower the fare of his passage as he finalised the account closure with the banker and retrieved his pitiful wealth, before strolling out of the cool shade of the building and into the warm sunlight of the city.

Before returning to his lodgings and suffering the frustration of watching a few more coins evaporate from his purse, he had one more important stop to make.

Less than ten minutes later, he pushed open the door to the church of Saint Titus, making his way through the narthex and into the side chapel – the parekklesion – where the heads of the saints, along with numerous other sacred bones and artefacts, rested in glory, surrounded by gold and mosaics that told tales of the Bible – the good, expansive Orthodox bible, rather than the constrained, scant pickings of the Roman one.

The church of Saint Titus was something of an oddity, though it probably bothered Skiouros less than it did the locals. Created as a good Orthodox church under Byzantine rule, it now housed a Catholic archbishop of the Roman Pope, appointed with the blessing of the Venetian authorities. Its layout and decoration was so achingly familiar to a man of Constantinople, and yet everything was curiously different, as though the whole church had shifted a little to the left of the real world. Moreover, while the clergy of the church were staunchly Catholic, there were small pockets of Orthodox priests who had fled the strictures of Ottoman Istanbul and sought refuge with their distant cousins in a land that was familiar to them in many ways.

Indeed, Orthodox churches and monasteries still outnumbered their Popish counterparts in Crete, despite the Catholic authorities. A thousand years of Orthodoxy among the population was not something that could easily be pushed aside.

Even now, while young novices and monks rushed about with their strangely-shaven tonsured heads, preparing for the great Ascension festival, priests tending to their flock in the naos of the church, a small group of exiled Orthodox priests in their black robes and cylindrical *skouphia* hats stood in a cluster in the parekklesion, paying their respects to the relics that sat behind an impenetrable steel cage, gilded and decorated with silver, several of which they themselves had brought to safety here.

Skiouros moved past them with a deferential nod, trying not to catch their eyes directly as he walked. It was extremely unlikely that any of them would remember him as the stowaway monk who had accompanied them here a year and a half ago, but if Skiouros had learned anything in his thieving youth it was that a careful man lived longer than an impetuous one.

Slowly, he approached the wooden pews at the fore of the chapel, brought at great expense and no small difficulty all the way from some important church or other in Venezia and, selecting the one directly in front of the reliquary of Saint Theodoros, he leaned forwards as if in prayer.

'The time has come, Lykaion.'

He waited for the inevitable reply. The church was in far more of a commotion than usual, the voices of priests trying to organise one of the biggest feast day festivals of the year intruding into every corner of the building and of the soul. And yet, despite the hubbub, he could just hear his brother's voice, reed-thin and distant as though the passing months were taking him ever further away into nothingness. He listened and pursed his lips before answering.

'You know as well as I that I have to do it. Would you turn me aside from the path now?'

He paused.

'No. I thought not. It is no act of brutality or sin in the eyes of God. It is a *cleansing*. The healing of a sickness. It is the excising of a boil upon the Earth.'

Skiouros sighed. 'I never thought, though, that it would be such a wrench leaving this place. Whether that is because of you or because of the different life Crete offers, I cannot say. But I do know that a piece of me will be torn out and kept by this island when I sail.'

He realised that his voice must have risen imperceptibly, as the small party of monks had hushed their own conversation and were looking in his direction. He shuffled to face slightly further away from them and loudly muttered something in Italian about needing God's guidance – an almost-replica of something he often heard other worshippers mumble.

Once the monks had lost interest, he returned his attention to the reliquary and bridled at Lykaion's voice echoing hollow in his head.

30

'It's no good being *angry* with me, brother. We agreed on this course of action a long time ago. I cannot back down now until I have completed the task, and I will likely never be more ready than I am now.'

His brow creased as he listened to the silent reply.

'Well be that as it may,' he grumbled, 'I have not the time, nor the finances to become any *more* prepared. I shall just have to rely on the skills I have always had and upon what I have learned in this place. And if I survive this, and if I make it out, I will return to this place, Lykaion, and we will leave Crete and go home.'

The disembodied voice sounded somehow snappy and disbelieving in its reply.

'Well whether this place could be *my* home or not, it will never be *yours*, will it? No. If we are both to be home, it must be where we started this: back in Constantinople. And when I return we will go there.'

He sighed and leaned back in the pew as though recovering from a soulsick prayer.

'All I ask is that you think on me and pray for me – if you can do that wherever you are. I go now to gather my things and prepare for the journey. I'll not be back until the deed is done. Wish me good fortune, brother.'

Standing slowly, he turned and made his way across the parekklesion and out through the narthex into the bright sunlight once more.

A day and a half.

The *Isabella* sat heavy in the water, laden more than usual with the supplies and cargo for the journey. The water lapped and splashed around the thick hull noticeably above the load line set by the Venetian port official, as the timbers and ropes groaned like the spectres of ancient ships haunting the jetty.

The moon shone silver and clear in a sky of deep indigo, creating a glittering carpet across the undulating surface of the water in the harbour. All activity had died away and the only sounds to pervade the night were the noises of the men on board the ships, still awake late into the night, sentries against cargo theft or unexpected trouble. Even the most outlandish carousing sailors were now either safely abed below or draped across one of the ornamental fountains in the streets of the city.

Unnoticed by all, a dark shape slid between two large piles of abandoned crates whose contents had long been emptied and stored away in the *Isabella*'s hold or that of the Neapolitan cog at the far side of the jetty.

The sole watchman on board the *Isabella* strode towards the stern, lurching and flatulating as he moved, before unlacing his codpiece and urinating into the sea with a relieved sigh.

The figure on the jetty slipped with the grace of a dancer and the silence of a ghost between the empty crates and the freshly-tarred hull of the Venetian caravel. A momentary glance would reveal only a figure clad in black, with a voluminous robe that fluttered about the legs as he moved, other details indeterminable.

While the stream of sailor's urine added to the filth of the harbour's water at the stern, the black figure slid into the shadows at the ship's side, its hand reaching up for one of the four ropes that anchored the rigging to the deadeyes on the hull. Under normal circumstances the ropes would be far too high to reach from the jetty, but Parmenio's commissions had exceeded the permitted load for this vessel class by Venetian law and the ship rode dangerously low in the water.

With a deft hop the figure launched itself up the side and rolled over the rail, dropping to the deck with a sound similar to the lap of waves against timber – bare feet slapping on wood.

By the time the sentry began to patrol along the deck once more, the figure had disappeared into the shadows of the stern housing, secure in the knowledge that of the twenty-five crew-members, twenty-two were safely ashore in the town, with only two sentries working shifts and one man suffering with gut rot in the hold below. It was amazing what knowledge one could glean from simply observing and listening – especially when one was effectively invisible.

Before disappearing inside and down into the bowels of the ship, the figure removed the drum-shaped *skoufos* priest's hat and the black veil draped over it, lest it brush the timbers of the ship's ceilings and give away his presence. With deft hands he produced a strip of black cloth and bound up the long, ragged hair so that the white bones threaded throughout did not clack together as he moved.

The Venetian sailor, still tying his codpiece back into position, stepped across the recent path of the intruder, oblivious to his passage, and peered off towards the port, ever vigilant in his duty.

After all, the *Isabella* sailed at the next tide. It would be unfortunate should anything go wrong at this point.

Chapter Three - Of the beginnings of journeys

Skiouros took a deep breath of the salty warm air and relaxed, sagging over the rail. He hadn't realised just how tense he had become over the past two days until he'd found himself finally aboard the *Isabella* and sailing west.

The sun was a mere dull umber glow at his back – past the caravel's bow – and the jagged, parched shores of Crete's westernmost spurs were little more than a purple smudge against the indigo sky to the east, past the ship's roiling wake.

All day the *Isabella* had kept up a good pace, cutting through the warm, pleasant waters of the Sea of Crete, the sailors in good spirits and the mood light and friendly. When one of the sailors had whispered to Skiouros that he was relieved they had made it out of port without being hauled over by the authorities for being seriously over-laden, the young Greek passenger had been beset with worries until he finally confronted Nicolo. The purser had easily smoothed over his fears, explaining that the *Isabella* was tougher, larger, steadier and heavier than the authorities had down in their records – a deliberate ploy to pay lower berthing fees and port taxes. While Skiouros remained sceptical that the load was truly safe for the ship – the water's surface rode well above the cargo line – he simply had to trust that Parmenio and his men knew what they were doing.

Despite the low-level background nervousness that the captain might have overburdened them in a desperate attempt to make his fortune, and the continual baseline acceptance that his entire journey was being undertaken in order to place him in the greatest danger he could imagine, he began to relax more than he had in some time. He was no great sailor

– he'd had precious few opportunities to board even small ferries or rowing boats in his past – and the only great sea voyage he had so far undertaken in his life had been less than comfortable.

Where his last trip had been spent mostly hiding below, dressed as a priest and feigning sea-sickness, this time he could stand upon the deck in the open air and enjoy the view and the rolling motion of the vessel as it plied its way towards the sunset.

The island of Crete – Candia as the Venetians would have it – had slid by to the south throughout the day, its spurs and coves, caves and villages creating an ever-changing backdrop to the glittering waters. Such a view of Crete had taken Skiouros by surprise. Though he'd seen the island on a number of maps he had perused in the past year and had even journeyed to some of the strange ancient ruins near the city – including the legendary home of the Minotaur that had frightened him as a childhood story – he had not realised Crete was really so vast. It was more than a mere island forming part of the Greek world or the Venetian empire. It was a great land – almost a country of its own.

Now as the chill began to set in with the loss of the sun's heat and the night started to take hold, the sailors began to work in shifts, some bedding down in their blankets on the ship's deck to get as much sleep as possible before being woken to take their turn.

Some captains would have plotted a course that took them along coastal routes and anchored in bays for the night. Not Parmenio. This voyage would not stop before Napoli, travelling day and night.

Part of the captain's reasoning revolved around the need for speed in order to be certain of fulfilling his contracts punctually and efficiently, and part came from the knowledge that the pirate vessels that operated in the eastern seas of the Mediterranean lurked in many such coves awaiting careless prey. Parmenio knew that traversing the open sea seriously reduced their chances of encountering such a threat. For their part, the sailors were equally happy with their tiring lot as it meant that, though they worked harder on the voyage, their cut of the profits from the captain would be slightly higher and their time spent in port at the end of the trip would be extended.

'Master Skiouros?'

His attention distracted from the all-but-invisible coastline, the young Greek turned at the voice to see one of the sailors waving at him from the doorway which led to the tiny, cramped rooms. *Master* indeed! It was distinctly possible that he would never become used to

34

being addressed in such formal terms, rather than the less formal 'Stop: thief!' that had become the soundtrack of his youth.

Bidding a final farewell to the land that had been his home for more than a year, Skiouros padded across the deck, barefoot for safety, towards the sailor.

'Yes?'

'The captain has called you to dine, sir.'

Skiouros chuckled. Such formality. If only the sailor knew of his real past, he would soon drop any such honourifics.

'Thank you,' he said, nodding as he strode past and in through the door. Responding to such novel formality in a manner that was fitting and betrayed nothing of the real Skiouros was becoming something of a talent.

The interior was extremely dim, with only the reflected light of the dying day through the doorway illuminating the passage. Four doors led to small rooms, the nearest almost cell-like in their tiny simplicity, the farther slightly larger yet still small. The room to the right had been allocated to Skiouros – a bunk that just fitted his fairly diminutive frame and would hardly suit a well-built sailor, leaving just about enough spare room to stow his single bag of worldly goods. The room opposite was occupied by the other passenger, who had yet to put in an appearance and who Skiouros had seen nothing of since boarding this morning.

The rear rooms consisted of the captain's cabin that now also played host to Nicolo in order to free up space for paying passengers, and the small social room where the officers' food was cooked and then consumed. It was a cramped way to live, though after the single rickety garret that had been his home in Istanbul the conditions were no hardship for Skiouros.

A flickering yellow light shone through the cracks around the edge of the common room door and guided Skiouros towards his evening meal. Pausing at the threshold to make himself slightly more presentable, he finally knocked.

'Come,' came Parmenio's muffled voice from within.

Skiouros gripped the catch and swung the door inwards, stepping into the light and blinking after the gloom of the corridor.

The table occupied roughly half of the small room, barely providing enough space for four people to eat. The chairs around it were so tightly jammed that they almost touched the walls of the room, the bench and tiny stove that served as the galley pushed back up against the far wall to make as much room as possible.

Captain Parmenio had changed from his daily rough attire into his best clothing – a slightly frayed and faded collection that had clearly once been expensive and well-tailored, before his girth had expanded just enough to put a strain on the ties that held the doublet closed. Opposite him, Nicolo sat in his ordinary work clothes, looking somewhat distant, as though solving an unspoken problem in his head.

The third seat held a young man, no older than Skiouros, and he was willing to bet more than a year younger. Wearing the sort of elegant yet understated sombre doublet and hose of the lower nobility of the Italian city-states, the fellow looked somewhat aloof and sour-faced.

'Allow me to introduce Master Cesare Orsini, nephew of the great condottiero, general and swordsman Virginio Orsini.'

'*Distant* nephew,' stressed the young man with a sigh.

Parmenio ignored the interruption and gestured at the new arrival. 'This is Master Skiouros, lately of Constantinople, an acquaintance and fellow traveller as far as Napoli.'

Orsini raised an eyebrow. 'What could possibly urge a man to visit that seething nest of Frankish and Aragonese vipers?'

Skiouros, somewhat taken aback by the quiet vitriol in the young man's voice, shuffled in the tight confines to his seat and squeezed himself in behind the table, before a wooden bowl of something brown and stew-like and a few chunks of hard bread.

Nicolo leaned slightly towards him. 'Tastes alright, so long as you don't look too closely at the lumps. *That* might put you off. I'm worried that Arnolfini dropped bits of himself into the pot.'

Skiouros shot him a worried glance and the purser grinned wickedly. Turning away from the joking purser, he studied the young Orsini. The young man had a two-day growth about his cheeks and chin, though it would likely mature to resemble more of a seeding dandelion than a manly beard.

'I confess I know little of the Kingdom of Napoli, Master Orsini. In truth I am merely alighting there en-route to the Papal States and Rome itself.'

He was rather proud of his answer. In his own head, he had sounded educated and classy. If Orsini thought so, he paid it no heed.

'Rome is little better – though the snakes are smaller and prettier, they are twice as fast and twice as deadly – and the Pope himself can only be seen when he crawls out of the pocket of the French King in order to breach holy laws with his simony. '*Innocent*' indeed!'

Skiouros leaned forward, his gaze taking in the other traveller, attempting to unpick the man's mind, conscience and soul through a simple examination, but Cesare Orsini was inscrutable, his outer a blank and impenetrable shell.

'I will defer to your knowledge on that count, Master Orsini, given that I owe my faith dues to the Patriarch Maximus in Constantinople.'

'Hmph,' was all the response the young man deemed necessary to this titbit.

'And where are you bound, Master Orsini?'

'Genoa. As far from the Neapolitan Kings and my dearest uncle as possible.'

'Your uncle serves the King of Napoli?' Skiouros frowned. His studies of the politics of the Italian peninsula had done little other than serve to confound him and bring forth a collection of headaches. The whole tangled web seemed to be more complex than even the Venetian port bureaucracy or the Medici banking system. And where the sensible Orthodox Church remained safely separate from the political morass, the Catholic Pope seemed to revel in miring himself down in the whole snarled mess.

The humourless, seemingly bitter shell of this young nobleman irritated Skiouros, and he would like nothing more than to break off the conversation and ignore him and his superior pretensions entirely, but something selfish deep inside prodded him to investigate further. He was bound for Napoli and Rome and if this young man knew things of import, Skiouros would be foolish indeed to ignore him merely for the sake of personal comfort.

'My uncle serves many masters. He is a prince among condottieri. The Orsini languish in vile state beneath the rich protective skirts of the sickening Pope and the treacherous Neapolitans, making themselves rich and powerful at the expense of their very souls, while shipping off the family's dissenters and their children to virtual exile on desolate islands – islands not even under family control.'

Skiouros nodded, his face a mask of concerned understanding for the plight of the young man – clearly a black sheep of his noble house – while beneath that manufactured expression, his mind raced with what use this might be. Perhaps he would be better staying on past Napoli as far as Genoa if Parmenio would permit it? Young Orsini could be an invaluable contact, particularly if Skiouros could nurture some sort of budding friendship with him?

'You have my sympathy, Master Orsini. Family can be difficult. My own brother caused me endless trouble' – a horrible stab of guilt – 'but then I fear I returned the favour tenfold.'

Orsini simply nodded, his expression as hard as ever, and Skiouros fought to avoid grinding his teeth. The man was less forthcoming a conversationalist than Lykaion, and the latter had been dead nigh on two years. Skiouros took a deep breath to try and engage the man one last time, but was interrupted by a rapping at the door.

Parmenio and Nicolo shared a concerned look. No one interrupted a captain's meal without good reason, even on a small trade ship like this.

Nicolo's jawline hardened. 'If I don't get to eat this swill in peace soon I'm going to start taking it out on the crew.' He turned to the door. 'Come!'

The portal opened to reveal two burly sailors in the gloom. It took Skiouros' eyes a moment to penetrate the darkness and pick out the figure that stood behind them. It looked pitiful – a thin, dirty figure, dishevelled and unkempt.

'What's this?' Nicolo demanded, narrowing his eyes to squint into the gloom of the corridor outside.

'Stowaway, sir. One of the lads found him down below while we was movin' things around to make room for Dimitri, sir, 'cause the poor old bastard's come down with the shi... something unpleasant, sir.'

Nicolo turned to Parmenio, a questioning look on his face. The captain simply shrugged, passing the matter back to his purser.

'Bring him in.'

Skiouros watched with interest as the two men reached back to their charge and then shoved him, none too gently, into the room.

Skiouros felt a shiver run up his spine as he took in the weathered skin of the Romani beggar, the bone-strewn hair tied up with a black band, a curious half-smile on his face.

'What in God's name?'

Every face in the room turned to Skiouros. 'What is it?' Parmenio asked quietly. 'You *know* this man?'

Regretting having spoken, Skiouros was forced to nod. 'I wouldn't say that I *know* him as such, captain. I've encountered him a few times back in Candia. I retained him as a guide when I first arrived, and he was a common enough sight around the city with his begging bowl, crying out for alms.'

'*That's* where I know him from,' Nicolo said suddenly. 'Always hanging around the port at the end of our dock. Should have driven him away weeks ago. Should have expected it. Paid far too much attention to the *Isabella*, he did.'

Parmenio pursed his lips. 'Why stow away? A beggar will do no better in any other port, so what difference whether you stay in Candia? Why risk so much trouble just for a change of scenery behind your bowl?'

The filthy man stretched his neck left and right, causing the bones within to click unpleasantly, and then opened his mouth, issuing a torrent of indecipherable syllables.

'What was that?' Parmenio snapped in confusion.

'It's the tongue of the Romani,' Skiouros replied, frowning at the man. The beggar spoke reasonable Greek – he'd discovered that early on – and at least a smattering of Italian, if Skiouros remembered correctly.

'You know their language?' the captain asked in surprise.

'No. Not a word, I'm afraid, but I have heard it spoken oft-times back in Istanbul. The Romani are not uncommon in the backstreets there.'

'Was he armed?' Nicolo enquired.

'No, sir,' the sailor replied quietly. 'Just a pile of clothes that we've confiscated and put in the deck locker. Weird stuff – looks like the robes them Greek priests wear, sir.'

'Peculiar,' Parmenio noted, looking the captive up and down. 'Well we're too far out from land now. Lucky little devil managed to keep secure until we were at open sea, and the next land we'll make will be Sicilia as we round the straits to head north. Looks like we're stuck with him.'

'Can you not simply tip him overboard?' enquired the young Orsini, peering at the beggar with some distaste.

'I'm no killer, Master Orsini,' the captain replied coldly. 'Besides, one doesn't cross the Romani, lest they curse one, eh Nicolo.'

The purser folded his arms. 'Oh I dunno, captain. I might be tempted to try, particularly if that ungodly ripe smell is him – though in fairness that could just be Arnolfini's cooking.'

'Did you say one of the crew is ill?' the captain frowned.

'Two now, sir' the sailor replied. 'One with the... with rear end trouble, and the other with gut rot.'

'Then we're two men down. Master Skiouros here has kindly offered to help out when needed, but I suspect he has all the sailing nous of a crippled sheep, and we could do with more manpower during the night if we're to keep up our pace. Take our friend here forward and dip him in the bathing barrel. Clean him up, feed him, and then show him how to furl, unfurl and reef a sail and where the deck cleaning gear is. He can work his passage to Sicilia at least.'

The beggar looked up for a moment, his eyes meeting Skiouros', and the young Greek felt a strange thrill as something indescribable and intangible passed between them. The hairs stood proud on the back of his neck and he shivered.

The door closed behind the three men as the sailors took away their charge to clean him up and put him to work. For a long moment Skiouros peered at the featureless wood panel of the door, and then turned back to the others. Parmenio and Nicolo had already largely dismissed the incident and returned to their somewhat miscellaneous meal. Cesare Orsini was watching him intently. Skiouros had the sudden suspicion that the young nobleman was far cleverer than he had initially estimated and that all this time of superior silence had simply given Orsini the time and leisure to examine his fellow traveller.

'You are a soldier, Master Skiouros? And a scholar? You have the makings, it appears, of a condottiero.'

Skiouros scratched his chin and picked up the three-tined fork from the table, stabbing a chunk of something brown from the plate and lifting it to his mouth while his eyes never left his opposite number.

'Forgive me, Master Orsini, but I am no soldier. A scholar, to some small extent, but nothing more.'

'Your doublet and breeches show the unmistakable signs of having recently had a sheathed sword slung alongside them, Master Skiouros, and a longer, heavier blade too, by my estimation.'

Sharp!

Skiouros made a mental note to withdraw into an even tighter caginess with this man. It appeared distinctly possible that Cesare Orsini might be able to unravel any mystery placed before him, given the time and the opportunity to do so. Chiding himself for having underestimated the man, Skiouros tried to see the lower left of Orsini's doublet, but could not get a good enough view to make any such observation about him. Still, he would be prepared to wager that the young man had a sword in his cabin that was every bit as lethal and beautiful as the Spanish blade Skiouros had brought aboard.

'I have had some training in the use of a sword,' he countered pleasantly, forcing a fake casualness into his manner. 'Not as much as yourself, though, I would wager.'

Something sparkled in Orsini's eyes and Skiouros suddenly understood. The young man was not only surprisingly clever and observant, but he was also playful, despite his dour appearance. He had been positioning conversational pieces in a game of investigation. In other times Skiouros might find such a pastime intriguing and alluring, but not with the dreadful, secretive goal that lurked at the end of his journey. In his current circumstances, he could scant afford this young traveller unravelling the tapestry of his life merely to keep himself entertained. He would have to head off any deepening of the game.

Time to take a chance, then, and kill the game in a move. A guess, or series thereof.

'You, for instance, I would say, have been training with the blade that sits in your cabin since you were old enough to stand the high guard. How old were you, might I enquire, when you and your mother were packed off to Crete?'

Orsini narrowed his eyes. 'Eleven,' he replied simply, his eyes daring Skiouros to delve further.

'I suspected so. Shortly after the current Pope came to power and your family began to prosper. Was your father a victim of his outspokenness, or did he remain in Rome – estranged from his own wife and child while they languished in exile – in order to repair the damage he had done?'

'Have a care,' Orsini murmured with a strange look.

'The former then.' Skiouros congratulated himself on his deductive reasoning. 'My condolences on the passing of your mother.'

There was a tense silence as Parmenio and Nicolo paused, forkfuls of brown sludge halfway to their mouths, and stared at Skiouros. Orsini sat in a stony silence.

And suddenly smiled for the first time since Skiouros had entered the room.

'Bravo and well played, my friend. The coming days of this voyage are finally starting to look up. I am beginning to regret my decision to leave my chess board back on the island.'

Skiouros returned the smile, hoping his face did not display his relief that said game remained absent. He had only ever twice even seen a chess board, let alone learned how to play.

'You and I will have to have a good chinwag at some point,' the nobleman laughed. 'Not now, though. Now it is time to investigate the mystery that is dinner.'

Skiouros nodded his agreement, eyes dropping to the unidentifiable brown meal before him, wondering whether it was supposedly fish or meat or perhaps neither. He would be very careful in the coming days to avoid every opportunity to be alone with the insightful young Orsini.

Chapter Four - Of the scourge

The heavy bulk of Methoni's powerful castle sat wallowing by the shore in the late evening gloom, off to the ship's starboard side. The great Venetian fortress marked the far south-western point of mainland Greece's Morea peninsula and projected out into the sea, providing a point of shelter and protection against the pirates and corsairs – both Ottoman and independent – who plied the waters looking for easy prey. Lights flickered along the battlements and in windows.

'Are we far enough away, Lord?'

Etci Hassan, captain of one of the most feared and powerful kadirga galleys in the Ottoman fleet, peered into the gloom at the twinkling lights of the Venetian defences. Soon. Soon that great monolithic structure would fall to the ever-advancing armies of the Sultan, and good Turkish sailors would not be forced to take such pains to stay out of the castle's reach.

'They are entirely unaware of us, Mehmi, for they are complacent fools. We could sail up to their walls and piss on their fortress and they would not notice us. In some ways I feel it is a pity that they *cannot* see. It would make such a glorious display for them, but we shall have to rely on the currents to do the job for us.'

'Now, Lord?'

'Now, Mehmi.'

Hassan stood at the rail, his arms folded, peering with distaste at the Christian fortress looming in the evening gloom. It had been a long journey from Avlonya, and there was a long sail ahead of them to meet up with Kemal Reis' fleet, but this trip had been worth the detour. Three unauthorised, but very successful, surprise raids on the island of

Zakynthos had filled the few spaces in the kadirga's hold with a great deal of valuable loot that would buy Hassan the goodwill of the Sultan when all of this was over – gold and silver crosses, reliquaries, coins and sundry treasure from the villages, churches and even a monastery. The great Kemal Reis could do what he liked with his honour and his respect, but when he stood before Bayezid, he would likely be torn apart and burned for his failure. The same fate would not befall Etci Hassan and his crew.

The resupply mission had been the perfect opportunity to leave the noble lord's side long enough to fill his coffers and slake his thirst for infidel blood. They would be cutting it fine taking so much time to skirt the Greek coast before heading west, especially if they tried to keep the coastline in sight as they sailed, but the chests of gold and silver in the hold made every extra moment worthwhile.

It had been a troublesome day's sailing from Zakynthos to the very edge of the Morea and the cursed Methoni castle. The captives had been no trouble, of course – how could they be after their throats had been slashed in honour of the great jihad? But still, Hassan's crew had become increasingly nervous at their continued presence on board the *Yarim Ay*. After all, it was one of the great taboos of the Ottoman world: to bring a corpse into a house was to invite a visit from death, and a ship could be counted no different to a house. So what trouble was their captain inviting when he brought two dozen stinking bodies aboard, and one of them a Christian priest, no less?

Such superstitions held no fear for Etci Hassan – beloved of Allah and the Prophet – of course. God kept him for greater things. But no matter how strong a captain might be, without a crew he was just a man.

Even Mehmi had been twitchy around the dead priest!

But now it was time to unburden themselves of their grisly cargo.

Time to pay the accursed Christians back for their temerity.

The smell of fresh meat assailed his nostrils and he breathed deep, savouring the odour. The two hastily constructed rafts were being lowered into the water and Hassan listened with satisfaction to the splash as they touched down.

Calmly, fingers resting on the rail, he watched with a nod of approval as the bodies of the men, women and children of Zakynthos, flayed and eviscerated and with the ridiculous three-barred cross of the Greek Church carved into their foreheads, were dropped unceremoniously into the rafts and then cast adrift.

44

The morning tide would bring them washing up on the beaches of Methoni, where they would horrify and frighten the cowardly infidels.

And as the charnel vessels bobbed off with their stinking, white-pink cargoes, Hassan turned his gaze west. That was it, now. Barring the loot hidden deep in his hold, the last evidence of his raiding that defied Kemal's orders was busy drifting away toward the shore.

Mehmi stood nearby, watching the bodies float away with a tangible sense of relief.

And at the rear, where he was working at fixing a broken oar, the ship's carpenter, already pale and wan, coughed and looked down at his hand, registering with dismay the blood clot that had spattered it.

Chapter Five - Of inevitable encounters.

'**S**hip ho!'

Skiouros turned from his conversation with Nicolo to peer up at the lookout who sat precariously on the mainmast yard, legs dangling and one arm wrapped around the spar for safety. Concern flooding through him at the news, Skiouros turned to the stern, where Parmenio stood in deep discussion with Cesare Orsini. The captain was also peering up at the lookout.

'Details?' he bellowed.

'Not sure, sir, but she's low and flat. Can't see oars yet, but she looks galley-style. Lateen sails... two masts.'

'Colours?'

'Blue and black, I think, captain.'

Nicolo, next to Skiouros swore under his breath and muttered, 'That rules out most friendly nations.'

'Can you see the stern? Or how the sails are rigged?'

'Stern's low and square, cap'n. Could be a Turk. Could be Venetian, mind, or even something else.'

There was a pause.

'Overlapping lateens, sir. A proper big overlap, too.'

Skiouros frowned, unfamiliar with sailing terminology, and turned a questioning glance to Nicolo, whose face had set grim.

'Turks,' he said in explanation. 'Unusual sail configuration with a heavy overlap.'

'Have they seen us?' Parmenio shouted.

'Don't think so, sir. No change, so if we drop the sails.... Wait!'

The crew collectively held their breath, each man pausing in his work, looking up expectantly at the lookout aloft. After a pause that felt like an eternity, the young man leaned down again.

'She's turning on us!'

'Shit!' snapped Parmenio. Still the crew paused, awaiting the command of their captain. Parmenio shielded his eyes with his hand and squinted over the rail – somewhat pointlessly, given that the enemy vessel was little more than a dark blot on the horizon from the deck, repeatedly lost behind the rolling waves.

'They'll come fast.'

Nicolo dropped the rope he'd been coiling and paced across the deck to his captain, Skiouros, unsure of what to do, scurrying along behind.

'Can we outrun them?' the purser asked as the two pairs of men met at the rail.

'Only if the galley's damaged or over-laden or their captain's a dolt. An Ottoman kadirga in full sail's a match for a good caravel on even terms, but with us so weighed down and them having oars to help close—'

Parmenio turned to the crew, who were still watching him expectantly.

'What are you waiting for?' he snapped irritably. 'Bring us around south by southwest and rig the sails for maximum speed.'

Nicolo nodded, but Skiouros frowned in incomprehension as the crew suddenly burst into life and the *Isabella* lurched and began to turn.

'I thought you said we couldn't outrun them?'

Parmenio tapped his lip with a twitching finger. 'We can't. But there are only a few places on the African coast where a Turk is welcome, and most of the Hafsid rulers are well-disposed towards Venezia because of the trade benefits. It's a small chance and it depends on how fast they're coming, but if we can get close enough to the coast before the bastards close on us, we might find a friendly Arab ship to help.'

Skiouros peered out at the dark blot over the waves as Parmenio and Nicolo turned and made their way back across the deck. To Skiouros' inexpert eye the ship looked considerably larger already, and larger meant closer.

'Parmenio fools only himself,' the young Orsini murmured, coming to stand next to him.

'How far are we from the safety of that Hafsid land he was talking about?'

'Days.'

'And we don't have days?'

'We might have hours if we're lucky – I've seen Venetian and Genoese galleys at full pace and they would easily outstrip this old girl. And we're a long haul from Africa too. Must be fairly close to the southern coast of the Italian peninsula by now.'

'Then why go south and not north?'

'You're not a sailor, are you.' Orsini smiled grimly. 'The wind is with us as we head south. If we went north we'd be into the wind, and the Turks' oars would soon close the gap.'

'Seems like we're in the shit both ways,' Skiouros sighed.

'Indeed. I know little of the Ottoman navy. Will they attempt to board us or just sink us? You're from their lands.'

Skiouros pursed his lips. He had little experience of the Turks' navy himself, but numerous times he'd seen their ships in the surrounding waters and harbours, and it was impossible to spend a decade living in the capital without hearing a thing or two and coming to understand a little of how the great captains of the Sultan's fleet worked.

'If he's a senior reis, he's likely to be politic. Since we're not at war, they will likely demand some sort of 'compensation' for the inconvenience of stopping us. They'll find some reason – checking for stolen cargo or Turkish slaves or some such. Senior captains have nothing to prove, but they do like to throw their weight around sometimes and make a little profit.'

'Otherwise?'

'If it's a junior captain with a lot to prove? To be honest, from what I've heard we might be better scuttling the ship ourselves and trying to swim to Africa.'

Orsini showed no sign of nerves, simply nodding to himself as he pondered the matter.

'Then might I suggest this would be a good time for you and I to go below and retrieve our blades, Master Skiouros? We shall see which one of us is condottieri material.'

Five minutes later, as Skiouros and his companion emerged from the doorway, their sheathed blades swinging at their sides, Parmenio, Nicolo and the steersman were in deep hushed conversation. The two armed passengers strode across to the senior crewmen, nodding their greeting.

48

'Skiouros' opinion is worth noting. No one here knows the Turkish mind like him,' Parmenio said, gesturing at the arrivals. The other two turned to look at him.

'Sorry?'

'There is some division of opinion,' Nicolo explained carefully, 'as to whether we would be better surrendering than fighting.'

Skiouros peered past them. Clearly any hope of flight or evasion had been abandoned, as the Ottoman kadirga was now near enough to make out details. They would close far too soon. Parmenio's jawline hardened as he spoke again.

'I believe that my fearless crew are suspicious of my motives. They put my urge to fight and not surrender down to the fact that the cargo we stand to lose is *my* livelihood, and not to an understanding of what it is that we actually face. Tell them what will happen if we surrender, Skiouros.'

The young Greek took a deep breath. It was hard to deny the validity of the crew's point of view. The preciousness of the ship's cargo would certainly have figured in the captain's decision-making but, regardless, he was almost certainly still correct in his conclusion. The fact that the Turk was so doggedly pursuing them suggested this was no mere 'bribe-and-run' situation.

'This hunter is intent on his target,' Skiouros replied quietly. 'A legitimate Ottoman captain would have given up by now, seeing how determined we were to get away. For most of them a difficult prey is not worth the effort. Which means that, no matter how official his command, this one's a corsair.'

'And that's bad,' Parmenio added, somewhat unnecessarily.

'Very bad. A corsair is only barely legal even in Ottoman terms so, unless they're preying on a nation they're at war with, they try not to leave any evidence. That means stealing the most valuable cargo, enslaving anyone they think they can make something from, killing the rest and then sinking the ship. Very bad.'

'Does the *Isabella* have any weapons?' Orsini asked quietly, peering at the approaching galley. 'I've seen none.'

'Clubs, swords and the like,' Nicolo replied. 'A few bows.'

'And them?'

Skiouros shrugged. 'Never been close enough to one to find out, but the Ottoman army prides itself on its guns. My brother used to enthuse about them no end.'

'It'll likely come down to hand-fighting in the end,' Orsini nodded to himself, peering with interest at Skiouros, perhaps wondering why his brother would have intimate knowledge of the Ottoman military. 'They will not wish to hole the ship before they can examine the cargo. Will they try anything before boarding, do you think?'

'Arrow storm, probably,' Parmenio sighed. 'Only a few shots, though – maybe three or four. They won't want to risk too many random deaths in case they happen to hit something valuable, but they'll want to thin the opposition, I'm sure. It's a play off. All depends on how greedy or violent the bastard who runs the ship is.'

Orsini squinted across the water at the ever-closing enemy galley. 'Turn into them, then.'

'What?' Nicolo, Parmenio, Skiouros and the steersman all stared at the Italian noble.

'If the biggest threat we face before combat is their arrows, run them down. The sooner we close on them, the less chance they get to fill us with arrows.'

Nicolo nodded slowly. 'Captain?'

'Do it.'

Skiouros watched in impotent dismay as the officers and crew suddenly burst into a fresh frenzy of activity, bringing the ship about in as tight a turn as they could manage in order to minimise the missile danger.

Orsini tapped him on the shoulder. 'Walk with me, Master Skiouros.'

The young Greek, his hand resting on his sword hilt, shuffled across the deck after his fellow traveller, trying not to let the pitch of the timber floor unfoot him as he walked. The nobleman reached the rail and leaned over as though examining the sea that roiled beneath.

'You've never killed a man,' he said flatly without looking around at Skiouros, and quietly enough that the working sailors would not overhear their conversation.

For a split second, Skiouros found himself standing in a shadowy memory of the Church of Saint Saviour in the fields, a heavy piece of stone poised to drop on the incapacitated Mamluk assassin, and then in the drenched street above the former Ottoman powder store, watching stone blocks the size of cattle falling from the sky. He closed his eyes and when he replied his voice was quiet and sad.

'I think I wish that were true, Orsini. In actual fact, I have killed at least three men.' He smiled hollowly. 'Never with one of these, though,' he added, patting the hilt of his sword.

'Never in battle. Are you sure you wish to do this? I will honestly think no less of you if you do not. My uncle is one of the greatest warriors in Christendom, and yet I would sooner favour a talented artist or a tuneful musician than such as he. The sword can be as cruel a mistress as the sea. It is not for everyone. An untrained and panicked soldier can be more of a hindrance than a boon to his own in the midst of battle.'

Skiouros peered out at the water. The *Isabella* was coming about rapidly and with every degree it turned, he was brought one heartbeat closer to a fight to the death. While he had been training and preparing himself for such eventualities this past year, he had truly expected only to find the need to draw a blade once he was in the heart of the Pope's realm with the traitor Cem Sultan in his sight – if such a thing were ever possible. To fight a bloodthirsty battle against pirates had not been part of his plan. Ottoman corsairs would be the enemy, of course, but not the seething object of hatred at the heart of his revenge. Could he really take lives like this? The three in Istanbul had been more a matter of survival than anger, but had been given the added impetus of having been responsible for Lykaion's death and therefore deserving of such divine retribution meted out by the hand of his brother.

But then what was *this* danger but another fight for survival, even if the enemy meant nothing to him?

'You'll not find me lacking, Orsini,' he said, praying to God that it was the truth.

The two men continued to stare out at the water and Skiouros could almost feel his companion nodding his understanding – perhaps even his approval – without looking round. Slowly, the vessel began to straighten once more, the sailors working madly to angle the sails just so in order to inch slowly north back towards the closing kadirga. The going was suddenly tough after sailing with the wind and Skiouros could feel the strain even through the boards of the deck.

As the minutes passed, the lookout regularly calling updates of distance from his lofty position, Skiouros tried to think back over what he had seen of the large galley vessels that formed the backbone of the Turkish navy. He'd never paid a great deal of attention, scarcely crediting the possibility that one day he might be staring down the bowsprit of one. But here and there over the years he had seen the ships

51

bobbing up and down in one of Istanbul's harbours, or plying the waters around the city.

Somewhat longer than the *Isabella*, the standard kadirga was a simple vessel, designed with speed and power in mind, like a hunter. It was rigged with an unusual sail system that actually gave it an edge over the standard western vessel and, with the addition of oars as a secondary system of propulsion, was capable of an astonishing turn of speed for short distances. Such vessels had occasionally put on displays in the Propontine Sea on state occasions. The cargo deck was wide and low, and the main deck above was given over almost entirely to benches for the oarsmen, the only flat walking spaces being the housing at the stern and the fighting platform at the bow, linked by a narrow walkway that ran down the deck's centre between the rows of benches. The bow platform would be where any guns would likely be placed, and where the dozen or so archers would likely be positioned, though a careful captain might have reserves in the stern. The rowers – galley slaves taken in battle or criminals condemned to the navy – would remain shackled to their oars while the captain's Turkish crew fought the battle, hoping their masters won so that the ship was not sunk, taking the chained oarsmen with it to the bottom.

Thus the great dangers came from fore and aft. The Turks might have as many as fifty fighting men aboard, while the *Isabella* held a grand total of twenty-eight souls, two of whom languished in their sickbed, one of whom was an old Romani beggar put to work hoisting sails, and the rest primarily sailors, bearing only a cudgel to defend themselves. It would likely be a short fight.

'It might be better not to be taken alive,' he said to Orsini. 'At best we'll end our days rowing that thing for them. The alternatives are less pleasant.'

The Italian drew his fine blade with a hiss and a rasp and smiled humourlessly. 'It is you for whom I worry, Master Skiouros. The mere mention of my name will likely be enough to buy my life. No pirate would pass up the ransom they would get from the Orsini, even for an ill-favoured relative. I fear you have no such financial backing.'

Skiouros fell silent and nodded as he drew his own sword.

Parmenio stepped out into the centre of the deck as the lookout gave the estimated remaining count of one minute.

'Essential hands only to ship duties. Everyone else arm up and head to the bow!'

As Skiouros and Orsini strode back along the deck towards the gathering crowd at the fore, Nicolo arrived, catching up with the captain and carrying two well-worn scabbarded swords with him. Passing one over to Parmenio, he strapped on the other sword belt and eased the blade from the sheath, listening to the sound as he chewed on his lip. Somehow, Skiouros formed the impression that Nicolo found the wearing of the sword unpleasant in some way.

Hardly had the four men arrived among the press of sailors at the bow when the lookout cried out a warning.

'Archers!'

With faces of grim determination, the crew of the *Isabella*, a variety of swords, daggers and clubs in hand, dropped behind the ship's rail, trusting to the high point of the bow to prevent the worst of the attack. It was only as he fell to the deck with the rest that Skiouros realised why the captain had called them all to the bow – the closest point to the enemy archers. It was, from a head-on angle at least, the only position on the ship that offered any kind of shelter. A dozen or so arrows swept through the air towards the *Isabella* and the cringing defenders could hear the points thunking into the timber of the bow less than a foot from their sheltered heads, only two missiles falling harmlessly into the water. Three of the flighted nightmares swept over their heads. One thudded into the deck, while a second struck one of the working sailors in the thigh, causing him to drop to the deck screaming and clutching himself. The third parted the hair of one of the men at the rail, drawing an angry red line across his scalp.

'Thirty!' yelled the lookout.

'Another volley then,' Orsini sighed, hunkering down low. Skiouros followed suit as the thrumming sound of the arrows came again. This time the sea claimed none, and a mere three struck the timber bow. The man to Skiouros' right shrieked as the steel point of the missile passed through his cheek, smashing teeth and bone and severing his tongue before emerging from the far side of his face, continuing on its flight and coming to a halt scraping along the deck. More yelps from back along the vessel announced further casualties among the working crew.

The disfigured and agonising man disappeared – Skiouros had neither the time nor the inclination to see what had happened to him – to be quickly replaced by another figure, and it was with a strangely juxtaposed mix of resigned acceptance and curious interest that he recognised the shape of the Romani beggar, gripping a studded club of ash.

'Fifteen!' bellowed the lookout and Parmenio rose, sure now that there would be no further missiles. *Good job*, thought Skiouros, as he mentally estimated the ship's active complement now at twenty or perhaps twenty-one men, including those required to handle the vessel itself. The next few minutes looked exceedingly bleak.

'Stand and make ready,' Parmenio barked, as Nicolo peered over the rail and shouted 'Brace!'

But the captain of the Turkish vessel apparently had no intention of ramming them, as Nicolo expected. At the last moment, as Skiouros stood and saw the looming shape of the kadirga, the Turkish ship banked sharply to starboard, withdrawing oars in a smooth motion. The ships, instead of colliding, swept past one another, their bows passing a matter of mere feet apart.

Skiouros frowned in surprise, his eyes crossing to the fighting platform at the front of the enemy vessel and widening at what he saw there.

'What... the fuck... are those?' asked Nicolo in a small, hoarse voice.

Skiouros realised that he was looking directly down the pitch black barrel of the artillery piece and instinctively stepped to the right. Two Abus guns swivelled on their tripods, picking a target on the *Isabella*'s deck. With a wide barrel and too heavy to be held by a man, these anti-personnel nightmares that fired iron balls three inches across had been employed by the Ottoman military at times, but he'd not heard of their use aboard ships before.

'Down!' he yelled, but not quite quickly enough.

The two guns fired as the ship swept alongside. A heavy shot passed through the space the young Greek had occupied a heartbeat earlier. Something warm and damp sprayed across the back of Skiouros' head, and he did not need to turn to see what the howitzer had done to the man behind his shoulder or how much of him was left as he slapped wetly to the deck.

A collective groan went through the *Isabella*'s crew and Skiouros ground his teeth. The Abus guns were hardly a suitable weapon for ship fighting. Indeed, two men with bows or muskets would likely have done just as much damage, but the effect on the defending crew's morale was instantly palpable.

A good Ottoman commander relied as much on fear unmanning his enemy as he did on the actual execution of battle.

The crew of the caravel reeled in shock and dismay, losing them precious time. The Turkish captain suffered no such difficulty. His crew leapt to the rail, bows discarded, and threw their grapples, hooking them onto anything and instantly feeding the ropes through the rail of their own vessel, anchoring them.

In the two heartbeats that the *Isabella*'s crew required to realise that they stood no chance against this enemy, six grapples and ropes tautened between the ships, the rowers of the kadirga smoothly back-oaring to ease the closing of the two vessels, the Turkish sailors dropping the sails to prevent the wind carrying them any further than necessary.

The ropes reached their anchored maximum length and strained with a groan. Both ships complained at the sudden pressure and the *Isabella*'s forward momentum was almost entirely arrested in seconds, every man aboard being thrown from his feet or against the bow.

'To arms!' bellowed Parmenio, struggling to his feet.

Skiouros scrambled from the deck, his ankle aching slightly from an awkward fall, gripping his sword hilt and trying to take stock of the situation as the world exploded into deadly activity around him.

Turkish sailors were pouring across the gap between the ships, heedless of the danger. One was caught a blow by an enterprising Venetian sailor before he managed to get his feet across the *Isabella*'s rail and the Turk disappeared down between the two hulls, his scream cut off sharply as the ships smacked together once more, crushing him instantly before he had a chance to drown.

The corsairs were everywhere.

Skiouros had experienced the infamous crowds of Istanbul during riots. He had fought for his life against deadly assassins and fled through a city in fear of his life. He had, in two short years, experienced more horror and danger than most men faced in a lifetime.

But he had never been in battle and, as Orsini had surmised, had never used a sword in anger. His heart fell as he realised at this critical juncture that he had no will to kill.

Even as a Turk leapt at him, sword raised high and ready to fall – to split him in two – he could not summon up the will deep in his soul to actually push a length of steel into the man's body, severing organs and ripping the God-given life from him. It was a dreadful realisation. His sword lessons had been utterly pointless. It mattered not that he knew exactly *what* to do – and he did; the corsair had left himself wide open

55

and Skiouros could easily skewer him in the blink of an eye – no amount of knowledge could overcome his soul-deep abhorrence at the thought of taking this man's life simply because he fought on a different side.

He should have died, then. Would have done, had not a blade whipped in from somewhere and punched a foot deep into the man's armpit. As the raised *kilij* sabre fell uselessly away and the Turk screamed at the realisation that a death blow had been struck, Skiouros glanced around in a panic to see Orsini giving him a look. The Italian's eyes dropped meaningfully to the clean blade in Skiouros' hands, and then he was off again, fighting another man.

Skiouros felt panic completely overwhelm him.

What was he to do? He felt his bladder beginning to strain, threatening to give way in a flood.

Suddenly he was knocked aside and, recovering, he turned in confusion to find Nicolo backing across the deck, his blade whirling and flashing as he parried and lunged at the heavy-set Turk with the drooping moustaches before him. Even Nicolo – a merchantman's purser – seemed to be fighting as though born to it.

The world swam and whirled around him as Skiouros staggered and spun in blind confusion. All about him sailors smashed down with clubs, splintering bones and crushing faces, or lunged with swords, puncturing hearts and lungs, cutting throats and severing limbs. Twice again a booming sound announced the firing of the Abus guns that turned good men into chunks of shredded meat.

Skiouros felt sick. Probably was sick. His bladder leaked just a little and it was only through a miracle of self-control that he managed not to completely piss himself.

Something struck him again, and Skiouros reached up to his shoulder in surprise. When he took his hand away it was soaked with blood. Well at least if he was going to die now, he would not have to face the ignominious failure he apparently was. What really kept him in the world, after all?

Lykaion…

'I'll miss you, brother.'

The throbbing pain in his left shoulder began to insist itself on his thoughts, and he focused on it, grateful for anything that distracted him from his utter failure.

A black shape suddenly blurred across in front of him. He blinked away sweat and realised that it was Cesare Orsini, backing across the deck, his blade whirring expertly, holding a Turk at bay, though the pirate was clearly also a master swordsman and continued to advance slowly.

It took only a moment for Skiouros to piece together what he was seeing and to follow the motions that would follow to their inevitable conclusion. Another Turk with a vicious knife in each hand was busy dispatching a Venetian sailor, the blood sheeting from the poor man's sliced throat. As soon as he dropped the body and turned he would have Orsini backing blindly towards him. The rest was too horrible to picture.

Despite his initial reservations about the disenfranchised Italian nobleman, Skiouros found at this last desperate juncture that he had warmed enough to the enigmatic man with his powerful intellect that he would truly be sorry to witness his demise.

He couldn't.

He could not watch another of his friends or even closer acquaintances die horribly before his very eyes. It seemed that at the very end he was a coward after all. And selfish, as the Romani had accused him of being just a few days – and a lifetime – ago back in Crete. For as he closed his eyes he knew, deep in his heart, that that was just a way to prevent himself having to suffer the sight of another friend's death.

He shivered with cold fear and hot pain simultaneously, the darkness of his eyelids doing nothing to prevent the images of battle and death assailing him, his ears filling with the din of cries, the scrape and rasp and clang of weapon on weapon, the smell of blood and death and shit filling his nostrils.

He was fairly sure he was crying.

A scream in front of him shocked his eyes open – Orsini's end appeared to have come.

Skiouros was more than a little surprised as his eyelids prised open slowly to see his own arm extended, the fine Spanish blade in his grip thrust deep into the chest of the Turk with the two knives. The corsair was staring at him, mouth flapping open and closed in horror.

Had *he* done that? How had he done that?

Before he even thought through what he was doing, Skiouros realised that he was twisting the blade in a half circle the way Iannis had taught him, before jerking it sideways to be sure of severe organ damage before withdrawing it.

As the Turk sank to his knees, a gobbet of blood coughing from his mouth, Skiouros stared in shock at the glistening crimson blade extending from his own hand.

57

'Thank you,' laughed Orsini, as he drove his own sword into the chest of the man with whom he'd been struggling. 'Most timely, my friend.'

Skiouros could not find his voice to answer as the Italian swordsman leapt off to find a new opponent. The Greek instead stared at the blade, his eyes jerking up and down, watching the droplets of blood falling from the sword's point to the deck.

Someone bellowed something in Turkish off to his left, and Skiouros turned his head to see another corsair with a curved blade stepping towards him.

'No,' he replied in perfect Turkish, turning and raising the sword. 'Not me. Not here.'

The corsair frowned in surprise to find a Turkish speaker on board a Christian vessel this far west, and he faltered for a moment.

'No,' repeated Skiouros as he took two steps forward and brought the blade round in an arc that the Turk barely managed to parry in time.

'No.' The swords met and rang again, and the corsair was forced to take a step back, surprised at the sudden ferocity of his opponent. Two more clangs of the blade. Two more steps back.

'No!' Skiouros snapped.

'Stop saying that!' demanded the Turk as he slammed up against the rail with nowhere else to go to escape this strange madman.

'No,' replied Skiouros, flipping his sword around with surprising speed and driving the point into the man's neck just below the chin, pushing hard and driving in the steel until he felt the blade meet the resistance of the back of the corsair's skull.

Something had happened and Skiouros would never be able to put it into words if he was asked, but it felt as though he had been pushing at an impenetrable wicker screen, unable to overcome it and fighting as hard as he could, and then suddenly he had burst through it. He had battled something and come out of the other side.

Something was different, though only time would tell what.

Pulling his blade out of the shuddering corpse, Skiouros realised that the battle was over. The Turkish corsairs were crossing back to their own vessel, delivering a last blow or two on the way.

Had they won? Surely that was impossible.

His eyes scanned the deck and took in the large number of bodies, most of whom bore the drab work clothes of the Venetian sailors.

No. They hadn't won. They had lost. Almost critically so.

A voice cut through the rapidly diminishing din – a voice speaking in fluent Italian, slowly and clearly enough that Skiouros found that he could follow what was said without any difficulty. The speaker had a Turkish accent, an Anatolian one.

'Lay down your weapons and surrender your vessel to Etci Hassan, Reis of the kadirga *Yarim Ay*. Submit and there is a chance that you will live. Refuse and you will all meet your infidel God with salt water inflating your lungs.'

Skiouros looked around and saw Parmenio and Nicolo nearby, both displaying minor wounds and both blood-stained, side-by-side. He followed their gaze and his eyes fell upon the Turkish captain, standing on the raised deck to the stern of the war galley. He stood next to a small crew of corsairs, who crowded around a bronze *sahalaz* cannon, angled – if Skiouros was any judge – such that its shot would punch through the *Isabella*'s hull just below the waterline.

'I would regret losing the opportunity of plunder,' the pirate captain added, 'but my hold is already packed, and I would rather not lose any more men. You have until the count of ten for your officers to step forward and surrender, else I will give the command to fire and we will watch you drown like the Christian dogs you are.'

Skiouros turned back to Parmenio and realised as he saw the captain's expression that there was no choice other than surrender.

Rome and the usurping prince Cem had never seemed so far from his grasp.

Chapter Six - Of captives and victims

'**S**ix!'

Parmenio took a deep breath. The count of ten, the Turk had said. Skiouros could see in his expression the hopelessness of an anticipated total loss. The captain had staked everything on this voyage with its large commissions, and he had now lost it all. He might not die – at least not yet. As a captain, he could be valuable or useful to the Turks as a prisoner. But whether he survived or not, he *had* lost his cargo and his ship, effectively bankrupting him.

That was all moot, of course.

Though Parmenio might be useful for now, the corsair captain would not be able to keep him around, providing living, breathing evidence of his piracy against the Republic of Venice, a nation with whom the Ottoman Empire was currently enjoying a rare, fragile peace. The captain's future looked no less grim than any other of the *Isabella*'s crewmen, even should he receive a temporary stay of execution.

'Seven!'

Skiouros looked around as Parmenio stepped forward, making himself known to the Turkish captain. There were perhaps a dozen or so men of the *Isabella* left moving on deck. Less than half. The grim looks on their faces told him everything he needed to know: their fate would not be pretty.

The corsair captain had stated that his hold was packed. If he had taken that much booty already, then his galley-slave complement would also likely be full, and he would not be looking for chained rowers. That meant that unless a captive displayed some sort of value, the Turks would have no use for them. At best they would be shackled and taken to a seething hive of depravity and sold as slaves. More likely they would be dispatched quickly and efficiently.

The only figures that stood proud – if equally grim – were Parmenio, Nicolo and Orsini. The former pair held the value of experienced ship's officers and might well see another day. Orsini might be worth a ransom to the corsairs.

Skiouros, of course, had no more value than any of the ordinary sailors.

The captain cleared his voice to address the Turk. 'I am Parmenio, son of Christos of Durazzo and captain of the Venetian caravel *Isabella*. As a son of the Republic, it is my duty to remind you that a treaty exists between our governments and this assault constitutes an act of war.'

Skiouros felt his heart skip a beat. The sort of Ottoman captain who would launch such an attack was hardly likely to be swayed by such rhetoric and might well become homicidally enraged by such a reminder.

An uncomfortable silence settled on the ships.

'Eight!' snapped the Turk.

'There is still the opportunity to label this a misunderstanding and go our separate ways.'

Skiouros had to hand it to Parmenio. The man seemed calm and in control, despite having no cards left even to bluff with.

'Nine!'

Parmenio's shoulders slumped slightly.

'On behalf of my crew and passengers, I hereby surrender the *Isabella* and her cargo to you in the knowledge that a good son of Allah will honour his captives and avoid excessive cruelty.'

Again, Skiouros winced at the captain's vain attempt to see to the survival of his crew. *Don't push him too far, Parmenio.*

The Turk turned to his man and rattled something off in Turkish. Parmenio and Nicolo looked across to Skiouros for a translation, but he shook his head imperceptibly, indicating that he'd not heard the exchange. A moment later, the corsair captain turned back to the defeated crew.

'The unranked crew of this caravel will assemble in the bow, unarmed, to be assessed by Mehmi here. He does not speak your vile tongue, but he is an excellent judge of livestock.' The short one called Mehmi smiled unpleasantly, displaying the black space where his two front top teeth were missing, a smile made all the more repulsive by the scar that ran from the corner of his nose to his jaw, heavily creasing one side of his face.

'The officers and passengers will come aboard the *Yarim Ay*, unarmed and bearing any documentation as to their identity, as well as the ship's manifest and crew listings. I give you three minutes to assemble the appropriate papers. Should there be any sign of betrayal on the part of any man, I will have the cannon fired and we will watch you all drown.'

Parmenio stepped back to join Nicolo in a position where the sails and rigging almost obscured them from their captors. Quietly, the captain addressed Nicolo and the purser nodded before walking towards the stern, pausing as he passed Skiouros and Orsini.

'Come with me,' he hissed to the pair as he strode on.

Surprised, the young Greek scurried along behind as the purser disappeared into the ship's gloomy interior, Orsini walking purposefully with them.

'What are we doing?' Skiouros hissed. 'You heard that bastard. He'll sink the ship and drown everyone if we get up to anything.'

Nicolo paused in the corridor and frowned at him.

'I had formed the impression that you'd had something of a misspent youth, Skiouros. A risk taker. Maybe a thief? I don't know. But whatever you've been, you need to start taking risks right now, 'cause if you don't you'll drown like the rest.'

Skiouros shook his head. 'They'll probably save you two and Orsini – you've slave value if nothing else.'

'You too. Come on. The captain has an idea, but we've only got three minutes. Go to the captain's cabin and look in the leather wallet on the top shelf. Find the book with the manifest in for me.'

Skiouros frowned at him.

'Just go. And Master Orsini, you had best fetch whatever papers you have to prove your connections.'

The Italian noble nodded and slipped into his room. Skiouros moved to the end of the corridor and entered the cabin shared by the captain and his purser, scanning the walls for the shelf. Finding it, he shuffled the leather case from the dusty surface, sliding it down and onto the captain's cot. As he undid the catches and retrieved a heavy bound book from within, Nicolo appeared through the door, laden with goods. Skiouros turned to him.

'Is this the book you... Hey! Is that my stuff?'

'Not any more, it's not. And get rid of that sword. Dead give-away, that is. And yes, that's the manifest. Pass it here.'

Confused and perturbed, Skiouros handed the heavy tome to the purser and began to unbuckle his sword belt, regretfully.

'How much do you know about the church?' Nicolo asked quietly.

Skiouros blinked. 'What?'

'The Church. God? Jesus? Holy Mother Mary? I presume you've heard of them?'

'Of course. I've been studying the Pope and his people this past year and I...'

'Not *my* church, you hare-brain. Yours!'

Again, Skiouros frowned. 'What? Well, more than some people, I suppose. Spent a lot of time in churches recently, and in the company of monks too.'

'Good,' Nicolo said, and cast a small bundle of dark rags at him. Skiouros dropped the sword he was still holding reflexively, in order to catch the bundle.

'Put those on,' the purser hissed. 'Quickly, now. We've less than a minute.'

Skiouros stared down at the rags and realised with a sinking heart that the strange lump in the pile was the drum-shaped *skouphos* hat of an orthodox priest.

'Oh come on!'

'Parmenio's idea. It's a gamble. Some corsairs are vehemently anti-Christian and will go out of their way to destroy priests and holy men, but some are less devout and more loot-oriented. The latter might think twice about just executing a man of God – even the *wrong* God. Sailors are a superstitious lot, believe me. It's a chance – a small one, admittedly – but a chance. Now put that on and start thinking Godly.'

Orsini appeared in the doorway, cradling a leather folder with the emblem of his family branded into it. 'Time to go, gentlemen,' he said quietly and purposefully. Nicolo turned to look at him as he rifled through the book, looking for the current journey manifest.

'Master Cesare Orsini, meet Father Skiouros, a monk of the Cretan Vrontisiou monastery, on a cultural mission to the Holy Father in Rome.'

'This will never work,' Skiouros grumbled, ripping off his expensive doublet and letting it fall to the floor. Nicolo kicked the offending evidence of a clothing change under the bed.

'You speak Greek as a native. You know a bit about the daily life of the church. You're thin and reedy like a monk. And you don't have to be letter perfect on your creed – I'm sure the Turks won't spot any cock-ups. You can pull it off, 'cause if you don't, you're going for a long swim.' The purser turned to Orsini. 'What do you think?'

'It might work. So long as the captain's not a crusading type, and the crew are not questioned over him, of course.'

Nicolo shrugged. 'They won't bother speaking to the crew, especially when they've checked the manifest.' As Skiouros shrugged himself into the dusty, smelly vestments, grunting with the effort and the unpleasantness, Nicolo found the entry for the passengers and added the honorific 'Fr.' to the name 'Skiouros – Candia'. 'There you are: we officially took on a monk back in port. Just remember not to curse or spit or fart.'

Orsini smiled his strange flat smile. 'I've yet to meet a priest who's not a past master of all three.'

The purser cocked his head, listening to a commotion outside.

'Come on, we've got to go. I'll take the manifest up... you two follow on as soon as you're ready.'

Skiouros glared at the back of the purser as the man ducked out of the room and ran along the corridor, brandishing the manifest book.

'At least it looks like they fit,' Orsini said conversationally from the doorway.

Skiouros, already tightly packed into the *anteri* cassock, struggled to pull the vest over his head. 'It certainly smells lived in,' the Greek grunted, sniffing the vest and pulling his face away in disgust, remembering its last occupant as the Romani beggar had been brought into the dining room.

Orsini chuckled. 'You need a hand?'

'Funnily enough, no. It might sound strange,' he added as he straightened the vest that hung to the knee, and reached for the outer *exorasson* cassock, 'but this is far from the first time I've dressed as a monk. In fact, I have the horrible feeling I've worn this very set of vestments before. I'm pretty sure I can still smell my own vomit on it.'

As the billowing outer cassock dropped over the top and Skiouros adjusted it, Orsini raised a curious eyebrow.

'You do seem to fit it well. I'll not pry, but I shall pray to God that the Turks think so too.' He smiled. 'I wonder if a good Catholic prayer for the welfare of an Orthodox monk is some kind of heresy?'

'I'm *not* a monk,' grumbled Skiouros.

'You are now. And don't forget it.'

Orsini watched with interest as Skiouros plopped the hat onto his scalp and arranged the veil so that it hung down the back neatly.

'How do I look?'

'Godly,' Orsini smiled. 'Dusty, but Godly. Get out there and don't forget to act like a monk.'

Skiouros sighed and stepped out of the room, Orsini ducking back and bowing respectfully as though the Greek was the real thing. Taking a deep breath and wishing he had more of a beard than the four-day growth of black bristles, Skiouros moved along the corridor and stepped into the bright sunlight of the Mediterranean.

A dozen Turkish sailors were aboard the *Isabella* now. Three of them were busy roping the Venetian sailors together at both hands and feet. *Slaves*, was Skiouros' first thought, until he noticed that behind them, unseen by the unfortunate men, one of the Turks was securing a heavy cannon ball to the rope. Skiouros felt sick as his mind leapt ahead to the conclusion of that particular activity.

He turned away from the pre-execution ritual, looking instead at the *Isabella*'s officers. Parmenio stood at the rail, along with Nicolo. Across the gap and past the rails, the Turkish captain stood aboard the *Yarim Ay* with his second, examining the log book, several armed men keeping a close eye on the *Isabella*'s senior men. The corsair looked up as the two passengers strode across the deck towards them.

'Cesare Orsini of Genoa and Father Skiouros of Candia.' He turned back to Parmenio. 'We are missing three crewmen of your ship's complement.'

'Two men are sick in their cots below decks,' Nicolo replied quietly, well aware of what would happen to the poor bastards – left writhing abed while the scuttled ship sank around them.

'And the third?'

'I have no idea,' Parmenio replied honestly and with a trace of bitterness. 'Possibly he went overboard during the unprovoked attack?'

The Turk lifted his face and fixed Parmenio with a piercing gaze, trying to detect any hint of falsehood but, appearing to find the captain's expression candid, he nodded once and struck a line from the crew list.

Skiouros examined the enemy as he busily ran down the manifest, deciding whether anything was worth taking. The Turkish captain was of an average height and build, not striking in any other way but for his face alone. His eyes were such a pale grey that they seemed almost white – a shocking contrast with his tanned, leathery skin and the pitch-black beard and moustaches that framed the lower half. His gaze seemed basilisk-like, and Skiouros found himself willing the man to blink, just to prove his humanity.

His heavy, gold-brocaded coat of dark blue hung over trousers of light grey that almost matched his eyes, high suede boots of dazzling bright sapphire completing the outfit. His turban was of a pale grey and a good size, the conical peak of the cap at its centre rising in deep blue from the top.

Well dressed and handsome, the captain should have exuded the charisma that seemed to Skiouros to be part of the uniform of the Ottoman officer class. Instead, what he gave off was a chilling coldness that sent shudders up the spine; a feeling akin to that of entering a cursed place, or the tomb of the recently deceased – both things that Skiouros had found cause to attempt in his time. Something about the captain of the *Yarim Ay* chilled the blood.

It was as he suppressed the shudder that Skiouros' memory dredged up the title the captain had assumed when he'd first addressed them: 'Etci Hassan, Reis of the kadirga *Yarim Ay*.'

Etci, he thought, his blood running cold.

The Butcher!

That a man would answer to such an appellation of his own volition said everything Skiouros needed to know about the captain of the *Yarim Ay* – the *Half Moon*. Hassan Reis would be a man to watch carefully, and certainly not to cross or antagonise, for a man called 'the Butcher' was hardly shrinking from a vile reputation.

Almost as if he felt Skiouros peeling open his soul, Hassan's chilling gaze came to rest on the Greek. Skiouros shuddered again involuntarily, feeling exposed and hopelessly at the mercy of this dangerous man. Under that grey-white scrutiny, he found himself thinking on everything that could very easily betray him without even the need to open his mouth.

Only young novices of the church went about without sporting the traditional great beards, and then only because they were uniformly too young to do so. Skiouros remembered questioning Father Simonides over the beards when they were children. The precise details escaped him, but it remained clear that more than one passage in the scriptures forbade a man of God trimming his hair and beard down. Fortunately, Skiouros' wild hair was easily concealed beneath the hat and veil, but the bristles would be difficult to explain away.

Similarly, should his vestments flutter up too much and reveal the scuffed but high quality leather boots he wore, their presence might be questioned on a monk. Even as he ran through what he would need to remember, he called to mind the signet ring on his left hand, purchased from a salesman in Candia while under the influence of drink. He could not for the life of him remember whether a priest would wear a ring, but it seemed extremely unlikely such a nice one would be found on the hand of a young, unmarried monk.

As he met Hassan's gaze weakly, he put his hand down to the prayer rope that hung from a loop on his cassock and unfastened it, pulling it up and working around the knots, his mouth moving in apparent prayer as, with the deftness born of a gutter thief, he secretly worked the ring from his finger with each movement of the rope until he was able to palm it to dispose of at the first opportunity.

The squat one called Mehmi curled his lip in sneering distaste at this overt sign of the infidel religion, though Skiouros noted out of the corner of his eye that the man also tugged at his earlobe, spitting and then sucking in air in an ancient Turkish gesture to ward off evil.

Superstitious? Good. That could be useful.

Hassan seemed to be less affected by this credulity. His gaze simply intensified as his eyes dropped momentarily to the rope and then rose once more to the young priest's face.

'You are shaved,' he said simply in Greek. Skiouros felt his heart skip a beat. God in Heaven, but the man was quick – not only to spot the mistake, but also to switch languages so smoothly.

'Lice,' Skiouros said quickly in Greek, his mind racing ahead.

'Lice?'

'With no wild nept, capsicum or quicklime aboard, all I could do was shave it. God in his infinite compassion will forgive the transgression, I am sure.'

He kept his face carefully neutral, though deep inside he congratulated himself, not only on the timely lie that had leapt to mind, but also on the fact that he had automatically placed a verbal emphasis on the word 'God', as he'd so often heard the Greek priests of Istanbul do when speaking to a Muslim. He'd never been sure whether it was supposed to draw a deeper division between the two or to highlight the connection, but that mattered not, so long as the Turk felt it came naturally.

Hassan narrowed his eyes as his piercing gaze peeled back layers of truth and lie from Skiouros, but eventually he nodded and looked back down at his ledger.

'You have some rich cargo, Captain Parmenio,' he said, returning smoothly to Italian as he paid no further heed to the monk. 'You are to be congratulated on your former fortune.' He snapped the book shut. 'Sadly, that fortune has now come to an end. While I value some of your cargo, it pales beside the silver, gold and other sundry treasures I already hold.'

He turned to Mehmi.

'Check on the space we have below – I am sure the past week's voyage has cleared out some of the supplies. Make sure there is room for three persons. Any extra space you find, you may fill with any of the goods from the top six lines of the cargo manifest. Select well, Mehmi, for it is our future we buy with it.'

Skiouros felt his blood run cold. *Three persons.* It was hard to picture a stray priest numbering among those three. As he began to sweat uncontrollably, his eyes locked on the Turkish corsair, Mehmi leaned close to his captain, a worried look crossing his face, and muttered something too quietly to be overheard. Hassan straightened and glared at his right hand man.

'He will be flayed, salted, gutted and drowned as all infidel priests deserve,' the captain informed Mehmi in Turkish, loudly enough to be overheard. Of course, Hassan would have no reason to believe that any of the captives spoke his language.

Skiouros felt the first wave of panic wash across him, as there was absolutely no doubt in his mind about whom the captain was speaking. Two of the Turkish sailors nearby paused in their work, tugging at their ears to ward off evil. If Skiouros wasn't busy pissing himself and panicking, he would have noted their reaction with interest.

Mehmi, his face a mask of panicked misery that probably matched Skiouros' own, started babbling quickly at his captain. The words were too quick, quiet and indistinct to make much sense of, but Skiouros heard the word '*dervish*' – a form of Turkish monk – and something about corpses and ghosts. As he finished, Mehmi began tugging on his ear so hard he was making it go a sore red, spitting until his mouth was dry.

For a long moment, Hassan stared at his man, then noticed the sailors nearby, the worried expressions on their faces, and took a deep breath, casting a look of utter disgust at Skiouros.

'It appears that today is your lucky day, priest, as my crew have petitioned me for your life.'

Skiouros almost collapsed with relief, aware of the warm, damp feeling in his trousers and the faint aroma of ammonia rising through his vestments to compete with the lingering scent of vomit. A quick glance at Mehmi told Skiouros that the squat man was almost as relieved as he.

Curious.

'Go to work, Mehmi.'

The second in command grinned his missing-toothed grin at his captain and bowed his head before stepping across the gap and onto the *Isabella*.

'Master Orsini, you will accompany your friends aboard.'

Cesare stepped forward. 'Respectfully, captain Hassan, you will no doubt be aware of my family. I can offer you a considerable reward should you find it in your heart to deliver me to the coast of Sicilia. Indeed, I feel certain that I can arrange enough of a ransom to make it worth releasing all four of your prisoners.'

Skiouros blinked as he turned to his fellow traveller. It had not occurred to him that the Orsini might be rich enough to make such an offer. Given Cesare's somewhat disenfranchised status, there was always a possibility he might be refused, of course, but such a magnanimous offer went beyond simple generosity.

There was only a moment's pause before Hassan shook his head.

'It is truly a shame, Lord of the Orsini, but the simple fact is that while I could always use a little more money – even the stinking currency of your vile nation – I have no wish to endanger myself by entering into dealings with the families of Italia.'

He straightened again, rocking on the balls of his feet.

'You will all live as long as it pleases me to see you do so. I suggest you put your minds to thinking how you might please me and my crew, or of what benefit you can be.'

Hassan turned his gaze to Skiouros for a moment, apparently weighing something up.

'You disgust me, priest. All of your kind sicken me, but there is something about *you* specifically that sets my teeth on edge. Had I the leisure to follow my whims, I would tip you over the side tied to one of the great gold crosses of Zakynthos that reside in my hold, and see whether your precious God would help you float.'

Skiouros felt his shaking intensify once more. 'But,' Hassan said, straightening and folding his arms, 'my crew are superstitious, as is the nature of sailors, and I would not have them fear ill luck brought on by your death. You will accompany the others.'

'As God wills.'

'No,' Hassan said flatly. 'As *I* will. You will join your fellow infidels below and prepare to sail. And I give you this one warning only: if at any time I hear your spiteful pleas to your vile God, I will have your tongue torn out and tossed in the sea.'

Skiouros nodded meekly and tried to stand quietly and control the trembling as he pondered the possible fates that awaited him, Parmenio, Nicolo and Cesare. Half a minute later Mehmi returned to the deck and began issuing instructions to the Turkish sailors before striding over to his captain and the four Christians standing by the rail.

Captain Hassan gestured one of his sailors over and rattled something off to him in Turkish before turning to the prisoners.

'This man – Kadri – will take you below to your accommodation for the journey. It is a little cramped, but I see no need to bind your limbs unless you prove to be troublesome.' He gave them a pointed look, which seemed to be mostly aimed at Skiouros. 'Do *not* prove to be troublesome.'

The Turkish crewman gestured to the gap between the ships and beckoned the four men. Skiouros fell in at the rear of the group, as he felt would be appropriate and fitting for a monk. As they crossed, slowly and carefully, trying not to lose their footing over the dangerous two-foot precipice with the roiling foamy carpet below, Skiouros became aware of two things:

Firstly, the sound of screaming and staccato splashes as the condemned sailors were kicked over the far side of the *Isabella*, roped to one another, and ultimately to a cannon ball.

Secondly, the one called Mehmi stepped close to his captain and asked a question that Skiouros couldn't quite hear, in a whispered, almost conspiratorial manner. Hassan frowned and leaned towards his second before answering in a similar voice. The conversation, whatever it concerned, seemed to be intense and secretive, and Skiouros found himself hurrying the prison party forward so that he could get closer to the pair, casting his signet ring into the sea between the ships unnoticed and with no small regret.

As the four captives were led towards the hatch that gave access to the hold, Skiouros listened as carefully as he could to the whispered thread of conversation, his excellent hearing managing to blot out the sounds of shipboard life, the sailors' grumbling, and even the executions, and focus purely on the one thing he needed to hear. It was a talent he had nurtured during his time living solely off his wits in the greatest city in the world.

Filing away the titbits of what he heard for further consideration later, he concentrated on walking in a monastic manner and not falling over. Soon he was past the pair and being urged on towards the hatch by a second Turk with a curved blade. As he moved reluctantly forward, Skiouros continued to strain his hearing to catch the last echoes of the conversation.

And then he was stepping down the ladder, following Nicolo into the gloom. Though he'd spent time below decks on the *Isabella*, this was an entirely different proposition. The hold of the caravel had been high-ceilinged and subdivided with bulkheads, creating individual spaces for different cargoes, some areas for the slinging of hammocks for the sailors not currently on duty above deck, a rudimentary sick bay and an area for the preparation and distribution of the crew's food and the distribution of same and their rations of drinking water. The *Yarim Ay*'s hold, however, consisted of one huge compartment the length and width of the ship and only a head taller than the tallest man, the only subdivision being the posts and struts that supported the deck above.

What was more impressive than the hold itself, though, was its contents. The entire vessel was packed with goods. Skiouros could recognise the stores by their shapes and containers, even if he could not read the Arabic script on their labels. From just an initial glance, he could see enough supplies here to keep a ship afloat for more than half a year, a fact that seemed to confirm what he'd heard above.

A narrow alleyway had been left down the centre of the hold, which smelled of wood, grease, sweat and spices, and a space had been cleared somewhere at the very centre of the ship.

The Turk in front of them gestured to the area and pushed them past to sink to their knees on the timber, not bothering to waste words on these human cattle. As soon as the four men were in their 'accommodation' the two Turkish sailors left, threading their way back aft and then up into the sunshine.

Below, all was gloom, lit only by the feeble sunshine that crept in through the tiny apertures along the hull below the main deck.

'Do you think they'll leave us un-roped?' Skiouros asked quietly, aware that the warning against trouble had been aimed at him for some reason.

'I imagine so,' Parmenio sighed. 'What harm can we do? We are at the mercy of that madman. Even Master Orsini's offer of boundless riches couldn't sway him.'

'Perhaps we could make it on deck at night and attempt to purloin a boat?' Orsini mused, his eyes gleaming.

'We would be dead before we struck a blow above deck,' Nicolo stated, shaking his head. 'These are not gullible men. They're corsairs, used to dealing with prisoners. Be damn sure that if they've left us unchained it's because they have nothing to fear from us. Dark in here, though,' he added. 'Do you think we could persuade them to let us have a lamp or a candle at night?'

'Not likely,' Parmenio replied, 'with the black powder that has to be stored in here somewhere. They had cannon and other guns.'

Skiouros shuddered at the memory of the huge stores of powder he'd seen as they travelled the cargo hold, and then at the more distant recollection of chunks of the Nea Ekklesia raining down from the sky during a torrential storm.

'Maybe we could find the powder and detonate it?' Nicolo shrugged. 'If the store's small enough and localised enough we could blow it and try getting to safety in the confusion while they attempt to save the ship?'

Skiouros swept the monk's hat from his head and scratched his scalp.

'I saw the kegs on the way down here – supplies I'd say for more than one ship. With the stores of powder in here, you don't want to even think about lighting a flame. If just one should catch, pieces of the ship will be coming down like rain as far away as Istanbul, and bits of us with it. Trust me – I have some experience in this area.'

Parmenio and Nicolo turned surprised expressions on him, but he seemed not to be inclined to elucidate further, and now was probably not the time for such tales of Skiouros' youth.

With a quick glance aft to check the ladder was empty and the hold clear of eavesdroppers, Parmenio leaned forward and lowered his voice.

'I saw you listening in to the captain as we were brought aboard. What did he say?'

Orsini smiled curiously. 'I should have guessed that you spoke Turkish, my friend. Monks' robes and gunpowder and now multilingual. You are a constant stream of surprises.'

Skiouros gave another conspiratorial glance about at the packed yet silent cargo hold, the only noises coming from above as goods were ferried across from the *Isabella* and the *Yarim Ay* was brought down from a war footing.

'It appears the crew are a little jumpy after some trouble they had when they left Greece – I think that's the only reason Hassan didn't have me flayed and left on the *Isabella* to drown. Didn't hear much about that, but it sounds to me very much as though there *is* a level of friction between this Hassan and his superior, a senior captain called Kemal. We're sailing west to join up with a fleet of two more kadirga near somewhere called Jebel Tariq. Not sure where that is, but it must be some distance away, as they're concerned about the possibility of Spanish ships intercepting them before they arrive.'

'That gives us plenty of time, I suppose,' Nicolo sighed. 'Best get used to our quarters for now, and hope that Fernando and Isabella's navy find us as we close on Spain.'

'Not likely,' Skiouros said, his mouth a grim line. 'There's to be a detour before the main voyage, to the Suq-al-Birka at Tunis.'

'Tunis,' mused Parmenio thoughtfully. 'The Suq-something or other, you say?'

'Suq-al-Birka,' repeated Skiouros. 'The slave market.'

Chapter Seven - Of disguises and superstition

It had been a cramped, sweaty and extremely uncomfortable night, and Skiouros had lost count of the number of times he had woken, disorientated and stiff, panicking at his unfamiliar, Spartan surroundings, only settling into the disconsolate realisation of his situation as he picked out the shapes of Parmenio, Nicolo and Cesare in the tight confines of their prison.

For Skiouros the morning was announced rudely as hands gripped him by the armpits and dragged him upright, jolting him jarringly from a pleasant dream in which he and Lykaion had been racing around their father's farm's perimeter fence, back outside the walls of Hadrianople, pretending to compete for the ancient Olympic wreath.

Blinking crusty sleep from his eyes in yet another confused panic, he fought his captors for a moment, elbows and feet jabbing and kicking, before remembering where he was and – more importantly – in what guise.

Settling, he allowed the two Turkish sailors to lift him to his feet. As he held up his hands in a gesture of calm and acceptance, the other three prisoners stirred from their uncomfortable slumber at the scuffling interruption, Cesare coming to his feet quickly with the look of a man about to react to the rough-handling of a servant of God. As the nobleman sprang upright, both Nicolo and Parmenio reached up and grasped his arms to prevent him doing anything foolish.

'Leave it be, Orsini,' Parmenio hissed, and Cesare held his arms out, stepping back. Neither of the Turks was armed, but any move against them would bring the prisoners into direct conflict with dozens of men above who were.

'What is the meaning of this?' snapped Cesare at the two Turks, who simply shook their heads in incomprehension at the Italian tongue and began to manhandle Skiouros along the narrow alleyway of the darkened deck towards the stairs. Again, behind them, Orsini made to follow, but his companions grasped him and held him back.

'Now is not the time,' Parmenio said. 'If you interfere, you might just get him – and the rest of us – killed.'

Skiouros turned his head as he was pushed roughly at the steps, and cleared his throat.

'The Lord will protect me,' he said loudly, aiming it at his three friends below deck, yet announcing it more for the benefit of those who waited above.

As he was urged into the light, Skiouros realised that the morning had progressed further than he had suspected from the tiny light sources below. The sun was well above the horizon and the crew were already busy at work, performing the arcane tasks required of a sailing vessel, the oarsmen waiting miserably for the command to begin rowing.

The stern platform of the kadirga was set up in much the same way as most Ottoman galleys, an ornate wooden rail – this one carved with beautiful images of Anatolian birdlife – around the periphery, a framework forming the bones of a small wooden structure occupying much of the stern section of deck. The captain's house was covered with a decorative, rich fabric roof, its tasselled edges secured to lines that allowed it to be hauled back to open the structure to the fresh air, removable screens of light decorative latticework allowing for the room to be fully enclosed or opened up, even to become bare deck, as it was now.

Standing proud and unyielding at the rear of the vessel, Etci Hassan seemed almost like some ancient Emperor or despot – or perhaps a *daemon* of Biblical lore – as he watched the approach of the prisoner. He stood calm, his arms folded, the squat ugly shape of Mehmi lurking by his side like some sort of homunculus. A number of the Turkish sailors – the ones not currently required to deal with the sails and ropes – stood around the rail, looking for all the world like some sort of court awaiting the arrival of a criminal.

The morning sea breeze wafted across the deck, cooling the ship's occupants, taking some of the heat out of the already blazing southern Mediterranean sun.

Skiouros kept his pace measured and careful, as might be expected of a monk. His vestments flapped in the breeze and he was immensely grateful that he had removed his expensive boots last night and hidden them among the cargo, returning to bare feet as an option less likely to reveal his true nature. The varnished boards seared the soles of his feet, having already soaked up an hour of sunlight.

The sailors at his shoulders let go of his arms and Skiouros wondered what he was supposed to do now. Unsure, he continued to walk for a few paces until he stood in the centre of the rough square of Turks, nerves beginning to play up and down his spine as he tried desperately to keep the stately, measured stance of a man who knows that God will save him.

Even if only that insubstantial part of him that cannot be sliced, stabbed and burned.

Skiouros' relationship with God had been something of a rickety cart ride over the past few years – his whole life, if he was honest. While he could hardly *deny* the existence of the creator – and the verbose ghost of his brother clearly indicated that death was far from the end – he could not say that his faith in his mother church was strong enough to deny the possibility that the Muslims had the right of it. Or the Catholics. Or even the Jews.

Yet for the time being, he had to put aside his uncertainties and his confusion and focus on what he knew of the church of his youth, bringing it into play as though that were the pillar that supported the ceiling of his existence. His very real physical life depended upon it for now.

While he had been extremely uncertain of the value of Parmenio's idea and of the monk robes, and while it appeared that Etci Hassan harboured nothing but the desire to butcher each and every Christian he could lay hands on, particularly priests, the crew were for some reason extremely nervous about him, and it was that strange and unexpected aspect that had saved him from Hassan's blade. The robes had, despite everything, saved his life so far.

He thought of those who hadn't been as lucky as them; Parmenio, Nicolo, Cesare and Skiouros had been saved only because of their value as slaves – experienced navigators and traders, a nobleman and a priest would likely fetch a good price for Hassan, while ordinary ship-hands would not be worth the trouble and cost of transport.

Those other poor souls were currently resting on the sea bed some leagues to the east, roped to a cannon shot. Whether or not Skiouros liked the monk's robe, and whether or not he felt it was some kind of blasphemy to wear it, without these stinking, dusty vestments, he would now be one of those still, silent denizens of the deep instead of uncomfortable but alive aboard the kadirga *Yarim Ay*.

His attention was brought sharply back to his current predicament as something thudded into the deck little more than an inch from his feet. Staring down in panic, Skiouros' eyes fell upon his fine Spanish blade, point driven into the timber, rocking back and forth with a curious wobbling sound. His heart skipped a beat and he felt the sweat begin to trickle from beneath his veiled headgear. Later in the day, such perspiration would be brought on by the heat and the thickness of the robes, but for now it was clearly caused by fear.

His legs confirmed the diagnosis.

Suppressing the panic he felt rising, he raised his face and cast a calm, questioning glance at the Ottoman corsair captain, trying not to worry about the nervous tic he could feel jumping beneath his left eye. He remembered the superstition about that from his Ottoman-oppressed youth. A tic below the eye was a warning of impending death.

'Pick it up,' Etci Hassan said quietly in Italian.

Skiouros felt his mouth opening to reply and forced it shut again, frowning and cocking his head to one side in feigned incomprehension.

'Pick. It. Up.' Hassan repeated, slowly and this time in Greek.

'Such a tool of wanton destruction has no place in the hand of a servant of God,' Skiouros replied flatly.

An uncomfortable silence settled across the deck, somehow emphasised by the crack, flap and thump of the sails, the creak of the wood and the splash of the waves below.

'PICK IT UP!' bellowed Hassan, still in Greek, spittle spraying across the deck. Skiouros noted with interest how the unpleasant gap-toothed imp Mehmi cowered slightly to the side at this outburst, and he remembered the unpleasant Turk's reaction to the arrival of a monk on board the previous day – hatred laced with fear that led to a warding off of evil. Was this cowering simply a response to his captain's anger – undoubtedly Hassan's anger would truly be a thing to behold – or something deeper-rooted, revolving around the danger of upsetting a man of God? If the latter, it could be played upon.

Slowly, as if handling something unpleasant – a gutted fish perhaps, or the unidentifiable detritus that littered the back alleys of Istanbul – Skiouros reached down and grasped the hilt of his sword. It had only been driven into the deck by the slightest fraction – just enough to keep it upright. He would have no trouble removing it, though he made a show of yanking it from the timber with considerable difficulty, straining his reedy priestly arms. Hassan's expression did not change an iota, though Skiouros felt it already had the distinct impression of a sneer.

'Is this your sword, *'priest'*?'

Once again, Skiouros felt the panic rising and had to fight it down, grateful that only his hands and face were visible and that the shaking and sweat were somewhat concealed by the robes – though such nerves would be fully understandable in a captive, even one with nothing to hide. He frowned in feigned perplexity.

'Captain?'

'Is. This. Your. Sword?' Hassan repeatedly slowly as though addressing a child – or an idiot.

Skiouros looked down at the blade in is hand, trying to let it dip and wave as though he was totally unfamiliar with its weight.

'I do not understand, captain. I am a man of God... I have no need for such a weapon.'

Mehmi, Skiouros noted, nodded slightly, made the warding sign against evil once again, tugging his ear urgently and sucking through his teeth, and then looked askance nervously at his commander.

Etci Hassan merely straightened his back for a moment and then unfolded his arms, putting them behind his back and clasping them there.

'Curiously, during our inventory of the goods taken from the stern cabins of the caravel, this blade turned up with no clear owner.'

'I have no knowledge of this thing,' Skiouros replied, staring with distaste at the sword in his hand and wondering for just a heartbeat whether he would survive the four steps forward that were all he would need to plunge the tip into the pirate's black heart.

Hassan rocked back and forth a couple of times on his heels and toes.

'The two officers we have below surrendered their blades to me when they came aboard, yet this sword was found in the captain's cabin. It is, I note, a very fine blade of Spanish manufacture. Considerably more expensive than the captain would wield, judging by his rather poor appearance.'

Skiouros shrugged.

'Perhaps it belongs to Master Orsini?' he hazarded.

'I think not.' Hassan raised an eyebrow. 'The Orsini's blade has already been located, identified by the family crest – the rose and stripes – stamped between the quillons. *This* blade appears to lack an owner – a wealthy one who is familiar with the martial skills – and that intrigues me.'

He narrowed his eyes. 'It intrigues me almost as much as the fact that when you gripped the blade to draw it from the deck, your fingers hooked through the side ring as though you knew precisely how to hold it. I abhor such decadent, womanish weapons, of course, but do not take me for a fool, priest. I have killed many a man as he affected that very grip.'

Skiouros looked down at the hilt, mentally chiding himself for such a basic mistake, but simply shrugged and frowned as though the grip had been entirely accidental.

'Raise the blade,' Hassan commanded.

Again, Skiouros looked up and frowned at him.

'I tire of repeating myself, priest. My revulsion at the very presence of your kind upon my vessel is almost unbearable, and the only reason I have not had you flayed to patch our spare sail, salted and then strangled, is that Mehmi here and a good number of his compatriots feel that your death and torture may anger Allah – may he be praised – and bring about vengeful spirits and unpreventable deaths. I am less convinced, but as captain it is as much my duty to look to the welfare of my crew as it is theirs to obey my commands.'

He glanced aside at the cowering homunculus. 'In ten years of service, Mehmi has never seen me wrong, and so I am inclined to indulge his foibles.'

The captain took a deep breath.

'However, *I* find you suspicious and troublesome, priest. There are too many infidel priests to my mind who hold ranks in military organisations founded with the simple intent of wiping my people from the world, and I cannot help but picture you in the garments of those cursed Rhodos knights. At this juncture it will take only a little more disobedience from you before I forget the respect in which I hold Mehmi and simply have you broken and quartered. If I have to repeat myself again, you will be able to confront your God in person with your complaints. Do I make myself clear?'

Skiouros nodded and bowed his head respectfully, suppressing the urge to point out that the Rhodos knights were in fact Catholic and a constituent part of those barbarian crusaders who had sacked Constantinople and ravaged the Orthodox church – a small piece of history drummed into the head of every Greek child by their priests at an

79

early age. But then, what would a Muslim care about the divisions in the Christian world?

Slowly, he raised the point of the blade into the air as Hassan had commanded, allowing it to tremble and wave as though he were entirely unused to the action. He hoped the nervous sweat running freely down his face would be taken for a symptom of the exertion rather than fear.

'Halil? Kadri?' the captain said quietly.

The two sailors who had escorted Skiouros from the depths of the vessel stepped forward, coming to a halt beside of the prisoner. The young Greek allowed himself a quick glance to either side. To his left, the man was bulky and well-muscled – a warrior born, with a neat beard and numerous scars, he was dressed only in a white linen shirt and orange sash, baggy blue trousers and a conical hat, the tip of which had slumped forward. To the other side, the man was somewhat shorter, though displaying the physique of the long-term manual labourer, his shoulders bull-like. Wearing similar clothes, but with the addition of a pale grey jacket, he was lighter skinned and bore only well-oiled moustaches.

Skiouros braced himself, aware that something was about to happen and sure it would be something unpleasant.

'Halil and Kadri, retrieve your swords.'

Skiouros stood perfectly still, the Spanish rapier wavering in his hand with his nerves as the two corsairs reclaimed their curved blades from their companions around the periphery before taking up position in front of and behind their prisoner.

'I have in mind a small test of your conviction, priest. I understand that an *imam* of your cursed faith is forbidden to take a life?'

Skiouros felt his blood begin to thump faster, the nerves getting the better of him. It was suddenly clear that sale into slavery was the very best Skiouros could hope for from this journey. He would be lucky to make it as far as the slave market of Tunis. Hassan's almost pathological need to humiliate, disprove and then execute him would not wane, and Skiouros would only be safe from the corsair captain's personal jihad when he had been enslaved by another. Hassan apparently cared not for the money his sale would raise – if he could prove Skiouros' lack of worth as a priest, he could execute him without the crew panicking. And the finding of the suspicious sword had given him that chance.

Clutching at any opportunity to bring the suspicious few of the crew back onto his side, Skiouros found himself saying in clear, loud Greek, 'I believe it is also forbidden in the Qur'an.'

Almost kicking himself over his inappropriate outburst, Skiouros tried not to shake. Not only did the near-accusation sound incredibly confrontational – and he was fairly sure that pushing Hassan was not a clever move – would it not seem odd for an Orthodox monk to have any knowledge of the Muslims' holy text? Unable to stop it now, he dredged his memory for the line that Lykaion had pounded into him time and again to illustrate his faith's validity: '"Do not take life, which God has made sacred." Is that not the word of your prophet?'

Hassan's mouth flattened into a hard line, his eyes becoming cold in their pale, almost-white eeriness.

'I believe Allah makes exceptions for those who do His work. The verse to which you refer completes: "except though the law and justice."'

He straightened again. 'The Qur'an also tells us to strike off the heads and fingers of all who do not believe. To "slay them, wherever we find them". Stick to your children's book of fables, priest, and do not befoul *our* holy text with your snake tongue.'

He glanced down at the form of Mehmi, whose face displayed open shock at this exchange, and sneered.

'My patience is at an end, even at the expense of my crew's goodwill. Mehmi will forgive me eventually, I am sure. I give you a simple choice, priest: use the blade in your hand and strike down Halil who stands before you, or Kadri at your back will send you to your God in person. For *I* believe you are no priest, but a killer of men, merely in the *guise* of a dervish – an abhorrence in the eyes of Allah and the prophet. My faithful children here would not have me execute a priest, but *you are no priest*, are you?'

Mehmi's eyes rolled in the manner of a panicked horse and his gaze shot back and forth between his captain and the captive priest.

Skiouros felt the atmosphere thicken around him, tension running high in nearly every figure present. The sailors around the edge of the ship, standing by the rail, displayed a mixture of emotions ranging from distress and worry through acceptance and interest all the way to to enthusiasm and ferocious hunger. Mehmi was almost vibrating with anxiety and Skiouros could hear Kadri behind him muttering a prayer under his breath with the vehemence of a man who is truly unsure of what he is about to do.

The only person who seemed utterly relaxed and unconcerned was Etci Hassan, his colourless basilisk stare fixed on Skiouros, displaying no emotion other than perhaps a mild curiosity tainted with disdain.

Skiouros looked up at the tip of his blade.

The big, bulky Halil, before him, slowly removed his shirt, displaying a bare chest coated with a thick rug of black curly body hair that was beginning to turn grey. The sailor seemed remarkably calm, given that he was being asked to offer up his life merely to tempt Skiouros into a blow, the only sign of his inner struggle a single tear that trickled down a cheek as he straightened and bared his naked torso to Skiouros' blade.

Almost immediately, Skiouros felt the tip of another sword tickle his vertebrae as Kadri raised his weapon in preparation.

Kill or be killed?

Skiouros hesitated, his bladder pulsing and threatening to relieve itself down his leg.

'Decision time, *priest*,' Hassan said calmly.

Skiouros took a deep breath. He'd never been much of a gambler. He liked to have all the good cards in his hand from the outset – to know the outcome before making a play. To actually *guess* was anathema to him even in a friendly game of cards, let alone with stakes as high as this. And yet he was left with little choice.

Inaction or indecision would simply give the captain all the excuse he needed to have Kadri run him through – a choice that would require some fence-mending with his crew, but which hardly benefitted Skiouros. But then, striking down Halil would prove him either a liar, a bad priest or a weak man, and all of those would provide Hassan with just as much reason to do away with him and probably with the crew's blessing. The captain had placed him in a no-win position.

All Skiouros could do now was gamble blindly.

The only thing he had on his side was the superstition of Mehmi and his crewmates that still currently held some sway and the hope that it was a powerful enough force to protect him from the captain's hatred, although the *reason* they should be so nervous about harming a Christian priest still escaped him.

Skiouros took a deep breath and cast his sword across the deck to one side with a clatter, stepping forward just a half-step, away from the tickle of the sword point, his hands clasped together in prayer.

'Forgive them Lord, for their mercilessness,' he said loud enough to carry to every ear in the court-like square.

He dropped his face to the deck, hunched over his clasped hands and rattling off the one hundred and fifty-first – the only psalm he could remember from the services of his youth – mumbling through the parts that evaded his memory, sure that the Turks would not notice.

He squeezed his eyes shut, awaiting the next move, his blood pounding, skin cold with anticipation.

'I was small among my brothers and the youngest in the house of my father; I would shepherd the sheep of my father.'

Hardly an appropriate incantation, given the circumstances, but to the uninitiated – many of whom would have no command of Greek – it would sound thoroughly spiritual, especially since he could remember the melody and had always been able to carry a tune quite well.

'My hands made an instrument... (mumble, mumble) harp. And who will report it to my lord? The Lord himself, for it is he who listens.'

Silence reigned in the space surrounding his words – the silence of an execution being carried out. But Kadri's blow never came.

The darkness behind his eyelids became an orange glow as the hulking figure of Halil moved out of his way and the sun blazed down on the praying monk. Falling silent, Skiouros unclasped his hands, allowing them to fall to his sides, and straightened, opening his eyes and blinking in the light. Hassan had folded his arms once more, Memhi beside him, wide-eyed and clearly relieved beyond imagining.

'It was he who sent his messenger and took me from the sheep of my father and anointed me...'

'Cease your prattle!' snapped Hassan, turning to regard Kadri only momentarily before returning his eyes to the prisoner. 'Take the priest back below.'

Skiouros held Hassan's blood-chilling gaze for a moment before nodding a curt bow and turning towards the cargo hatch from whence he'd emerged. Kadri, his sword still out and looking almost as relieved as Mehmi had been, gestured to the ladder with the weapon. Back across the deck, Halil hurriedly retrieved his shirt and dressed once more. Skiouros eyed with regret his expensive sword, lying gleaming on the timbers, and stepped onto the ladder, disappearing into the gloom once more.

'You are brave, priest,' Kadri said quietly once they were below deck again. 'And the luck of the prophet – may peace be upon him – is with you.'

Skiouros paused at the bottom of the steps and waited for the sailor to reach the floor.

'Why *are* the crew so uneasy about me? The captain has surely killed my brethren before?'

Kadri looked nervous, his eyes rising to the square of light above, beyond which the crew were returning to their tasks.

'There has been... trouble,' he said so quietly that Skiouros had to strain to hear.

'Trouble?'

'We killed a priest – along with his whole village – in Zakynthos and delivered their peeled remains to the Venetians at Methoni, a day's sail to the south. The captain despises the masters of Methoni more even than he despises your kind. We shouldn't have done it, though. We lost three men in three days – to the priest's spirit, of course. You *never* bring a dead body inside! *Never!* And we brought a dead *priest* aboard.'

Skiouros nodded slowly – that was one of many Turkish superstitions he remembered from his days in Istanbul: to bring a corpse into the house was to bring about the death of three of its occupants. He was beginning to understand why Mehmi and his friends displayed such nerves. Of course, there could be myriad reasons for unexplained deaths aboard ship, though three in three days was a little out of the ordinary, admittedly.

Luck? Or was God lending him a hand after all?

'Etci Hassan Reis appears not to suffer such concern.'

Kadri looked surprised at the statement.

'The captain is impervious to such spirits. Allah shelters him; protects and preserves him for great things. He is beloved of the prophet – peace of Allah be upon him – but such protection does not extend to the rest of us.'

Kadri's voice dropped to an even quieter whisper, if such a thing was possible, and he leaned close to Skiouros, holding his sword safely back out of the way.

'If the captain decides you are to die, the decision will be unpopular, but no one will contest it. Remember, though, that I was good to you. When your spirit roams free and vengeful, do not come to claim me.' He looked about nervously. 'I will bring you all food,' he added, pleadingly.

Skiouros almost smiled. A few random unlucky deaths had fed enough uncertainty to the superstitious crew to overcome their general hatred of the church and accept the presence of a monk, however uncomfortably.

It was either the most extraordinary stroke of luck, or the Hand of God truly was moving pieces in the great game of life. So many things had fallen into place. For there even to have been a priest's vestments on board the *Isabella* was miraculous enough. For Parmenio to have thought of using them? For such a random happening of events to have struck the kadirga on their journey to have put the crew in a receptive frame of mind – enough even to sway their captain, who clearly denied all superstition and harboured the most bloodthirsty hatred of the Christian faith?

It was almost mind-boggling to Skiouros that such a chain of events should fall into place.

Kadri gestured towards the prisoners' accommodation, back along the deck.

'Go. I will bring food soon.'

As the sailor turned and clambered up the steps to the main deck, Skiouros smiled to himself and shuffled along the narrow alleyway to the space where the other three sat nervously, waiting.

'What happened?' Parmenio asked, as Skiouros entered and sank to the floor once again, relief flooding his system.

'I think that God just moved in yet another mysterious way. It seems that Captain Hassan is currently at the mercy of a superstitious crew who are afraid to kill priests. It's a long story.'

'We seem to be overly-burdened with spare time,' noted Nicolo wearily.

'True. And now we might have something of a small ally among the crew – or at least a man who will not cross me for fear of my ghost making a tasty morsel of him. And we need to bear in mind that the second in command – Mehmi – is particularly jumpy and superstitious. Could be useful.'

He sighed.

'Let me tell you something about Turkish superstitions…'

Chapter Eight - Of the bones of an empire

Skiouros grunted with discomfort as he squeezed between the containers in the hold – barely enough room for a cat to crawl, let alone a human being. Behind him, only just visible in the cramped circumstances, Parmenio, Nicolo and Cesare stood tense and quiet.

'Can you see yet?'

Skiouros, small and agile and yet still experiencing extreme difficulty in crawling between the tightly-packed supplies, shook his head.

'Almost,' he whispered. 'Nearly there.'

Taking three deep breaths to prepare, he exhaled, making himself as thin as he could manage, and pushed between the two huge wooden crates, feeling the rough wood scraping the flesh of his ribs even through the inner, light cassock that protected him. He had left the vest, hat, veil and outer cassock with the others, as they were far too bulky to even contemplate wearing for such activity.

His eyes fell once more on the tiny apertures below a ceiling that was far lower than in a caravel such as the *Isabella*, due to the shallow draft of the galley. He could hear the water lapping against the hull somewhere around half way up the wooden wall and the thought that most of him was actually below the waterline was somewhat unnerving.

The small holes that were his objective were there – according to Parmenio – to allow air circulation in the cargo hold and prevent rot, and were at most four or five feet above the water at any given point, exposing the peripheral cargo to occasional slops of seawater whenever the surface became too choppy. The corsairs had, of course, accounted for this and stacked the goods that would not be at risk from salt damage at the perimeter.

As he pulled himself through the narrow gap and collapsed, breathing heavily, on a rare high and flat surface, he peered at the stores that he was moving amongst and thought back over the illicit inventory the four prisoners had carried out yesterday.

It had become painfully obvious that unless the captives could work out some method of escape, they were doomed to sale and enforced servitude among the Arab states of the Barbary Coast. The first step had been an inventory of the goods in the hold, as quietly as possible during the early morning, when there was enough light in the hold to see by and the galley-slaves above were engaged in the first major rowing session of the day, the noises disguising the searching below.

Clearly the fleet that this kadirga was sailing to rejoin was planning to stay in circulation for some months yet and were expecting action. The *Yarim Ay*'s hold was packed with stores, but not with livestock or victuals – ordinary food and water could be taken by trade or by force in small unprepared village harbours. These were supplies for a campaign: a small section – close to the hull as it would not suffer from seawater – held packed salted beef, prepared in the halal manner, which would feed the officers, the crew living from whatever could be taken or foraged on coastal forays. The rest was black powder, timber and tools, spare sails and heavy-grade linen for patching, yard upon yard of rope of varying thicknesses, sealed buckets of pitch, leather goods, cleaning equipment and the like.

A surprisingly large section had been put aside for the plunder of Zakynthos, and the four had stared in open-mouthed awe at the unearthly value of those chests. Skiouros had found himself clutching his prayer rope as he peered at the great crosses and other religious silver- and gold-ware, praying as though he were a real priest, and chided himself irritably for succumbing to the garb he wore. Despite his vow to Lykaion that his thieving days were done, Skiouros had dipped into one of the chests and scooped out a handful of gold coins with Venetian designs. After all, it was more an act of rescue and restitution than theft, when he thought it through. Clearly the others agreed, as they had also purloined a handful of ducats. The hiding of such coins was no trouble, slipped into boots, codpieces and the like.

Of the rest of the hold's cargo, there was little they could use to effect an escape. Certainly no weapons – barring arrows, cannon shot and the three-inch balls for the Abus guns. Although there would almost certainly be weapon stores, they would presumably be kept up top where they could be easily accessed at short notice by the crew.

And away from the prisoners.

Just in case, the four had taken some spare tool handles that could serve as clubs, a few handfuls of black powder wrapped carefully in sail fabric pouches and tied with twine, and two arrows apiece, which could – at a push – serve as thrusting weapons. Now hidden behind a crate next to their prison area, the collection was more than they could have hoped for, but was still paltry and ineffectual when weighed against the opposition above deck. Any overt move would soon see them to their deaths.

And so they had concluded that their only hope of escape would lie between disembarkation and their grisly destination. Until their feet touched land there was simply no hope, and once they reached the slave market all hope would be lost. A narrow window of opportunity.

Parmenio and the others had settled into a quiet discussion of how a break could be effected during that time and Skiouros had listened to the conversation progress, aware that any useful input on his part would likely involve revealing something of his past that he'd hoped to keep from the others – particularly from the noble Orsini.

'We are all trained with a blade,' Parmenio had said, 'even if for some of us it was decades ago. The four of us might well be able to take care of ourselves if we manage to arm ourselves and make some space to take the Turks on. I have a little knowledge of Tunis, from trading there many years ago, as does Nicolo, so we might be able to find our way around the city, but beyond that, we're somewhat left to flounder in our plan. So do you two have anything to add?'

He and Nicolo had looked to Cesare – who had simply shrugged and shaken his head – and then to Skiouros, who had closed his eyes for a moment and taken a deep breath.

'I have some experience in the field of slavery and flight.'

Raised eyebrows and frowns had greeted this revelation. Carefully, Skiouros had gone on to elucidate, telling the story of his selection in the Devsirme, along with his brother, and of their travel to the great city of Constantine, the lucky moment and his escape into the city. He glossed over Lykaion's objections somewhat and said nothing of his life beforehand or what had happened after he fled into the streets of

Constantinople, but Parmenio had nodded as though it was much as he'd expected, as did Nicolo. Cesare had smiled a fascinated and surprisingly warm smile.

No one had pressed him further, and he'd been glad of that, though he knew that he'd now removed the first brick from the wall that surrounded his innermost private secrets and that, should they make it out of this, his friends would begin to hack away at the rest of the wall.

Parmenio had gone on to outline what he knew of Tunis, which turned out to be a surprisingly detailed account, albeit restricted to the areas that a Christian trader would visit, which ruled out the slave market and its locale. It had become clear that the only chance they had of flight would be on the trip through the city, relying on Skiouros' skill at trickery and evasion, Parmenio's local knowledge, and their collective martial skills. Skiouros would have to pick their moment, as soon as he saw the best opportunity, and Parmenio and Nicolo would then have to steer them as best they could until they reached relative safety.

This was all dependent upon them getting away from their captors without a hitch, of course.

As they had continued to look at every angle of the so-called 'plan' for the last evening, it was somewhat disheartening to hear how many times the phrases 'if', 'as long as' and 'might be' arose. Too often for any of their liking.

But, sparse and barely-formed as it was, it was the start of a plan that would have to wait until they reached Tunis to develop further.

And finally, ten minutes ago, the kadirga had come to a halt. That fact, combined with the sound of dozens of gulls shrieking at the ship and the crash of waves breaking on rock somewhere nearby had led them to assume they had reached their destination.

Parmenio had pondered at the sounds outside and come to the conclusion that Hassan had settled for anchorage somewhere in the outer reaches of the Gullet – the wide series of harbours that led from the open sea to the very walls of the Hafsid capital. Given the simmering enmity between the Tunisian Emirs and the Ottoman Empire, Hassan was probably playing it as safe as possible and staying within reach of the sea for a clear run, should the authorities take exception to him.

Their anchor position would dictate the route and distance they would take to reach the heart of the city and the slave market, and the end result was what now led to Skiouros lying, scraped and bruised, on a crate of salt beef a few feet below one of the small apertures that would afford him a view of the great port of Tunis and allow him to provide some points of reference for Parmenio to work with.

He could hear the rowers only just above him, resting and rubbing their sore muscles, drinking the precious water that was handed around to them from a bucket. Through the holes, the oars themselves were now visible almost at the collar, which rested at another set of apertures from the top deck only a foot above these ones.

'Well?' demanded Nicolo in an impatient hiss, unseen in the dark hold.

Skiouros heaved himself up and peered through the hole.

'Come on!' snapped Parmenio quietly, back among the crates with the others.

'This Gullet...' Skiouros hazarded. 'What does it look like?'

'It's a wide harbour with different port sections and docks, jetties, warehouses and so on down both sides. If you can see the fortified mouth of the place, then we're still anchored outside in the bay. If you can see down the mouth and to the walls and the city itself, then we're a lot further down and near Tunis, but I don't think that's the case, from the sounds.'

Skiouros pinched the bridge of his nose and took another breath.

'And Tunis. It's a big, thriving walled city, yes?'

'Yes. Bigger than Candia and home to thousands of Arabs and Berbers. Full of markets, mosques and palaces. The walls come right down to the port, and you might be able to see the Bab el Bahr – the sea gate. The twin towers stand quite high above the docked ships, and they usually have the Hafsid flag flying.'

'I don't think we're at Tunis,' the Greek breathed quietly, his gaze darting back and forth.

'What?'

Skiouros squinted through the hole again, his eyes unaccustomed to the bright sunlight. His gaze took in the surroundings once more, and he shook his head in defeat.

'Unless there's been some sort of Biblical disaster – like Sodom and Gomorrah – this isn't Tunis.'

'What can you see?' Nicolo urged, panic tinging the edge of his voice.

'We're in *some* sort of harbour,' Skiouros said, his eyes ranging across the scenery for landmarks. 'It's sort of curved and I think there's a small island in the middle, although it could be a headland, it's hard to tell from this angle. It's covered in ruins; looks like smashed up warehouses. Very old. Sort of like the ruins of the older emperors back in Istanbul – maybe as old as the hippodrome or the Blachernae ruins? And there are what look like city walls, but they collapsed centuries ago, I reckon. There's a big hill and it doesn't look like there are many signs of life.'

Parmenio groaned.

'What?' asked Skiouros with a frown, unable to see his friends back across the hold and past the crates.

'Sounds like Carthage,' Parmenio sighed. 'Does the hill have its own walls? And the edges of the circular port – are they covered in the same sort of ruins as the island?'

Skiouros peered into the heat haze and blinked.

'Think so.'

'That's the ancient harbour. A lot of it's silted up and it hasn't been used by anything bigger than local fishermen for a thousand years. Caravels can't really get in, but a galley has a nice low draft. Best get back here quickly.'

Skiouros took one last look at the outside and then began the scramble back between crates and bales, finally dropping into the open space where his friends waited, to see Parmenio scratching his golden-bearded chin thoughtfully.

'Where is Carthage, then?' Skiouros asked.

'Just outside Tunis. Maybe three leagues from the city, but only a league from the Gullet. Wily old bastard Hassan's decided to anchor in an abandoned ruin, where the Hafsid authorities won't be looking for intruders. He'll be a lot safer here, and it's only a short hop to the city.'

'Does that improve our chances,' Cesare asked quietly, 'or worsen them?'

'Hard to say.' Parmenio shrugged. 'It means we'll have a longer trip, which has to be useful. More opportunity, I suppose. But it also means that Hassan can concentrate on taking us to the souk and the sale, and won't have to divide his attention between us and the security of his ship. His eyes will be all the more on his prize.'

Skiouros shrugged. 'Attention can always be diverted. I see this as an advantage – a greater opportunity to slip away.'

Without further delay, the Greek began to shrug into his monastic garments, straining with the effort and pulling faces at the ever-worsening smell that clung to them: vomit, ordure and more than a week's worth of sweat.

Orsini tapped his lip, deep in thought. 'What are the chances that we could actually get the local authorities on our side, if they hold the Empire in such disdain?'

'Low,' Parmenio sighed. 'Doesn't matter what the *official* stance is, very few questions will be asked if Hassan brings quality slave merchandise for sale in the city. Only the higher authorities would baulk at our arrival, and they'll never hear about it. A few copper fals slipped to the guards on the gate and no questions will be asked. If Hassan is careful – and my guess is he's a *very* careful man – we'll be at the market and sold before anyone ever raises the fact that there are Turks in the city. He'll be back aboard and to sea before the Emir's government hear anything about it, if they ever do.'

He glanced across at his purser.

'You've been to Carthage itself if I remember rightly. Anything useful you can add? I've only seen it from the coast.'

Nicolo shrugged. 'I just took an hour or two to look around. They say if you look carefully enough, treasures can be found lying on the ground. I only found dried shit and dead animals, myself. The whole place is one big, shitty ruin. People still live there, but they're peasants in tents or badly-built huts. I think they're the Berber desert-dweller types.'

Parmenio nodded. 'I've heard tell that the poor and those of dubious professions live there, 'cause they don't have to pay taxes to the Emir the way they would in Tunis. Doubt we'll find any help there. We'd be more likely to be murdered as Christians than aided as enemies of the Turk.'

Skiouros, finally patting and smoothing down his outer cassock, jammed the hat on his head and allowed the veil to fall at his neck. Reaching up, he rubbed the burgeoning beard that now filled out his chin, two weeks' growth making him look ever more priestly. 'In fairness, this Hassan is a piece of shit, but I would hardly call myself an *'enemy of the Turk'*. In fact, Sultan Bayezid still has my allegiance. Better the Ottoman than the Mamluk, for certain!'

'Can you hear what they're saying?' Parmenio asked, blithely ignoring Skiouros' comments and gesturing upwards with a pointed finger.

Skiouros lifted the veil and cupped his ear. The murmur of Turkish was dampened by the deck that lay between, and he could almost make out the odd word, but not enough to make sense of it all.

'Not really. Think I can hear the boats being lowered into the water though.'

Nicolo nodded. 'Me too. I suspect we're about to go ashore.'

'What do we do with all these supplies?' The purser gestured to the crate, behind which the store of purloined goods lay hidden.

'We'll have to leave them,' Parmenio sighed. 'It was a nice thought, but we'll never get them past the guards.'

Skiouros shook his head, a sly grin crossing his face.

'If you'd ever had to live off your wits, you'd know there's always a way.'

Crossing the space, he edged aside the crate. His hand closed on the eight arrows and he withdrew four.

'You'll never hide them,' Nicolo frowned.

Skiouros laughed and took the missiles by head and flight, one at a time, snapping them across his knee and discarding most of the shaft. As he finished and threw aside the broken remnants, he offered an arrow head with three inches of shaft jutting below to each man.

'You can put these in boots or up your sleeves for when you need them. I'd advise against the codpiece as a hiding place unless you're happy with diminished chances of fatherhood.'

As the three men took the proffered arrow heads and peered at them before searching for a good place to secrete them, Skiouros turned to the next article, retrieving three of the four-foot lengths of rope they had cut from the stores.

'These will go around your waist, hidden beneath your doublet. Just make sure you get them beneath your underclothes so that they're well padded, or the shape might stand out too much.'

Leaving his friends desperately trying to secrete the ropes as suggested, Skiouros hooked out a tool handle – an ash shaft some three feet long.

'No way you can hide that.' Parmenio shook his head.

Skiouros simply raised an eyebrow and crouched, taking one of the spare lengths of rope. Lifting his cassocks, he tied the shaft to his thigh, such that only a foot of the wood jutted out below the knee on the outside of his leg. As soon as the cassock fell back and he stood once more, there was not a sign of the handle – not even a tell-tale shape in the material.

'You're good at this,' Cesare noted with a sly smile. 'Someday I will draw from you the tale of your past, Master Skiouros, and you can enlighten me as to how an escaped slave of the Turk managed to

94

learn the high guard, speak several languages, and has *'experience'* with black powder.'

'Speaking of which,' noted Skiouros, reaching into the space once more and withdrawing two of the small linen bundles, 'there is always a chance we might find a use for these.'

The three men instinctively stepped a few paces away from Skiouros as he stuffed the small parcels of powder down beneath his robes, attaching the twine ties to his vest so that they hung to either side of his torso beneath the armpits.

'Not entirely comfortable,' Skiouros smiled, 'but quite well hidden, wouldn't you say?'

Parmenio opened his mouth to suggest that Skiouros not flap his arms so much unless he wanted to detonate them, but then closed it again, pointing down the hold towards the stern. Skiouros turned to look and saw the booted feet of the Turkish sailors descending the ladder to the hold. Stepping to the side, he pushed the evidence of their theft deeper into the darkness and shifted the crate back into position, hiding the remnants.

'Alright,' Skiouros said with a deep breath. 'No one makes any move to escape until I give you the nod. It'll all have to be using hand signals or winks and the like – Hassan speaks Italian and Greek, and we can't be sure none of his men do the same. Just watch me as closely as you can. As soon as I see a chance open up, I'll let you know, but you'll need to be ready as we'll have to move straight away. I'll get us away from them if I can, and then Nicolo and Parmenio will have to take over guiding us. If anything goes wrong, we'll just have to improvise and fight our way out.'

'Or die doing so,' Nicolo sighed. 'Better dead than a life lived as a catamite to some toothless, horny old Berber bastard.'

'Just be ready,' Skiouros repeated, his voice falling to a whisper as two sailors paused at the far end of the narrow passage along the hold and started shouting at them in Turkish, demanding they approach, and beckoning with the hands that didn't hold a curved blade.

Skiouros stepped into the corridor first, aware that he would need to take the lead position if he were to spot any opportunity and be visible to the others.

'Let's get this over with.'

Chapter Nine - Of freedom's call

Skiouros felt the crunch of the gravel beneath his feet, hastily shod once more in his fine – if scuffed and dirty – boots before leaving the hold. It felt as though the world had reached out and grasped him once more, clutching him to her bosom. It was hard to countenance just how much of a relief it felt.

A quick summary of Skiouros' seafaring life left him in no doubt as to how strongly he belonged on land: a voyage from Istanbul to Crete in the guise of a sick monk, spending his entire trip taking emetics and vomiting, and then a voyage from Crete to... well, *from Crete...* in which he had been captured and humiliated by a renegade Turk and was now to be sold into slavery. Two for two – hardly a good record. On the bright side, unless they managed to break out between here and Tunis, he would hardly have to worry about future sea voyages, since he would most likely end up in the deserts to the south playing pretty boy to a Berber chief, tending caravan animals or labouring on a farm scratching out agriculture on the edge of the desert.

The crunch of gravel.

Bliss, despite what it heralded.

Parmenio and Nicolo looked less enamoured with their new situation, though Cesare Orsini seemed to be taking the whole thing remarkably stoically. Strangely, since they had first met on board the *Isabella*, Skiouros had only seen Orsini show a strong outburst of emotion once. Irrespective of slavery, pirates and fighting for their lives, the only thing that seemed to have raised a strong response from the nobleman was the mention of his own family and their links with the Pope and the King of Napoli. The man certainly was an enigma.

Skiouros peered across at him as the Italian stretched and rubbed the small of his back, his eyes closed as he relaxed in the searing sunshine, almost as though rising from his morning's bed without a care in the world. The Greek shook his head.

Parmenio and Nicolo, on the other hand, were glowering with deep-seated hatred at their captors as they took in the Turkish force surrounding them.

It appeared that Hassan was taking no chances, not that Skiouros would have expected him to – the Butcher was clearly not a man given to error. He had left at least two dozen men on board the *Yarim Ay*, including the homunculus Mehmi – enough armed men to be certain no trouble could arise from the chained galley slaves, and sufficient men and officers to put the ship to sea and find a safe haven should the Emir's own galleys happen by and spot the Turks languishing on their coastline. This left two dozen more men under the command of Etci Hassan Reis himself, rowing ashore to escort the prisoners to the market in Tunis. As the armed and brutal sailors continued to arrive from the ship's boat and form up around the prisoners, Skiouros felt their chances of escape ebb with every fresh set of footsteps. Four men against almost thirty? It seemed unlikely, to say the least.

The first boat had brought the captain ashore with seven of his men. Four of those had armed themselves with matchlock muskets, slow-matches sizzling away, which had stayed unerringly trained on the prisoners as they were loaded onto the second boat and then ferried across. Skiouros had made no suggestion of an escape attempt as they first landed, aware – from the fact that the barrels of their guns barely wavered and remained locked on the targets' breastbones wherever they moved – that these men were good shots. To attempt to run at that point would have been plain suicide.

And then the rest had arrived and Skiouros had begun to wonder whether he'd have been better running and taking his chance with a musket ball.

All moot now, of course.

A quick glance around at the ruins among which they stood revealed that it had once been a large structure, perhaps even large enough to accommodate a war galley like the *Yarim Ay*. Now the walls were little more that knee- or waist-high remnants and rubble had piled up next to them like the snowdrifts that plagued Istanbul in the harsher winters.

There were signs that this particular ruin had been used as accommodation fairly recently, piton holes in the stone where a tent roof had been stretched across, using poles to create the pitch for height. The remnants of bedding, tattered rugs and the bones of past meals lay scattered, and along with them numerous pieces of debris from shattered jugs to leather fragments to snapped spoons.

Skiouros paused and noted the position of some of the more interesting debris.

Now two dozen men surrounded them, and one of those was approaching with a solid-looking iron chain hanging between his hands. The sailor glanced between the four prisoners and, seeing Skiouros watching him intently, strode across, a comrade at his shoulder. Gesturing to his friend, the man found the end of the chain and looped a few feet of it. The second guard stepped behind Skiouros and grasped both his hands, yanking them around behind him painfully and holding them in a vice-like grip. As Skiouros winced at the pain, the first sailor dropped the loop of chain around the prisoner's neck and slid it close so that the thing was tighter than any collar, biting into the skin whenever Skiouros swallowed or moved his head even fractionally. Satisfied that it was tight enough and would never stretch to go over the priest's head, the sailor produced a small padlock from a pouch at his side and slipped the lock's shackle through the chain before snapping it shut with a gentle click that might as well be the doom-laden sound of a tomb door slamming shut as far as the captives were concerned.

Secured, the two men let go of Skiouros and he stretched his arms and rubbed his painful hands, swallowing painfully within the choking loop of chain. At least they'd put him first in the line, Skiouros thought as he saw a guard escorting Orsini over, while the other looped a few more feet of chain a mere two yards down the line from the first padlock.

Skiouros shuffled himself so that he could just see the padlock's edge out of the corner of his eye if he strained to look down, though most of it remained hidden by his chin and burgeoning beard.

He smiled.

The Turks were master engineers and great inventors and innovators – the ease with which the once-great Byzantine Empire had fallen to Mehmet the Great stood simple testament to that. But a padlock was a simple thing and not much improved on since the days of the great founder of Constantinople. A padlock hardly presented a difficulty to a man who'd spent a decade in the world's greatest city, living by theft and subterfuge. It would be a lot easier, of course, if he had the tools, but these things could not be helped.

His eyes dropped to the debris he had been investigating earlier and it took him only a moment to re-locate what he was looking for: a broken eating utensil, cast aside among the wreckage before the shabby, impoverished inhabitants moved on.

Just right. That sharpened metal spike which was all that remained of the spoon would be ideal for tripping the pins in the lock at his throat. Trying to look casual, he turned to Cesare, who was now fastened in the same manner a couple of yards away while the guards went to work on Nicolo, third in the line. With a jerk of the head, Skiouros beckoned Orsini towards him and, as soon as the man took a step, easing the tension on the chain, Skiouros dipped and scooped up the broken spoon, using a finger to push it up the sleeve of his cassock. As he came upright, the metal spike disappearing into his cuff, Skiouros made sure to stagger the other way also and then clutch at his head as though he'd been caught momentarily off balance.

'A picklock?' Orsini whispered. 'You are a constant surprise, Master Skiouros.'

'I don't know about that, but I'll surprise myself if I can work out a way to get all four locks open without being noticed. Mine I can do in moments without drawing attention, but the other three…'

Orsini pursed his lips.

'Can it be taught in minutes? I am a fast learner.'

Skiouros frowned. Under normal circumstances he would have said no, plainly. But there was just the faintest possibility that a man with Cesare's sharp wits might be able to pick it up almost instinctively.

'No better time to test that,' Skiouros muttered, turning so that the guards who could see them were busily involved in a discussion and comparing their weapons, not paying a great deal of attention to the prisoners.

'Try to look like you're attempting to loosen the chain for breath,' Skiouros advised quietly, and Cesare obliged readily.

'Right,' Skiouros muttered. 'I'm going to do mine and talk you through it, just once, and quite fast, else we'll be noticed. Ready?'

Orsini nodded, still pulling at his neck chain.

'Here goes,' Skiouros whispered, grabbing at the padlock, allowing the pick to slide out of his sleeve and into his grip. 'Thumbnail in the keyhole, jerk the cylinder as far to the left as you can, so that it's very slightly misaligned.'

Cesare nodded, peering intently while maintaining the fiction of struggling with his own chains. His view was partially obscured by Skiouros' flapping black veil, which aided him in keeping the activity so well hidden from the Turks.

'In goes the pick, making sure that you don't knock the cylinder back into line. Push the spike in to the full extent and then angle it to feel upwards. You'll find a sort of springy pressure. Push up until you hear a faint click. We're lucky as these are really simple locks with only three pins. Pull the pick slightly out until you feel the second pin and repeat the procedure. Then same again with the outer pin and then...'

Skiouros' padlock snapped open with a click, though he kept it in place and pushed it so that it was almost closed again, sliding it around so that it sat beneath the back veil of his skouphos hat.

'Astounding,' Orsini smiled. 'And why do the pins not drop back into place as you leave them? Because of the cylinder's angle?'

Skiouros nodded. 'It's a simple failing of all padlocks. Unless the cylinder cannot be misaligned, it is only a matter of patience and practice.'

Orsini grinned and Skiouros whispered 'here', palming the broken spoon to the Italian. The nobleman almost dropped it as the chain jerked and the pair turned to see that all four of them were now fastened together, the far end looped around the wrist of a very burly guard. The captives were each separated by two yards of chain.

Already the guards were starting to move, and Skiouros found that the organisation of the prisoners had placed him at the back of the slave line, and not the front as he'd expected. Another setback.

How could he possibly get signals to the others from behind?

It would have to be done through whispered commands, passed down along the line. That would seriously slow any attempt to flee.

Skiouros ground his teeth. Every moment was bringing another setback.

'Memorise what I said. You need to have the padlock open long before the time comes to break.' He turned from scanning the ruins to see Cesare smiling at him and settling his padlock so that it appeared still closed. Once more Skiouros was forced to reassess this man. He was a *natural*. What they could do together! A month of practice and they could own the world.

Hassan bellowed the order to move and the guard at the fore jerked the chain, almost pulling Parmenio from his feet and starting the slave column moving. Skiouros shuffled slightly forwards and whispered, 'I doubt Nicolo and the captain will find the lock as easy. As we move, whisper the explanation to Nicolo and pass him the tool and we'll just have to hope he's more nimble than he looks. We may have to find a way to help them, though I have no idea how. We're going to have to play it all by ear. You're the one who's closer to them and can see what's going on, so if they can't do it, you may have to be the one to let me know when we can help them.'

Orsini simply nodded and moved forward, head down as though dejected and accepting his lot – in truth trying to further conceal the fact that his padlock was not properly fastened.

The two dozen men with them were taking as few chances as Hassan himself, making sure they kept on all sides of the column at all times, providing no easy escape route. What did they expect a bunch of chained prisoners to do?

The column moved out of the ruins and Skiouros peered to left and right. Another set of low, ramshackle broken walls betrayed the presence of a once thriving street – an arcade of shops perhaps – through which they passed. Ahead, a low colonnade indicated that the huge, square shape had once been something of import – perhaps a market or a temple, or a forum such as those that could still be found in Istanbul if one explored a little.

The once-elaborate building had become the home of an extended Berber family, their huge black desert-style tent anchored on the walls and held up in the centre by three broken columns of varying heights, carpets and coloured, patterned wall hangings dividing the space up. The tribe sat watching the motley parade, each one dressed in dusty black and with the walnut-coloured leathery lined skin of the desert tribes. Even the children looked weather-beaten and wizened, and the beasts that were tethered in the same space as the family were threadbare and slightly mange-ridden. They put Skiouros heavily in mind of the Romani people he was used to seeing in Istanbul and the thought prompted him to wonder what had happened to old 'bone-hair'. Had he died on the ship? Skiouros didn't remember seeing him among the executions, but where else could he be, really?

And then the column was moving on, tramping through the eternal beige dust of the ruined city. Time passed tensely for Skiouros, his breath catching at every sight and sound and move of the Turks as his mind

101

churned endlessly, cycling through possibilities, sifting the information his eyes and ears fed him and trying desperately to turn it all to their advantage.

All in vain.

The guards were sharp and attentive, and Hassan had everything worked out well. The route they were taking through the ruins of once-great Carthage utilised main streets and open barren spaces, where little of use could be seen, let alone taken or put to work. The indigenous folk were unlikely to be of any help and the bulk of those – sparse occupants really – were Berber families pitching camp among the ruins or the poor and disenfranchised of Arab stock, inhabiting ramshackle shanty buildings among the fractured walls.

All in all, the atmosphere of the ruins did little to lift the spirit.

Skiouros noted as they moved that, through the ruins and trees and undergrowth, he could see the great harbour-lake that lay inside the Gullet occasionally, at first ahead, and then off to their left as they curved away from the morning sun to head west. The land was relatively flat, broken only by the occasional small rise or dip, though the flora broke up what might otherwise have been a good clear view of the countryside. After some twenty minutes of marching at a pace of which the military would be proud, the slave train finally left the ruins of Carthage and entered the barren wilderness that lay between the ancient capital and its later counterpart.

A trail led between the two, though it was unsurfaced, dusty and rock-strewn and clearly used only by the poor and wretched inhabitants of the ruins beside the sea or by the few farmers that eked out a living in the lands around and about. There were certainly no tell-tale marks of vehicle passage.

Skiouros, finally accepting that nothing was going to happen until they reached some kind of civilisation – unless they were suddenly set upon by random travellers – settled into the endless tiring crunch of footsteps on the uneven, uncomfortable surface, the guards watching them intently.

It had been the same a decade ago, of course. There had been no real hope of escape on the journey of the Devsirme intake to Istanbul, until they had passed into the built up area. Clear, open space meant no opportunities. *People* meant *possibilities*. And the more people, the more possibilities.

He leaned forward.

'Relax until we reach Tunis. I can't see any possibility arising until then.'

'Agreed,' hissed Orsini over his shoulder.

'How are the others doing with their locks?'

There was a brief pause of murmuring further forward as Orsini enquired, before hissing over his shoulder once more: 'No luck. Nicolo cannot get the hang of it.'

Skiouros cursed silently under his breath, using a number of words that sat at serious odds with the vestments in which he was clad.

'Tell him to keep at it. We've clearly got plenty of time.'

'Perhaps you could pray for him, Father.'

Skiouros glowered at the back of Cesare Orsini's head, unable to see his face, but imagining the smile upon it. Gallows humour. It had no place in the real world.

Skiouros ran through everything he knew over and over again. Everything about Hassan and his crew and ship; about Ottoman corsairs in general; about the Arab nations of Africa (which was unfortunately little more than legend and rumour to him) and about the geography of the land; about what advantages they had, what stolen equipment they had concealed about their persons, what they could do if all four managed to slip their shackles.

No new conclusions could be drawn, of course, but the desperate search for an epiphany at least kept him occupied on the long walk as the minutes stretched out to a dusty, hot, painful hour, and that hour dragged on into a second and then finally a third, the landscape barely changing.

As they moved, the lake harbour started to pull away from them on their left and was finally lost to sight. Then the path began to turn slowly southwards. The road skirted the busier areas near the ports and came at the city from an inland angle, presumably so that the less-than popular peasants of Carthage were kept away from the commercial region.

Finally, as the third hour of stamping on rocky dust drew to a close, a thicket of acacia, bulked by dry grasses and musk thistles, gave way to their first view of Tunis, down a gentle slope. Skiouros felt his lead-heavy heart lift just a little.

After the claustrophobic, enclosed world of ships and the wide, neat streets of Venetian-controlled Candia, Tunis – at first sight – looked almost heart-warmingly familiar. Despite the difference in the ruling nations and the vast geographical gulf between this city and the great metropolis of Istanbul, the similarities were evident even at a distance. The walls were Arabic, clearly, squat and squared and with exotic point-arched gates and unusually-shaped merlons, but behind them Tunis seethed like a living creature, no great western city planning having touched the organisation of the maze-like alleys, streets, souks and bazaars. If ever they had a chance to slip their captors, it would be in that heaving mass of sweating, disorganised humanity.

Cesare had clearly come to a similar conclusion, as he looked over his shoulder, raising an eyebrow before having to turn back in order to breathe past the tightened chain loop.

'Be prepared,' Skiouros murmured.

Orsini simply nodded as far as his shackles would allow.

The Greek felt a certain tense excitement build as they watched the gate from the top of the low rise and the column came to a halt. Etci Hassan barked out commands in Turkish to his men and Skiouros smiled to himself. The captain still had no reason to assume that Skiouros spoke his tongue and therefore never guarded it. Hassan had ordered his men to split up. Only ten of them plus the captain himself would enter the city, the other fifteen or so waiting here, so as not to provoke the Hafsid military. Any more than a dozen entering the city would be too strong a force of potential enemies for even the most selfish guard to turn a blind eye to.

So their chances continued to improve – now at odds of only three-to-one and moving into an enclosed, seething environment. It felt so familiar.

The slow descent to the city began, the four prisoners now watched all the more closely by their diminished guard, Hassan leading the way, removing a pouch of coins from his waist and weighing them as they approached the heavy bulk of the city's gatehouse.

Hafsid warriors moved back and forth along the wall tops, spear points and conical helms gleaming in the sun, white linen cloaks, tunics and turbans dazzling. Two more stood beside the gate, one at each side, ready to challenge anyone desirous of entry to the city.

Skiouros paid scant attention to the guards as the column closed on the gate. His mind was already beyond the arch along with his gaze, picking out every detail of the cramped street beyond, which seemed to be one of the few, rare long straight thoroughfares in the city, stretching away to its heart. Yet for all its linear form, it was still relatively narrow, cluttered with life – stalls, tethered animals, beggars and the general bric-a-brac of a thriving city. Narrower alleys led off it periodically, some through small arches of their own, one or two covered with canvas roofs to guard against the sun.

Much now rested on Parmenio and Nicolo freeing themselves of the chain.

A quantity of purloined Venetian ducats changed hands at the gate – a part of Hassan's Zakynthian loot, presumably – and the Hafsid guards nodded, their unsympathetic stony expressions showing no greater respect for the Turkish pirate than for his captives. Money talked in every language, though, and in moments the column was moving through the arch.

'How's the padlock?'

Cesare didn't bother turning.

'Still nothing. We may have to try and help somehow.'

Skiouros chewed his lip. He could almost certainly see himself slipping the grip of their captors and melting away into the city as he'd once done in Istanbul, and he could even see Orsini following him, despite the man's background of privilege and law. The two Venetian sailors, though, were a different matter. They might know the city a little, but they were not men of dubious skills or instinctive quick-thinkers – they were too honest for that. Unless Skiouros and Cesare could help free them, they would be doomed.

'I'll try to think of something. We're in the best place now, but we're running out of time.'

Skiouros continued to bite his lip deep in thought, his eyes darting this way and that, looking for something to give him hope; an idea; a way out.

'Christ is risen!'

Skiouros was so taken aback at the sudden voice that it took him a moment to drag himself from his deeper thoughts. The voice had called out in Greek! His mind raced as quickly as his gaze, the latter trying to divine the source of the shout, the former attempting to put it into context.

Christ is risen – a standard mode of salutation between priests and the more pious of the Orthodox Church. What was the response, again?

'Indeed he is risen!' Skiouros shouted in reply, grateful that he'd spent so long in the company of priests and monks that the response came to his lips before it filtered through his brain.

His eyes fell upon the speaker just as the haft of a matchlock musket cracked him between the shoulder blades, the guard behind him punishing him arbitrarily for calling out. As he staggered forward, gasping at the pain in his spine, Skiouros lost sight of the man for a moment, but then the crowds parted and he saw the speaker again.

An Orthodox believer? Here?

The man was wearing the white *sticharion* liturgical vestment of a priest, with the plain three-barred cross about his neck – no hat or hood, but the long grey hair and almost white beard that hung to his chest as much a badge of his office as any headgear. Skiouros reeled, partially from the blow, but mostly from the shock of such a sight deep in the Arab and Berber city of Tunis.

The man was pointing at him now and shouting to people around him.

'A priest! In chains!'

Skiouros' heart jumped. The opportunity was upon him. God had apparently provided, and Skiouros found he was grinning suddenly as Orsini craned his head painfully to see what was happening behind him.

The priest and his companions were a short way up one of the side streets, and Skiouros was interested to hear the man speaking in both Greek and Arabic to his people.

'For shame!' he then bellowed in Greek, and suddenly the priest was barrelling through the crowd, half a dozen people with him, helping him push through towards the slave train.

The guards seemed to have suddenly noticed what was happening. Three of them to the rear turned and hefted their swords, preparing to fight off any attack, continually on the alert in this city that held no love for the Ottoman Empire.

'Release that man!' the priest bellowed in Greek, and then 'release him, I say!' repeated in Arabic. Skiouros's darting gaze took in the priest and the half dozen people accompanying him. He was clearly native, born to the region, looking for all the world like the Arab and Berber population around him, and his friends were all apparently of Berber blood from their skin, hair and clothes, and yet Skiouros was interested to see crosses dangling around their necks.

His mind continued to boggle at this sudden, most welcome and most unexpected encounter, but his instincts took over without the need for conscious thought or decision making.

Chaos had broken out, an explosion of activity around him.

The guards were distracted, most of their attention suddenly devoted to this new potential threat. Even Hassan seemed to have taken his eyes off the prisoners, as had the man who still held the end of the chain.

Skiouros slipped the padlock's shackle open and allowed it to drop from his neck. The chain unravelled and fell away.

'Orsini,' he barked, somewhat unnecessarily as the Italian had clearly shared his thought and was already moving.

'Nicolo!' he shouted, and Cesare nodded, stepping forward to help the *Isabella*'s purser with his padlock. The crowd in the street had reacted to this sudden activity in the same manner as any crowd in any city would: with keen interest. Some were shying back from the Ottoman guards with their bared weapons. Others were shouting angrily at them, enemy warriors in their city. Yet more were flooding to prevent the Christians from reaching the street, while others were trying to help them through. Most, however, were simply trying to get a better view of the commotion without putting themselves directly in harm's way.

Skiouros had lost sight of the priest again, but he no longer cared. The man had served his purpose as a distraction and could safely be ignored now. A little back and to one side, where they had passed moments earlier, stood a narrow alley with a canvas roof, packed with stalls selling enticing-smelling things.

Perfect.

'Street back there with the spice and fruit stalls,' he hissed to Orsini in Italian. The guards at the rear seemed miraculously to have become bogged down in spectators, attempting to seal off the approaching Christians. Skiouros was actually unfettered and with a clear run.

Hassan was bellowing at his men in an attempt to bring them back into a semblance of order, but the Turks were beyond such discipline at that brief, distracted moment.

Skiouros turned back to his companions. Orsini was shouting something at Nicolo and in that sudden, stupid, goddamned sick moment, Skiouros' eyes saw Nicolo's fingers fumble, blood welling up where the metal shard had ripped his thumb. The shattered spoon that was their lifeline to freedom pinwheeled, arcing through the air, to disappear among the legs of the guards and the citizens they were fending off.

Given time and planning, Skiouros would be able to come up with an alternative method of springing the locks, and if he crossed those few precious paces to them, he could do it in a heartbeat with an appropriate spike.

But there was nothing easily to hand.

And there was no time.

Even as Orsini dropped to try and pick up the broken spoon shard, the guards were beginning to come back to order, obeying their captain's furious shouts.

No time.

'Cesare!' He didn't really know what he was trying to convey to his friend; it just seemed important to spur the Italian into some other activity. In response, the young nobleman looked up and about, realising that the men whose feet he was scouring around were stepping back into line and that the guards had noticed the state of the prisoners.

The nobleman rose, and received a musket butt to the back of the head from one of the quicker guards.

Skiouros felt the panic of impotence. What could he do? Nicolo and Parmenio were still chained, and Orsini was in danger.

'Get out of here!' Cesare bellowed at him, as a guard smashed the hilt of a sword into the nobleman's stomach, doubling him over in pain.

Skiouros stared. The world seemed to slow to a crawl, the very air a tar-thick substance the crowd moved through. The escape had failed. Nicolo and Parmenio could not break from their chains and were now already back in the grasping, angry, abusing hands of their captors, Hassan busily snapping out orders. Cesare came upright, waving Skiouros away, only to receive a punch to the face that snapped his head sideways and almost threw him from his feet.

Skiouros simply stared.

'Selfish...'

Despite the desperate situation, Skiouros found himself picturing the old Romani beggar in the taverna in Crete, accusing him of selfishness.

Was he a selfish person?

Could he truly be? He'd always considered himself quite the opposite, particularly in light of the amount of effort he had put into trying to rebuild his relationship with Lykaion and to pull their family back together.

'Selfish?'

Skiouros broke into a run for the alley.

He hadn't really planned to.

In fact, somewhere in his heart, he had fully intended to run in the other direction – for Orsini, to push aside the big corsair brute that was even now landing blow after blow on the nobleman. To rescue him or at least to succumb to the same fate, as a true companion should; to show support and solidarity for his only true friends in the world – the men who had helped, sheltered and befriended him when no one really should have done. Men who had taken him in unquestioningly, despite his deliberately hazy past and occluded plans for the future.

Shame flooded through Skiouros, freezing his heart and chilling his legs, yet bringing red flames to his cheeks as he bolted, leaving his friends to their fate and racing for that narrow alley and its promise of escape.

Moreover, he had completely ignored the fate of the priest who had so unexpectedly attempted to come to their aid, along with his companions. Perhaps they were even dead, butchered by Hassan's men in response to some sort of perceived attack. What then of the old man who had greeted him like a brother – which he, to all appearances, was – and who had shouted so defiantly at the enslaving of a priest?

The corner loomed ahead with only a few boys and old folk in between, none of whom were likely to step in to stop him.

Shame.

Flooding, freezing, burning, lead-heavy shame.

And yet his feet were pounding the road as if he were moving with a single-minded purpose, taking him ever further from his friends and their unpleasant fate. The alley.

Perhaps he was right to run? Orsini had *told* him to go, after all.

But while Skiouros was an expert with a lifetime's experience of fooling people, there was simply no way to fool himself in this regard. Not just selfishness, but even cowardice! With no sense of relief, just the dreadful knowledge that he had proved the old Romani beggar absolutely correct in every way, he rounded the corner...

... and smashed into an outstretched arm.

A big man in the white tunic of a local Hafsid guard, curved sword slung at his side, stood like a mountain of toughened meat, barring his route to safety. The Hafsids were no lovers of the Turk... but then *he* was an escaped slave.

As Skiouros staggered to regain his footing, the big man shoved him, roughly, sending him tottering back out into the main street. Skiouros, now in a panic that almost overrode the shame pressing down on him, spun in a mad daze. The crowd were closing in on him, angry now. An entirely Muslim crowd. They might – surprisingly – have nothing against the Orthodox Church, as the other priest who had contacted them seemed to indicate, and they might dislike the Ottoman Empire, but they were in no mood to let trouble brew on account of an escaped slave. All exits were sealed off now.

Skiouros turned to see Etci Hassan glaring that awful pale grey glare at him, a guard by his side levelling his musket and aiming for the priest-slave's face, his slow-match glowing and giving off a trail of smoke as he prepared to squeeze the trigger and fire.

The Greek closed his eyes for his death, too cowardly in the end even to face that like a man.

After half a dozen heartbeats with no fatal bullet grinding its way through his skull and brains, he opened one eye. While the musket remained trained on him, two guards were approaching, weapons in hand.

Another failure.

Not one of them had made it to freedom.

He could not even find the strength of character to resist or object as the two guards grabbed him, punched him a few times, kicked his knees out from under him and then dragged him back to the slave train, his toes dragging in the dirt.

He watched miserably as Hassan beckoned to a guard – the one who had padlocked them all together back in Carthage's ruined port – and quietly, in a voice like icy death and accompanied by the freezing white glare of his eerie eyes, told the guard that he was a worthless fool and an incompetent. The guard lowered his gaze to the ground, muttering desperate pleas to his commander, unable to meet that disconcerting glare.

Skiouros noted with no surprise or pleasure just how fast Hassan's sword arm was as it swept his blade from its sheath in a tight arc and down through the man's lowered neck, sending the penitent sailor's head bouncing across the road with unpleasant bony, meaty noises, where it rolled among the legs of the watching crowd.

A jet of arterial crimson pumped from the severed stump and Hassan negligently stepped closer and pushed the still-standing sailor's corpse backwards to fall flat on the floor, the spray of gore now pumping onto Skiouros' own black vestments.

He didn't care. He was beyond such cares now.

Parmenio and Nicolo had received a couple of blows from their captors despite having never moved. Orsini was being held up by a guard, his own legs no longer able to support him. Hassan had been pushed to a dangerous point, where his anger was so hot and powerful that he had authorised punishment of the captives despite the fact that such damage could seriously reduce their value at auction.

And it had been Skiouros' doing. *He* had exhorted them to escape. *He* had showed them the time and the method and had essentially given them up to a beating from their captors while he attempted to flee to safety.

And yet, as Parmenio and Nicolo turned to look at him while another Turk retrieved the padlocks from the floor for refitting the chains, both regarded him with a strange respect for his attempt, tinged with pity that he had been recaptured. They held him in no way accountable.

If only he could say the same for himself.

His heart felt heavier than it had ever done.

'Chain them properly, bind their hands and then we move on to the Suq-al-Birka immediately,' Hassan snapped. 'I want to be back at sea and making for the rendezvous as soon as possible. And any further stupidity will be met with the edge of my blade, be it on the part of slave or crewmember.'

Skiouros stood like a sheep, uncaring and unfeeling as the chain was replaced around his neck and the padlock fastened once more.

It appeared they would be sold after all.

Chapter Ten - Of human traffic

The four prisoners were shoved roughly into a stone room of surprisingly large dimensions, given how jumbled and confused the Suq-al-Birka had appeared from the outside. Light was provided by a square opening in the roof at the huge chamber's centre and even that was secured with a grille of metal that destroyed all hope of escape. Two corners of the huge room – roughly a third of the total space – had been sealed off with cage-like bars, creating two animal pens – one for men and one for women, as was evident immediately, given the occupants. Skiouros briefly raised his forlorn gaze from the floor to take in the room, not with any hopeful view to escape, but from the depths of a miserable, self-interested depression.

The men and women in the cages were mostly very dark, even ebony-skinned Africans, stripped naked and festering in their own filth. In the open space between the cages, a post stood – resembling a pell for sword practice – but the use of this post was no such happy exercise. The shackles attached to the top and the dried blood that coated the floor around it told unhappy tales of its usage across the months and years.

Another corner held a large trough of water, fed by a pipe and trickling away down a drain, keeping the supply full. Three buckets stood next to it, one with a ladle.

As soon as the captives and their Turkish guard appeared, the cages broke into an uproar of pleadings, screams and imprecations, and Skiouros dropped his gaze again. He could feel the disapproving looks of the other three. For the last ten minutes through the streets, his companions had kept themselves alert and hopeful, watching for any possibility of a further attempt. Skiouros, disgusted at what he had discovered in his own soul and having abandoned all hope, had merely shuffled along meekly, keeping his gaze down. His friends were silently urging him with their eyes towards further hope.

But there was no hope.

Not on the journey, and certainly not now they had arrived and were to become caged animals to be bought and sold at the whim of their captors.

The room had two doors. The one through which they had entered passed through a well-guarded room. The other one was equally secured with locks, though where it led, who knew? Probably the sale place. It would have interested Skiouros, had he been of a more positive outlook, to note that Hassan deliberately stayed outside the door with a few of his men, sending only four sailors to push them inside, and then allowing the Hafsid guards to deal with them from that point. Clearly Hassan had no faith in the word of the locals and no intention of endangering himself and his crew by walking willingly into a slave chamber.

The corsair captain began to speak with the commander of the Hafsid guards, rattling away in Arabic. Skiouros wished that he had ignored the Latin that the scribe had been pushing on him in Crete and devoted some time to the study of this eastern exotic tongue. But then how could he have known that he would wind up here in the slave market of Tunis, unable to comprehend his jailers?

'What are they saying?' hissed Parmenio, shrinking away from one of the native guards who glared at him for opening his mouth unbidden.

'No idea,' sighed Skiouros. 'It's Arabic, not Turkish.'

'They negotiate,' croaked a voice from the male cage, the Italian words heavy with an Arabic accent.

Skiouros, despite his misery, looked up and spotted the man sitting cross-legged by the bars of his cage. The old fellow with the shaved head and the grey beard scratched his scalp.

'You remain the property of the Turk until a sale is agreed, and then the degraded filth – that is, the Emir's men – will take their cut and your friend will walk away with his fortune. They negotiate because the standard procedure is to strip you naked and sell or burn your possessions, then give you a good check over, perhaps abuse you a little depending on which guard it is and whether he's recently been sated, and then you are washed and imprisoned until the event.'

'And the negotiation?' asked Parmenio, frowning.

'Your Turk believes you will fetch a good price as you are, because the clothes identify you as worthy stock. Without them, you are just another group of Christians taken in a raid. He is probably right, but the guards still do not like this.'

Skiouros nodded sadly. It was hardly their concern any more. Degradation would be their lot now.

After a few moments the guards grabbed Nicolo and pushed him against the wall. The purser bellowed out in anger and struggled futilely, given the number of guards that were now in the room. Skiouros could not quite see what was happening as three men surrounded the sailor, but a moment later there was a bark of triumph and the length of rope that had been around Nicolo's waist was cast into the open area of floor. A few seconds more, and the broken arrow followed. For another minute or so, Nicolo was searched roughly, though nothing else of interest appeared – only a few coins and personal objects being cast onto the pile. As soon as the search was complete, Nicolo was pushed aside and left to refasten his clothes while the guards moved on to Parmenio and repeated the sequence, finding the hidden tools and various other personal goods and throwing them on the growing pile. Having ascertained that no violence or other abuse was likely, since Nicolo had remained untouched, Parmenio simply surrendered himself to the search and was shoved aside when it was completed.

Hassan watched from the doorway and then rattled off some more Arabic with the guard – a short exchange of some subject on which they finally apparently agreed, before the Turk disappeared out into the other room, taking his sailors with him.

It appeared they had now been delivered into the hands of the Hafsids.

'What did they say?' asked Parmenio as he adjusted his shirt from the rummaging.

'Your Turk just gave them a preferential cut in order to get you into this afternoon's sale. He seems to want to be away in a hurry. No surprise, being a Turk in Tunis.'

As the old man in the cage watched, Cesare was subjected to the same search, the rough handling causing sharp intakes of breath as they touched the bruises and damage of Hassan's beating.

'Looks like our cache of tools will be of no aid?' Parmenio grumbled, watching the pile of goods on the floor grow with the third rope and arrow head.

'If I had a source of flame,' Skiouros sighed miserably, 'I could destroy the whole building in a heartbeat.' To illustrate his meaning, he lifted his arms just a little. Parmenio and Nicolo backed away a few paces instinctively.

'No matter, though.'

As Cesare was pushed towards his friends, holding his side painfully, one of the white-clad Hafsid guards rattled something off at Skiouros in Arabic.

'I don't speak your language,' he said in Turkish, frowning. The guard glowered angrily.

'He demands that you surrender all your goods, including the rope and arrow that he is certain you have.'

Skiouros nodded bleakly. 'Tell him I will.'

'They won't search him?' Parmenio asked in surprise.

'Christians are a people of the book. Our faith demands that we treat you with respect.'

'That I'd not heard before.'

The old man shrugged. 'Theory and practice are different in every field. The guards will not go easy on you, for you may be Christians, but you are also slaves. Yet they would rather not anger a holy man any more than they must, and they would certainly rather not force a search upon him. Deliver your goods to them and they will be satisfied.'

Skiouros began pulling out the arrow head and rope from his vestments.

'They don't expect anything else,' hissed Parmenio meaningfully.

The 'priest' nodded. 'But it will show good faith if I go beyond expectations.' With a sigh, he bent and unfastened the tool handle from his leg, throwing it onto the pile. Turning to the guard, he gestured at the prayer rope at his waist. There was a brief discussion among the jailers – after all, it could be used in an emergency as a noose – but they finally reached a consensus and shook their heads, indicating that he could keep it.

'I see your good faith only goes so far?' Cesare smiled, subtly indicating his own armpits gingerly. Skiouros gave a weak, hollow smile.

'We may yet find an open flame and I would like to think it would be better to be engulfed in the flames of freedom than chained, whipped and abused for the rest of my short, painful life.'

'Never give up hope,' smiled Orsini. 'A man of God should have more faith than that.'

115

As two of the guard gathered up the pitiful pile of possessions and hauled them out into the other room, the rest opened the door of the cage, using their clubs to batter fingers away from the bars, two of them with swords drawn to ward against any trouble.

As the door swung open, three of the more desperate, naked Africans inside made to run. Club blows rained upon them for half a dozen heartbeats and then their bruised, bloodied forms were roughly shoved back into the throng.

The Hafsid guard spoke quickly to them, the old man in the cage translating.

'You are expected to make no trouble. It would be unfortunate for your owner if the guards had to '*damage*' you. You will be kept in the cage for only one hour, until the afternoon sale, when you will be taken out and added to today's stock. He also says that you all smell like a camel's rectum and that you should be washed.'

Nicolo glared at the guard. 'No man gets to soap me down without buying me dinner first!'

'Do not worry unduly. If they decide to wash you it is a short and painless process.'

'Not for them,' grunted Nicolo meaningfully.

'Come on,' Skiouros sighed, walking into the cage. The others followed quickly and as soon as the door was shut and locked and the guards made their way out of the chamber, Parmenio approached the old man.

'I'm surprised to find an Arab who knows Italian?'

'Not all of us are thugs and killers.'

'What's your story?'

The old man simply shrugged. 'I mean no offence, friend,' he said to the captain, 'but we are slaves to be sold and abused, and I will languish here a week or more yet, while you will go to the block and have a new master in an hour. I have no desire to make new friends only to lose them moments later.'

Parmenio stared at the man, but the Arab simply climbed to his feet and shuffled off among the other captives. A few were looking hungrily at the four new arrivals, probably deciding whether an attempt to take their clothes would be too costly in blood and pain. A few others were looking at them with clearly very different – and highly disturbing – ideas.

The four prisoners drew slightly closer together in the cage's corner close to the door.

116

'What now?' Nicolo asked quietly.

'Now,' Parmenio sighed 'we try and think of a way out of here.'

'Now,' Skiouros corrected, 'we stay here and try not to get raped or attacked long enough to be sold into slavery and die a slow, long death in captivity.'

Orsini turned to Skiouros, his eyes narrowed.

'This defeatism does not become you, Master Skiouros of Constantinople.'

'Leave me alone.'

'Hardly. You are our best hope for freedom, and you still carry the only tool to that end which we possess.' The young nobleman pursed his lips and cast a quick glance at the two sailors beside them before leaning close to Skiouros and hissing with clear irritation. 'I care not whether you are wallowing in self-pity because you ran from us or because you got caught again, but know this: you went with our blessing and returned with our pity. We have no time for you to explore the depth of your soul and just because you wear the robes of a priest does not make you any the less the man who drove a sword through a Turk to save my life. Send this self-pitying heap of blubber back to where he came from and sit up and think.'

Skiouros stared at Orsini. This was only the second emotional outburst he had ever heard from the nobleman and the strength in the words jerked him some way out of the fug of misery that had settled upon him.

'Good,' the Italian said quietly, looking deep into his eyes. 'Shame at your flight, then. Stop wallowing and turn your anger away from yourself and to our captors, for they are the ones who deserve it. Now what can we do?'

Skiouros shook his head.

'Nothing.'

'There is always something. And you are resourceful.'

Skiouros stared helplessly at his friend and realised now that Parmenio and Nicolo were both peering intently at him too.

'Honestly. There's nothing. This cage has locks that I may be able to pick given the time and the tools, but I have neither. And if we did get out, we're then sealed into the room. Through the door from which we entered is a room full of men who would love nothing more than to cut us down. The other door likely leads to the sale area, and if the auction is in less than an hour, they will be out there too, preparing. There's no escape.'

117

Orsini nodded sharply.

'Alright. So what about when we get out there?'

'I have no idea. I've never seen a slave auction.'

'I have,' Parmenio said quietly. 'In Cairo. Not pretty. It'll be busy as all hell, swarming with buyers round the edge. We'll be dragged up to the block one at a time, which is the only place where there's any space. We'll be manacled, of course. And then we'll be auctioned, and bought. If they're anything like the bastard sons-of-whores Mamluks in Cairo, we'll probably be branded then for our new owners.'

'Security?' Orsini prompted.

'Tight. All exits will be heavily guarded and there'll be plenty of guards around the sale block. As soon as the money's exchanged hands it's the responsibility of the buyer, but most of those will bring their own thugs with them and will take an even more proprietorial approach to us.'

'So our best opportunity will be after the sale itself, but we will likely be separated by then. That presents difficulties.'

'It would still be our best chance,' Skiouros replied, the veil of depression falling away a little further, his mind beginning to churn the possibilities. 'Until the sale we will be far too closely guarded. The situation afterwards we cannot predict, but it will still be our best chance.'

'After the sale, then.' Orsini nodded. 'We will have to keep our wits about us and move as soon as an opportunity presents itself. Will Hassan be present, d'you think?'

'Most likely,' Parmenio replied. 'He has a hefty interest in the sale. If he expects enough remuneration to have diverted his voyage to Carthage and risked unfriendly territory to sell us, then he's going to want to see it through.'

'Shame, else we could probably speak Greek without people understanding us. It's still likely our best option.' Cesare turned to Skiouros again. 'We shall look to you for our lead unless something sudden happens. Keep your chin up and your wits about you.'

'And pray,' Parmenio added with a bitter smile. 'We could use all the help we can get.'

The minutes dragged on in the cage, Parmenio and Nicolo playing some sort of betting game involving hand movements to keep their minds from the tedium and the worry, Orsini mostly sitting with his hands on his knees, eyes closed and leaning back against the bars as though sunning himself peacefully in a garden.

Skiouros was a maelstrom in a skin sack.

Cesare's keen insight was frightening. And helpful. It had certainly lifted him from the fog of despair, though it had done little to kill off the horror that had lain at its heart: the sudden discovery that he was not half the man he thought he was.

And yet it had done something to that core of self-loathing. Instead of the revulsion eating away at him as it had been, chewing on his hope, it had instead formed into a hard shape – a bullet – that had begun to drive him, to make him think, to provide new hope. Yes, he had failed his friends just as he had failed himself, but allowing it to eat him up was no use to anyone. Instead, he would redeem himself. He would put things right. He would make up for his selfish attempt at self-preservation.

'Lord,' he asked silently, lips barely moving above his quiet breath. 'I don't deserve your love, and I know that. But these people do. Give me some sign – some hint that there is a chance for them. If you can see a way in your infinite wisdom and mercy to lift them out of bondage, there will never be a better time.'

He became aware with a strange smile that he was automatically working his way along the prayer rope at his waist, without having intended to. Wearing these vestments was starting to affect him and he wasn't sure whether that was a good thing or a bad one.

Leaning back against the bars in the same manner as Orsini, he began to reminisce in his memory about the days of sermons and services under Father Simonides back in Hadrianople. In his happy recollections, he must have fallen asleep, since he did not even hear the jailers enter the room until the cell door was rattled open and the Hafsid guards snapped out commands in Arabic. Skiouros looked around blearily for the old man to translate, but there was no sign of him among the press of prisoners, who cowered back from the guards. No matter. The commands were fairly self-evident.

One by one they were led from the cage and into the open space beneath the light well, where they had their hands bound with iron shackles. This time they were not chained together – their sales would be individual – but their chances of escape yet were, as predicted, nil. More than a dozen armed guards filled the room.

One wandered across to the trough and dipped a bucket in, filling it and hefting it as though ready to throw it at them, but the man who had given the orders shook his head and gestured for his man to put the bucket down. Pungent they might be, but their clothes labelled them high class and worth far more than the average slave. Bedraggled, they would not impress as well.

'Keep your mind focussed and be prepared,' Orsini said quietly, addressing all three.

The others nodded, as Parmenio was thrust towards the far door, his arms shackled like the rest, behind his back.

Despite the illumination of the light well in the large room, the four prisoners blinked in the searing, white-gold sunlight as the door opened and they were pushed through into an open courtyard. It was now mid-afternoon, past the worst heat of the day, yet still sweltering, dazzling and dry.

The courtyard sale area was little larger than the room they had left, slightly bigger than a large monastery cloister and bearing a curious resemblance to one. A colonnade stretched around the edges, beneath which sat the richer buyers on cushions of silk and colourful rugs, their attendants and guards keeping the riffraff at bay while they sipped cool drinks and ate sweetmeats. The less wealthy – farmers, merchants, craftsmen and the like – crowded in the sunny square, keeping to the edges near the colonnade.

Skiouros' practiced eye picked out the two pedestrian exits other than the door through which they had entered. Each was guarded by two men in white with swords and turbans. Those doors would likely be locked until the sale was over. They would certainly be tough to leave through in a hurry, guarded as they were.

A large heavy wooden gate stood on one side, unguarded but barred and locked in more than one place – probably an access point for animals and carts. A dextrous man could probably easily get up to the top of the surrounding colonnade, and from there onto the building's roof, but it was such an obvious route that Skiouros was certain beyond doubt that it would be protected somehow.

A large wooden podium stood in the centre, steps leading up to it. More than a dozen guards stood around it, keeping the crowd at bay and prepared to deal out damage to any commodity that decided it might try to flee. Another dozen or so guards stood around the sale table, where the deals were finalised and the coins changed hands. Skiouros noted with unpleasant interest the brazier and the branding irons that stood close to the table, attended by a leering guard.

As they were led towards the block, Skiouros' eyes roved around the crowd. The exits were difficult, to say the least, so perhaps there was hope among the audience? The people watched with interest – some with hunger or desperation. Etci Hassan stood near one of the doors, beneath the colonnade, two of his crewmen with him, present to watch their profits increase and see their transaction complete.

In a small knot, half a dozen other slaves selected for the afternoon auction ahead of them were already being checked over prior to their sale and a careful listen suggested that more were being prepared back in the room inside. The four prisoners were roughly shoved over to join their naked slave counterparts, where an Arab doctor started to look in their eyes and ears, a guard gesturing for them to open their mouths so that the doctor could look inside. Muscles were tested, limbs moved around. Skiouros closed his eyes momentarily as the doctor grasped one of his wrists and yanked his arm this way and that, horribly aware of the small pouch of black powder that nestled in his armpit. An image of the branding brazier passed across his vision and he smiled for a moment.

As soon as the doctor had finished and given the guards a nod of approval, the four captives watched intently as the first of the naked slaves was pushed at the stairs and made to walk up onto the block. A man in a rich, fine, embroidered gown stepped out from the sale table and climbed onto the podium next to the slave, a small black stick in his hand. Taking a deep breath, the auction master began to speak to the crowd, his Arabic fluid and musical with the pitch and tone of a born salesman, rattling out all the information the crowd could wish for in an almost theatrical manner, his stick pointing at various facets of the goods to illustrate his words. The crowd listened quietly, the richer buyers in their shaded positions nodding their interest and understanding, some already counting through their coin purses with their assistants.

Finally reaching the end of his river of words, the auctioneer took a deep breath and snapped out a short phrase which clearly opened the sale.

One of the richer men beneath the colonnade shouted something and received a reply from the auctioneer. Two of the less wealthy, yet reasonably dressed patrons – merchants perhaps – near the front began to shout, attempting to outdo one another, the auctioneer pointing back and forth between them. The rich man called out another number and one of the merchants gave in, falling silent. The other continued on for a moment, but another offer from the rich man clearly outweighed his purse and he finally fell silent.

All through this exchange, which lasted less than a minute, the slave had stood silent and unmoving, like a side of salted meat hanging in a shop. Skiouros felt at once sorry for the poor creature, his lips mouthing a plea to the Lord to look after the man, and angry that the slave did nothing, simply standing and accepting his fate meekly.

But then, had Orsini not chosen to rant at him, that poor figure who even now was being pulled down the stairs towards the branding irons could easily have been Skiouros.

There was barely even a whimper as the slave had a mark sizzled into his flesh, the smell of roasting pork adding to the whiff of sweat, spice and dust that formed the bulk of the atmosphere.

The procedure was repeated for the next prisoner and then the next, these 'cattle' presumably lower grade, since only the lesser bidders put in offers, the rich visitors remaining silent. Skiouros could see nothing different from the first lot, so it must have been something in the auctioneer's words that prompted the change.

The fourth slave was apparently more special, prompting something of a bidding war between two of the wealthy, cushioned buyers, and he had the effrontery to smile in satisfaction as he was brought down from the podium. He was a handsome, clean-shaven young man with a lithe physique and Skiouros noted the lascivious look on the buyer's face as his factor moved to the sale table, leaving him in no doubt as to what the destiny of this young man was.

Again, the last two slaves were led up one at a time and raised a reasonable sum from the mid-range buyers, leaving only the four of them waiting, the next bunch still being prepared inside. Skiouros took a deep breath.

'Now's the time for us *all* to pray,' he hissed.

The others nodded, their eyes darting around the courtyard.

'You be show together.'

Skiouros blinked in surprise as the auctioneer addressed the four of them in stilted Italian.

'Sorry?'

'Four. Show together. Sell not together.'

Skiouros frowned in response.

'Show together!' snapped the man again, irritably, gesturing to the podium with his stick.

'Come on,' Parmenio said, taking a breath and stepping forward. The others fell in behind him as he approached the steps and they clambered one at a time up to the podium, carefully, aware that with their arms shackled behind them, a misplaced foot could lead to a very painful fall. As the four men stepped out onto the flat surface, the dry timbers creaking beneath their feet, a murmur of interest passed through the crowd.

The auctioneer started a rolling announcement in his sing-song cadence, using his stick to gesture to one or the other of them here and there, pointing to their heads, their shoulders and chests, their feet and so on – and, fairly disturbingly, at Skiouros' crotch more than once. Though he could understand none of it, the gist of what the man was saying was clear. The four men were being presented together as a great find, which might then increase their individual value.

A number of the wealthier buyers looked shrewdly at one another, gauging their opposition and preparing for the coming sale. As the man's speech finished and the four were gestured towards the steps once again, a voice from the depth of the crowd shouted something and everything went ominously silent.

The auctioneer turned to the collection of buyers, seeking out the source of the voice. Skiouros caught a glimpse of the salesman's expression as he turned, and he frowned. The man had been almost struck dumb with astonishment, but behind the surprise and interest there, Skiouros had recognised overtones of overwhelming greed.

Whoever it was had made an offer impressive enough that it had halted the proceedings. Seeking confirmation, Skiouros turned and scanned the colonnade. The looks on the faces of the rich bidders clearly backed up that theory: astonishment, tinged with disappointment. One or two of them were struggling with the decision as to whether to make a counter-offer, but the fact than no one spoke suggested the sum offered had been an undreamed-of figure.

Skiouros felt a rush of excitement. Whatever was happening, it had to be better than a slow, calm sale to some fat nobleman for his personal use and abuse.

The other three were now facing the same way.

'What's happened?' Parmenio asked, voicing the question that was also clearly hovering on the lips of the others.

'Someone's made an offer – onc that can't be refused, too, by the sound of it.'

'For who?'

'I guess for all of us, since they didn't wait for the individual sales to begin.'

Skiouros' eyes rose to meet those of Etci Hassan, standing in the shade by the door. The captain's cold basilisk stare was only slightly tinted with avarice and satisfaction, though the surprise and pleasure was more evident on the faces of his two sailors, who were sure of a small cut of all profits.

'It's unbelievable. Which fat bumhole was it?' Nicolo asked, scanning the faces in the shade.

'Not one of them. Someone from the main crowd.'

Skiouros' eyes roved around until he spotted the figure now pushing his way forward, holding a sack of money, a few gleaming gold coins displayed in his other palm – enough to buy him attention and preferential treatment even over the rich men under the colonnade.

'Him... look,' the Greek said, pointing, and as he looked back along his finger, he realised that he recognised the man with the pouch and the coins. Wearing a very utilitarian smock of a local cut and a small turban, he easily blended in with the local crowd – he looked as good as native after all. But even without his earlier liturgical vestments and the three-bar cross, Skiouros recognised the priest that had called after them near the city gate and almost facilitated their escape. His hair was bound up in the turban, but the white beard was very evident, and he made a very passable Muslim. But how could he possibly have so much money?

The guards were now hurrying them from the podium and towards the sale table. The local 'priest' was converging on the same spot, along with the auctioneer, the heavy bag of coins hanging from his hand and attracting hungry looks from the buyers around him.

The auctioneer gave a few quick orders and the next set of slaves was brought out of the cage-room door to the courtyard, freshly washed with a thrown bucket of water and miserable as hell. Most of the crowd, disappointed at having no chance to bid for these interesting specimens, turned their attention to the fresh meat. As soon as the four reached the sale area, the auctioneer lost interest and returned to his task on the podium. Now, two clerks took over the sale at the table, surrounded by Hafsid guards to be sure of their safety. The priest approached the clerks at the table, hefting his bag and displaying the coins.

The clerk asked something and gestured to the brazier. The priest shook his head and Skiouros noted with relief the disappointment on the face of the guard with the branding irons as he placed them back in the sizzling coals.

The priest rattled something off in Arabic to the clerks and gestured to the three figures who came to his side. They were dressed as locals, with curved knives at their waists, but Skiouros was fairly sure they had been the faces he had seen alongside the priest a couple of hours ago, struggling along a crowded street.

In response to whatever he was saying, one of the guards unfastened the shackles on Cesare, who stretched his arms as much as he was capable after the heavy beating he had taken an hour earlier, rubbing his wrists. Another reached for Skiouros.

'Christ is risen,' the priest said in conversational Greek to Skiouros.

'Indeed, he *is* risen,' Skiouros replied, the rote reply inflected with real feeling. Had his prayers done this?

'We will have to move fast,' the man replied as the clerk examined the sample gold coins the priest handed him.

'Why?' Skiouros hissed, almost disbelieving. 'How did you manage to get so much money?'

The priest placed the sack on the table and rolled his shoulders.

'I didn't.'

Skiouros stared at the priest, his eyes widening. The old man smiled. 'Run!' he snapped.

Before Skiouros realised what was going on, the old priest and his three companions were pushing aside the buyers around them, making a space through the crowd.

Skiouros stared at them as the clerks and guards frowned in confusion. The men at the table grasped the coin bag and tipped it up, releasing a torrent of shale and flat pebbles that slewed out onto the surface. The guards were equally slow on the uptake and by the time the first of them shouted in alarm, Orsini had grabbed Nicolo and Parmenio and almost thrown them after the priest into the crowd, their arms still painfully jammed up and fastened behind their backs. Skiouros felt his shackles fall away, unlocked just in time, as he leapt out from behind the table. His hands went into his vestment sleeves and pulled down with a jerking motion.

He was already in the crowd, barrelling after the priest and his companions as well as the other three captives, when the two bags of black powder ignited among the coals of the branding brazier. The Hafsid guard who had been reaching for his sword and shouting a warning looked down to see what had been thrown by the escaped priest and his eyes widened for a fraction of a second before his face disappeared in an explosion that shredded his entire body, almost obliterating his head. The sale table was blasted twenty paces across the courtyard, the guards and clerks around it killed or badly wounded not

125

only by the explosion of the powder, but also by the flying orange-hot coals and the shards of sizzling metal which were all that was left of the brazier. Men staggered around screaming, clutching faces from which slivers of black iron jutted, the blood spraying from some, cauterised by the searing explosion on others.

Skiouros felt the blast as an almost unbearable heat on his back as he caught up with the others. Ahead other apparently friendly spectators had managed to fling open the wide cart-gate. The nearest guards were having trouble fighting their way through the crowd.

It was unbelievable. Skiouros had tried again and again to find a way out of their predicament. He had fought and struggled, planned and schemed and all to no avail, but the Lord had apparently provided.

He felt an almost overwhelming sense of relief as he passed through the gate and out into an alley, wide enough for a cart but little more. There were few locals about and they were content to watch with interest rather than embroil themselves in the action.

'This way,' shouted the priest, haring off up the alley at a turn of speed that belied his age and physique. The three who had accompanied him to the table ran alongside while behind Skiouros four more left the slave market, slamming shut the large gate and rolling a heavy barrel in front of it before running after them.

'Shit!' bellowed Parmenio from the front, drawing Skiouros' attention ahead once more.

Etci Hassan and his pair of Turks had stepped out of the door they had been close to and ahead of the fleeing slaves, weapons at the ready. Skiouros felt a moment of panic. Hassan was a fine swordsman, as he'd displayed while executing one of his own men, and the pair of sailors with him were likely to be the best he had. On the other hand, Skiouros was unarmed, Orsini the same but also badly beaten, the other two still manacled, and the rest apparently Christian townsfolk with small knives at most.

A straight fight would be fatal for many people, and it was unlikely any of the Turks would be among them.

As he ran, Skiouros swooped his arm down and picked up a heavy stone from the floor. He hefted it for only a moment and then flung it at the three men. It was not aimed specifically, but it was not his intention to do specific damage with it. Instead it struck as he had envisaged, causing the men to turn aside, the stone glancing off one of the sailors' hips and spinning him around slightly.

Barely pausing to think, Skiouros reached out and grasped the knife on the hip of the man running beside him, wrenching it from its sheath.

'Take the left,' he bellowed, at no one in particular, but fairly sure that Orsini would try to oblige. Paying no further attention, Skiouros ran at the quickly-recovering Hassan at the centre of the trio, whose blade was coming up to defend himself against this pitiful attack. What could a man with a knife do?

Skiouros had learned the use of the Spanish rapier from the expert Don Diego de Teba, and the standard moves of military sword fighting from Iannis of the Duke of Candia's staff. Both might be of some use against Etci Hassan, had Skiouros a blade and plenty of room. But beyond the lessons of the former guard and the Spanish nobleman he had also had a few useful lessons from Draco, with his broken nose and brown stumps of teeth.

Skiouros hit the ground in a roll, angled past the captain's legs.

In a blur of movement his dagger came down in mid-roll, punching through Hassan's tough leather boots, plunging on through the flesh and the delicate bones of the corsair's foot and then the sole, driving into the ground. Skiouros rolled on, leaving the blade standing proud from the foot.

Hassan let forth a great bellowing cry of rage and pain as Skiouros came out of the roll another four yards behind them. The man with the bruised hip was still recovering himself.

Cesare and two of the Christians had kept the other sailor busy as the rest ran past, but Skiouros could see blood on them and realised that they had paid heavily for their passage.

Skiouros didn't linger to take in the situation but ran on, along with the others, attempting to put as much distance as possible between themselves and the Turks before Hassan managed to remove the blade and unpin his foot.

A dozen heartbeats passed and they rounded a corner into another street, the priest leading them, his companions herding them as fast as they could. Skiouros glanced back for only a moment as they turned the corner to see the three Turks struggling exactly where they'd left them. Skiouros wished for a moment that he'd had the time and leisure to do away with Hassan and it came as a sudden surprise to him to discover that the Turk who until now had simply been 'the enemy' had suddenly taken on as much a dark hatred in his heart as had the conspirators who had led to Lykaion's death. He would happily drop a heavy marble column capital on the head of *this* Turk too, now.

It was only as he turned back to run on that he felt his leg almost give way and looked down.

His vestments were glistening black and wet below a ragged hole that had been rent somewhere around his middle. He stared in shock as the pain in his waist blossomed, alongside the realisation that Hassan had been every bit as fast as he and had managed a counter-blow as he had rolled past, striking home with a far better accuracy than Skiouros' delaying blow.

How bad was it? A torso wound was never good, Lykaion had once said.

Skiouros felt the desperate grip of hands grabbing him as his world slid into blackness.

Chapter Eleven - Of the butcher's rage

Mehmi lurked outside the gilt door of the audience chamber. His squat, brutal frame had never looked more out of place than here in this vestibule of gold, blue and white, with its banners bearing the sword of Islam, the blue lion of the Hafsid dynasty, the three crescents on blue of Emir Zakariya the Second, the white-on-red crescent of the Tunisian Emirate and countless other decorative designs of peacock feathers and gilded fretwork. The diminutive, slope-shouldered pirate with his curled beard, Ottoman turban, salt-stained rough sailor's trousers and jacket and heavy boots shuffled uncomfortably from foot to foot.

Not only was he extremely unhappy at simply being in the court of the Hafsid Emir, who had every right and every reason to execute them on the spot for making landfall in his demesne, but two other things were preying on his mind almost as much as their potential predicament:

First was the fact that they would already have to sail as fast as the *Yarim Ay* could manage – a killing pace for the galley slaves – in order to reach their rendezvous with the great commander Kemal Reis in the straits, and the delay caused by the side trip to the market in Tunis had stretched their schedule to snapping point, but now to further delay over such a lost cause as the four slaves was making him twitchy. The whole of Hassan's crew were loyal to the death to their captain, of course, but they also all knew that he rode a fine line of unpopularity in the fleet and that he could still theoretically be removed from command and sent home in disgrace by Kemal. Angering the fleet commander through further delay was ridiculous.

But the thing that was *really* making him twitch was the priest. Mehmi's mother – may the blessed nineteen keepers of the fires of the abyss spend the rest of eternity torching the flesh from the old hag's bones – had always impressed on her malformed child, in between beatings, that the Christian priests were not men of God. They were sorcerers and witches and purveyors of infidel, heretic, evil spells. Mehmi had never paid too much attention to the idea, despite his loathing of all Christians, but the journey from Greece had brought all those painful lessons flooding back.

Priests *were* magicians of the blackest kind, abhorred by the prophet – may Allah protect and keep him. God had turned his back on these wicked black-robed creatures in a way he had not for the other peoples of the Book. Hassan himself had cut the throat of the Zakynthian priest on his altar, watching the red stain blossom on the ivory-coloured altar cloth. But it had been Mehmi who had nailed the man's wrists and ankles to the crossed benches while the sailors had systematically peeled away his flesh, leaving a twisted pink parody of the great Christian symbol.

Mehmi had thought at the time that this dishonouring of the prophet and Masih Isa – whom the Christians called Jesus – could only bring them trouble, but Hassan had been adamant in his thirst for their blood.

And then they had compounded their sins and crimes by bringing the priest's corpse *on board* the kadirga! Madness.

It had come as no surprise to Mehmi when Kepci the carpenter had suddenly collapsed the next morning, fountaining blood from his open mouth, gore flooding down his front – Kepci had been one of the men who had flayed the priest. A corpse brought inside meant three deaths, though, and after Kepci had been unceremoniously cast into the sea – Hassan was resolute that the death was an illness rather than a curse and he would not have the body kept among the living even for the appropriate rites a good Muslim deserved – Mehmi had spent the next two days checking his skin, his spit and his breathing each time he stood still, panicked that his part in the priest's death would make him one of the three.

It had come as an immense relief when over the following days Halil and Nebi had vomited their innards onto the deck, marking them as dead men and announcing the end of the curse.

But not the end of the troubles.

Yes, they had brought a dead priest on board, but beyond that they had angered God and the Prophet by their disrespect and in return he had sent them the Greek priest and his companions. Mehmi had pleaded with the captain not to kill them – and he had agreed – but where Mehmi had advocated they be dropped on the coast of Sicilia unharmed and free where they could end the curse, Hassan had instead seen them as an extra profit for the voyage and planned this diversion to Tunis.

Hassan Reis did not know that Christian priests were also witches – he had not the benefit of Mehmi's upbringing. But the priest had almost led them into chaos and a riot in Tunis when yet another of his accursed brotherhood had appeared from a side street and somehow his witchery had freed him and his companion from their chains. And then when the slaves were about to be sold and finally out of Mehmi's hair – so to speak – the priest had produced an explosion from nowhere and managed to escape, wounding the captain in the process.

As soon as the messenger had returned to the ship telling Mehmi that they would remain in port for a day, and that the second in command was to join his captain in the city, Mehmi's heart had sunk, for he knew that the priest and his cursed magick had struck again. As Mehmi had attended upon the captain, Hassan had been tending to his wounded foot with the aid of a local doctor – a Jewish one, no less; a son of fallen Granada, possibly rescued and transported to Africa in their very own ship these past two years.

The captain was renowned for his temper – cold and calculated as it was – and Mehmi had seen the man in moods that would make djinn and demons shrink away, but he had never seen Etci Hassan Reis as angry as he had been while his foot was being bound. Mehmi would swear he had seen the first real colour ever in the captain's eyes as flames like the very core of Jahannam – the place the Christians simplified as Hell – burned in his eyes.

The captain had told Mehmi that as soon as he felt comfortable walking, they would be enlisting the aid of the Emir. Mehmi had almost fainted at the proposal, but the captain seemed unafraid of the ruler of Tunis – a man who was their enemy almost as much as the Mamluks and the Christians.

The guards who had accompanied them had been told to wait outside the palace gate, while Hassan alone would be granted an audience if it pleased the Emir to do so. Mehmi had felt panic grip him once more.

'What shall *I* do, master?' he had asked, hoping the captain would send him back to the ship where he felt relatively safe. Instead, Hassan

Reis had given him very specific instructions, and Mehmi had left, with only one man accompanying him, and extremely unhappy, to carry out those instructions.

The task had taken him almost three quarters of an hour and he had returned to the palace to find with surprise that the captain was still in the Emir's chamber in deep consultation. He had half expected to return to find Hassan's head on a spear point over the gate, and when instead he had been invited into the vestibule to wait for his captain, he had felt fresh chills, but tinged with wonder and pride. Only the great Etci Hassan Reis could charm – or more likely frighten – an Emir into peaceful negotiation.

Ten minutes he had stood here now, waiting for his captain or for the Emir's guards with their beheading sword. When the door opened with a click, Mehmi almost urinated a little, but relief flooded through him at the sight of Etci Hassan, striding with purpose – and only a slight wincing limp – out into the corridor.

'Come, Mehmi.'

'Master,' he replied quietly as he fell in at Hassan's heel, trying to get a glimpse through the doorway, but failing as it swung closed with another gentle click.

'Have you completed your task, Mehmi?'

'Yes, my captain. But, Lord…'

Hassan stopped dead, rocking slightly as he finished on his bound foot, and turned his head to regard the squat sailor.

'What?'

'With the deepest respect, Lord, we need to sail west at the first tide. The commander is waiting for us and…'

'I have been insulted, tricked and cheated, Mehmi.'

'Yes, Lord, but the money we have…'

'Is as nothing weighed against our reputation and my personal honour. The Shaytan-born whore-fodder fake priest and his three djinn companions will die for what they have done. I would sooner throw the most holy imam from the highest minaret than let that dog live free after what he has done.'

'But Lord, we have enough treasure to…'

'Money is now immaterial, Mehmi. I have promised a chest of Zakynthian silver and gold to the Emir. In return he will seal the city gates against all unauthorised traffic. The cursed djinn' – a pause to spit on the tiled floor – 'will not leave this city alive.'

'The Emir's guards will help?'

'No. They will seal the city, but nothing more, though I offered further coin for further assistance. Now come. Show me the result of your task.'

Mehmi fell in behind once more as his captain strode on. He wanted to beg Hassan to leave the matter and sail on. He wanted to tell him that the witch-priest had already cost them too much and to pursue him further was to cost them all the more, probably their lives, even. Perhaps their souls. He wanted nothing more than to get back aboard the *Yarim Ay* and sail for their rendezvous. He would even be glad to see the arrogant Kemal Reis and his pet captain, Salih. Anything other than pursuing this accursed slave.

But Hassan's mind was not for turning, and Mehmi could go no further – he knew how far he would be allowed to push before snapping the Butcher's fragile patience and he himself becoming the target of the captain's rage.

All the way back through the palace, under the baleful eye of the Hafsid guards, he tried to think of an argument that would work, but failed and finally, as they stepped out into the dazzling, searing Tunisian sunshine, Mehmi knew that as long as those four men were trapped in the city, the captain would not leave.

'Where do we go?' Hassan said, quietly and with purpose, as his half-dozen sailors re-joined them and fell in behind, their hands on their weapons and eyes suspiciously dancing around the faces of the locals as they passed.

'There is a khave house a few streets away, where the man said he would meet us. He told me you were to come alone, barring me as a guide.'

Hassan's expression did not change, nor did his pace falter, as he snapped, 'I will not be dictated to by an Arab criminal. Come – show me this khave house.'

Mehmi, his short legs scurrying to keep the pace, led his captain around a few corners, where the locals backed away into shady doorways or alleys, keeping out of reach of this Turk and his men. Finally, a minute or two later, they came to a heavy, low white building with a single doorway covered with a colourful rug, and two arched windows that gazed out of the wall like dark, unseeing eyes.

'Here?'

'Yes, Lord.'

Without preamble, Hassan strode through the door, pushing the rug aside with a negligent hand and pausing to allow his pale, strange eyes to adjust to the darkness within.

Mehmi followed in, nervously aware of the guards entering behind him.

The building consisted only of one low room, with small circular tables and heavy leather cushions for seating, a timber bench in the corner serving as a counter, while a raddled old woman in black sat at a stone block with a shallow depression, grinding coffee with a single-mindedness of purpose. The level to which she was intent on her work might, however, have had something to do with the khave house's occupants, which seemed also to be forcing the owner to take an obsessive interest in the cleanliness of his cups.

Mehmi looked around at the leather cushions, of which only three were free, and counted more than twenty men who, he would be willing to bet, had spent the majority of their lives raiding trade caravans and butchering the merchants. In short, they looked a lot like the crew of the *Yarim Ay*, but without the naval uniformity.

'I told your pet toad, no guards.'

Mehmi's jaw muscles twitched as his hand went to the pommel of his knife. Regardless of danger, witches and curses, he was not the sort of man to allow that kind of insult to pass easily. The captain's restraining hand clamped over the top of his own without Hassan's head even turning. Mehmi relaxed into a seething mass, glowering at the motley collection of killers and bandits around them.

'I am a captain of the great Sultan Bayezid's fleet. I go nowhere without my guard, thief. Are you interested in proper negotiation, or would you like to puff and bluster like a Christian for a little longer?'

The room fell into an unnatural silence as hands gripping small cups of strong, gritty khave paused halfway between table and mouth. The man who was addressing Hassan – an older man with white hair and beard and a dirty saffron-coloured turban – stared at the captain in stony silence for half a dozen heartbeats, then finally grinned and leaned back, sipping his khave and then folding his arms behind his head.

The tension dissipated in moments.

'You interest me, Turk. An enemy of my people, and yet you dock here and enter as though you owned the city, seeking an audience with both the Emir and myself. What could *I* possibly do for you that he cannot?'

134

Hassan strode across and dropped into the leather seat, almost completely suppressing his limp by sheer force of will, though Mehmi saw the strain on his face.

'It is a small matter of some property I have misplaced,' the captain said quietly.

The other man gestured to the table, sliding across a small cup of khave. Hassan waved it away.

'You will not accept my hospitality? Perhaps you think I mean to poison you?'

Hassan's lip curled slightly. 'I would credit you with more sense than that, *Sidi*.' An over-formal honorific for such a man, in Mehmi's opinion, no matter how much power he wielded.

'Very well. Your property... four Christians, yes? Escaped from the Suq-al-Birka this afternoon?'

'You are well informed. I should have guessed as much. Yes. They are somewhere in the city and the Emir has closed the gates to most traffic. I want them – or at least their heads – by the setting of the sun tomorrow. Can you do such a thing?'

The old man laughed.

'Of course, my friend Turk. I could have them for you before sun-up tomorrow if they are, as you say, trapped within the city. But such a thing I do not do from the goodness of my heart, or because I am a good man. I have many mouths to feed.'

Hassan waved aside the comment as meaningless.

'I offer you more silver and gold than you would take in a year of picking off trade caravans. A chest full of Christian treasure. For one day's work.'

'You have my attention.'

'I must be away from Tunis as soon as possible – I can delay only a day or two – but it would vex me to leave without seeing these men dead. I would prefer to take their heads with me. If you deliver them to my ship in the port of Carthage, I will give you treasures that would pay to feed all your mouths until the day the Prophet – peace and blessings be upon him – walks once more. Have we a deal or must I find another?'

The old man smiled. 'You will find no other such man, and unless you know Tunis, you will never locate your property in such a short space of hours. You have a deal, Turk. Know, though, that if we deliver them and you renege on your part, you and your crew will leave Tunis bobbing on the surface of the sea, your limbs separated from your trunks.'

Hassan simply nodded, ignoring the open threat.

'The treasure is there. Can you deliver?'

'Most likely,' the old man said. 'There are but half a dozen places such men could hide in this city. We will root them out in a matter of hours. The only difficulty will come if they have had help from certain quarters. If they were quick and lucky, it is possible that they have already passed beyond the walls before our precious fat Emir sealed the gates, and are even now free men out in the countryside. If this is the case, I cannot deliver them to you so easily.'

Mehmi felt his captain tense at the thought that his slaves might even now be fleeing across the African landscape.

'If they have been so fortunate, we will come to a further arrangement, though I look forward to seeing you – with a bag of heads – in the morning. Thank you for your time, Sidi Najid.'

With a simple nod of the head, Hassan rose once more, turning and making for the door, his limp once again only in slight evidence, though Mehmi could see the slit in the boot leather that had been hastily patched and the slight discolouration of the blood that had stained it.

As soon as they were outside the khave house, in the bright street once more, Mehmi cleared his throat.

'Can we trust them, Lord?'

'As long as there is money in it, they will do as they promised, Mehmi. My only fear is that he is right and they have already slipped from the city. They had to have had aid from those disruptors at the market, and such men may have ways and means.'

Mehmi felt a weight lift from him at the thought that the priest and his friends might be gone forever. 'And if they are away, lord? We put them from our minds and return to the fleet?'

Hassan paused and peered down at his diminutive second.

'We must indeed return to the fleet, my friend, but I will pay every ducat and lira in that hold for their heads. They will have to run to the end of the world to escape, for Sidi Najid and his cutthroats will pursue them forever if I pay them enough.'

Mehmi nodded, uncertain as to how he felt about that. In a way, he hoped the slaves had escaped the city, for they would then be the problem of Sidi Najid, the master of Tunis' worst criminals, but he would still rather they remained unmolested altogether. Nothing good would come from continuing to pursue the priest-witch.

Even Etci Hassan Reis was no match for dark magick.

136

Chapter Twelve - Of peril and rescue

S kiouros awoke in a panic from a well of blissful blackness. The light was not brilliant bright, coming apparently from two or three small flames, but was certainly enough to shock after the stygian darkness formed by his eyelids. With an instinctive reaction he sat bolt upright and memory flooded through him, surfing on the wave of pain that accompanied the movement...

Ah yes.

Recollection of a wound in his side returned as he slumped back down, whimpering and gritting his teeth.

'For the love of God lie still, young man,' a voice snapped in Italian.

Skiouros opened his screwed-up eyes once more and took in his surroundings through a constant needling of pain in his side. The room was small and cave-like – even sepulchral with its lack of windows. The only holes in the walls were a dark doorway revealing a set of rough steps leading upwards, and a small aperture containing small vessels of liquid. The presence of a high altar with a plain wooden cross hanging above and a wide, low font that was clearly older than anything else in the room confirmed the space's consecration as a church.

Skiouros tried to voice his surprise, but found that the pain had quite stolen his breath.

The man standing nearby was very familiar. His hair and beard were matted with blood, and his plain white linen robe was soaked crimson and dark and glistening, but he was without doubt the priest who had set all of this in motion. The pair appeared to be alone.

'Where am I?'

The priest smiled and held out his hands in a gesture that encompassed the low room with its half-barrel-shaped ceiling apparently moulded of concrete.

'This, my young friend, is the grand unified church of Tunis. Welcome to the very heart of our faith.'

'Church? Tunis?'

The man produced a bowl of water from somewhere below and began to wash the worst gore from his hands. The water was already deep red. Skiouros strained his eyes and noticed the slick of dark red on the floor and the number of discarded cloths all stained crimson.

'Am I...?'

'You are almost certainly a very lucky young man. Though most all of the credit must go to the will of the Almighty and, of course, a small amount to my own considerable skill as a chirurgeon.'

'I'm very confused. What...?'

'We brought you here a few hours ago. You took a very bad wound in the side facing your pirate friends, and I have been forced to resurrect – apologies for the terminology, Lord – skills that had long since rusted. It seems I have good recall, fortunately. The sword blow went rather deep and severed a few of the smaller blood tubes but miraculously slid between your gut and your kidney and seems to have missed everything vital. I have dealt with the internal bleeding as best I can and stitched your side – though it is distinctly possible you have just torn some of those stitches.'

'So... so I'll live?' Skiouros asked weakly.

'Barring infection, pestilence, starvation, Turks and accidents – and the wrath of the Lord for your wickedness – you should make a full recovery.'

'Wickedness?'

'The impersonation of a priest? I will not delve too deeply into your motives, but know that I disapprove of such an act on an almost monumental scale. Had I known that you were naught but a fake priest I might not have been tempted to risk my diminished flock in aiding you. Clearly God has some purpose for all of this, and so here you are, bleeding onto my table in my church, bringing with you the deepest of dangers.'

Skiouros shook his head blearily.

'I am weak. Can I stand?'

'All things are possible in this world.' Despite his harsh words and disapproving look, the priest held out a hand to help Skiouros. The young Greek very slowly and carefully, and with a great deal of hissing and grunting, swung himself sideways and dropped to the floor. He almost fell – would have done had the priest not held him upright. Tentatively, he took a step. It was excruciatingly painful, but possible. He felt relief wash across him. The strength would return.

'How does there come to be a church here?' he asked quietly. 'A priest of the faith here, and one who speaks Italian and Arabic? And your cross is a plain Romish one, while you greeted me in Greek?'

The priest shrugged and let go of Skiouros, leaning the young man's hands on the table for support instead as he removed his white linen smock to display his ordinary clothes beneath, also stained with blood. 'There has always been a church here. In the old days there were many of them, but time tears the faithful from this Muslim world and sends them across the water seeking the safety of Catholic lands and the shelter of the Pope. When I first came to these shores I attended service in the last overground church in the Emir's domain, and there were still half a hundred of us in Tunis and Carthage and the surrounding lands. Now there are nine and we are all old. Soon the light of the true faith in this land will be extinguished forever.'

He sighed as he dried his hands on a rare clean cloth. 'Even if there is some great crusade to take this once-sacred land back into the faith, it will be too late for us. My flock are a motley collection of survivors, both Orthodox and Catholic – they speak mainly Arabic, with a smattering of Latin. Truth be told, we should be two churches but, with a combined flock of nine, who has the inclination to uphold the age-old divisions between our churches? Even I, who am shepherd of the flock, do not deign to hold my services in Greek.'

'But it is nothing short of miraculous, then, that we found you,' Skiouros breathed, trying to straighten.

'I think if you dredge your memory, young man, you will discover that it was *I* who found *you*. It so happens that my congregation and I were on our way here when we came across you in the street.'

'You will have incurred the wrath of the Arabs,' the Greek sighed as he took a tentative step once again, wincing.

'I doubt that. The great Emir has more to occupy his mind than such a little hiccup. He will not worry too deeply that a corsair's slaves escaped and that a Turk is somewhat out of pocket. There is an age-old understanding with the Christian community here. He is tolerant of us and we cause him no grief – he knows that our days are numbered and that the church here fades. To allow us to fade away peacefully fulfils an ancient vow of the Hafsid Emirs of Tunis and grants him an aura of mercy and respectability that few of his contemporaries can claim.'

Divested of the worst blood-soaked garments, the priest stepped forward and grasped Skiouros by the wrist as he staggered.

'Your strength will return. It is mostly the loss of so much blood that makes you weak rather than the wound itself.'

Skiouros nodded and noted for the first time the paleness of his skin. He shuddered in the slight chill harboured by the underground temple. He had the strangest feeling that he had escaped death by only a hair's breadth, and even that only because God had willed it so. 'God has some purpose for all of this,' the priest had said, echoing speculations he himself had made in the days aboard the pirate kadirga when he could so easily have died a dozen times over.

'What of the others?' he asked quietly.

'They are in the room above. The church remains below ground, where the less tolerant of the locals cannot daub their slogans upon its walls, and the room above serves as our meeting house and a place we can sit and drink wine or khave in peace.'

'Can I manage the stairs?'

The priest furrowed his brow. 'I somehow feel that little can stand in your way when you set your mind to a task, young man.'

'Will you help me?'

The priest nodded and held out his hand, aiding his young patient to cross the room to the stairs.

'You make a good medic for a priest?' Skiouros enquired hesitantly.

'And you make a good priest for a killer.'

'Sorry?'

'The number of sword cuts in your shirt, breeches and boots. Strangely, though, with no matching marks on your flesh as far as I can see. You are clearly a lucky man or impervious to blades.'

'Sword practice,' Skiouros explained, noting with interest that the priest had even sewn the fresh rent in his shirt along with the wound itself.

'I said I wished to know nothing of your past, and I hold to it. God brought me to you and I am not a man to flout the will of God, but I have no wish to deepen my knowledge of your strange world. I would as soon have you gone from under my roof.'

Reaching the stairs, Skiouros began to climb very slowly and painfully, the priest gripping him carefully and gently and yet with a vice-like grip that would prevent him from falling should his legs give way. Skiouros still had a hundred questions, but not only was he sure that the priest was unlikely to answer them; the sheer effort of the climb stifled him, requiring every ounce of breath he could muster.

It seemed an hour, though it could only have been little more than a minute or two, before he stepped out onto the old, threadbare rugs that covered the floor of the upper room. The building was almost as low as the church-cellar beneath, though with a flat ceiling. A large room was filled with low cushions, a table and three chairs and two old, worn cupboards, with two windows and a closed door giving out onto the street. The windows were covered with white hangings that afforded privacy, but let in plenty of light and swayed in the breeze that kept the worst of the heat from the room. The curtains glowed and from the bronze quality of the light, Skiouros estimated the time as perhaps an hour before sundown.

The opposite side of the room held two more doorways, each covered with a draped rug. Skiouros was relieved to see Parmenio, Nicolo and Cesare all seated in the main room with cups of something, the young Orsini relaxing back into a cushion with a contented – if puffy and discoloured – smile despite the beating that had almost knocked him into the arms of Morpheus for good. Three of the priest's congregation sat with them in silence, the Arabic-Italian language barrier almost uncrossable for the two groups.

'Jesu, look at you,' Parmenio whistled as he caught sight of Skiouros appearing from the stairway. 'You look greyer than a Donatello marble.'

'I have to admit to having felt better,' Skiouros replied with a weak smile.

'Come here and have some wine. Puts red back in your blood.' The captain peered down into his cup. 'And given the pedigree of this local hooch, probably puts hair on your eyeballs too. Tastes like it's already been drunk a couple of times.'

Nicolo nudged him, causing wine to slop from the sides of the older man's cup. 'If you don't like it, pass it to me.'

'I don't dislike it *that* much,' Parmenio said defensively, cradling his cup away from the purser.

'Wine dulls the wits,' Orsini announced quietly without looking around. 'Khave seems to sharpen them. Well met, Master Skiouros.'

As the young Greek staggered across to one of the seats and lowered himself into it, painfully and grunting every inch of the way, Parmenio looked across at the priest.

'Now that you're back, I have to enquire as to what our next move should be? I won't burden you with too many of our troubles, but you know we're escaped slaves and with little or no knowledge of the city. It's more than likely that Turkish bastard is still in the city, especially now that brother death-wish over there has given old grey-eyes a wound to remember us by.'

Skiouros frowned irritably. 'I helped us escape.'

'And you just had to give him a nasty wound in the process, didn't you. I'd have liked to have run the bastard through myself, but barring that I'd have left him well alone. That way he might have cut his losses and left us alone. But you've met Hassan, the Butcher. Can you imagine for one moment old grey-eyes letting us go free now? He'll turn over every rock and kick in every door in Tunis to find you now.'

Skiouros blinked. It hadn't occurred to him, but Parmenio was almost certainly correct. His blow against Hassan had given them the chance to escape but had also sealed their fate as prey to this most vicious of hunters.

Damn!

Behind him, the priest wandered across to a barrel of water and stripped down to his breeches, dropping the bloodied clothes in a pile and scrubbing the stains from his flesh before dipping his head in and rinsing the blood from his beard and hair. After a moment he rose again, water droplets falling to the sparse dry rugs.

'I have already arranged matters, Master Parmenio,' the priest announced. 'Two of my congregation deal in ivory and rare woods that the Amazigh – the Berbers as you call them – bring from beyond the deserts. They are busy unloading their latest cartload along with the desert people who brought it into the city. The cart will then have to return through the walls and back out to the camp of the traders a mile from the city. When it returns, the four of you will be aboard it.'

'You take a serious risk in providing such aid, Father,' Cesare noted quietly.

'The greater risk would be in keeping you here, and as a good man of God I could hardly abandon believers to their fate...' he shot a quick glance at Skiouros 'no matter how underhand and suspicious they may be. You must be gone as soon as possible for all our sakes. Faysal and Shukri will take you to the camp as soon as night falls. I would move you sooner, but there might be questions at the gate. As the sun sets the guards are always tired and less attentive, and the lengthening shadows add a touch of obfuscation to any trickery.'

Orsini nodded his understanding.

'What can we do from there, Father?'

'I have already spoken to the brothers. The Amazigh people have always had a healthy respect for the Church despite their nearly all being Muslim these days – in the years Byzantium ruled here, many of their people were of the Orthodox faith. Faysal and Shukri will negotiate with the traders to transport you away from here.'

'Where can we go?' Skiouros asked quietly. 'This is not a land filled to bursting point with helpful and sympathetic people. We really need to be making for the peninsula of Italia.'

'That,' the priest said quietly, 'would be a very bad idea. If you are being sought by this Turk you would be very unlikely to make it to sea. Plus there are very few Hafsid sailors who would be willing to transport Christians without serious recompense. We can talk the Berber traders into taking you for almost nothing. Unless you have hidden wealth, your seaborne options are all but nil.'

'So where?' Skiouros repeated, aware that they would be unable to afford even a ferry across the bay, let alone to Sicilia or beyond.

'It is a lengthy journey and a tiring one, but the network of desert traders can take you from here, across the old roads of the Romans and the hidden ways of the Amazigh almost to the great western sea. The ports along the coast between here and there will be generally unfriendly to you, but if the traders can keep inland and take you far enough, there are cities on the far coast that belong to the Portuguese. There you may find sympathy and aid.'

Parmenio sat up straight.

'There is nowhere nearer? What about going east?'

'Into Egypt and the Mamluk world? Hardly an option, captain.'

'How far are these Portuguese ports?' Skiouros asked quietly.

'Three hundred leagues if they're a mile,' Parmenio answered in an equally low voice. 'I've sailed it from Sicilia a few times. Takes nearly a fortnight at best, leastwise to Ceuta, which is where I'm assuming you're talking about?'

'Indeed,' the priest said with a smile. 'By desert route and trade road, plan on perhaps a month and a half.'

'A *month and a half*?' demanded Skiouros incredulously.

'It's not a fast business. But it is the most sensible choice; the *only* sensible choice,' the priest added.

'There must be a better way,' Parmenio sighed.

'*Six weeks*?' boggled Nicolo unhappily.

'It is,' Orsini said with a shrug, 'the sensible decision. No one will think of looking for us there and even if they do they will not have the local knowledge these Berber traders do. We will disappear from Tunis without a trace and Hassan will be left nursing his wounded foot and his wounded pride. We cannot hope to acquire transport on a Hafsid vessel, so we must look to our fellow Christians for aid, and the nearest safe port is a month and a half away. I for one would rather move slowly and safely through the desert than face the extremely hazardous ports of the coast here. Besides, I ache as though I have been bear-baiting with my open hands, and I would appreciate the time to recover my strength as, I'm sure, Master Skiouros would too.'

Skiouros nodded slowly. It was a delay but safety was worth the time, and the idea of spending a month or more lying cushioned in a cart appealed, given how much it had hurt simply lowering himself into the seat.

'Agreed,' he said quietly. 'Besides, towards what are we all rushing? Parmenio and Nicolo have lost their ship, Cesare has only troublesome family to return to, and I...' He fell silent as the others looked expectantly to him. 'I have nothing pressing,' he finished feebly.

'God preserves you for something,' the priest said with a strange smile 'and I would not stand in the way of my Lord.'

The whole room fell instantly silent as the door clicked and then swung open. The four Christians' hands went to the hilts of swords that were no longer there, but the local congregation seemed unconcerned as two men scurried inside, shutting the door and babbling away in Arabic, though their expressions warned of trouble.

'What has transpired?' Orsini asked sharply, glancing at the priest before crossing to the window and peering out with his good eye, the other still puffed and rosy from the beating.

'It seems that your Turk is sharper than we expected,' the priest replied, struggling into clean clothes. 'I assumed he would attempt some sort of bribe with the authorities, but he has also enlisted the aid of Sidi Najid, who already has men scouring the city.'

'Sidi Najid?' Skiouros hazarded, noting with alarm how the six locals were scrambling from their seats and retrieving the knives that had sat at their waists when they attended the slave auction.

'A local villain. More powerful in some ways than the Emir himself.' The priest turned and spoke in Arabic to the two men who had just entered.

'They have seen men who are known to work for Sidi Najid in the souk two streets away asking after Christian priests. It will not take them long to learn of this place, and then we are in trouble. We can no longer wait for nightfall – we must go now and trust to God to see you safely out of the city.'

Skiouros shook his head. 'What about you? Will you and your people not be in danger? You could come with us?'

The priest smiled wanly. 'This is not the first time I have had dealings with Sidi Najid. Can you wield a blade?' This last was clearly aimed at the other three as he turned his face from Skiouros while he spoke.

Parmenio and Nicolo both nodded, but Orsini stepped back from the window and turned.

'With some skill, Father.'

'Good. Take this.'

Reaching down behind the water barrel to a small cupboard, the priest hauled something out from behind it. Skiouros' eyes widened as the man retrieved a heavy, well-used sword – old fashioned and utilitarian – and crossed the room, presenting it to Orsini, who took it with a raised eyebrow, turning it over in his hands to admire it.

'A soldier's blade.'

'Upon a time, yes.'

Skiouros peered at the sword as Orsini tested it and both noted at the same time the symbol on the crosspiece: a cross pattée. The symbol of the Order of the Knights of Rhodes, the Knights Hospitaller. The old priest's past became at once clearer and more occluded.

'This is from…'

'Yes. Use it well in God's grace. I am more familiar these days with this.' Reaching down behind the cupboard once more, he drew out a long, curved blade of Arabic manufacture.

'These will be a trifle difficult to conceal,' Orsini noted.

'We will be moving quickly through small alleys to the cart. They can then be secured and hidden. Better to be prepared than not, young man.'

Skiouros stood, slowly and painfully, and one of the locals thrust something at him. Skiouros noted with dismay that it was the battered, dusty and frayed vestments of his monk persona.

'You want me to wear this?'

'Certainly not now – you would be far too conspicuous in the streets for those who are hunting a priest. But you will need them for the journey. The Amazigh will respect you a great deal more in vestments, may God forgive me for perpetuating your deception.'

Having finished dressing, the old priest slung the sword at his waist and, without any Christian accoutrements, bore more resemblance to a Hafsid warrior than a priest.

'Are we ready?'

'As we'll ever be,' Parmenio muttered.

One of the local flock crossed to the front door, flicking the latch and swinging the door slowly inwards. The sudden force of a kick from the far side slammed the heavy wood into the poor man's face, smashing nose and teeth and hurling him back from the doorway to collapse against a table. The room erupted as three men crossed the threshold wielding heavy blades, faces made ugly with expressions of hate and lust.

'Run!' barked the priest as he pushed his way past the others towards the intruders. Two of the locals ran across to join him, drawing their small curved knives.

Orsini hefted the solid knight's sword and stepped next to the priest to help deal with the attack.

Skiouros felt himself panic, aware of the danger, but feeling the need to go to the aid of Orsini and the priest. He took a painful step towards them, picking up a heavy wine jug as a makeshift weapon, but Nicolo and Parmenio grasped him and turned him away. The other two locals had hauled aside one of the rug doors into a back room and while one held the rug aside for them, the other crossed the small chamber and opened a back door that led out into a narrow alley.

Skiouros felt panic at the thought of turning his back on Orsini and the priest, but was being propelled towards their escape route by his friends and harboured too little strength to resist.

Cesare Orsini leapt into the fray with a speed and dexterity that belied the beaten aspect of his body. Only those who knew him well would note the slight stagger as he landed on his right foot, the slightly off-mark thrust, thrown aside by his lack of depth perception, one eye almost swollen shut.

The priest – at the centre – was engaged in a duel to the death with one of the grunting, black-teethed villains, while the intruder at the far side busied himself with dismembering the two flock members who desperately fought him off with their knives, taking horrifying wounds as they did so.

Orsini took half a heartbeat to weigh up the man facing him: a thug of some size, with great ham hands and tree-trunk legs. The sword that would be a weighty thing for most men to swing was nothing to this beast, yet he was far from fast. He favoured his right leg, twisting oddly on the left. It could be an old wound still causing some discomfort, though Cesare was willing to wager that this was the man who had kicked the door inwards and, not expecting there to be a man behind it, he had badly jarred his knee. He could manage one good thrust, but without room to swing or slice downwards in the confined circumstances, his great strength had become more a liability.

Ba-thump. Cesare's heart pounded and he back-footed a single pace to the side – knowing the man's injured leg would prevent him from reacting fast enough – and readied himself a fraction of a moment before the thug's sword thrust through the empty air where he had been. Cesare suffered from the same lack of space as the big man, though for a smaller, lithe man it was no setback. With a deft flick of his hand, he brought the heavy knight's sword around and ran it through the brute's ribs just below the armpit. The sword slid in the full width of the man's huge torso, the point scraping on the inside of the ribs at the far side, scything through vital organs as it passed.

Ba-thump. His heart beat again as he ripped the sword back out, smoothly, just as the big body fell forwards, astonished and already in the throes of death, heart and lungs all pierced in the same strike.

Another glance around to take in the situation: the priest had managed to dispatch his opponent, but had taken a painful shoulder blow from the third assailant, who had already butchered the two men with knives. A shout drew Orsini's attention to movement outside the door, and he realised that there were more thugs coming up the street to back up the three.

'We have to leave,' he shouted at the priest.

'Go. Find the cart.'

Ba-thump. The indecision lasted only that one heartbeat. Cesare Orsini had played chess many times in his life and had won the lion's share of the games. He knew when the game was in danger of being lost, and it aggrieved him deeply to have to sacrifice a knight like this, but he also knew that to stand and argue would lead to his own death and they would have lost *both* knights.

'God be with you,' he yelled to the priest as he turned and hurtled through the room, out of the curtained door, where he paused only long enough to pull a heavy cupboard down with a crash, partially blocking the door, before dashing out into the narrow alley.

There was no sign of life already in this crawl-space perhaps two feet wide and filled with dust, rubble and detritus.

Pausing for another heartbeat, he could just hear a minor commotion in the distance to his right. His teeth gritted in irritation at having to leave the priest to his fate and, clutching his bruised ribs with his free hand, Orsini pelted off along the alley in the direction of the distant commotion, sword held close.

There was no longer any doubt. The desert traders were their best hope at a successful flight.

Chapter Thirteen - Of desert traders

Skiouros burst from the latest in a series of identical alleyways, clutching his erstwhile disguise to his side, Parmenio in front and all but dragging him by the bunched-up shirt, Nicolo pushing him along from behind and the two locals scurrying ahead. The small square into which they emerged was little more than a junction of two streets that widened to create just enough room to swing a cat. A rickety wooden cart stood in the centre, hitched to two sorry-looking, flea-bitten donkeys that twitched and whickered.

Two men who could only be Faysal and Shukri were overseeing the cart's unloading, dressed in the same white, yellow and peach colours as seemed to be the norm among the common folk of Tunis, their heads bare. Around them, half a dozen of the Berber traders lugged stacks of elephant tusks tied with leather straps as well as stacks of rich dark wood and boxes and bags of miscellaneous goods. These men were fitted out for desert travel, with long billowing robes of deep blue, their faces almost entirely concealed behind veils of a similar hue, black turbans wound atop their heads.

Skiouros staggered to a halt as Parmenio and Nicolo finally relented from their propelling of him, and he looked down to note with some concern that his shirt was once more wet with fresh blood where his stitches had come apart from the painful exercise.

He felt like collapsing between the effects of the throbbing pain and the weakness, but knew that such an act was not an option right now. Soon he would be in that wagon and relatively comfortable, though. It was a pleasant thought.

As Parmenio and Nicolo stood with him impatiently, the two locals who had brought them from the church scurried over to their friends, and the four men began to talk animatedly in Arabic. The three former slaves watched for a moment, feeling the desperate pressure to move as fast as possible, but unable to do anything about it.

After a brief discussion, one of the trader brothers called out and the door-curtain to what could only be their warehouse was swept aside.

The woman who issued from the building took away what was left of Skiouros' breath. He noted Nicolo and Parmenio's grips loosen as they too had the bulk of their attention diverted. Wearing a long billowing robe of bright flame-orange and a head covering of saffron yellow, she was tall and elegant, tendrils of her shining black hair peeking out from the confines of her headdress. Her face was blessed with high cheekbones and flawless caramel skin, her dark, almond-shaped eyes glittering with life and intelligence. Tattoos of delicate designs with whorls and lines and branches extended from her lower lip down her chin and neck and along her jawline to the ears, complemented by a small but beautiful design on her brow between her eyes.

The woman turned to the trader brothers and addressed them in a voice like honey flowing slowly over a spoon.

The two men replied, hurriedly but clearly respectfully. Skiouros noted with interest that the language seemed to have changed. He had no grasp of Arabic, but he had heard it enough to know that this tongue was not it; bore no similarities, in fact. These desert folk were like nothing he had encountered before, and he was rapt – particularly with this latest apparition.

The woman was clearly in charge – a fact that surprised him as much as her delicate and stunning appearance. She listened, asked a couple of questions of the brothers and then nodded her agreement. Stepping out towards Skiouros and his friends, she placed her hands together and smiled.

'*Oy ik?*' she asked in her honeyed tones. '*Mani eghiwan?*'

Skiouros coughed uncomfortably, while Parmenio and Nicolo simply gave her nonplussed looks. The woman frowned and then spread her hands. '*As-salam alaykum?*'

The two sailors shared a baffled look, and Skiouros cleared his throat. 'It's an Arabic greeting. They use it sometimes in the Empire. Means something like 'peace be with you'.'

'What's the reply?' Parmenio asked quietly.

'I haven't a clue. I'm a monk, remember, not a dervish!' he replied petulantly.

The three men smiled at the lady and nodded in feeble reply, and she turned to the brothers who owned the local business and rattled something off again in her own language, opening yet another conversation. The men were clearly explaining something – presumably how none of the Christians spoke any useful language and how none of their own could speak the peculiar Christian tongues.

Skiouros almost laughed at the absurdity of the impasse. Here they were trying to arrange to sneak out of a city and travel with these people, and no one spoke Greek, Turkish or Italian. Skiouros remembered that the priest – who would hopefully be here soon to interpret – had mentioned that Latin was held by some of his flock, but Skiouros had not paid a great deal of attention during those Latin lessons and was very much aware of his failings in the dead tongue. He would hardly be able to communicate beyond telling the brothers that *nauta vacca amat* – 'the sailor loves the cow'. Hardly helpful.

The last goods were unloaded and empty cloths and bags and straps were thrown back into the cart.

'How are we going to hide under that?' asked Nicolo.

The four locals held another brief discussion and then two of them touched their foreheads respectfully in the direction of Skiouros and his friends and ran off into the streets. The brothers remained and gestured at their Berber companions.

'Yes?' Skiouros prompted, hoping for more details, perhaps in the form of sign language.

The Berber lady began to rattle off an explanation in her own tongue, which was strange and otherworldly and yet musical and attractive, given her voice. Skiouros realised he was bathing in the words and grinning like an idiot and pulled himself together. Still clutching the priest robes to his bleeding side, he held out his other hand imploringly.

'I am afraid we do not understand.'

The woman repeated her phrase slowly and loudly and Skiouros shook his head at the wonder of the fact that people of any race when confronted with incomprehension simply raised their voices and talked slowly and deliberately.

'We do not speak these languages. Shall we get in the cart?' he asked, gesturing to the vehicle. Parmenio and Nicolo nodded helpfully, Nicolo echoing the gesture.

Again, the Berber lady spoke, gesturing at her companions.

'We... do... not... understand,' repeated Nicolo slowly.

'She is telling you to don their robes!' bellowed Cesare Orsini breathlessly, bursting from the alleyway, bloody sword in hand.

'What?'

'Try to read everything in a conversation, not just the words.'

Indeed, as the friends looked past the woman, they realised that two of the menfolk were holding out their arms, proffering bundles of blue cloth.

Without delay, Cesare ran past his three friends, pausing to bow respectfully at the lady, and then over to one of the blue-clad traders. With a nod of thanks, he jabbed the sword into the gritty earth and grabbed one of the billowing robes, pulling it over his head.

Stung into action, Nicolo and Parmenio rushed over to don the gear themselves, leaving Skiouros tottering and almost falling, weak and unsupported. Grumbling irritably, he righted himself and shuffled over to the proffered robes, still clutching his side as he moved and only dropping the dusty black priest robes to the floor as he reached for the blue garb.

One of the men mimed something to Orsini and then gestured to the sword. Cesare nodded and the Berber tore the blade from the ground and moved over to the cart, tying the tell-tale Christian sword to the underside of the cart's slat bed.

Dressing was hell for Skiouros. Every move seemed to pull at whatever stitches remained in place and it felt as though someone was trying to insert a boiling khave pot into his gut through his side. On the third attempt, with a lot of puffing of breath, he got the robe over his head and let it drop.

'What happened back there?' Parmenio asked the young nobleman as they changed clothes rapidly. Cesare simply shook his head and it took Skiouros but a moment to realise what news Orsini was imparting. Yet another fallen innocent in his quest. A true man of God a thousand times more pious than Skiouros.

More bodies in his wake.

Clenching his jaw, Skiouros settled the robe in place and looked down at the priest's black gear on the ground with distaste. Could he really justify wearing it again? Yes. Of course he could. It was not just a matter of survival, now. Nor was it about his end-goal: the demise of that traitorous cur the usurper Cem Sultan. A new head had risen from the Hydra that plagued Skiouros and his friends: Etci Hassan.

Hassan's anger had destroyed the priest in Tunis, not Skiouros, and he would no longer allow himself to feel such guilt over unsolicited aid, given freely by a good man. But regardless of what the old Romani had said in Crete about selfishness and revenge, Skiouros remembered the old saying 'an eye for an eye and a tooth for a tooth' – a favourite of Father Simonides' back in Hadrianople. The old Tunisian priest-knight, whose name Skiouros had never even known, would rest in the knowledge that somehow, somewhere on his ever-growing quest, Skiouros would drive three feet of steel through the black heart of Hassan the Butcher.

One of the Berbers strode across and collected the priestly garments, cradling them respectfully while wrinkling his nose at their odour, and placed them among the wrappings and bags on the cart, where they blended in and became yet another miscellaneous empty container.

By the time Skiouros had finished struggling into his robe, his friends were busy having turbans bound round their scalps and veils strung across their faces. As the process was repeated for Skiouros the others shuffled around impatiently.

'We need to move now,' Orsini declared as soon as a Berber tucked the loose end of Skiouros' turban away and hooked the veil across. 'They will be searching for us and we're still dangerously close to the church. They could come across us at any time.'

With signs and hand motions, Cesare explained to the Berber lady their need for urgency. She simply smiled and bowed her head.

'This is going to be a long and lonely journey if no one speaks our language,' Nicolo grumbled as he settled in with the other Berbers alongside the cart.

'Remember not to speak until we're fairly certain we're safe,' Skiouros hissed through the indigo veil across his face. He felt stifled from the neck up, with the veil and turban, though the billowing robe was easy enough, and he could imagine that with baggy clothing beneath, it would be the perfect garb for the blistering sun of Africa.

The Berbers made noises and chatted for a moment, and then the donkeys started walking, the cart clunking and bouncing off the uneven street. The traders fell in alongside and the lady strode across and climbed aboard the cart, taking position on the seat up front while her people walked as an escort, the brothers who had purchased her goods walking out ahead, leading the vehicle through the streets.

Skiouros fell in behind Cesare and tried his best to walk normally, despite the pain in his side that had now subsided to a constant heavy throb after his brief rest. Parmenio and Nicolo walked alongside, the captain in front, Berbers before and behind them all. Veiled and with covered heads, as long as they kept their eyes averted or lowered and their paler hands from view, the four friends were indistinguishable from their escort.

Skiouros, aware that on this ever-troublesome journey the unexpected could always be expected to occur, took note of their route as they moved through the edge of Tunis, marking any points of interest that he could later use to find their way should anything go wrong.

After five minutes of travel, the cart emerged, bouncing, out into a major thoroughfare and a quick glance ahead as they turned revealed one of the city gates. In a structure heavy and squat and of glowing gold-brown stone, the pointed arch was dark. The gates were shut! Had the Arabs and the Berbers accounted for this? Perhaps it was normal to close the gates at sunset, and the sun was now sinking behind the hills ahead, leaving only an amber glow tracing the indigo sky with lines. Men in white with shining armour strode across the towers that flanked the gate, while others stood beside the forbidding dark portal.

'Closed!' hissed Skiouros, receiving shushing motions from his friends in reply. Skiouros turned back to the gate, noting just in case the position of the priest's sword where it lay fastened just out of reach beneath the cart.

Skiouros realised he was holding his breath as they closed on the guards and forced himself to breathe as normally and calmly as he could. Parmenio and Nicolo looked equally nervous, their hands twitching and constantly gripping and ungripping, though Orsini strode calmly as though born to the role. The man never ceased to amaze – and slightly irritate – Skiouros.

The cart trundled slowly to a halt and the two Hafsid guards stepped out from their position at the side of the gate. Skiouros could just see another white-clad soldier in the gloom beneath the arch. One of the guards – perhaps an officer? – approached the cart and nodded at the lady, offering some sort of challenge in Arabic to the two local brothers who stood before them.

The one with the neat beard – whom Skiouros had decided could be Faysal, since they couldn't communicate enough to determine which brother was which – spread his hands and bowed his head, answering the question. With a curt nod, the guard looked up at the

Berber lady. His voice took on a strange tone. Skiouros could not quite determine whether it contained respect, fear or disdain, or perhaps a combination of the three.

The Lady answered in her languid, honeyed voice and the guard actually smiled. Skiouros felt something ease within him. How could any ordinary man argue with this goddess?

More conversation. More questions, easily answered, the brothers interjecting as required, and after perhaps two minutes of discussion, the guard officer nodded and, stepping back, bowed.

Skiouros had not seen any coin exchange hands during the conversation, but he did notice the officer's closed fist disappear beneath his cloak, apparently securing some bribe or payment at his waist. With a single command, the man stepped back further, his companion alongside, clearing the road before the cart. The guard beneath the arch moved and there was a series of clunks before the great wooden gate swung ponderously open.

Skiouros felt the hackles rise on the back of his neck in an almost preternatural warning. Risking a casual glance over his shoulder, he confirmed his fears. He thought he'd heard a distant commotion and now he could see, back some way along the wide, straight street, figures moving apace.

The killers had caught up with them.

Skiouros bit into his cheek in tense desperation. He wanted nothing more than to shout a warning to the others, who had not heard and were standing there blissfully unaware, waiting for the cart to begin moving. But there was no way he could speak without drawing deadly attention.

He turned his wide eyes forwards again, where the second leaf of the gate was being slowly swung wide. Simultaneously, the cart began to creak and then trundle forwards, so slowly Skiouros was starting to wonder if they would ever leave the city. Beyond the gatehouse, the open land stretched out towards the irregular humps of the hills that lay to the west of the city. It was a fairly dry and open stretch of land, though there were the tell-tale signs of farming on the more distant slopes, shadowed by the setting sun. It was a wide expanse, framed by low peaks with no great sign of habitation beyond these walls.

But that was only a small part of what that landscape meant to Skiouros and his friends. That wide space with its fertile slopes, scrub grass and intermittent farmland was freedom. Freedom from Etci Hassan and his corsairs. Freedom from this Sidi Najid and his criminals. Freedom from the grip of the Hafsid Emir.

Out there was the only way forward and, while it required a lengthy journey in the company of these strange desert folk, it was safe. It was freedom.

It was also on the other side of this gate and past a cart that was being drawn by two of the slowest donkeys Skiouros had ever encountered. His ears picked out voices back along the street, but he dared not turn his head again, not least because of the childhood fear that seeing the pursuers would bring them somehow closer.

His heart almost skipped a beat as he realised he was moving and passing beneath the shade of the heavy gatehouse's arch. It was progress, but his somewhat acute hearing told him that it was not fast enough. The voices behind were now clear enough to be heard. If he had understood Arabic, he would have been able to hear what they were shouting.

The guards clearly had.

Skiouros glanced in the direction of the sword once more, picturing the way it had been loosely tied and how he could retrieve it. The others had finally realised that something was wrong and their heads turned towards the noise.

The guard holding open the gate through which the donkeys were about to pass faltered, his grip on the wood tightening as he prepared to close it again, trapping them in Tunis. The guard commander turned a look of consternation on the traders and his fierce, uncertain gaze met that of the Berber lady, who raised her eyebrows and turned, spitting imprecations back down the street. She cast a malevolent look at the guard officer, who actually took a couple of paces back in shock, and snapped something out at him in Arabic.

Skiouros and his companions stole the opportunity to share a quick glance of confusion and surprise and then, suddenly, the guard officer and his companion rushed past them, taking up a defensive position behind the cart and its escort, preparing to defend them against this new threat from within the city.

The soldier holding open the gate smacked the donkeys on the rump, stirring them to heightened speed, and the cart bounced and jolted through the gate, the men at the front jogging to keep control of the vehicle, the Berber lady holding tight as she was shaken about. The escort picked up the pace and suddenly Skiouros and his friends were through the gate and out into the open countryside.

Freedom?

The idea that they might have evaded the thugs back in the street did not sit well with him. The criminals would argue their position with the Hafsid guard and it all came down to whether the officer found more value in the opinion of a foreign desert trader or a local thug. Not much of a choice to make, he would guess.

Behind them, the man beneath the arch slammed the gate shut and Skiouros could hear the sounds of bolts and bars being rammed home.

Perhaps they were free after all?

Of course, there was every chance that after a brief explanation, the gate guard would let the thugs out to chase them down. And even if not, Sidi Najid and his men seemed now to know when and where they had left the city. Skiouros was an experienced enough tracker and fugitive – in city streets at least – to realise that they would not be hard to find with that knowledge. The sooner they could put a few leagues between themselves and Tunis, the better.

He shared a look with Parmenio and mouthed something at him. The captain frowned and shook his head – the level of light was too low for him to make out what his friend was saying. Skiouros exaggerated the shapes as he mouthed again 'why do we not speed up?'

Parmenio shook his head. 'We do not want to look like we are running,' he mouthed back slowly. Skiouros nodded to himself. They were playing it above board as proper traders in the hope that the thugs in the city would be recognised as Sidi Najid's men and dismissed as criminals. If the cart suddenly fled, it would lend credence to whatever the thugs were claiming and the various sharp weapons of the men atop the walls and towers would find targets among the Berber traders.

Skiouros instead held his tongue and his breath as they slowly moved out across the open ground, away from the walls of the city. With every step he expected to hear the creak of the gate opening behind them, yet they reached the top of a low rise with no such trouble and as the cart sank behind the hummock, Skiouros allowed himself to breathe easier.

The Berber lady turned with a smile and said something unintelligible to them. Skiouros frowned, but decided that she meant it was now safe to speak.

'That was about as close to capture as I ever want to come again.'

Parmenio sagged with relief. 'Looks like we've seen the last of Tunis. Nice enough place, but I won't be hurrying back if you get my drift.'

'Indeed I do. But you know that's not the end of it, don't you?'

Parmenio nodded. 'Hassan's not going to let this go. Not after you lost your brains for a moment and stuck him in the foot.'

Again, Skiouros bridled. It seemed so damned unfair that Parmenio kept blaming him for the Butcher's wrath, but it was also hard to deny the consequences of that act of desperation. The captain was right, but did he have to keep ramming the point home?

'Of course, Hassan had some appointment to keep with his superior, and he won't leave the coast and his ship in unfriendly waters long enough to chase us,' he said quietly.

'No. But you saw how much silver and gold he had. He can pay Sidi Najid enough to keep those cutthroats on our tail right to the edge of the goddamned world and chasing us until we're too old to run any more,' Parmenio replied. 'I won't even countenance the word 'safe' until I am in a Christian city with a bloody great wall between me and the Muslim world.'

It was sad to have to think like that, and it particularly rankled for Skiouros, who had been raised as a Christian, yes, but within a Muslim culture that had shown itself to be refined, educated and tolerant. Having given almost everything he had to save the life of the Ottoman Sultan, it seemed appalling that he was now driven to seeking the protection of Christian states and turning his back on all things Islam just because of yet another bastard using a position of authority to carry out his own personal jihad.

But the captain was absolutely correct, regardless – as he often was – in that until they reached the Portuguese controlled port of Ceuta they would never be safe.

'We'd best be on our way into the desert as soon as possible. I hope these Berbers plan to leave in the morning.'

'*I* hope one of them speaks Italian,' grumbled Nicolo, kicking an errant stone on the dusty road and watching it skitter among the dry grass alongside.

'I would not hold your breath for such an eventuality,' Cesare smiled. 'But whether we can communicate or not, they appear to be friendly, and for that I am grateful.'

The other three nodded and gave up their own silent thanks to the Lord for this latest miracle.

Perhaps ten minutes they walked, the donkeys matching a standard walking pace, until they crested a low saddle and gazed down into a shallow bowl-shaped depression.

The light now was little more than the glow of the silver moon and a few low streaks of copper that stained the western horizon, but the size of the merchant camp was impressive even at night – perhaps

158

more so at night. A collection of tents and low huts sprawled across the centre of the dip creating a shifting temporary settlement larger than many villages Skiouros had visited in his time.

Fences had been erected at some time creating animal pens that contained horses, camels, cattle, sheep, goats and other miscellaneous livestock. Closer examination revealed that the tents and huts, for all their sprawling appearance, were actually organised into tight groups – families or clans? Perhaps trading parties? Torches and lamps burned throughout the camp, giving it a glittering appearance, like a reflection of the stars above, and large fires blazed in the five or six open social spaces that had been left between the habitations. Music and voices issued forth into the night. After the last week or two, the very idea of a place filled with song, laughter and happiness seemed so alien to the four friends that they had already descended halfway down the slope towards the camp before they began to smile.

'Looks friendly,' Parmenio said with a grin.

'I wonder if they have wine?' Skiouros muttered hopefully.

'Don't prepare yourself for carousing,' Cesare laughed. 'Remember that you're a monk. As soon as we get down there you need to change and start being all pious again.'

'Piss off.'

The three men laughed, and Skiouros spared each of them a caustic glare in turn, but his ire bounced off their happy relief at this turn of events, and as he thought about it, Skiouros realised with a sinking heart that they were serious. And they were right. The only reason the old priest had managed to secure a deal with the Berbers to take the four travellers had been because one of them was a holy man. While none of them knew anything about the desert folk, and none of them could converse, it seemed very likely that, given the deal, 'no monk' meant 'no help'.

He glanced with distaste at the dirty robes in the cart.

'At the very least, if I'm going to be trapped as Brother Skiouros again, I expect you three to help me. And the first thing is to wash these robes. There must be a source of water here somewhere for the camp to survive, and I refuse to spend the next six weeks travelling through the landscape smelling like a pile of vomit and excrement.'

'We can only wash clothes, not work miracles,' grinned Nicolo, staggering to the side as Skiouros landed a punch – only half-playfully – to his upper arm, deadening the muscle.

'I may be a monk on the outside, but I'm a severely aggravated swordsman underneath. Stop pissing me off.'

The party descended the last stretch to the encampment laughing and shouting, three men poking fun at the fourth and eliciting the most impressive series of spiteful reactions. The Berbers strolled alongside them, grinning at this display of humour from their new travelling companions.

Passing the animal pens, the cart came to a halt. The lady dismounted and held a brief, friendly discussion with the brothers from the city. The pair bowed and then turned, grasping the donkeys by their reins and hauling the vehicle back towards the city.

'I assumed they'd be coming with us,' Parmenio noted. 'Not that it really matters who it is we can't converse with. And the lady's a sight prettier than that pair.'

Nicolo rolled his shoulders and smiled. 'Can't argue with that.'

One of the Berbers entered into a deep discussion with Cesare, using hand gestures and signs, pointing somewhere ahead. Skiouros watched with interest. The pair seemed to come to an understanding, though the whole thing looked thoroughly arcane from outside.

'We're staying the night in their tent group,' Cesare announced when the conversation had ended, turning back to his friends. 'Apparently, they're called the Tuareg, I think, and they move in some sort of family or clan. It sounds like we're going to be on the move before the sun rises in the morning, but it seems they have some sort of celebration first tonight. We're to follow them to our tent, where they've got clothes for us all.'

'Excellent.'

'With the exception of yourself, of course, Brother Skiouros. On the bright side, I think they're offering to wash your vestments for you. At least, the man held his nose and pointed at you.'

'Wonderful,' Skiouros grumbled. 'Thank the good lord that priests are allowed to drink wine. I need enough right now to drown myself in.'

The other three laughed, and the friends breathed easy, free air for the first time in many days as they made for the heart of the trade camp.

Chapter Fourteen - Of fallen empires and dangerous men

S kiouros straightened and brushed out the creases and kinks in his vestments, looking around the dim interior of his temporary lodging. The small, stone room which was perhaps a dozen feet across consisted of ruined ancient walls that reached up to Skiouros' head height and the Tuareg – as they were apparently called – had used a wooden pole and a patchwork tent cover of tanned goat skin to form a roof, adding a large carpet on the floor and a colourful hanging-rug door to complete the enclosure. All in all, it was surprisingly warm and homely once he had placed his sleeping pallet and traveling gear inside and he had spent the first hour since they arrived lying back on his bed and relaxing.

It was certainly a step up on the first night of their journey, when they had camped in open farmland and the four travellers had shared a tent with two Tuareg, whom Nicolo had quickly named 'Honker' and 'Farter'.

As the sun had begun its descent toward its bed in the western hills on the second day, the four had looked upon their stopping place with interest and wonder while the Tuareg made their plans on the approach.

Skiouros had had a mental image of the terrain their journey would take them through, born of childhood tales of deserts and the accounts of odd travellers who had regaled him in Crete with their experiences of Africa. Mountainous dunes of sand, rippling heat that distorted the horizon, occasional mirages and other devilish troubles, but mostly endless sand and rock, stretching to infinity around them, punctuated hundreds of miles apart by oases of green water and palm trees.

So far, he could not have been less accurate in his imaginings.

As the caravan had moved away from the coast and southwest into the hills, it had soon become apparent that at least this region of the Emir's lands was far from desert, consisting mostly of fertile farmland tended by weathered villagers and green hillsides roamed by herds of cattle, sheep and goats. Occasional olive groves added regularity to a landscape that undulated with verdant, rolling hills.

They had passed the fractured jagged fangs of stone and brick which marked the ruins of cities that had already begun their decline when Constantinople was little more than a provincial town, the Tuareg barely paying any attention. Indeed, the blue-veiled men had laughed at their passengers when they took enough of an interest to move off to the side of the trade caravan, exploring ruins of temples, fortresses, churches and homes.

But nothing they had passed in the first two days could hold a candle to their second night's stop.

Tugga, as the Tuareg called the place, was a vast sprawl of ruins scattered across a hillside, its summit and the plain below, with great edifices – temples, arches, colonnades and the like – standing almost as if their occupants had simply left them that same morning and not yet returned.

As the caravan moved up from the low street, through an elaborate grey arch inscribed with Latin, and along streets of irregular paving that twisted and curved, always climbing the side of the hill, Skiouros had noted with interest other groups – presumably of Berber traders – camped among the ruins. It appeared Tugga was a stopover for many traders on the road to Tunis.

It would be a wondrous place to explore at leisure, he was sure, though he knew the traders would be up and gone before dawn, and he would have little chance to look around.

Still, it was nice just to rest here.

Skiouros looked down at his priestly form. His robes had been washed and were relatively clean and black, scented with some strange, exotic, almost nutty oil. He looked truly pious and serene, though the effect was somewhat spoiled by his strange bandy-legged stance and lurching walk.

Despite his wound, which had been re-stitched by one of the Tuareg that first evening amid the cries and hisses of the agonised patient, Skiouros had discovered that the pleasant cart-ride he had expected was as far from the truth as his visions of sandy dunes.

No carts or donkeys. *They* were used by the city dwellers. Out here on the trails, the traders used strings of camels tied together, loaded down with goods. Most of the trade group walked alongside the pack animals for hours on end, and only the womenfolk were given mounts. Indeed, even Parmenio, Nicolo and Cesare had found themselves trudging along on foot beside the caravan. In deference perhaps to his priestly profession, or perhaps to his wound, Skiouros had been given one of the few spare camels as a mount.

After the first half day, he had seriously considered giving up the mount and walking the six weeks to Ceuta. It was hard to imagine there could possibly be a less comfortable mode of travel and he was beginning to reassess the apparently favoured position of women in Tuareg society. Perhaps they were not so revered if they were made to ride these beasts that resembled nothing so much as a collection of broken tool handles tightly crammed in a rough, hairy skin sack. There was quite simply nowhere on the creature's awful hide where a human being could rest without something angular jabbing into his nethers.

Slowly and painfully, grunting with each move, Skiouros stepped to the rug door and lifted it aside, hissing at the pain in his side the movement caused. His guts had been so jumbled up and tossed around on the camel ride that he was beginning to wonder if before long he would have to eat with his backside and crap out of his face.

Evening had descended on Tugga – a balmy, warm evening with an indigo sky glittering with the first shining of the stars. The purpled hills stretched away before him beyond the ruins, and the hum and buzz of insects that filled each day had been replaced with a calm silence broken only by the braying of an insomniac goat somewhere nearby and the muted sounds of socialising from the trader camps spread wide enough apart for privacy among the remains.

Immediately outside the door, he looked around. A wide square surrounded by the stubs of broken columns sat before him, a low wall enclosing the plaza on either side. The northern edge, where his accommodation lay, was formed of five such small enclosures, and four had been turned into rooms for the traders' guests.

The room next to his own reverberated with the ripping snores of Parmenio, who had announced upon arrival that he would be lucky if he managed to undress before sleep took him. A less sharp but more insistent snore came from further along, where Nicolo matched his captain rasp for rasp, and Skiouros smiled warmly in the direction of his slumbering friends. No noise issued from Orsini's room, but that was no surprise – the man seemed to sleep absolutely silently.

To the south, at the far side of the columned square, a low ruined wall was split in the middle with a doorway and Skiouros strode quietly towards it. The rest of the traders, he knew, had pitched their tents off to the left some distance away and higher up the slope, where much of the ruined city was low and covered with grass, and he could just hear them laughing and talking, but he felt the need more for peace and solitude than revelry, especially revelry among those with whom he could not communicate.

At the doorway, he looked down. Each new corner or threshold in this place revealed fresh wonders. From the gap, old steps led down to what appeared to be an ancient theatre. Row upon row of stepped seats in a gentle arc sat as silent, empty witness to a flat orchestra backed by a chest-height wall and a series of six decorative columns. Beyond that wall, the hillside must drop away sharply to the sprawling ruins among the fields.

And at the wall the figure of Cesare Orsini stood, his elbows resting on the stonework, gazing out over the city and the hills beyond. That sleepless goat bleated forlornly off somewhere to the left, stirring its dozing companions to life in a short frenzy of warbling, wavering noises.

Orsini looked around at the animal commotion and spotted the black-robed monkish figure lurching bow-legged down the steps towards him. With a smile, he returned to his leaning. Carefully negotiating the fractured broken area of seating towards the bottom, Skiouros stepped out onto the flagged auditorium floor and across to the wall, where he placed his folded elbows atop it, mirroring his friend.

'Blissful night,' Cesare said with a sigh. His eye had now opened once more and the swelling was receding, though the colour of his bruises had intensified.

'Better than a corsair galley or a Hafsid slave market, for certain.'

The Italian nobleman gave a light chuckle.

'I think you could probably have safely left your robes in the room tonight. No one is going to question you out here. Unless you're starting to believe your own fiction?'

'I hardly think that the divine creator would take me into his priesthood willingly. When my time on this mortal plane is up, I think I'll have to sneak into heaven unnoticed!'

'He might consider taking you on now that you no longer smell like the alley behind a tavern at throwing out time.'

'Thanks.'

The pair fell silent, looking out across the ruins which stretched across the grassland, scattered with arches, walls, columns and a strange tall needle-like monument, before giving way to the farmland which stretched across the valley and up the slopes beyond.

'This place is amazing,' Skiouros said quietly, his eyes tracing out the twining streets and alleyways. 'I mean, I went and saw some of the ancient places near Candia that people enthused about, but this place is *ten times* the size, and some of it might as well still be a living city.'

'Rome fought across here with her legions when she was just a small republic,' Orsini said in a matter-of-fact tutor's voice. 'This land was Carthage's empire then, until Rome crushed her utterly. Rome always wins. Even now, long after the days of the Empire and under the rule of that scurrilous creature Innocent the Eighth, may God rot his bones. Glorious Genoa, ophidian Venezia, Pisa, Milano, even Napoli and Sicilia may claim to be independent, but those who do not owe their power to the Papacy manoeuvre and ally purely to prevent that happening. And the east languishes under the Turk only because the Pope will not call a crusade, such is his power. Such is the power of Rome. When that decrepit wall-eyed monster '*Innocent*' finally descends to Hell and the role falls to a true Christian, you might find the Grand Turk ejected from your homeland once more. Imagine that, Master Skiouros? Being able to go home.'

'I *could* go home,' Skiouros conceded, 'if I were truly sure where home was any more.'

He turned to Orsini.

'Do not write off the Turk so easily, though – the Ottoman army is the best in the world. They rolled over the lands of the Byzantine Emperors hardly pausing for breath. My grandfather died on the walls of Constantinople when Mehmet came and my father told me the stories of those early days. The Empire is there to stay, Cesare, and I think your so-hated usurious Pope may well be the one to have to look to his defences. Even Sultan Bayezid, who is just and reasonable and no hater of Christians, harbours further designs on the Greek lands and Venetian territory, or so it's said.'

165

Orsini narrowed his eyes.

'Why is it that you sound almost proud of them, despite what you have been through?'

Skiouros took a deep breath and sagged on the wall. 'You don't know what I've been through, Cesare. And to be quite honest, I *am* sort of proud of them. Don't forget, I grew up in the Empire and, for all my faith and my tongue, I am a son of the Ottoman world. Do not judge the Turk by the yardstick of Etci Hassan, for it's an unfair comparison.'

'I can imagine that is so.'

Cesare turned to him, a curious look across his face, and adjusted the knight's sword that he wore slung at his waist.

'Will you tell me what happened to you?'

'I thought you were more interested in where I was bound.'

'I am almost certain the two are bound up together. How far do I have to go before you will place your trust in me?'

Skiouros smiled weakly. 'It's not you, Cesare. I... I tell no one. Not even Parmenio and Nicolo, who are the closest thing I've ever had to friends. There is too much pain and danger tied up in it, for me and for any audience I choose. There was once a man I *could* have told.'

'Lykaion?'

Skiouros frowned. 'How did you...?'

'You spoke the name a few times in your fevered sleep when you were first wounded. I helped the priest clean you up in his church. Lykaion was your brother?'

'Yes.'

'Dead?'

'Yes. Partially through my inquisitiveness and selfishness, but mainly through the designs of a group of wicked men, almost all of whom are now themselves dead.'

He blinked. He had really not meant to impart any information at all, let alone so much.

'I think I've said enough.'

'So do I,' Cesare smiled, returning his gaze to the hills opposite. '*Almost* all, eh? And the ones who live remain your enemy? Vengeance is hollow victory, Skiouros, and as oft destroys its perpetrator as its target.'

Skiouros clenched his teeth. The honesty and sympathy in the words surprised him almost as much as the fact that Cesare had

166

directly addressed him by name, without 'master' for, as far as he could remember, the first time.

'I really don't want to talk about it.'

'When you do, seek me out. I owe you more than one life-debt, Skiouros. We may be from different worlds, you and I, but continual and shared peril creates bonds that cannot easily be severed. And remember that a danger sought is no less troublesome than that which falls on one unexpected.'

Again, the pair fell silent for a moment, with only the bleating of irritable goats as an aural backdrop.

'What is it with those creatures?' Skiouros smiled. 'I thought they slept at night.'

Orsini turned to him, a look of deep thoughtfulness on his noble features. His eyes passed across Skiouros and then over the slope where the goats, somewhere unseen, continued their gentle cacophony.

Pain lanced through Skiouros' wounded side as Orsini grasped his shoulder and threw him none-too-gently to the floor.

Scrabbling around in panic, Skiouros felt below his ribs, certain several of the stitches had popped once again. He looked up and began to rise, but Cesare pushed him back down as he ducked to one side himself.

A cracking noise resounded through the evening air and Skiouros stared at the two-foot-long black shaft, falcon-feather fletching slightly ruffled, reverberating as it stuck from the stone wall where Skiouros had been leaning.

'What?'

Cesare reached down, grabbing Skiouros by the shoulder and hauling him back toward the stairs, only to pause again. Skiouros scanned around in something of a panic to spot three figures stalking slowly down the steps like purple phantoms in the indigo night. They were dressed in much the same manner as the Tuareg traders, though their faces were unveiled. Skiouros had only spent two days with this enigmatic people so far, but it was already clear to him that all menfolk after puberty wore the veil, and none removed it in public. And that meant that, regardless of their mode of dress, these figures were not Tuareg.

The veils had likely been removed for ease of combat, as blades glinted in the hands of all three as they descended. Another chorus of bleating – that and Cesare's sharp mind had been all that had saved Skiouros' life – gave way to a rushing sound as another arrow clattered against the wall, its passage close enough to ruffle Cesare's hair.

'Hellfire,' the Italian snapped, looking up at the figures cutting off their escape route back towards their escort. The arrows were coming in from the side from where the goat noises issued. 'Parmenio!' Orsini bellowed a warning. 'Nicolo!'

With no apparent regard for Skiouros' wound, the young nobleman then yanked him back across the auditorium and to the wall at its rear, behind the fractured columns. The three robed figures advanced cautiously, spreading out to cover the wide arc of the stepped seats as they descended. A fresh chorus from the goats indicated further activity from the unseen archer.

'Get over the wall,' Cesare hissed.

'*What?*' Skiouros said incredulously, rising just enough to look over the parapet again.

'Jump!'

Skiouros looked down. He'd a reasonable head for heights, unlike poor Lykaion, and under normal circumstances a drop of perhaps twice his own height would not even faze him enough to make him pause. Now, however, he was stiff as a board from two days of camel-riding, with aching bandy legs, jumbled insides and a still-fresh wound in his side that could very easily have killed him. The very idea of dropping that short distance to the paving of the narrow road below was unthinkable!

'I...' he began, but clamped his mouth shut as he suddenly found himself hurtling out into empty space, Cesare's grip as he hauled the Greek over the parapet strong and solid. Skiouros had the presence of mind not to scream as he dropped like a stone towards the flagged road, using the single heartbeat it took to push out his arms to prevent him landing head first.

The shock and pain as he hit the road was intense, and for a moment he panicked that he'd broken his arm, but a brief exploration revealed only bruises and scrapes, albeit painful ones. What was Cesare thinking? If he hadn't put his arms out in time, his head would have burst on that paving like an overripe watermelon!

The answer came to him as he rose painfully and slowly, testing his side that was – yes, he confirmed – leaking once again:

Skiouros had been wounded, encumbered by his robes, and entirely unarmed. The young nobleman had not been meaning the two of them to evade their attackers by leaping the wall. He had been meaning to save Skiouros' life. Above, unseen over that parapet, the Greek could hear the ring of steel on steel as Orsini fought for his life against three opponents, with an archer still hidden and aiming to take them out. It was all well and noble to sacrifice himself to save Skiouros, but the Greek could hardly countenance Cesare falling to an assassin's blade out here, especially one that might have been meant for him.

It took only another two heartbeats to formulate his plan.

Crouching, his hand closed around a heavy, jagged piece of marble, about the size of a small wine jug and perhaps an inch thick. As he began to jog up the street, keeping low and close to the wall, ignoring the throbbing insistent pain in his side, he noted with interest that the slab was covered in incised Latin words. It seemed almost divine ordination that the only word he could fully make out was NEMESIS.

With a grim smile, he moved on towards where the high wall became gradually lower. Dry scrub grass and rubble formed the majority of the landscape above the low wall that bounded the north edge of the street and led across to the auditorium where Cesare fought desperately, the clang, grate and smash of swords still echoing around the night.

It occurred to Skiouros that other trade encampments could probably hear the noises of combat, and probably their own travelling companions too, but it would take too long for them to work out where the echoing sounds came from and they would be too late to save at least the Italian.

Gritting his teeth against the inevitable pain, Skiouros placed the marble fragment on top of the lowest section of wall he could find and then hauled himself up to the grass before retrieving it.

A large, bulbous cactus stood a few feet up the slope, and Skiouros ducked behind it, taking care not to get too close to the spines. After a quick deep breath, taken to a soundtrack of traded sword blows, he glanced around it and scanned the slope.

His gaze had passed across the whole area twice before he spotted the figure crouched behind a low wall. Peering into the dim starlit landscape, Skiouros could see the bow stretched taut in the man's hands, swinging gently to left and right as he sought a shot at Cesare without the likelihood of striking one of his own companions. Half a dozen arrows jutted out of the ground next to him in a line, awaiting their turn.

Noting the man's position, Skiouros hitched up his black robe, tucking it up at the waist and dropping the veiled hat to the floor, and ran to his right, keeping low as he skirted around the edge of the grassy slope. The ache from the camel ride loosened a little as he ran and he did his best to ignore the discomfort. As subtly as he could manage, he skipped across the grass, horribly aware of the warm trickle from his open wound that would be gradually weakening him once again.

He was not quiet. He was, in fact, far from quiet. Fortunately, the combination of the archer's concentration on his target, the swordfight's clamour, and the nearby bleating and shuffling of goats masked the worst sounds of brushed grass and grit crunched underfoot.

Suddenly, he was around a low acacia bush and directly behind the archer. His arm coming back with the rock, he went into a low run, all pretence of silence now abandoned.

The crunch of a stick breaking beneath his foot alerted his intended target and the archer's head snapped round, his eyes widening as he noticed the assailant bearing down on him from behind.

Skiouros felt his heart pounding as he raced against the archer, his silent voice offering up a hundred prayers to a God he felt sure he had offended, just to make him that tiny bit faster; to allow him the time to close before the archer got off his shot.

The man was turning, his bow still drawn back, arrow still sitting in position awaiting release. Skiouros was almost on him, the rock ready to bring down as a weapon. Running. Turning. Running. Turning. A heartbeat.

It was only when he was less than two yards from the archer that he knew he was not going to make it. The archer finished turning and released as Skiouros dived, the rock now closing the end of its swing out in front of him, descending on the man's head.

The marble-slab blow struck the Hafsid thug just above the left eye, smashing the socket so that the eye revolved loosely and lolled, blood flowing out of his broken face. Beneath the smashed skull and the river of free-flowing blood, the tiniest hint of white-pink brain showed, confirming the efficacy of the strike.

Skiouros could not arrest his desperate leaping attack in time, and crashed painfully into the slumping body of the senseless archer, the two men collapsing in a heap, blood from the pair mingling on the ground beneath them.

The young Greek stared at his victim, at the hint of brain visible and the gushing blood, at the misshapen eye socket and the pupils that had rolled – unevenly – upwards as the man fell unconscious in the precursor to a slow and painful death.

A *sure* death.

Skiouros hit him again.

And then again, just to be sure.

170

A quick check brought no sign of breath from the man, but Skiouros hit him again, in case.

Then he looked all over his chest and side, his arms and legs, felt his neck and face and shoulders. No arrow wound! Nothing other than the unhealed cut in his side.

What the hell had happened?

It was as he was lifting himself upright that he looked down at the marble slab in his hand and began to laugh. The M now had an extra stroke to it where the arrow had struck and been deflected off to the side.

Coated with crimson and damaged by the arrow, the slab stared back at him.

NEMESIS.

'I couldn't have put it better myself, Lord.'

Crouching, he drew the curved sword from the scabbard at the thug's waist, admiring its keen edge and simple design. He had never held one of these Muslim blades, even in his most unusual training sessions, but it bore a close resemblance to the swords of the Ottoman army.

It would take just a little adjustment, but the basic fact of which end did the damage was not lost on him and he hefted it, grimacing at fresh waves of pain from his waist.

Figures were now coming over the low ruins at the top of this grassy area – the traders who had finally been drawn by the commotion. Paying them no heed, since they wore veils identifying them as the real thing, Skiouros ran over towards the desperate sounds of sword-fighting, commandeered Arabic blade in one hand, ancient Latin, blood-smeared rock in the other.

At the small auditorium's perimeter wall, Skiouros took in the scene and was once more impressed at the skill of his Italian friend. Despite being outnumbered three-to-one, Cesare had managed to dispatch one of the thugs, who lay on the lower steps, his head at an unnatural angle, half-cleaved from his neck. The other two were, however, pressing in; they had him backed into the corner by a column, and soon Orsini would probably make a mistake. He was clearly tiring and had suffered several small cuts.

Pausing at the wall, Skiouros hefted his 'nemesis stone' for a moment, wondering whether he could remove one assailant from the equation from here, but there was at least a small chance that he might err and brain Cesare, so he quickly put away that idea, left his stone on the wall, and dropped from the top onto the auditorium floor with a gentle slap.

The two men were busy with Orsini and had not noticed Skiouros' quiet approach and so, trading speed for silence, he moved quietly across the flagged floor on the balls of his feet until he was a few yards behind them.

Cesare could not have helped but notice him and yet, professional that he was, he made no sign that he had spotted the approach, keeping the two men's attention on himself as they cut, thrust, swiped and parried.

Skiouros smiled as he took two steps forward, sword coming up and to the right, gripped in both hands. As he swung with all his might, he realised how his companionship with his three friends and the experience of their shared nightmare had changed him. There was no fear now, in battle. No hesitation or panic while his eyes closed to whisk him away to his safe place. The fact had been simple: Cesare was in danger and without his help, the noble would be dead. And so he had killed the archer without a second thought, and now...

The keen edge of the curved sword cut through the thug's arm just below the shoulder, severing it completely and continuing on a foot deep into the man's chest, wedging into the spine. One of many simple facts of the swordsman's art that Don Diego had drummed into him early on was that straight weapons were born for the thrust. Curved weapons were designed for the slice. Now he could see how effective the Arabic curved scimitar was when used so.

The thug was already almost dead as Skiouros slid the blade back out of his chest, the severed arm with the sword still gripped in its hand bouncing away across the flags, blood jetting from the stub at his shoulder and joining the torrent flowing like a crimson waterfall from his scythed chest.

With a strangling sound, the dying man fell.

The sudden surprise attack was enough of a shock to distract the other swordsman and he swung wide, presenting a perfect target for Orsini, who thrust his own straight, old-fashioned blade up into the thug's armpit and deep into his chest.

Twitching, the last man fell and Orsini met Skiouros' gaze and slowly broke into a weary smile.

'Timely. Thank you. Just what I needed – another life debt to you!'

Skiouros laughed and winced at the pain in his side.

'I think we could just about call that one even, though I'd be grateful if, next time you throw me over a wall, you try and make sure I'm the right way up!'

'I was a touch pressed for time.'

The two laughed and sagged in that post-battle relief period.

'You found the archer then?'

Skiouros nodded and strode back over to the wall.

'Did you kill him?'

Retrieving the marble slab, Skiouros nodded, proffering it to Orsini, who read the inscription and laughed. 'You hit him with this? You have a great sense of irony, my friend.'

'Irony, no. *Marbly*, perhaps?' grinned Skiouros.

Footsteps from above announced the arrival of others. The pair looked around to see Parmenio and Nicolo plodding wearily down the steps, barefoot in just breeches and shirt but with swords in hand and both spattered with blood.

'You're alright then?' Nicolo asked with relief.

'Yes. You?'

'Just about. Good job you shouted,' Parmenio grinned, wiping blood from his face. 'Your commotion woke me up just in time to see a cloaked bastard pulling aside my door with a knife in his hand. Just got to my dagger in time. They'd have killed us in our sleep without your warning.'

Nicolo nodded his agreement.

'I think it is a family of goats to whom you owe the thanks, captain,' smiled Cesare, wiping his blade on one of the cleaner parts of his victim and then on a rag from his belt before sheathing it, almost pristine clean.

The Tuareg were now spreading out across the site, making sure there were no more attackers.

'Perhaps we should have left one to interrogate?' Nicolo grunted.

'Hardly necessary. I think we can be fairly sure who they are and why they were here,' Parmenio answered.

'Yes, but was that all of them, or are there any more?'

'Time will have to answer that for us,' Orsini shrugged. 'I suggest, gentlemen, that you arm yourself from their weapons and we take anything of value. Let us be prepared in future. Where are you going?' he said, this last aimed at Skiouros, who was strolling back towards the grassy area and climbing wearily over the wall.

'There's a basin of water down there. I need to wash my wound before one of you helpful gentlemen gets to stitch me up again. Besides, I have a souvenir that's rather sticky and I think I might want to wash.'

He hefted the marble slab as he turned away once more.

'Peculiar lad,' sighed Parmenio behind him and started walking.

'And where are *you* going?' muttered Nicolo.

'You think I'm going to let the foolhardy boy wander round on his own in the dark after this?'

By the time he had reached the wall and climbed up, following Skiouros, the other two had joined him, swords in hand.

Chapter Fifteen - Of the journey

'**E**leven days.'
'Are you sure?'
Skiouros shrugged at Parmenio, wincing. 'I've been marking them off on my camel stick with a knife.'

'Eleven days since Tunis. It feels like a bloody lifetime. I cannot remember a time when I smelled anything but camel or when I spoke to anyone but you three. You realise that means we're only about a quarter of the way,' the captain said with a weary sigh.

'At least it's been quiet.'

The pair lapsed into silence as Skiouros examined his stick – the badge of office of a camel handler, used for everything from directional control and goading stick to scratching pole. Eleven notches.

His eyes strayed up to the countryside, still green and cultivated, as it – surprisingly – had been all through the journey, though it was gradually becoming noticeably less verdant and more interspersed with dry brown dust as they moved westwards. The locals all, he noticed, nodded in greeting at the Tuareg, but on the whole the caravan kept to itself. Three in every four stops or so had been open country pauses, pitching tents together as an insular group, but on occasions they came to stopovers like the one at Tugga where numerous caravans would meet, exchange news or goods and even socialise before departing their separate ways in the morning.

Such a place, apparently, was Sedif, which loomed ahead half a mile away – a sizeable town from all appearances. In deference to the fact that trade caravans were not always welcomed in civic areas, they would camp along with any other groups on the edge of the town.

Skeletal trees reached up to the grey-blue sky on both sides of the old road that had brought them from the previous night at Tajenanet. The road – little more than a flatter, greyer line in the dirt – drew them towards Sedif and, as much exchange of sign language had revealed, the lands of the Zayyanid Sultan Abdallah the Fourth. While the physical change between the two realms was impossible to identify, that invisible line marked an important point, as they were finally in the domain of a ruler who had no knowledge of them and no contact – as far as they knew – with Etci Hassan. While there had been no sign of further pursuit since Tugga, Skiouros remained watchful and suspicious, almost certain that, though nothing had been seen, more hired killers were out there somewhere regardless. Perhaps things would be easier now, in Zayyanid lands?

'Looks like we'll be in the big tent with Honker and Farter again,' Parmenio gave an exaggerated sigh with a touch of humour. They had grown accustomed to, and somewhat fond of, the tall, thin trader and his bear-shouldered companion who were in truth very friendly and generous. If only any of them had a clue what the pair were saying...

Skiouros nodded. 'I think we'll be camping as if we're on our own in the countryside, despite the town beside us.'

Both men pictured the noisy pair that would be sharing their tent that night with a smile and then lapsed into mindless chatter until a few minutes later one of the more senior, older Tuareg wandered up to them, nodding in greeting.

Taking a breath, he began to launch into the usual signs and signals that the four travellers had become rather used to translating, voicing his message in his complex language for his own ease, despite their incomprehension.

'Tomorrow? Moving west?' Parmenio nodded.

The man nodded in return, turned and pointed south.

'South?'

Nod.

'West *and* south?'

Nod. Point, point, point, point.

'I'm lost already,' the captain grumbled. 'Seven words. That has to be a record.'

'No,' Skiouros held out a hand. 'Look. He pointed at us and then west; then at himself and south.'

'We're splitting up?'

176

Parmenio waved his hands to clear the conversation as if wiping chalk from a slate, and then pointed at the man and the camels and then off to the south. The Tuareg nodded. The captain then pointed at himself and the west. Again, the man nodded, but this time also gestured to the town of Sedif ahead.

'No. Still lost.'

'I think,' Skiouros hazarded, 'that he's telling us that we're swapping over to another caravan here as they're going south.'

Parmenio grunted. 'Wonderful. Having to break in another set of incomprehensible desert dwellers.'

'I doubt it'll be the last time we change, though,' Skiouros sighed. 'It's a long way and the chances that one caravan will be going all the way from Sedif to Ceuta have to be tiny.'

Now, they could see the goat-skin tents that betrayed the presence of other Tuareg caravans, pitched in the lee of a barren hill to the south west of the town, and the camels at the head of their line were beginning to peel off the road and head in that direction. Skiouros nodded his thanks to the Tuareg, who smiled, returned the nod and then shuffled off back to his own concerns ahead.

'Looks like they'll just be settled in time for the *Maghrib* prayer. Tents are going to go up slow then,' Skiouros said wearily.

'Bloody prayer times every ten minutes. I swear this caravan hardly moves sometimes. Some of these lot would stop in the middle of a shit if the call to prayer went up!'

Skiouros smiled. Most of the Tuareg clung to their strange old faith, but perhaps a quarter of them followed the Muslim doctrine – adopted from the settled Berber cousins in towns and villages across the landscape – while curiously still carrying the idols and talismans of their old gods. How they reconciled the two apparently irreconcilable faiths fascinated Skiouros and he really wished he could converse enough to ask them about it. His own complex feelings on the blending and blurring of borders between the Muslim and Christian faiths could, he felt sure, benefit from understanding such a working dichotomy. The practical effect on the caravan, however, was five pauses a day for the Islamic prayer ritual.

Unsure at first what to do, given his guise, Skiouros had joined the Tuareg Muslims in their devotions, given that their faith was closer to his than the strange ancient beliefs of the others. While they knelt and faced their holy place, reciting the prayers, Skiouros kneeled among them, muttering what he could remember of the Nicene Creed from his days in

177

church – surprisingly, it had almost all come back to him – and adding a couple of personal prayers for himself and his friends. Curiously, he had found over the past few days that he had begun mouthing the Muslim prayers alongside when he had finished his own, so often had he listened to their escort repeating the words. In a way, it was comforting. After all, Lykaion had tried to tell him again and again that Allah was the only true God and Mohammed was his prophet, and it felt reassuring that he add a few words in favour of Allah in addition to the religion of his youth... just in case Lykaion had been right.

It had earned him odd looks from the Tuareg Muslims, but in time they had come to accept it as some quirk or some facet of his specific piety and had smiled at him as he tried to wrap his mouth around the unfamiliar syllables. The words and the language might be different, but the intonation and the meaning were clearly very similar to his own devotions.

'Best get my prayer rug out ready,' he smiled.

'You worry me.' Parmenio rolled his eyes. 'Bad enough that you're starting to believe your own disguise, but now you're starting to turn into one of them!'

'There's no harm in an open mind.'

'Tell that to the Dominican inquisitors. They'd peel a man for heresy. Our Holy Father's got a thing about witches, you know, and he's no lover of the Arabs! Stick to your prayer rope and your liturgy. Rome may not be a big fan of your Greek church, but they won't burn you for it, like they might if they saw you out here.'

Skiouros shrugged. 'Then it's a good job they can't see me.'

The captain rolled his eyes again. 'Think I'll go back and talk to Nicolo. He may have a head full of mad goblins, but he's ten times more balanced than you.'

Skiouros grinned as he watched the man leave. In truth he was grateful to be left alone for a while. For some reason, his friends had spent most of the day walking alongside him as he bounced up and down on this hairy sack of broken hammers, and when they hadn't been there, some of Tuareg had always been present.

And there was something he'd been waiting to do when he had a moment alone.

Now he looked up and down the line. No one ahead was paying a jot of attention, and those behind were busy, the three Christians in deep conversation some way back now that Parmenio had returned to them and the rest minding their animals.

Angling himself so that his actions were somewhat obscured from behind, Skiouros gently, carefully lifted the side of his outer cassock, hooking his fingers under the inner garments and shirt too and lifting them.

A faint odour of chicken broth rose from his side, tinged with some underlying current of foul sweetness. Why it should smell like chicken was beyond him, but it was the only way he could describe it to himself. The stitches were all still in place, but the wound had lengthened a tiny amount and the area around the stitches and the incision itself had turned a yellow-orange colour. Skiouros peered at it with dismay. It had become noticeably worse just in the last few hours.

One of the most regular subjects of his prayers in those strange Muslim/Christian pauses had been the decline in health of his gut wound. He knew it was infected and, whatever priests usually claimed, no amount of beseeching the divine seemed to be making a difference, whether he called him God or Allah. He should have told the Tuareg who re-stitched the wound after Tugga, but Skiouros had watched him and come to the conclusion that he was some sort of artisan, trained in piecing together the hides that made the tents and coverings of the Tuareg, and not a medical man at all, and bringing the infected cut to the man's attention seemed like inviting some rather unskilled probing he would rather avoid.

The downside was that he knew as well as any man that an infected wound would almost certainly eventually lead to a painful demise.

Orsini, who had suffered a similar wound once, had informed him after Tugga that the stitches would need to stay in for two weeks, which meant that they would be expecting Skiouros to have the sutures out and be exercising to return to full health in the next few days. In truth, he was starting to feel distinctly unwell and his decline showed no signs of slowing.

Despite the difficulties involved, he resolved to try and find someone in Sedif that night who might be able to help. It was the largest town they had passed since Tunis, and if he was going to find a medic anywhere in this region, Sedif seemed a likely place.

Lowering his robe once more he breathed in the warm, late afternoon air of the Tamazgha – as the Tuareg seemed to call this land – trying to drive the stink of the suppurating wound from his nostrils.

Yes, he would have to do something tonight. Prayer was doing nothing and the problem would hardly go away on its own.

For the next ten minutes or so, as the caravan moved off the track and gathered on the edge of the trader camp, Skiouros ran through everything he could think of saying in signs that might help when they stopped.

His deep concentration was interrupted as his three friends wandered alongside once more.

'Ho, Master Skiouros,' Cesare smiled. 'You look uncomfortable. No matter as you'll be down and in a tent soon now.'

'A pleasing thought,' he replied. 'But I have something to do first.'

'Ah yes. Time to raise your voice in prayer along with our friends.' Orsini smiled.

'I think God may have to start without me tonight. I have a mind to go into the town and look for a physician.' He noted the concerned narrowing of the eyes in his friends and shrugged. 'Time these stitches were out.'

Orsini nodded slowly, his eyes still suspicious.

'There are men in the caravan that can do that.'

'Tent makers and the like, yes, but a doctor would be a little more careful and delicate, I feel.'

Again Orsini nodded. 'Then I will accompany you.'

'That's really not necessary.'

'Piffle. It's more than just necessary. You have no idea how these people will react to a Christian monk in their midst. We're not in Hafsid lands now, you know.' He turned to the others. 'Will you two gentlemen be joining us?'

'Better than standing around watching the tents not going up, 'cause they're all busy praying,' grumbled Parmenio, raising nods of agreement from Nicolo.

'Very well. As soon as we've stopped, we'll head off.'

Skiouros sighed. He'd wanted to avoid company. The fact that he'd hidden his declining health from them for days now was embarrassing, and they might be insulted by his decision not to tell them. Clearly they were determined, but perhaps he could make them wait outside if they found a physician?

The camels were being corralled as most of the trade party moved around removing the tent sections, ropes, poles and so on, preparing to make camp. Six of them moved off to one side, where they could kneel and carry out their devotions. They would have to do so without his company tonight. God would understand.

One of the Tuareg threaded his way between the rest and approached them, beckoning. With a frown, Skiouros and his friends followed the man, who led them past the unloading of the camp gear to where the elegant lady in charge stood with a small group of Tuareg Skiouros did not recognise.

Skiouros bowed with a hiss of pain, and smiled at the men.

'*Oy ik?*' he asked, mimicking the greeting he had heard so many times over the last week and a half. '*Mani eghiwan?*'

'Much good,' one of the Tuareg said from behind his veil. He was a short, heavy man with bulky arms and large, bulging eyes, and though his accent was thick with the desert dwellers' inflection, his Italian was surprisingly clear.

'You speak Italian?' Parmenio said in surprise.

'Little. Few word. Trade tongue.'

Parmenio sagged with relief. 'That makes things somewhat easier.'

'You come us now. We west seven days at Khemis.'

Skiouros nodded. 'Before we do, I must see a doctor. Do you know of one here in Sedif?'

The man frowned in incomprehension.

'Physician? Medic? Healer?'

Still the trader frowned, shrugging. Skiouros bit his lip. 'We go into town to find healer,' he said in the end.

'Show him your stitches,' Parmenio urged. 'Then he'll understand.'

Skiouros swallowed. *Damn it*. Taking a deep breath, he turned so that the wound would face the man and away from the others and slowly lifted his vestments.

The smell emerged once more and the Tuareg's eyes widened. Skiouros dropped the black robe once more, but Cesare caught it falling and lifted it again.

'Infection?'

'Sadly,' Skiouros replied with a sigh.

'Why didn't you say anything?'

'What could you have done?'

'Nothing, but we might have helped you on and off your camel and perhaps enquired with the traders as to whether there was anyone who could help.'

'Precisely. Nothing.'

The Tuareg had gone into a brief discussion and finally the short leader nodded and scratched his forehead.

'*Timaswaden*,' he announced. '*Boka.*'

'Erm. Alright?' Skiouros hazarded.

'*Boka! Boka!*' the man repeated, earning more shrugged agreement from the four travellers. A moment later, another Tuareg appeared from somewhere behind them and bowed.

'*Boka.*' The leader said yet again. Skiouros frowned and the two Tuareg fell again into deep conversation. When it ended, without further discussion, the new man – the boka? – beckoned to them and began to walk away. The four friends exchanged glances, shrugged, and then followed.

The man rattled away in his own language as they walked, apparently not expecting them to answer, since he left too little pause in his words for reply, and the friends followed with mixed interest and nervousness as they moved into the edge of the town. Unlike the great Hafsid city of Tunis, Sedif sprawled out across the flat landscape, having expanded beyond its ancient containing city walls, which now stood in ruined fragments at the sides of streets, houses built into the defences. There were no guards or figures of authority in evidence and, as they moved along a wide, dusty street, Skiouros looked about and realised that many of the houses were empty shells, gradually falling into disrepair. Sedif, it appeared, had seen better days.

Along the wide thoroughfare the Tuareg led them, before taking a side street just short of a shattered ancient bastion of the walls. The call to prayer began to echo across the roofs, warbled by some imam high in his minaret in the town's centre. The men walked on to that exotic aural backdrop and finally arrived at a plain door in a house no different from any of the other white, squat buildings. The man knocked, and a few minutes later the portal opened and a local appeared, speaking Arabic.

Skiouros stepped back with the others as the Tuareg launched into an incomprehensible conversation, occasionally using the word 'boka'. As the house's occupant seemed to nod in some sort of agreement, the Tuareg grasped Skiouros by the shoulder, taking him somewhat by surprise, and dragged him forth, lifting his cassock, inner vestments and shirt to display the infected wound.

The old, bearded man stepped from his house and bent to peer close to Skiouros' side, sniffing at the wound. Straightening, he nodded and beckoned them inside.

Orsini and the others stepped forward and Skiouros shook his head. 'You three stay out here and keep watch. I'm not too sure about all this.'

Unhappy with his decision, the three men scowled, but remained in the street as the Tuareg and the local led Skiouros inside, closing the door behind them. The older man who owned the house lit an oil lamp and beckoned Skiouros over to a low table, while he removed his own long gown and flexed his fingers. Skiouros eyed him nervously as he slowly sat on the table and then turned and lowered himself so that he lay on his back. The doctor – if that was what he was – gestured him to lie on his side instead and Skiouros did so with some discomfort. His vestments and shirt were pulled up to beneath his armpit and his breeches pushed down below the hip, revealing the entire area around the wound.

Skiouros stared at the wall, feeling utterly helpless, while the two men held a brief discussion. As he felt fingers probing the tender area around the wound, Skiouros resolved to learn Arabic when he finally returned to civilisation and had some time on his hands.

He drew in a sharp breath as the first stitch was snipped. A few of the sutures were the original ones put in professionally by the knight-priest two weeks ago, and they were now a little embedded in the flesh and painful to remove, the others less neat and put in by the Tuareg tent-stitcher, but fresher and therefore less painful.

After his first hiss, there was a pause and then the 'boka' leaned over him with a vial and a stick. Skiouros stared at them, and the man mimed tipping the vial into his mouth and then proffered it. Skiouros frowned nervously, but as a particularly painful stitch was snipped, he grabbed the vial and tipped some of its contents into his mouth, swallowing the sharp, spicy cocktail. As he opened his mouth to take another swig, the vial was lifted from his hand and the stick was jammed gently between his teeth. Skiouros simply bit down, knowing now what they were about.

He began to run through the Orthodox litany in his head as he tried not to tense and jump with each fresh stab of pain they inflicted as they removed the stitches one by one and allowed the infected wound to open up once more.

The local said something he could not understand in a soothing tone which was followed a heartbeat later by a probing that caused such intense agony that Skiouros almost bit through the stick. Raising his head to see what was happening he quickly wished he hadn't and lowered it again, closing his eyes. The local physician was mopping the inside of his wound with some sort of swab, while the Tuareg stood by with what appeared to be a jar of honey.

Before he realised what he was doing, Skiouros found he was muttering by rote the sounds of the Muslim prayer. It must be about the right time, given the recent prayer call he'd heard, and either the doctor was not a Muslim or he took his work so seriously he was prepared to bend the rules of prayer.

Skiouros could not say how long he lay on his side, and he certainly passed out briefly, but suddenly he awoke with a start as the Tuareg wafted something beneath his nose. The pain in his side bloomed as he moved, but whatever they had given him from the vial – poppy juice among other things, he suspected from the smell – had floated his mind and senses on a cushion of drug-comfort and the pain seemed somehow removed from him, as though he were having it described to him rather than enduring it himself.

He moved slowly, peering at his side. It had been padded and dressed, and a linen wrap wound around and around his middle.

The physician smiled at him and nodded in an encouraging manner before entering into another discussion with the Tuareg. Skiouros tried to sit, but immediately slumped back, woozy. One thing he had discovered in that sudden move, though, was that apparently they had not put in any new stitches. There was no tell-tale tug as he moved, just the dulled pain of the wound moving.

As he tried to sit up again, the two men scurried over and helped him until he dropped his feet over the side and to the floor. He tried to plaster an expression of mixed gratitude and enquiry on his face, but the two men either failed to notice or declined to react, instead grasping him by the elbows and slowly hauling him to his feet.

The following five minutes or so were a blur once again, and the next thing Skiouros could remember with any clarity was the door opening and being escorted outside, where the Tuareg continued to support him. The physician smiled and nodded encouragingly again, and then passed a small pile of linen and a vial of clear liquid to the Tuareg.

No money seemed to change hands and Skiouros suddenly felt both guilty and beholden. Had his unnamed saviour healed him for no recompense? He scrabbled round his middle, wondering if he had anything of value to give the physician, but the man simply smiled, shaking his head, and closed the door.

Skiouros turned, and the sudden blurring movement almost blacked out his senses again. When he focussed, he realised that his friends were no longer outside the door.

Panic gripped him and he tried to pull away from the Tuareg, but he was still shaky, in fairly serious pain and very much in danger of passing out into comfortable bliss, and the man hardly had to struggle to hold onto him.

Helplessly, Skiouros staggered back through the town, the Tuareg both guiding and supporting him, and eventually, with some relief, he spotted the tents of the camp.

Everything went black.

When he came round again, he was lying on his travel bed in the confines of a familiar Tuareg tent. The panic hit him as he remembered leaving the physician's house to the empty street, and he started to struggle upright, the pain ripping through him, until Parmenio's hand landed on his shoulder and gently pushed him back down. Skiouros blinked and turned his head. Nicolo and Cesare were seated beside the captain on leather cushions.

'What happened?' His voice was thick and difficult to follow, his tongue still tied with the juice of the poppy, but Parmenio smiled.

'You've been out for a while. Probably a good thing from what we were told. Our new trader friend helpfully translated everything for us. This *boka* fellow is some sort of herbalist and took you to a proper physician he knew in the town. He's been given instructions to change your dressings and clean the wound every day, and you've got some sort of poppy-juice potion to take while he does it. They reckon you'll be alright so long as the wound stays clean and you're sensible. We'll know for sure in a week, he thinks.'

Skiouros slumped, his feeble strength giving out.

'They're putting together some sort of litter so that you don't have to ride a camel. Should be nice and comfortable,' Parmenio smiled. 'I'm thinking of sticking myself in the side so that I can have a nice ride too.'

Skiouros tried to smile but it turned into a wince.

'Where were you?'

His friends shared a look, and Parmenio leaned forward.

'We saw people – unveiled but shadowy like the ones back at Tugga. Tailing us as we moved through the town, we think. We tried to find them, but they melted away into the streets like ghosts and it took us some time to find our way back here. We cannot be sure, but it seems highly likely that Sidi Najid's men are still tracking us.'

'It is to be hoped this new caravan we're joining is large or well armed enough to put off potential attackers,' Orsini added. 'Anyway, you've only been out for an hour, so you should try and get some more sleep. We're on the trail with our new friends at dawn.'

Skiouros sank into the comfortable bed with a sigh. More than four weeks still to go.

Chapter Sixteen - Of Gods and fevers

Parmenio struggled to control the writhing form of Skiouros, his teeth clenched, his hands gripping the young Greek by the shoulder as slowly, gradually, the fight went out of the recumbent form and his friend subsided into a fitful slumber once more.

Peering down at him, Parmenio sagged as he took in the waxy complexion and the sweat that ran freely from his friend's hairline and face, drenching the covering of the bed upon which he lay. His torso was swaddled with fresh linen and his priestly garb sat on a chair nearby, freshly laundered, stitched and folded.

The captain's eyes rose to the figure opposite, who was now letting go of Skiouros' other shoulder with visible relief. The physician nodded and then used his eyes to motion them across the room and away from the patient.

The caravan had pulled into the small trade post of Miliana the night before last, seven days out from Sedif, and Skiouros had already been deep in the throes of his fever by then, his temperature controlled as best the travellers could with wet rags and kind words. Miliana was little more than an overgrown village built upon the fragmentary ruins of some lost ancient site and scattered across the ground at the foot of a range of heavily wooded hills, but its position at the meeting point of trade routes that ran east to west, south into the desert, and north to the coast had secured it a position as a regular stopping place for many caravans.

Consequently the populace, small as it was, was open to contact and exchange with the passing traders and the people there showed signs of a number of different racial roots in their physical makeup. Upon arrival, Parmenio, Nicolo and Cesare – along with the caravan's herbalist and the short, bulky, pop-eyed man who spoke traces of Italian – had approached the village's central square and made enquiries. The locals had happily directed them to the house of one Eleazar ben Tabbai, who turned out of be a Jewish doctor and apothecary who had settled in Zayyanid lands a few months earlier, having been ejected from his beloved home in Cordoba by the new laws of the despots Fernando and Isabella.

The caravan that had brought them to Miliana had moved on the next morning, taking their herbalist and translator with them, and passing them into the care of a group of traders out of Al-Jazair and bound for Fas – another caravan who shared no common tongue with the travellers.

The four had stayed on, waiting for their new guides to be ready and grateful for the pause on behalf of their sick friend. Ben Tabbai had readily agreed to look at Skiouros, and the young Greek, already delirious and sweating, had been taken to the house by his friends.

The Jew, a middle aged man with sad, hollowed eyes and a drawn face, had announced that contrary to their fears, the fever that currently gripped Skiouros was almost certainly a good sign. He was battling the infection and, while there was always the chance that he would lose that fight and his health would decline once more, ben Tabbai believed his patient to be strong and taking the upper hand in the war.

A quick examination of the wound had earned another positive reaction, and the physician had nodded in satisfaction at the cleanliness of the wound, confirming that the young Greek was ridding himself of the evil within. Fearing to stitch in case he caused further infection, ben Tabbai had smiled at the half-healed incision and rebound it, tighter and tidier than before, announcing that as long as Skiouros won his battle, the wound should be fully closed and healed in little more than a week. Then a further week or so to regain his strength and he should be well on the path to full recovery.

It all sounded like a fabrication to Parmenio as he held his friend down during the worst of the thrashing and raving, yet he could do nothing but trust the physician. He had asked whether some sort of soporific could be administered to prevent the worst of the fevered movement, but ben Tabbai had shaken his head and very clearly stated that any interference in the young man's struggle could lose him the fight. It was all down to Skiouros' body now.

And so while Cesare and Nicolo had organised everything with the traders and gleaned what information about the coming journey they could, Parmenio had stayed with the doctor and his patient overnight and through the day, helping wherever he could and restraining Skiouros as required.

'Say what you like, Master Eleazar, but every time he lapses into stillness, I fear he is on the way out. Are you *sure* he's improving?' Parmenio queried in passable Spanish – a tongue he had used in trade dealings in the west for many years.

The physician smiled.

'He needs to rest between fights, as any soldier does. However, you might note that his periods of rest are lengthening, and his struggles for control are ever shorter. Unless something causes a down-turn we should see a change by sunrise tomorrow.'

'Do you think he'll be out long?'

'Who can say? Though I believe, God willing, that he should be at rest for an hour or two now.'

'Then if you're amenable, I will go and find the others and get myself a quick bite to eat.' He pictured the other two now, as it was nearing the evening meal time. Nicolo would be sitting in his tent preparing a dinner from the meat, cheese and bread they had bought upon arrival, waiting for the captain to return and join him. Though Cesare dropped in regularly, he had taken to eating and drinking khave with the friendly – if incomprehensible – village elders, though he'd not explained why, only tapping the side of his nose infuriatingly when pressed.

Ben Tabbai nodded with a smile. Parmenio had gratefully accepted his offer of a meal the previous night, but it appeared that slow-cooked kosher mountain goat was not to the captain's taste, and since then, he had sought the company of his friends to eat whenever time allowed.

Parmenio paused only to lay his hand palm-flat on his recumbent friend's shoulder, wishing him a speedy recovery, and then strode across to the door, noting again with interest the table full of goods near the door. In the past day as he'd stayed with his friend, he had realised just how often the local populace and passing traders visited the Jew for help and advice, paying him in whatever manner they could, from eggs or cheese or vegetables to curios, clothing, even furniture. Eleazar ben Tabbai might be a poor man, monetarily speaking, but he clearly wanted for nothing.

With a small smile, Parmenio opened the door and breathed in the warm evening air, infused with dust and animals and the heady scent of rosy garlic and bay laurel that covered the slopes above. It was not difficult to imagine why the Jew had found this place worthwhile as a replacement home. It may be smaller than his native city of Cordoba, but the climate was similar, the scents and landscape intoxicating and the villagers respectful and friendly towards this most welcome settler.

Parmenio sighed and stretched on the step.

The arrow thudded into the doorframe three inches from his eye.

Parmenio stared as in his peripheral vision the feathered shaft vibrated in the timber.

Half a heartbeat later, he was ducking back into the room and slamming the door, just in time to hear the thud of a second arrow smashing into the wood.

'Shit.'

The physician looked around in surprise.

'Captain? *Ma koreh?*'

'We have trouble.'

His mind racing, Parmenio tried to decide what to do, drawing the slightly curved blade he'd taken from a body at Tugga and hefting the sword somewhat inexpertly – he'd little experience with such an exotic Arabic-style weapon.

Dashing across to the wall, he shuffled next to the table of foodstuffs and gifts and peered through the gap between the ill-fitting shutters that covered the windows. It took a moment for him to pick out the shapes of men moving between the buildings on the far side of the street.

'Do you have a back door?'

'Well yes. What is happening?'

'Bandits,' Parmenio hissed.

'Here?'

'They took a personal dislike to us on the road a while back. They must have followed us into Miliana.'

'Are they godless men who would trouble a sick patient?'

Parmenio pictured Sidi Najid's men. 'I think they'd rob and rape a corpse if the mood took them, doctor.'

'Then you should not leave your friend to them,' the Jew admonished.

'I wasn't planning to. I didn't mean to use the back door on my own. We can take him out the back and try and sneak to the traders' camp. Hopefully we can be streets away before they know I'm not in here any more.'

Eleazar shook his head. 'Such a route is not feasible. Besides, it would be bad for your friend to be rough-handled through the streets.'

'Worse than being cut into strips by angry bandits?'

'If you open his wound up again with such rough movement you risk new infection, and with the young man being already so weak, I do not think he would survive a second bout.'

Parmenio sighed. What was it about pious men that they could not see the worse, more earthly dangers right in front of their face?

'If they find him here, infection will be the least of his worries, doctor. We have to get him out of here. I cannot protect him from three or more bandits and, unless you happen to be a physician *and* a swordsman, I see no alternative.'

Ben Tabbai smiled infuriatingly. 'Such plans are rendered moot, I fear, by the fact that the rear exit of this building leads only into an alley that emerges onto this same street, unless you feel you could carry your friend up onto rooftops.

'Shit,' Parmenio repeated, peering between the shutters and now counting four men visible in the street. 'So we're trapped and outnumbered.'

'It would appear so. I trust that these men would not be willing to listen to a well-reasoned argument, if I were to step out and speak to them.'

'Take one step out of that door and they'll pin you to the wall, doctor.'

He lapsed into silent, desperate thought, his gaze straying across to his friend. 'If I could think of a way of getting word to the others...'

Ben Tabbai shrugged. 'The locals say that the people once urged Mohammed to call Mount Safa to come to him to prove his holiness, but when he did so and it did not come, he reminded the people that, had it done so, it would have crushed them, and so instead *he* went to the mountain.'

'What?'

'A meshuggah story, I know, but the meaning holds true. You cannot bring your friends to the bandits. But you *can* bring the bandits to your friends.'

Parmenio narrowed his eyes.

'That's an exceedingly dangerous gamble on whether or not they know Skiouros is here. It's quite possible that one of them followed me here this afternoon and was waiting for his friends before he moved, but what if they have been watching the house for a while and they know the lad's here? They'll just come in and kill you both once I leave.'

'And what will they do if we simply all wait?' Eleazar asked with a crooked smile.

The captain sighed. 'Come in here and kill us all.'

'Precisely.'

Parmenio knuckled his forehead in anguish as he tried to decide on a course of action. Finally, sighing again, he straightened. 'If they come, protect him.'

'As God protects us both. *Mazel tov*, Captain Parmenio.'

'Good luck.'

Ben Tabbai smiled that infuriating smile again and watched as Parmenio reached for the door handle. Taking a deep breath, he swung it inwards, stepping into the gap, but maintaining his grip on the handle. Sure enough, the tell-tale sound of an arrow in flight cut through the night-time air and Parmenio slammed the door to again just in time to block it. As soon as the arrow hit with a thud, he threw it open once more and was out into the street and running.

There were five of them. That much became quickly plain as the four men with drawn blades burst into activity following him off down the street, the fifth – the archer – emerging from a side street. Though it seemed unlikely he could loose an accurate arrow on the move, Parmenio deliberately zigged and zagged from one side of the street to the other, presenting as difficult a target as he could manage.

Another thing that quickly became apparent was that the thugs on his tail were younger, fitter and faster than he. He risked a momentary glance over his shoulder and could see already how much they had gained on him, though the fact that the street outside the Jew's house seemed to be empty was heartening. The archer was busy attempting to shoulder his bow and draw his sword as he ran.

Parmenio tried to picture the layout of the town. So sudden was the attack and so unplanned his response that he had turned from the door in the direction that would give him the greatest head start. Sadly, that direction was also leading him further into the town and away from the traders' camp.

In a desperate attempt to right himself, he charged into a side alley, bouncing off the white walls as he disappeared into the shadows. They would be on him in a few moments and, while he could do with putting some distance between them, he could not afford to lose them, lest they go back to the house and find Skiouros.

Breathing deep and trying to regulate himself as he ran, Parmenio burst out into another small street and skidded to a halt, his feet kicking up chips of stone, gravel and dust. The way ahead was soundly blocked by half a dozen more thugs, their naked blades gleaming in the evening light as they advanced slowly on him.

Parmenio grunted as he backed towards the doorway of a house. The thought of turning and running back the way he had come occurred to him, the odds being slightly better in that direction, but already his pursuers were emerging from the alley behind him. He was trapped in the street by eleven men with no way out. They had outmanoeuvred him, herding him into a trap. Now, as soon as they'd done away with him, they could stroll across to the Jew's house and put the doctor and his patient to the sword before dealing with the others at the camp.

Desperately, Parmenio scrabbled with the door handle at his back, but the house was sealed tight and there was no exit. Had he been twenty years younger and considerably fitter, he might have managed to vault up onto the low roof and run from here, but he knew for certain that he would have a blade in his back before he gained the parapet.

Clenching his teeth in preparation, he hefted the curved sword in his hand, waiting for the first move. He would take at least one or two with him and was determined that if his time was up, he would go in the fight and not let them take him alive to slowly torture to death later.

'Come on then, you pieces of fetid camel dung. Who's first?'

The advancing thugs paused and one of the new arrivals stepped out – a large man, naked to the waist and with a wicked blade in hand. He grinned a malicious grin, made uglier by the scars that had misshapen his nose and knocked it out of line.

The bandit said something in gravelly tones that Parmenio could not understand, though its meaning was fairly clear.

'Alright, lad. The bigger they are, as they say…'

'Apologies,' came a voice from somewhere hidden, 'but this big one, I think, is mine.'

Parmenio grinned at the voice, recognising those tones even before he spotted Cesare Orsini sitting on the flattened roof of a house a few doors down, his heels kicking the white wall, sword balanced across his knees.

'I thought you'd be eating?'

'While you get all the fun? Please, captain.'

193

With a flash of white teeth, Cesare dropped to the floor and straightened, testing the swing of his old knight's sword as he stepped across the street towards Parmenio, keeping between him and the big bandit.

'Very stylish and funny, I'm sure,' the captain said quietly, 'but even back to back that's still more than five men apiece. You might have been better staying quiet and out of the way. You could have gone and got Skiouros to safety.'

'Master Skiouros will be fine,' Cesare smiled, figure-eighting his blade in the balmy air. 'Friends are already with him.'

'Friends?'

'Friends. I'm sure even *you* have them, captain. I appear to have many.'

Parmenio gave a mirthless chuckle and then fell silent, his eyes widening as a dozen figures emerged from the alleys and doorways around them, a few armed with swords, but more with cooking knives, sickles and staves.

'What the...?'

'I have been cultivating a relationship with the locals,' Orsini smiled. 'You would be surprised how much they themselves dislike bandits. They were quite incensed when I told them there would be some in their own town. So we decided to trap them in their own trap.'

Parmenio shook his head. 'We *wondered* why you were eating in town and not with us.'

'I was beginning to become heartily sick of being pursued. Time to deal with the problem altogether. I'm pretty certain that we have them all here. We have been tracking them across the town.'

He opened his mouth to speak further, but at a command from one of the thugs, the eleven men of Sidi Najid's criminal enterprise rushed the pair, triggering a second charge from the locals behind them with their mismatched weaponry.

Parmenio swung his heavy curved blade as they approached, more trying to keep them at arm's length and out of the way than to actually hurt one. He smiled in satisfaction as the blow caught an unlucky bandit on the arm and cut almost to the bone, causing him to shriek and drop back. A second swing claimed no such result and, had he been facing the men alone, he would soon have been lying a bloody hacked lump on the floor. However, as he pulled back to swing a third time, the thug closest to him, snarling and pulling back

194

his blade to swipe, suddenly stopped, his eyes rolling upward to try and see what had arrested his movement.

The dark skinned local farmer wrenched his sickle tip back out of the top of the man's head, bringing pink and red matter with it, and swung the wicked implement again, this time low and facing upwards, where it disappeared into the thug's torso, the curved tip cutting up inside the ribs.

Parmenio felt a sudden elation – a thrill he rarely felt without watching a sharp ship's bow scything through the waves. With a shout, he swung the sword again. Beside him, Orsini was fighting three men on his own, including the big half-naked bully. His heavy old sword danced and flashed through the air, already gleaming metallic crimson. A stray blow caught him in the leg and for a moment, Parmenio worried that his friend was done for, but Cesare lurched upright again, using his wounded leg to pivot instead of step, and his blade lanced out, taking the big thug through the neck, cutting through windpipe and muscle, smashing bone and cartilage before ripping out below the base of the skull.

Cesare laughed as he almost staggered before heading back into the fray.

Chapter Seventeen - Of fever's grip

Skiouros stood in the white marble and golden latticework room, at the centre of the decorative floor, almost as though on trial. For some reason, although the only light source he could determine was the triple arched window that looked out over charming gardens, the periphery of the entire room remained in gloom and shadow, even the window. Any doors or exits were lost to sight and he stood in a shaft of light with no apparent source, almost as though God was illuminating him for the perusal of a hidden audience.

Curiously, even though he knew this was a dream, in the same way as he'd known the previous dozen horrible, peculiar experiences were flights of imaginative fancy, this one felt slightly different. It had the feeling of something that was at once total illusion and yet real and vital, akin to his conversations with the ghost voice of his brother in the church at Candia.

But one thing he also knew from those other dreams – nightmares? – that had beset him was that he would not be able to drag himself from this until the story had played itself out, when he would briefly surface into a sweating, uncomfortable world of swirling agonies.

He was dressed in his vestments. No surprise there. The monkish robes had become such a part of his life recently that they had figured throughout each and every dream-scene in which he had taken part.

Gradually his eyes picked out some details of the audience in the shadowed edges of the room and he realised that each of the four sides was like some sort of royal court, with its alcove or exedra containing a throne-like chair and an occupying figure.

Sultan Bayezid the Second, the Just, was familiar enough a sight that he could easily identify him, despite never having seen him except over the heads of a large crowd. The man at the opposite end, though, was similarly dressed and bore a heavy resemblance. There was no doubt in Skiouros' mind, despite his unfamiliarity with the figure, that this was prince Cem Sultan, the usurper and anathema to all things in Skiouros' heart.

To one side, below the bright windows which cast no light, a man with a stretched aquiline face wore a beehive-shaped hat and a collection of heavy robes. Of the fact that he was the Roman Pope there could be no doubt.

And opposite him…

Skiouros' already laboured and tortured heart pumped all the faster as he saw the familiar shape of Etci Hassan Reis seated, watching him with something akin to disgust.

The many other figures standing shoulder to shoulder about them were their courtiers – pashas in civil and military roles about the Ottoman brothers, officers of the navy around Hassan and robed priests about the Pope.

'What am I to do?' Skiouros asked quietly. What was the purpose of this?

He turned slowly in a circle, taking in each and every figure. Though too shadowed to make out, he could identify Mehmi standing beside his master, his squat form a giveaway. Not wishing to learn anything more than he already knew of Hassan, he crossed away from the captain, approaching the other shadows. The robes and cowled monks there were Catholic ones, not Orthodox in the manner in which he was garbed, and Innocent the Eighth watched him impassively as he approached.

'Why?' he asked again. No sounds emerged from the room other than his own breathing, and nothing moved, even the various robes staying still in the slight breeze from the window, as though every figure in the room but him had been carved from marble.

Irritated, particularly in the knowledge that this was a dream and therefore a situation of his own devising, Skiouros stepped into the edge of the penumbra, squinting, and reached out with a mix of panic and anger, grasping a monk's hood and throwing it back.

The Rhodian Knight from Tunis simply stared blankly past him. Anger gaining the upper hand, Skiouros ripped the cowls from the heads of two more monks, finding only two tonsured men he did not recognise – one grey with wild hair and the other neat and dark, with a squared beard.

'So what is this? Who are these people? Why? I don't understand.'

But somehow, somewhere deep in his soul, a small flicker of understanding *had* been lit. A fourth cowled figure among the many was of slightly below average height and thin bodied. Skiouros had a nagging, unpleasant feeling, and backed away from the shadowed monk.

'So what? I'm no monk, and I know it. As soon as I can, I will stop wearing the robes, believe me!'

Spinning, he scurried along the room's longer axis towards prince Cem Sultan.

'The same here? I know what I'll find!'

He stepped towards the men in their turbans, their faces hidden in shadow, and wrenched the first head-covering from its owner, prepared in advance and totally unsurprised to see Qaashiq the Mamluk, master of assassins and would-be killer of the great Sultan. His hand tore the turban from Hamza Bin Murad and he resisted the urge to spit at the man and punch his intolerant, hate-filled face. His hand hovered over the turban of the smaller man next in line, but he paused.

'Ah no,' he waggled his finger admonishingly. 'You'll not make me play that way. Nor will I touch Etci Hassan's imp or his friends.'

Skiouros turned and strode purposefully along the room, footsteps rapping on the marble floor and creating the only sound in the chamber. Almost eagerly he approached the pashas – the council members and generals and administrators of the Ottoman Empire – his hand coming up.

'For I know where I am and I know who I am, and I know what needs be done. And I know that when I rip the turban from this head it will be me that…'

His voice tailed away as his hand fell to his side, still gripping the turban, only to find Lykaion staring at him, a jagged red line drawn around his throat, marking the end an assassin had made of his life. The very fact of standing face to face with his brother – even recognising that Lykaion was dead and that this was in truth a fevered dream – almost unmanned Skiouros; it brought crashing in so many emotions he had kept buried.

'Lykaion…'

198

Somehow, he knew that Parmenio and Nicolo and Cesare would be in this room somewhere, and probably other people he knew and cared about even as there would be more people he loathed like Bin Murad and Etci Hassan. But while he loved and trusted his three friends, he knew that in the end, when all of this was over, his place would not be amongst them, but by his brother's side, under the benevolent gaze of the great Bayezid the Just. He could *play* the Orthodox priest all he liked, but his real place was in Istanbul, and the further he got from that great city that had been his home, the more it became true. When he had been there in the wake of Lykaion's death, he had dreamt of Crete and foreign climes, but he had not realised that those dreams were only luring him out into a great circular route that would eventually carry him back. The time was coming when he could no longer endanger his friends and he must look to the future. He smiled at the two figures who stood beside Lykaion.

Nodding his acceptance of what must be, he reached out and took the turban first from the old Romani who stood on the far flank and then – in the centre – his own head, experiencing a certainty and a feeling of peace that he had not known since the days he and his brother had lived beneath the walls of Hadrianople.

He smiled.

Blinding light struck him dazzlingly and painfully as he opened his eyes.

'Shalom,' said a friendly voice, and Skiouros felt his muscles melt in relaxation.

Chapter Eighteen - Of the endings and beginnings of journeys

It was with a certain mixed sense of relief and sadness that Skiouros eyed the crucial port city of Ceuta from the heights of the landward hills. Grateful that he had finally discarded the priests' robes, he relished the sun on his face and arms, though the black garb remained bundled with his gear. It had saved his hide more than once now.

Turning, he watched Parmenio and Nicolo bidding their friendly farewells to the latest in the chain of Berber trade caravans that had seen them safely over a thousand miles of African mountain, scrubland and wastes to the very threshold of the Kingdom of Portugal. Cesare Orsini had said his goodbyes earlier and was even now resting a little apart on a large grey rock, easing the load on his leg which, though he had managed to avoid the infection that had almost claimed Skiouros' life, was still weak from the wound he had received from the bandits in Miliana.

Relief and sadness.

The relief was palpable and obvious, and was shared by the other three friends. Though the caravan would turn south here and head for Tanjah or Fas, the defences below them marked the end of the Muslim world they had traversed – a world of wonders and greatness, and a place where they had found friendship in the most unexpected places, and yet still a world full of dangers for the four friends. His gaze returned to Ceuta. The city was crammed onto a narrow spit of land that marched out from the African coast to a large hill surmounted by a heavily fortified castle. The place seethed with life, hardly an inch of open space left within the defences.

At the near end of the spit heavy, squat walls in the Arabic style marched from one side of the isthmus to the other, a powerful drum tower at each end and a crenellated gate in the centre. A narrow channel had been dug, effectively allowing the sea itself to create a moat, and the bridge showed signs of being capable of being drawn up to render the moat impassable. The entire perimeter could not be more than three hundred yards. A small force could hold the city against a land army for ever. Of course, the production of boats by that army would soon see the place fall. Even with the scattered towers and wall stretches along the sea front, Skiouros could not see how this place remained in Portuguese hands. It could only be with the blessing of the Wattasid Sultan, for a determined man with a small fleet could surely take the city. Presumably a number of the ships wallowing in the water nearby were Portuguese warships determined to keep the Sultan's armies at bay.

Suburbs stretched out beyond the wall, filled with souks and street markets, and Skiouros felt he could see further – perhaps earlier – defensive walls almost lost in the seething centre of the city.

But despite its life, its defences, even its great castle on the hill, the sight that drew their attention and brought such relief was the port with its multiple docks housing cogs, galleys, caravels and carracks. The port meant safety. The port represented a means to finally leave Africa and return to the lands of Europe.

Relief and sadness.

Sadness likely for Skiouros alone. Turning back again, he watched the two former officers of the *Isabella* wave their thanks and then start down the slope towards him. Sadness because he knew that somehow he was going to be leaving his friends soon. Whatever path the future held for Parmenio and Nicolo, they would tread it together, perhaps seeking loans from the Medici bank in order to purchase a small Portuguese carrack and re-found their commercial 'empire'. There was no room in such a plan for Skiouros, though he felt sure they would offer a place anyway. That was what friends did. And Orsini had some – probably tedious and political – future in Genoa or possibly in the heart of the Papal lands. The nobleman would invite Skiouros to come along with him, he felt sure – their shared experiences had bound them as tightly as friends could be. He would try to help Skiouros, because that was what friends did.

But the simple fact was that Skiouros knew his future, and there was no room in it for friends. He could invite Parmenio and Nicolo and Cesare into his vengeance and he felt sure they would take his task for their own, but to do so would be to place their lives in direct peril. And Skiouros could not in conscience lead the others into the kind of danger he would face. He would cast them adrift rather than endanger them. Because that, also, was what friends did.

Somehow he would make his way from Ceuta to the states of Italia, preferably separately from Orsini to save further trouble, and there inveigle himself into the court of the Pope his friend so despised until he discovered the location of Prince Cem the usurper. Then, he would hunt down the vile enemy of the Empire and slay him, finally avenging Lykaion and the whole Ottoman world.

And somehow, he knew he would live. Since he had first decided upon his path in Crete he had been certain that the task would also see him dead, though hopefully *after* completing his task. But that almost-real, prescient dream that had wrenched him from the grip of the fever in Miliana had changed things. He knew now that he would live, because he had seen his future in that courtroom vision. His future lay in Istanbul, along with Lykaion – albeit his ghost – and the great Sultan Bayezid the Just. But it did not lie alongside Cesare or Parmenio or Nicolo.

Sadness.

But also relief for, in parting company with his friends, he saved them from the terrible dangers that would await him in Italia, and freed them to rebuild their lives after the awful fate that had almost befallen them at the hands of Etci Hassan.

Ceuta. Portugal. Europe. Safety.

'Are you coming?' Parmenio grinned as he fell in beside Skiouros, slapping him on the shoulder in a friendly manner. Even Nicolo, who only ever seemed to smile when he was joking at someone else's expense, wore a wide grin.

Relief.

'Indeed. Do you think we will be able to secure passage with what we have or will we be forced to work a few weeks as dockers to raise the funds?'

Nicolo snorted. 'Dockers? You wouldn't last a day with muscles like early-picked peas in a stringy pod.'

'No.' Parmenio smiled. 'I've done a couple of deals with our friends back there and sold on most of what we took from the bandits.

I've a purse of coin that should see all four of us back to Europe. Of course we'll be broke when we get there, but they say the world is full of possibilities in the new Spain of Isabella and Fernando.'

'Unless you're a Jew or a Moor,' Skiouros noted archly.

'Well we're not. We can sort something out once we're safely across, and we're hardly rich, so it might be a working passage, but I can talk some captain into taking us, I'm sure. Now come on. Let's get to that port and find ourselves a ship.'

Parmenio was the most animated Skiouros had seen him since their first capture and it occurred to him that the captain was only truly comfortable at sea. Two months of being trapped on land must be for him what two months at sea would be for Skiouros. Of course, the young Greek knew he had the worst record with sea travel, but the trip across the straits would be a matter of hours at most, and in relatively secure conditions.

He began to relax a little as they strolled on down the slope, collecting Cesare where he reclined on the rock and helping him to his feet. The leg wound had ruined the muscle in his left thigh above the knee and the Jewish doctor in Miliana had shaken his head and told them that it would be months before he could expect full strength, and that he would need to rest it as much as possible while it healed.

The four friends walked slowly down the slope at Cesare's stilted pace, gradually joining the coast road that led into the suburbs and towards the walls. A few locals – farmers, traders and the like – went hither and thither along the dusty road. Insects buzzed and birds chirped. The sounds of port life rose from the city ahead. Orange trees and eucalyptus provided a strange yet enticing scent to welcome them to the western terminus of their journey.

Slowly but happily they strode down into the suburb and past markets, shops, gardens and houses, Parmenio and Nicolo stepping out ahead, deep in some sort of naval and mercantile discussion, presumably planning the coming journey.

Skiouros was happy enough to amble along behind at Cesare's pace, as long as the others stayed close enough.

He smiled.

'You will not lose *me* so easily, you realise, Master Skiouros.'

The young Greek turned, frowning, to his friend. 'Sorry?'

'I can see the battle in your heart. It is as clear and as troubling for you as the war you fought against your fever. You would love to revel in our newfound security in the same happy manner as our friends, but you cannot. I have seen the way you look at them; at me. As soon as we cross the straits you will drop us all in the kindest fashion you can manage, and then rush off on your vengeful task.'

'I just want to get to Spain or Portugal.'

'Drivel. You have ever been a man of purpose, even though sometimes that purpose has taken a back place to current necessities. And since your fever broke, I have seen that resolve harden to a diamond. You are on task and with a goal in mind.'

'It is *my* goal, though. My task. My danger to face.'

'You can leave Parmenio and Nicolo. They'll argue and regret it, but they'll let you go, because they think that you have some great, glorious future planned. You and I know that where you go there is naught but peril and pain. No man worth his salt would leave a friend to that alone.'

'I cannot ask for help.'

'Then don't. Just accept it when it is offered.'

'You don't understand...' Skiouros said quietly.

'I fear that I do, Master Skiouros. You hunt the one remaining man responsible for your brother's death. I do not know who that man might be, but he is powerful and well protected, else you would have gone for him long ago and not spent years preparing yourself.'

'How could you...?'

'You are transparent,' Cesare interrupted with a smile, 'to a man with keen eyes. You're a man who abhors of death and killing. You are no warrior, and we both know that. You fight when you must, but you take no joy in it, and you handle a blade as though it might bite you. And yet you paid good money to learn how to use one. So wherever you go, you expect a great deal of trouble. And a Greek living in the Ottoman Empire studies Italian, and maps of the peninsula, and even learns what he can of the Pope and his lands? I think we can dispense with the dissembling. Whoever you seek is in my homeland and tied up with the court of Innocent the Eighth, yes?'

Skiouros sagged. He hoped it was only his intuitive friend who had pieced all this together and that he was less transparent to others.

'Yes, Cesare.'

'How do you plan to achieve your goals?'

'That I must work out when I am closer to them.'

'And how much easier will your task be with a native nobleman who has access to wealth, transport and the ears of the powerful walking the path by your side?'

'Considerably,' Skiouros conceded.

'Then when we are safely in Cadiz, I will seek a banker, withdraw funds and we will take ship for Genoa. I have distant familial connections with the Visconti family on my mother's side, and they still maintain a palazzo in the city, despite having lost their rule to the Sforzas. The Palazzo Visconti will be a comfortable home for us while we plan your next move. I am in no hurry to return to the bosom of my sickening family, so a rest in Genoa would be most welcome.'

'I have nothing to offer you in return.'

'I was not aware I had asked for payment,' Cesare smiled. 'Money is one thing my family do not lack. Morals, yes. Piety, yes. Love, yes. Money: no.'

Skiouros smiled at his friend. 'It is a shame Lykaion will never meet you. I suspect you would have liked each other.'

The pair lapsed into easy conversation as they passed beneath the gate in the city walls, Parmenio and Nicolo ahead having spoken to the Portuguese soldiers on duty and gained entry into the city. Ceuta was a strange place – a mix of the Arabic and the European. Very ornate buildings that would not look out of place in the great cities of Spain or Italia stood to either side of souks with covers to shade them from the sun, dark skinned men of Berber descent selling their wares in the shadows and drinking khave. Lighter skinned men served wine in taverns – a sight unseen since they had left Crete and entered the Muslim world. With a great deal of relief the friends drank in all the sights, smells and sounds as they made their way to the port at the centre of the isthmus.

'You said you'd been here before,' Skiouros smiled at Parmenio. 'I can see that now. You navigate the streets like a native.'

'I've done business here and in Melilla, and at Tanjah too. I've traded in Malaga, Cadiz and even Faro. Not been this way for a good seven or eight years now, but it feels a little like home.'

'I speak three languages,' Skiouros laughed. 'More than anyone I knew back home. And yet still we find ourselves in a place where I cannot communicate, for they all rattle on in Arabic and… Portuguese, I'm guessing that throaty language is?'

'It's like a sharper Spanish, yes. You'll be alright with people in the port. Nearly any captain, ship's officer or trader out here has at least a little command of Italian. Between the Medici financial Empire and the traders of Genoa and Venezia, Italian is the international language of commerce.'

A few minutes later, as Parmenio chattered away on the subject of trade and Empires and languages – some parts of it fascinating, many altogether lost on Skiouros – they arrived at the port.

Two wide arms of shaped stone reached out to embrace the sea, forming a harbour of calm water with gentle, lapping waves. Ships of all shapes and sizes sat at berth and Skiouros noted with interest the vast array of different colours denoting the nationality of the traders. He could see Venetian vessels as well as those bearing the infamous colours of aggressive, expansionist Spain. Others that were faintly familiar would be Genoese or Neapolitan or even Sicilian.

'What is that one?' he asked, pointing at a large carrack as they passed.

'That flag is England's. A nation of cold, hard men and frigid women forever warring amongst themselves. See also the French vessels and there, a Swede of the Hanseatic league.'

Skiouros narrowed his eyes as they strode across the dock.

'If there are so many nations here, could we book passage elsewhere?'

'Such as where?'

Skiouros faltered for a moment.

'Perhaps for Cesare to return to Genoa?'

Parmenio laughed. 'You've clearly never dealt with a Genoese trader. With apologies to Master Orsini here, the Genoese are tighter than a mermaid's underwear. Their purses have three padlocks on them. Even their wives won't lift their skirts without a sign of coin! If we pooled all the money we have it would not buy passage for *one* of us to Genoa. No. Our best hope is for a cheap journey to the other side of the straits and to see what we can do from there.'

Skiouros sighed. For a moment he had pictured Cesare and himself sailing out over the great sea towards that Palazzo Visconti of which his friend had spoken.

'This one,' Parmenio announced, pointing to a carrack that had clearly seen better days, its hull peeling and discoloured and pock-marked with barnacles. The sails had been patched so often that there was little to be seen of the original material. Skiouros peered at the ship's name, the paint almost faded to the same colour as the hull.

'*Repolho*?'

Nicolo grinned. '*Cabbage*. Says it all. Think it reminds him of the *Isabella*!'

Skiouros couldn't help but laugh despite the sharp irritated look Parmenio threw at them both.

'Ho!' he shouted up, and a sailor with ridiculously wild curly black hair and a neat beard, naked to the waist, leaned over the rail.

'*O que tu queres?*'

Parmenio cleared his throat and began a brief conversation that flowed completely over Skiouros' head. A few moments later the curly haired sailor disappeared and then returned with a man in elegant red and gold doublet and russet breeches, his hair tied back from his eyes in a tail with a crimson ribbon.

'*O que voce gostaria?*'

'Do you mind if we speak Italian, Captain?' Parmenio replied. 'So that my companions can understand, you see.'

'If you wish. What can I do for you? Danilo tells me you wish to book passage to Cadiz?'

'That's right. We are not overburdened with funds, I am afraid, but two of us are professional sailors and even the other two are hard workers. We can supplement our payment with labour?'

'That is not the issue, my friend. We go not to Cadiz, but to Palos. Is that of use to you?

Skiouros shrugged and looked across at Parmenio. 'Is it?'

'Best part of twenty leagues further up the coast. Fine by me. I can always make my way back to Cadiz, or perhaps we can move round to Faro. That's another big port. Palos is big and busy enough, but it's too closely scrutinised by the authorities for my liking – favourite port of the Spanish crown.'

Skiouros rolled his eyes. The *Isabella*'s captain would walk at *least* twenty leagues to save paying an extortionate berthing fee.

'I see no problem. At least we're in Europe then. Cesare?'

Orsini nodded with an easy shrug.

'How much do you have?' the captain asked.

Without replying – it would have been difficult to list the coins in his purse, given the varied nationalities and denominations – Parmenio simply unhooked the purse from his belt and tossed it up to the *Repolho*'s captain, who deftly caught it and examined its contents. His face, for the briefest of moments, took on a disappointed cast, and then he smiled.

'You'll have to work quite hard! Alright. Four men to Palos de la Frontera. We sail on the morning tide, which should see us in Palos for sunset. Get yourselves somewhere to sleep for the night. I would recommend the Plucked Chicken three streets along. It's a little on the cheap and dirty side, but I figure that's what you need. Here,' he added, flicking a coin back down. 'You'll need this.'

Skiouros smiled. After the trade caravans, even a poor inn would be a palace to the friends.

One more night in Ceuta and they would leave Africa for good.

Chapter Nineteen - Of old adversaries

Mehmi, son of Ibrahim the goat thief and a black-hearted motherless mother, lurched as the ship's boat bounced against the solid dock, shedding fragments of black and red paint. His eyes remained fixed on the curve of the wide river as it swept around the headland on which the town stood and on out of sight, past the wide marshy land on the far bank. Somewhere, a mile and more back that way, lay the three kadirga galleys of Kemal Reis' fleet.

His eyes swept slowly up from the broad expanse of water and the variety of ships that rode at anchor along its length, past the low cliffs and up the steep slope of brown, parched grass, past the great church of San Jorge, to the squat, russet coloured fortress that dominated the top of the slope and marked the summit of the town. Streets of low white buildings curved and wound about the hill below that weighty reminder of Spanish power.

It should irritate him to be here, in the same way it was clearly irking the officers of the three boats. That castle was built in the Arabic mould, and would not have looked out of place in a good Muslim city – as one would expect, given that it had been built by the faithful and had remained in their hands for more than four centuries until the Christians had begun their scouring of the peninsula. The fact that a Moorish-built fortress dominated the sprawling, grand church beneath it was of no comfort. The very sight of the once important bastion of Islam that now lived happily under the rule of the heretical Christian church had set the captains Kemal, Hassan and Salih's teeth on edge, though clearly for different reasons.

Mehmi knew the three men well after years of service. He knew that the fleet captain – his excellency Ahmed Kemaleddin Reis, most honourable Defender of the Emirate of Granada and representative of the Sultan Bayezid the Second – saw it with sadness as a sign of his failure to protect Muslim interests here; as a reminder that he was mopping up the mess of his own impotence and loss. Captain Salih Bin Abdullah saw it with some trepidation. The taciturn lesser Reis had voiced his unhappiness about all three commanders entering such a place with inadequate guard, and his concerns clearly still plagued him.

But Mehmi knew Etci Hassan Reis best of all and, looking at him now, standing erect in the boat despite its bouncing and swaying, his ice-grey gaze razing the strongholds and churches as it passed, he could see the captain's nails biting into his palms. Hassan felt no sadness or loss; no trepidation or worry. Etci Hassan Reis felt only bitter, icy rage. To him the city represented a plague that had ruptured the skin of the world and which should be incised with the sterile knife of Islam.

Hassan burned to fire the non-Muslim world and watch it turn to ash.

Mehmi shuddered.

Him? He felt some fear, for certain. No hate or sadness, but the very idea of setting foot in this place, which was beloved of the Muslim-hating queen Isabella, made his blood run that little bit colder. His eyes dropped back again to the headland that hid the distant ships.

All three vessels had been left with almost full crews at anchor out near the river's mouth, in the narrow channel that separated the Isla de Saltes from the far bank, where they were out of sight – and therefore out of mind – of the Christian ships bobbing about in the river. Indeed, they were well positioned, under Kemal's orders, just so as to be out of sight of all shipping and yet ready to put to sea quickly and easily if placed under pressure.

Even the cannon were loaded ready.

Mehmi had felt a little better and that tiniest bit more relaxed every day since they had left Tunis and the cursed priest behind, though his relief had been stunted somewhat by the captain's mood. Though the curse had apparently lifted from the ship and nothing untoward had occurred since Tunis, the events there had soured Etci Hassan's mood to such an extent that he had begun to wake in the night, pacing the deck of the *Yarim Ay* and cursing the world for sending him Brother Skiouros and his companions. The captain's already infamous temper had amplified alarmingly, and no crewman now willingly approached their commander, generally fighting to stay out of his way.

For Hassan had put to death three men in that first week alone for minor infractions of his rules that warranted no more than a slap on the hand. The captain had become a curse to his men with just as harsh effect as that which had taken three men near Greece. Hassan appeared – to Mehmi at least – to be on the verge of becoming dangerously unbalanced. The second in command gave himself a mirthless smile at that little private joke as he watched Hassan step up onto the dock, tottering for a moment on his still-weak foot.

Even if Hassan's smashed metatarsals ever fully healed, which seemed unlikely given the absence of sympathetic medics along the African coast and Hassan's unwillingness to consult a Jew, Mehmi doubted now that the captain would ever lift his sights from the priest who had so wounded him. The *Yarim Ay* had been in the straits of the Jebel Tariq for weeks now and still no word had come concerning the escaped slaves. Even Mehmi felt sure that unless the villains had managed to flee the net completely, Sidi Najid would have sent word to them by now.

The meeting with the fleet commander and Captain Salih had been smooth and remarkably quiet. Mehmi had expected some remonstrance over their delay, but had not really been surprised that the two other captains had seemed to have been happy with Hassan's prolonged absence. He himself would quite like to be out of his lord's company for a while.

The supplies had been ferried between ships quickly and efficiently, even in the seething summer heat, and no hint of the small remains of their private treasure – little more than a pittance compared with that which they had carried before Tunis – had been uncovered by their counterparts on the other two galleys.

Mehmi watched as Hassan righted himself on the dock and took stock of the city, and stepped forward resignedly to join his captain. His hand went reassuringly to the knife at his belt as his eyes scoured the Christian city above and before him.

The blade was a beautiful piece taken from the body of a Mamluk sea captain some years previously. Damascus steel and with only a six-inch blade, it was decorated in a Turkish twisting pattern, with a hilt and sheath of gleaming silver. A single emerald set in the pommel provided the only colour to a knife otherwise the hue of shimmering moonlight.

A strange brick structure stood before them, close to the dock, and it took Mehmi a moment to notice the babbling stream of water that issued from beneath its quadrifons arch and down into a flat brick channel, where a drain emptied the overflow into the river next to the dock. There were fragments of stucco clinging to the brick with clumps of ruined paintings. This once rich decorative fountain held a prominent position and a number of sailors were filling small barrels and skins to transport back to their ships, while local women and urchins filled buckets and old men dipped in mugs to recover from the sizzling early August sun.

Behind the structure, an open area of flat ground and then grassy hillside ran up to the oppressive, almost featureless brick walls of the large church, though a market covered almost all the open ground. Presumably a permanent feature, given the state of the ground and the form of the stalls, this appeared to be the main mercantile meeting place of Palos' dock area. Behind the huge market and inland from the church, the town spread across the slope, shimmering in the blistering temperatures.

Mehmi turned as he stepped fully onto solid ground, the six accompanying crewmen clambering ashore behind him. Half a dozen large ships sat in the wide open channel of the river – caravels, carracks and a cog, their numerous ships' boats intermingling with the local skiffs and fishing vessels to create a swarm across the river's surface that made it look as busy as the market ashore.

Palos de la Frontera teemed with life.

'Mehmi!'

The diminutive Turk almost leaped from the ground at the sudden snap of the captain's voice. He turned and tried not to look panicked as his heart thumped fast and loud in his chest.

'Lord?'

'Keep your gaze on the crew. If a single eyeball strays to those infidel djinn-ridden stalls, I want it ripped out and pinned to the ship's hull as a reminder of what we are.'

Mehmi shuddered, but nodded and gave a half bow to cover his apparent weakness. Hassan seemed not to notice. Hardly a surprise. The captain spent most of his time these days wandering the corridors of his own mind, winding the cogs of hatred and bile and sinking ever deeper into a pit of violence and irrationality.

Etci Hassan took a few paces and fell in beside the grey-bearded form of the great Reis Kemal and the genial face of the handsome captain Salih. The three men could hardly be any more different, and yet between them they represented not only Ottoman interests in the western sea, but also those of *all* Muslims in this particular place.

Kemal had made sure they knew that in their last meeting the previous night, aboard the flagship. He had impressed upon his captains and their seconds that he would brook no failure in diplomacy or manners on this most delicate visit. The relationship between their majesties Fernando and Isabella and the great Ottoman Empire were tense and not a long stretch from open war, and despite the provocation it might cause, it was quite conceivable that the local authorities might just decide to hang the entire Turkish party as pirates or coastal raiders without preamble. Ironic, really, in Mehmi's opinion, given that they had practiced piracy halfway across the great sea and only here, in these waters, had they fallen back into legality.

'Remember,' Kemal Reis said, his wise eyes, surrounded by the creases of age and care, playing across the men under his command, 'that we are here as an embassy in the name of the Sultan and not as an invading force... *or* a "cleansing fire of Islam".' This last had clearly been aimed at Etci Hassan, on whom the commander's gaze had finally come to rest.

Salih Bin Abdullah smiled as he bowed and Mehmi noticed a sly flick of the eyes towards his fellow captain. Hassan simply stood silent and impassive, his cold eyes busily killing, raping and pillaging everything they fell upon.

A man in a red robe that almost covered a large paunch wrapped in black silk and wearing some sort of chain of office around his fat neck strode over towards the new arrivals. His puffy, bald, sweaty face was filled with officious power and Mehmi could not help but notice the small knot of half a dozen men in tunics which bore the arms of Castile – red lion on white and gold castle on red – standing close behind him, ready for trouble with their pikes held aloft, yet in tight grips.

The man babbled something in their strange, ophidian tongue and the entire party turned to look at Salih Reis. While Kemal had some small ability with the tongue, only Salih had a full command of it, and the smiling captain nodded his understanding and turned to his companions.

'This is the dockmaster. He is, I surmise, unhappy with our presence.'

Mehmi almost smiled. He had seen the dockmaster's face and could well imagine the sort of words the man had truly used – Salih had paraphrased fairly heavily.

Kemal Reis sketched a deep bow in the Spanish fashion, drawing a sneer from Hassan, and then smiled.

'Forgive us, Excellency' – almost certainly an over-pompous honorific for such a minor bureaucrat, but one that eased the tension in the man's face as Salih translated – 'We are here in the form of diplomats only. We seek to cause no distress or harm to the inhabitants of your fair city; only to negotiate the freedom of a number of enemies of your crown that remain in custody.'

He waited as Salih translated and then the official paused in thought before replying.

'The dockmaster says that you must mean the *'moros'* in the *carcel* – the jail. He says that many are calling for their death and that you will have to be very persuasive if you wish to convince the Duke of Medina Sidonia's senior representative to release them.'

Mehmi sagged a little. The name of the brutal Medina Sidonia was well known for his hatred of the Moors that he saw as having infected and enslaved his nation. The negotiations would be tense, even if it were just some lackey they dealt with – which it would be, of course.

The information that almost thirty Muslims had refused to convert to the Catholic Church, but had also failed to leave the country, had reached Kemal Reis through contacts in the ports of Africa. The imprisoned group had been attempting to live a quiet life, unnoticed and forgotten in a small village in the hills below Monte Cebollar, but their religious practices had been observed by a passing merchant and they had found themselves in short order in a locked cell in nearby Palos. Their fate remained uncertain until Medina Sidonia confirmed his decision, but Kemal had decided that such men deserved rescue more than most and so had risked the lives of his men to negotiate with the Spanish lords.

'Inform the dockmaster that we would like to visit the Duke's officer and open negotiations with him. Could he direct us to the appropriate building?'

Another pause for translating and Mehmi clenched his teeth as he saw the fat man shake his head and spread his sausage-like fingers in refusal.

'The dockmaster says we are not to be permitted our freedom in the city. By civic law he should report us to the Duke's man and we should be allowed no further than the dock until he authorizes it, which he undoubtedly will not do. Even so, should permission *be* granted, we will be forbidden from bearing arms in the city.'

Etci Hassan's gaze slid slowly to the man, his ice-grey eyes flaying the flesh from the fat man's bones.

'Tell this piece of pig offal that if he speaks to us with such disrespect again I will tear off his face and mount it on my ship.'

Kemal's restraining hand came across and pressed on Hassan's chest, causing him to turn an all-the-more furious look on his own commander.

'You will say no such thing,' Kemal said quietly to Salih, though the other captain was unlikely to have done so anyway. 'You will ask the man, using every honorific you can dredge up, whether there is any way we can be escorted to the official in charge and preferably not entirely unarmed, since we are emissaries of a foreign power.'

Salih relayed the question and an expression more open to possibilities began to fall across the fat face.

'The dockmaster says he will be willing to escort the commanders to the office, but their *'pirates''* – a smile at this word – 'must remain on the dock.'

Mehmi experienced a moment of relief at the possibility that he might have to remain 'safely' by the water. Kemal gave a genuine chuckle, though Hassan looked as though he might burst into flame at any moment.

'Tell the man that I am most grateful,' the senior captain replied. 'Would his excellency be willing to extend the offer to our seconds in command? He must understand that they serve in a clerkish fashion as well as being sailors and we are loath to leave behind their expertise.'

Mehmi felt his spirits sink once more – he would have to go after all.

'I will not place myself in peril at the hands of these heathen animals,' Hassan spat. 'I will remain here with the soldiers while you walk into their prison, and when you fail to return I can take your ships back to sea and do something more productive with them.'

Salih's eyes shot across to his counterpart, while his hand went to the pommel of his sword, causing a ripple of similar action throughout the crowd. More guards suddenly appeared as if from nowhere, bringing the sum of local men-at-arms to around two dozen. Salih carefully took his hand from the pommel and rattled something off in Spanish to the dockmaster, presumably trying to explain that any threat had been meant towards his own companion and not the locals.

Kemal, his usually benevolent features displaying a rare true anger, turned to Etci Hassan, whose own hand was now resting upon his sword hilt.

'Your words come dangerously close to mutiny, Hassan. Bear in mind what punishment I might consider meting out in response to treachery from my own.'

'I am no traitor,' Hassan snarled. 'I mean only to protect our backs here while you walk into the lion's mouth.'

'Under no circumstances will you ever persuade me to leave you alone, armed and with soldiers under your command in the company of Christians. You are not to be trusted, Hassan Reis. You will accompany us, where I can be certain of your actions and that they do not embarrass both myself and the great Sultan Bayezid. Take your hand from your sword before I have it sawn off and present it to the dockmaster as an apology for the insult.'

Mehmi actually stepped back at the words, moving a little away as if pushed aside by the commander's ire. Even Hassan actually blinked in surprise. The great Kemal did not lose his cool. He was almost famed for his even temper and carefully considered words, and it was a sign of just how close to the edge Hassan was treading that he had managed to elicit such a response.

Not for the first time these past months, Mehmi wondered about the health of his captain's mind. Was Etci Hassan coming apart at the seams?

The captain of the *Yarim Ay* was so furious that he was vibrating ever so slightly, controlling his own anger through clenched teeth. After almost a minute of visibly forcing himself to calm down, Hassan spoke through gritted teeth, his hand falling back down to his side, where it continually gripped and ungripped, his nails digging into his ruined palm.

'My apologies, great Reis. I meant no insult. My wounded foot aches and drives me to unnecessary anger.'

It was a fake act of contrition and they all knew it, but it appeared to be enough to mollify the commander for now, and he nodded his acceptance and turned back to the dockmaster. Behind him Hassan moved sharply, taking the weight from his bad foot, and Mehmi had the momentarily but very real fear that his captain might draw his knife and murder the commander there and then.

216

It would be easy and, were it not for the presence of Salih and the crews of the other two kadirga, he might well have done so. For sure, the Spaniards would not intervene to save a Turk.

Now, they were surrounded by an arc of local soldiers bearing the arms of Castile, with the water at their back.

Mehmi turned his head and looked longingly at the river and its promise of freedom. Spanish ships wallowed as small boats continually ferried goods and supplies across to them from the dock and the shoreline. It almost looked like a fleet preparing to sail and it worried him for a moment that the authorities were moving against the Turkish ships near the river's mouth. But they could not yet know where the kadirga were, and could not possibly have had the time to begin preparations for sailing against them this quickly.

'They shall not take my blade,' Hassan said with quiet steel, drawing Mehmi's attention back to the confrontation.

'They have not asked for it,' Kemal replied equally calmly and with an arched brow. 'But nonetheless you will keep it sheathed unless *I* command otherwise.'

A silent battle of wills appeared to be waged between the two captains and Hassan was the first to break their locked gaze as he reached out to one of his men standing behind Mehmi, snapping his fingers. Without the need to enquire further, the sailor unshouldered his matchlock musket and passed it over.

Kemal's arched eyebrow rose a little.

'Going hunting, Hassan?'

'I prefer to arm myself adequately when walking into the arms of my enemy, Lord,' Hassan replied in his quiet, deadly tone.

The dockmaster burbled away in Spanish and Salih coughed and pointed at the gun over the captain of the *Yarim Ay*'s shoulder.

'His excellency is asking what this is?' Mehmi smiled as he realised that the Spaniards had probably never seen muskets in action. These people were so backwards and barbaric they had only just learned to use cannon.

'Tell him...' Kemal glanced at his underling and sighed in resignation. 'Tell him it is a badge of office. Nothing more.'

Hassan glared at the Spaniards while the next round of translation began and finally the dockmaster shrugged and gestured towards the town.

Mehmi watched as his captain fell in line behind Salih at the rear, his piercing grey gaze raking the guards and the locals alike as he cast his displeasure and disdain around at Palos and its occupants. The captain of the *Yarim Ay* cared not for his situation.

With a deep breath, Mehmi followed on, throwing a last longing look at the water and its seething collection of small craft and large merchant vessels.

He would give good money to be out at sea right now. And it would be nice to say that he was free of cursed witch-priests at last, but his nervous gaze strayed once more towards the great russet bulk of the church of San Jorge above them.

Resigned to a troubled fate he sucked air through his teeth and spat on the ground, tugging madly at his earlobe, trying to protect them all from the hell into which they walked.

Chapter Twenty - Of merchants and madmen

'It's almost as busy as the Theodosian harbour back home,' smiled Skiouros as he leaned over the rail between his friends.

'Not bad for a small town with only a riverside dock,' Parmenio nodded. 'Looking at what's going on at the moment, there's probably as many people on the river as there are in the town. Palos is not large.'

'I've never seen anything like it. Captain Agostinho must be a damn good sailor to navigate all that.'

Parmenio turned a sour look on the young Greek. 'I've done as much myself a dozen times. Sometimes in this very river.'

The journey from the open sea, perhaps five miles or more, had been an education for Skiouros in the fine art of ship steering. The river was many hundreds of yards across – far from a narrow channel – but the sheer volume of craft clogged it tight, from large mercantile caravels and carracks, through a smaller cog, down to perhaps hundreds of fishing vessels, barges, small traders, tugs and ship's boats. The good ship 'Cabbage' had been forced to move at the most inordinately slow pace, allowing tiny boats to paddle and edge out of its path, while itself weaving between the larger vessels moored in the deeper water at the river's centre.

Not once had they touched the hull of even a small fisherman. Skiouros was certain that had he been on the tiller, they would have sunk two dozen ships by now. But then, had he been on the tiller they'd have run aground before ever they had reached this shipping maze.

219

Now, they were finally drifting to a halt, not far from the heavy cog that displayed the Portuguese flag and two heavy, low barges which must have come down from Moguer and Huelva. Even as Skiouros peered at the riverside dock which teemed with life, he heard the strange garbled Portuguese tongue and the splash as the anchor dropped, signifying the end of their journey and their long-awaited return to Europe.

It was almost over.

Skiouros watched briefly as the ship's boat was lowered to the river's fast-flowing surface with a splash and two sailors descended to it on a rope ladder. As they began to load a few small bags and unshipped the oars, Skiouros returned his attention to the town on the hill, dominated by a heavy, low fortress and a featureless Catholic church. Most of the town was of white plastered walls, winding around the hill above a market that would give even Istanbul's bazaars a run for their money. But despite the market, as a conurbation Palos was, in his opinion, nothing special. In the last few years he had seen the seething metropolis of Istanbul, the great fortress city of Candia on Crete, the sprawling ruins of Carthage and Tugga, the steaming souks of Tunis and the powerful port of Ceuta. Somehow, this small, almost provincial hill town with its disproportionately busy dock and market seemed a deflating sight, considering its importance and what it meant for him personally.

Somewhere among those stalls behind the dock or between the white houses on the hill, Skiouros and Cesare would have to say their farewells to Parmenio and Nicolo and then make their way towards the fractured ever-warring states of Italia. He hoped the two sailors would understand; was fairly sure they would. Cesare had stated his intentions to draw extra funding from the Medici House when he found it and pay the sailors a heavy subsidy that would give Parmenio a leg up to rebuilding his life. Shared adversity made brothers of the most dissimilar of men.

'*No barco!*' shouted a sailor nearby and Skiouros frowned.

'Into the boat,' Parmenio translated as he made his way along the rail and prepared to climb down. Nicolo followed, then Skiouros and Cesare. Negotiating the rope ladder and its wet, salt-encrusted surface with legs made unstable by the rolling gait of the ship was interesting, and Skiouros was forced to divert all of his attention to the task, sending up a quick thank you to the divine for not fumbling as he set foot in the small boat and took his seat.

It was only as they started to move and his eyes fell upon that hulking church on the hill that he realised once again the prayer he had cast up was of the most strange, eclectic type, consisting of part doctrinal Orthodox prayer, part heartfelt personal gratitude and part learned-by-rote Muslim offering. If God – whoever he truly was – was actually listening in to the prayers of this particular fabricated priest, the random mix of faiths and languages must be giving him an almighty divine headache.

As they crossed the river, nipping lightly between other boats with the two men on the oars yelling at their counterparts nearby and his other three companions watching the dock approach, Skiouros amused himself by wondering what the local Catholic priest would say if he dropped in at that monstrous church and sent up such a prayer in a mix of Greek and Arabic. This particular worshipper would probably find himself stretched to snapping point or burning at the stake within an hour.

One thing he had heard about the Spanish church during his sojourn on Crete and his constant visits to Saint Titus was that they had absolutely no sense of humour. Another was the dim view they took of 'heresy'. Perhaps he would give that brooding building a wide berth.

The four men had their gear – such as it was – in the boat with them. One meagre bag apiece, along with the swords they had acquired from the brigands in Africa – in Cesare's case the old knight-priest's plain blade. Not much to show for a lifetime's possessions but, when added to the fact that those lives were still being lived despite everything, it was something to be immensely grateful for.

Skiouros reached out, as the boat rocked in time with the oars, for the blade wrapped in his cloak to examine its strange curved, exotic beauty but saw Nicolo shaking his head with a dark expression. In the climate of the new Spain bearing an Arabic weapon openly might be a fast track to losing one's liberty again.

Instead, he watched the boats around them as they approached the shore, making for an area of gravelled landing rather than the purpose-built dock that seethed with a constant ant's nest of activity.

Even discounting the numerous fishermen, there were still a huge number of boats and small vessels carrying goods ashore from some ships and from the land to others. Traders and barges sold their wares to the merchants of Palos, while other boats supplied their vessels for new journeys.

Skiouros leaned back with a smile.

It was pretty much unprecedented.

221

A sea journey without incident.

He had been beginning to think that he was cursed with regard to ships, and had undertaken their latest voyage with the greatest of trepidation, wondering whether God would choose this time to sink them – sinking was about the only naval horror that had so far passed Skiouros by – or perhaps have them eaten by a giant fish like the 'sheol' of the prophet Jonah. But now they were here, perhaps fifty feet from land – certainly not deep enough water for a man-swallowing fish no matter how angry God might be. And even with his somewhat poor swimming skills – once likened by Lykaion to a blind bear on a spinning top – he could make it ashore if the worst happened here

The young man drifted off into a pleasant reverie filled with images of his youth and the brother he had lost, before the days of the Devsirme and of plots and murders. A minute or two later, the boat hit the gravel and crunched up onto the shore, shaking him from a pleasant image of the village church he had once climbed with his brother – the trigger as it happened of Lykaion's fear of heights. Skiouros lurched from his seat with the sudden thump and almost fell into the bottom of the boat, reaching out and gripping the side to stop himself.

Parmenio thanked the sailors on behalf of the four of them and stepped out of the boat onto the riverbank, reaching up and stretching, then retrieving his bag and wrapped sword. Nicolo followed, and then the other two, and Skiouros felt an unexpected thrill run through him at his return to Christian lands, albeit rabid Catholic ones that probably considered his native church every bit as heretical as the Jews and Arabs.

His boots crunched on the gravel and he smiled as they moved off onto the narrow stretch of grass that separated the river from the huge market. As soon as they were on flat, solid ground and the men of the *Repolho* had departed to locate the official on the dock, Parmenio stopped and held up his hand for the others to do so.

'I don't know what the plan is from here, gentlemen, but I would heartily recommend that you leave all the talking to me.'

'That should not be a problem,' Cesare smiled, 'given that we do not speak the language.'

'And I know this place and its people and how to handle things in a port.'

Nicolo nodded his agreement. 'He's right.'

222

'Very well,' the captain smiled. 'We've not truly discussed it before except in the barest and vaguest of ways, but what are the plans from here?'

Skiouros felt the lump rise in his throat. Now that the time was upon him, he found that he could not quite summon up the words to say farewell.

'Perhaps we could think about that in the morning?' he suggested in a hoarse voice. 'We're finally here after months of trouble and the possibility of spending a normal evening and night in a Christian inn with a good strong wine and non-dogmatically-authorised foods. Let's just have a night to reward ourselves.'

Orsini, who had clearly seen through Skiouros' words to the heart of his difficulty, took pity upon him and smiled. 'Yes. Let's have a night to remember.'

'You are aware, I presume,' Parmenio sighed, 'that our entire monetary reserve might just stretch to a crust of bread. Unless you intend to take up brigandage, how are we to pay for our night of debauchery? The sun is already starting to sink to the west and we cannot even afford a room for the night without selling one of our swords. You two young 'uns might be able to sell your arses on the docks for a comfy night, but Nicolo and me wouldn't raise a copper for our efforts.' He smiled.

Cesare pursed his lips. 'I presume there is a house of the Medici in this place, given its busy mercantile nature?'

'There is. Up near the church, in the main square.'

'Then the grand Orsini coffers, filled with the profits of Papal usury and Condotierri murderers, shall pay for our revels and for the grandest rooms Palos can spare.'

'That is extraordinarily generous, Master Orsini.'

'It is the least I can do. And believe me when I say that you could offer to buy the good ship '*Cabbage*' and it would be little more than a drip in the cistern that is the Orsini's account. My friends, we will live tonight if not like kings, then at least like minor dukes.'

Parmenio grinned and a look passed across Nicolo's face that Skiouros could read without a translator: 'Drink. Meat. Whores. Comfortable pillow.'

'It is settled, then,' Orsini laughed. 'Lead us to the Medici house, captain, and we will begin the first evening of our new lives.'

And the last of our old, Skiouros added mentally, still filled with a surprisingly powerful sense of loss at the thought of their impending departure.

With a strange sad smile and the sagging frame of a man who has surrendered himself to relaxation after tense weeks on end of privation, Skiouros traipsed off into the market, following the others. As they passed, Nicolo and Parmenio occasionally paused at some stall or other, examining the items on sale, commenting on their value or lack thereof. Orsini occasionally joined in their comments, but regularly threw a worried and sympathetic glance back at the young man at the rear. Skiouros, for his part, trudged along behind, his mind blessedly free of almost all thought. The simple fact that nothing urgent demanded his attention was fresh and relaxing.

It seemed that perhaps half the stalls at most were actual repositories of wares. The rest were stands where merchants could display samples of the goods they had warehoused. Palos must do a vast trade – it was no wonder that it charged exorbitant docking fees and was so beloved of the crown.

'See that idiot?' laughed Parmenio as he waved aside a merchant and stepped on up the gentle incline. 'Two pistoles for the whole consignment. How do people like that turn a profit? I couldn't buy such goods in Venezia or Candia for less than four. I could *sell* it for *eight*. I'd forgotten how much I like this place. The uncertainty of its proximity to the southern emirs brings all sorts of desperate and unsavoury types. A man could get rich here, so long as he can afford the port fees.'

Skiouros smiled. Given what he knew of Parmenio's struggle to maintain his business in recent years, he had to wonder how many bad investments the captain had made if he could have become rich from the markets of Palos but instead had scrabbled for cheap commissions in Crete.

Orsini, a few steps in front, attacked the thought from another angle.

'You say you could turn a hefty profit?'

'Undoubtedly. If I could guarantee the safety of the ship between here and Venezia or Candia, I could double my investment at the very least with each trip. Probably triple it!'

'And if you were willing to sail longer journeys, you could stay close to the coast around Spain and France, where piracy is all but erased?'

'It would eat into the profit a little, for sure, but it would still be a lucrative run, especially with Nicolo here involved. Guaranteed that if

224

I can spot half a dozen sound investments here, my acute friend has already seen twice that many and mentally ear-marked them.'

Cesare smiled.

'Then we will have to see what funds my unwholesome family are willing to extend me as it drips through the grasping claws of the Medici. Perhaps the *Isabella* should sail again?'

Nicolo narrowed his eyes.

'Never the *Isabella*.' He crossed himself. 'Worst luck possible to name a new ship after a sunken one.'

'Then perhaps the *Candia*? It matters not to me. Like the Medici, the Mozzi, the Peruzzi and all the other avaricious nobles of Italia, my family are always open to a sound investment and, while I may not have direct control of the accounts, I have enough sway to accomplish such a transaction, I am sure, given time.'

He turned to Skiouros as they laboured up the slope of the hill between the tightly packed market stalls while still addressing those in front.

'I'm sure that whatever business we each have planned can be delayed long enough to secure such a thing, can it not?'

His eyebrows rose and Skiouros shrugged. He had been delayed in his murderous task for two months, pushed in the wrong direction and subjected to seemingly endless deprivation and pain. What might another week matter, especially if it were accompanied by taverns and comfortable beds? Besides, given his imminent vengeance, he could do with some time to work through ideas with Cesare. Perhaps they might even travel back to Genoa and the Palazzo Visconti with Parmenio and Nicolo if they could secure a ship? It would delay their parting a little longer and save his anguish for a time.

'Good,' Cesare announced. 'Then let us seek the Medici house. I will draw a small fund for living expenses and then remain to negotiate a larger investment sum while the three of you take our funds, locate a good tavern, a tailor, a cobbler and – most importantly – the bath house. You can then meet me at the nearest tavern to the church.'

The four friends smiled as they climbed the hill. The very thought of clean clothes and even cleaner skin was truly appealing – almost as appealing as wine and beef, a pretty tavern girl and a feather pillow. Nicolo was already shaking his hand with his wrist twisting, practicing his dice throwing.

The hill began to level out and the market stalls – which for the last hundred paces or so had been raised on brick piles to keep them level –

thinned out as they approached the heavy, featureless rear wall of the huge church, its thick brick buttresses strengthening the apsidal end above the slope.

'The square lies on the far side,' announced Parmenio. 'There are mercantile guilds and banks around it and in the nearby streets, along with a couple of the palaces of the wealthy and the main approach to the castle. As soon as we...'

Parmenio's sentence dropped off sharply and at the back of the line Skiouros looked up in interest to see what had halted his friend's conversation so suddenly.

His stomach turned over and his heart froze in his chest at the sight of the half dozen Turkish officers who had rounded the church corner from the far side and were face to face with Parmenio across at most thirty paces of roadway.

The older officer with the grey beard Skiouros did not recognise, nor three of the others, two of whom were clearly lower-ranking sailors.

But Etci Hassan and his homunculus...

Skiouros fought the urge to turn and bolt back down the hill. Such a move would be ridiculous. They were in a good Christian town and the Turks were no friends of Spain. Surely they would not be so foolish as to...

'You!' bellowed Hassan in a voice that carried a fury with a keen edge and the weight of generations of jihad. Mehmi, next to him, jumped slightly, a look falling across his face that was a strange mix of disbelief and outright panic.

The senior Turk with the grey beard turned in surprise.

'You know these men, Hassan?'

Parmenio seemed frozen to the spot, uncertain whether to run, shout for help or draw his blade.

'These are the filth that wounded me. Pirates!' Hassan denounced, spitting at them. 'They attacked the *Yarim Ay* and attempted to sink us. We were lucky to make the rendezvous!'

Skiouros blinked at the ridiculous bold-faced lie.

'These sorry creatures challenged *you*?' the older Turk said with an element of disbelief.

Hassan shoved Mehmi on the shoulder. 'I will keep them here. You will go back to the river and rouse the men.'

'You will do *no such thing!*' snapped the old man. Mehmi moved from foot to foot in panic, his eyes rolling like a distressed horse as he struggled with conflicting commands.

'I think it is time for us to depart,' muttered Cesare, taking a step sideways towards a gap in the stalls that would lead him around the rear of the church.

Skiouros could not agree more.

The young Greek watched in disbelief as Etci Hassan drew his sword – the musket over his shoulder would take too long to load, but the blade…

'Run!' shouted Orsini from the dubious safety of the market stalls.

The word cut through their indecision and confusion, and a moment later, Parmenio, Nicolo and Skiouros were after him, ducking into the gap between the stalls.

Hassan made to follow, but was surprised to feel a hand clamp down on his shoulder.

'Let go of me,' he snarled.

Kemal Reis fixed the lesser captain with his own almost fatherly eyes which carried even now a look of paternal admonishment.

'May I remind you that we are here under the sufferance of the Duke of Medina Sidonia and as guests of the Spanish Crown. We have almost concluded the negotiations for the release of dozens of good men whose very lives are in our hands, and you draw your blade *in public*? Are you out of your mind, Hassan?'

'I say once more, let go of me or I will take off your hand, you impotent, wizened, Jew-loving old goat!'

All elements of fatherliness were swept from Kemal's gaze with the words and Hassan wrenched himself from his commander's grasp, stepping two paces down the slope and turning, pointing his drawn blade threateningly at the old captain.

At that moment their Spanish escort, who had been only paces behind in the square, some laxity having crept into their duty with the monotony of the task, swept around the corner and realised that their charges – who had been allowed to stray too far ahead for comfort – were bearing arms.

'Halt!' their captain shouted, drawing his own Spanish rapier. The soldiers with him followed suit, some drawing blades, the others levelling their pikes.

Mehmi stared in horror at what was going on around him: his captain, threatening death to a senior captain of the Sultan's navy; the dozen guards drawing and levelling their own weapons to move against them; the great Kemal Reis wearing an unprecedented expression of utter outrage. The diminutive sailor's eyes darted for a second to the market stalls. *And*, of course, the four cursed ex slaves.

None of them had been wearing priest's robes, but that no longer mattered. He knew them by sight, and he knew that the taciturn one at the rear was the witch himself – the black priest who had almost ruined them all. A rock and a hard place did not come close to describing the situation.

'Mehmi!' barked Hassan. 'Come!'

And with that the rogue Turk was descending the hill after his fleeing quarry, his gait made strange and unstable by his limp – an ever present reminder of the men who had defied him.

Behind them, Salih Bin Abdullah was desperately trying to talk down the guards, who were moving towards them threateningly, assuring them in his best Spanish that they meant no harm. 'Look! Our blades are sheathed! This man is mad. Let *us* handle him.' Platitudes and pleas that were falling on deaf ears. Three Spaniards grasped the great Kemal and held his arms tight, jerking them behind his back. Along with him, the senior captain's second in command was also restrained. Others moved on to Salih and his companion. The younger of the two remaining captains turned to his second and pointed down the hill after Hassan, hoping the man was up to the task.

'Go, Cingeneler. Stop that lunatic.'

Even as guards grabbed Salih's arms and the captain bellowed for more members of the city watch, Salih's second in command nodded and broke into a run, following Hassan and Mehmi into the market stalls.

Kemal, his arms painfully restrained, looked at Salih.

'You warned me time and again, my friend. Sadly, my ears were clogged with misplaced trust. I am so sorry.' He looked across at the angry faces of the guards who held him.

'Tell them I submit without hesitation and will do whatever I can to help them take Hassan.'

But there was little more that could be done.

It was in the hands of Allah now.

Chapter Twenty One - Of escape and evasion

The stalls went by in a blur of white canvas, crates, baskets, copper pots, sacks of goods and the bronze colour of the late evening sun. Somewhere on the hillside Skiouros had found himself at the front of the fleeing foursome instead of the rear where he had begun, the two sailors built for stamina and strength rather than speed, and hampered a little further by the decade and a half they had on the Greek, and Orsini slowed by his unhealed leg wound.

No one had set a destination for their escape. The simple mechanics of unanticipated flight had taken them directly away from Hassan by the most direct route, which meant straight back downhill away from the church. Indeed, once they were among the stalls and running, it had occurred to Skiouros that perhaps matters could have been resolved with the aid of the old captain and without the need to flee, but the fact remained that it was too late now. They had run. And Skiouros knew full well that Hassan the Butcher would not have let them live, no matter his position, so perhaps it had been for the best.

Rounding a corner, Skiouros narrowly avoided collision with a stall owner carrying an armful of baskets. Apologising pointlessly in a language the man would be unlikely to comprehend, Skiouros scooted past him, ducked around another stall, and emerged, surprised, at the riverbank.

As the other three slowly arrived behind him Skiouros looked this way and that, his head cocked and his ears picking out what detail he could from the overall din. A decade of surviving on his wits in the

229

world's greatest city had given him a keen sense of hearing, particularly in relation to the chase and evasion.

Three Turkish voices emerged as threads from the tapestry of sound that was Palos in its last flurry of the day's activity. One: Etci Hassan, bellowing orders to his lessers; and not just Mehmi, from the phrases – cut them off... secure the dock... do not let them escape. The second voice was Mehmi. Skiouros knew those oily tones well enough. Mehmi sounded unhappy, but was relaying his commander's orders to some unseen group – presumably the crewmen he had mentioned by the river. The third voice was an unknown, but clearly not the target of Hassan's commands, given that his own bellowed words were orders for Hassan to cease his chase. It occurred to Skiouros once again that with some sort of division among the Turks, they might not have needed to have fled if they could only have determined who might be friendly. But now there was no hope. Even though it seemed they might have friendlies among the Turks, there simply was not time to unweave that tapestry and determine which threads went against the warp. If the past two months had taught them anything it was not to underestimate Etci Hassan Reis.

'Where now?' Cesare asked as he lurched out from the market, his bad leg shaking with the effort of the run. He was coping well with the flight, but Skiouros could see the effort he was expending simply to stay upright on that weak leg. There was not a lot more run left in him.

Skiouros' head snapped back and forth once more, taking stock of the situation. The dock-side proper was thronged with people loading the last boats of the day and offered a certain anonymity and the possibility of vanishing among the crowd. The other way – downstream – was clear, barring three wide boats pulled up on the gravel of the shore. His eyes narrowed as he picked out the detail of those boats. Two of good polished dark wood, well-cared for and plain, barring a little gilded embellishment at the bow. The third was red and black.

'The dock!' Skiouros said, even as the detachment of Turks left to guard their boats burst out of the maze of stalls next to the boats, less than twenty yards downstream, weapons drawn in response to Hassan's bellowed commands that rang out across the market. Even as the other three turned and ran, heading for the dock, Skiouros saw the Turks spot them and burst into renewed activity, racing along the riverbank. Behind them, three Spanish soldiers emerged, shouting angrily at the foreigners bearing arms in malice in their city, but staying far enough back from the corsair force that outnumbered them four-to-one so as not to engage them prematurely. Suicide was clearly not on the guards' agenda, so they were of little use to Skiouros.

The young Greek turned to follow his friends, just in time to come face to face with two more Turks who burst from between a set of stalls into his path, sealing off his escape. Skiouros watched his friends beyond the two men, running and unaware of his peril. Arresting his paltry momentum, he whipped the curved blade from his pack, allowing the rest of his meagre worldly goods to fall to the ground, where they rolled gently into the edge of the water and were tugged at by the current until finally whisked away.

The curved blade still felt unfamiliar in his hands and Skiouros felt the irony of being a European, trained with a Spanish rapier and standing in a city where those blades were the norm but bearing an Arabic sword. Despite his unfamiliarity, his practiced and almost professional grip clearly alerted the two Turks and they straightened and came to a complete halt, sizing him up.

Skiouros looked over his shoulder. He had a matter of mere heartbeats before he was caught between these two and their friends back along the river, and then the matter would be resolved in a bloody end.

Desperately, he tried to effect the 'hanging point' guard, raising his blade so that it arced down forward from above his forehead, with his arms crossed at the wrist. It looked different from the many times he had practiced it in the courtyard with Don Diego, but that was the simple matter of the curved blade. His positioning was spot-on, and he knew it.

'Come on then, ass-for-a-mouth,' he snapped in Turkish. Of all the many insults he knew – and had practiced – in his years in Istanbul, that particular one had never failed to raise a response.

This occasion was no different, judging by the ire in the Turk corsair's twisted expression.

Goaded, the two Turks attacked, the one to the left lunging forward with his blade, while his companion swept his sword in a slicing stroke at Skiouros' side. From his perfect defensive guard, Skiouros twitched his hands and knocked the lunge harmlessly aside, bringing the blade across to block the swipe in the same swift move. As both sailors recovered from their failed attacks, Skiouros uncrossed his wrists, the simple action bringing his curved blade around in a wide swing, biting into the hip of the man who had sliced at him. The sailor shrieked and staggered back, his leg ruined and useless, blood slicking down his thigh.

231

With no time to effect any other clever guard of Don Diego's teaching, Skiouros fell instead to his natural instincts and the basic methods of defence taught him by Iannis. The second man was faster in his recovery than Skiouros could have anticipated, his blade whipping back again and then forth at the Greek like a snake striking. Skiouros barely managed to get his blade in the way and turn the blow aside, himself staggering wrong-footed.

He knew this moment for what it was. So often in his bouts with Don Diego he would manage to stay in control of the fight, utilising the appropriate guards and strikes, but sooner or later he would falter. Something would take him by surprise and he would fail to recover, and from there it had always been a slippery slope to destruction and humiliation at the tip of the Spaniard's sword.

He was lucky indeed that as he ducked panicking to the side, he spotted – in the blink of an eye and reflected in his opponent's blade – a Turk behind him approaching with a raised sword. Allowing himself to stagger further aside than necessary, he barely avoided being skewered in the back by the new arrival.

Now he was in real trouble. Two men was a challenge, but a dozen was an impossibility. His eyes flicked up to try and determine where his friends had got to, but he had neither the time nor the freedom to search the shoreline for them. Instead, he spun, his hastily raised blade clattering off three swords of the group of sailors coming from behind. Something sliced through the air by his ribs and he felt the sharp edge grate across his flesh, barely grazing him, but leaving a hot, wet line.

Desperately, he turned once again, just in time to knock aside another blow.

He was clinging onto life by the fingernails and he knew it. He'd managed to stop them sticking him so far, but more through luck than judgement, and the constant flailing to defend himself left him no time to actually try and deal with one of them.

Another spin and more blades.

A line of fire drawn with a razor edge along his knuckles.

More blades.

A pain in the shoulder.

The ring of steel on steel.

A sharp pain in the calf.

Turning back…

His eyes widened as his original assailant's grinning head slid slowly from his shoulders, bouncing off the shoulder of the wounded kneeling man who clutched his ruined hip. Skiouros stared at the headless body, an arterial jet pumping into the air where his head had been.

A Turkish officer in a fine crimson jacket and hat – one of those he'd seen on the hill, he thought – drew back his dripping blade.

'Go,' he snapped, glaring at Skiouros and then shifting his attention to the advancing pirates, eying them warily.

The young Greek needed no further inducement. His legs propelled him towards the dock, out of the reach of the various blades coming at him from behind. Even as he ran, he realised that his unlikely saviour had disappeared off among the stalls. The officer had saved his life, but had only bought him a little time in the grand scheme, as the rest were now on his trail again, brandishing swords and baying for blood. Clearly the single Turk had no intention of dying at the hands of his countrymen, and who could blame him for that.

The other three had stopped at the edge of the dock and were looking back at the martial activity, concerned. As Orsini spotted Skiouros out front at last, he alerted the others, pointing back along the riverbank, then at the Turks following him.

Skiouros' ears picked up another shout from the market and he realised that Hassan and Mehmi were cutting across towards the dock, cutting off his escape route. The others seemed not to have noticed but at any moment the belligerent pirate would emerge from the market almost on their position, possibly with more men.

Skiouros felt his spirits sink.

The three of them had halted to allow him to catch up, but Skiouros also knew how much they needed to rest. Parmenio and Nicolo were out of breath, as evidenced by the fact that they stood with their hands on their knees, heaving in deep lungfuls of air. Orsini leaned against a mooring post to save the strength in his injured leg.

It didn't take Skiouros long to take stock of what was happening.

The town was in uproar high on the hill, officials and guards yelling, soldiers' pikes flashing in the sun near the church and above the market. There would be a couple of men on the dock, probably, but not many – just enough to watch for trouble. The three Spanish soldiers who had chased the Turkish sailors out to the riverbank were now themselves under attack. In all, there were guards here and there, but not enough and in too small a concentration to be of any real benefit to Skiouros and his friends. Conversely, there were the best part of two dozen angry Turks converging on them. The four of them could fight, but not against that many and, with the weariness and weakness of the others, Skiouros would have to carry the lion's share of the fight, which he knew was beyond his ability.

His eyes scoured the crowd beside which his three friends stood.

The large skiff next to them had a strake that was painted in white and red and bore the inscription *Orgoglio Genovese*. Genoese pride. The boat was almost loaded to the brim with goods, but there was just about room for a few men. The sailors were busy untying the lines.

Skiouros felt his future – his destiny – slipping away from him, like a man hanging over a drop, trying to grip a slippery sill with numb fingers. That boat – that ship – could carry him to where he needed to go, along with his friends. But the sailors were leaving and if Skiouros tried to reach them and join them, he would simply bring all the Turks who were converging on the dock right to them.

What had that damn Romani said a lifetime ago in Crete? Selfishness. And he had proven that to be true – despite his hopes to the contrary – when he had attempted to flee in Tunis and leave them to their fate. He had told himself then: never again. Never again would he put his own good over that of his friends.

'Climb aboard!' he yelled.

His friends frowned in his direction and so Skiouros took a few loping strides forward, waving and pointing to the Genoese skiff. If the three of them made it aboard that ship, they would be free of the Turk.

'No!' Cesare shouted.

'Yes. Climb aboard!'

Orsini was shaking his head and Skiouros waved his arms, demanding they board and get to safety. He couldn't go with them without damning them all, but he could see the three of them safe first. He waved madly but suddenly his view of the others was blocked as Mehmi and Hassan burst out of the market to the riverside between Skiouros and his friends.

That sealed the matter. Nothing else for it now.

With a deep breath and a sad smile at the shapes of his friends in the distance behind the bellowing, furious corsair, Skiouros ducked back into the market and began to pound along the narrow ways between market stalls. Hassan and his second in command were immediately on the move.

As he ran up the slope, Skiouros could hear the bellowed commands and replies of Turks, moving back into the sprawling collection of stalls. He smiled to himself. That was perhaps his only remaining advantage: they had no idea he spoke their language – all barring the headless one by the river. He listened, training his hearing to the thick accent of the easterners among the Spaniards. There were sounds of local guards all over the place but, despite his incomprehension of their tongue, the locations suggested that they were creating some sort of perimeter to prevent the Turks escaping their grasp. Sensible in a way, but of little help to him right now. They would slowly move in, tightening the net until they trapped the Turks by the water, but that left the pirate crew plenty of time and space to deal with their fugitive in the market beforehand.

Within the Spanish net, the Turks were forming their own. The bellowed commands and answers spoke of men arcing round to both sides, curving in ahead to seal off his escape route, driving him back to the riverside. He could hear his doom being planned in the shouts. Ducking left between a stall displaying copperware and a wool merchant, he aimed for the one area he hoped would bring him some relief – an area with no Turkish command yet – but even as he angled towards that side of the slope he heard a voice bellowing from a new position up there. He was surrounded, and all the corsairs needed to do was move slowly into the centre to catch him.

Somewhere behind him down the slope, slowed by wounded foot and short stature respectively, Hassan and Mehmi were in pursuit. Despite the rabid hatred the captain bore Skiouros, and the man's clear skill with weapons, back downhill had become the sensible option – two men as opposed to two dozen. Clenching his teeth and shifting his sweaty, slippery grip on the sword hilt, Skiouros spun on his heel and headed back towards the shouts of the corsair captain.

Two stalls further back, he paused to listen to the shouts once more and as he did so, his eyes fell upon the stall's contents. The trader had his back to Skiouros, deep in discussion with a fellow merchant at the stall behind, and the former thief, despite his vows, offered up a quick apology to God as his hand dipped into the nearest sack. A cloud of white powder bloomed up into the warm air as he patted the fine flour onto his face and lower arms. The white dust clung to his damp skin, absorbing the sweat of his palm and securing his grip as he swapped hands again with the sword. The beads of sweat that trickled from his hairline, brought on by all the exertion, drew strange, pink-grey lines down through the white, giving his skin a streaky, mottled effect.

Half the battle in any encounter was surprise. How often in Istanbul had he avoided a direct confrontation simply by startling his opponent into inactivity long enough to escape?

Pale as ash and curiously streaked, he ran on, ignoring the angry shout of the trader who had noticed the cloud of flour.

Four stalls and two turns further on, he rounded a corner and came face to face with Mehmi.

The squat officer's eyes bulged as he beheld Skiouros.

The young Greek shifted his grip on the hilt in preparation, but Mehmi's sword dropped forgotten to his side as he sucked and spat, sucked and spat, his free hand coming up to pull at his earlobe so hard that Skiouros wondered if it might come off.

Thank God it was Mehmi and not Hassan. Skiouros knew full well that in a duel with the corsair captain, he would be dead in half a dozen traded blows. Grinning a rictus mask, Skiouros ducked into the next line of stalls and descended the hill. He would have precious seconds on the diminutive Turk now and when you were the hunted, seconds were more valuable than gold or jewels.

He could hear Mehmi one row over, still unmoving, chattering out a prayer to Allah to preserve him from witches and vengeful djinn. *Thank you God for making the imp so superstitious*!

Back down at the lower reach of the market slope now, he was moving towards the river bank. More shouts issued from Hassan close by, and the focus of the closing net of Turks shifted to centre on him, even as the net of Spaniards closed outside that.

A new hope began to grow in Skiouros' heart.

If he could reach the river bank ahead of Hassan and his men, perhaps he could get out to the river? Perhaps the *Genovese Pride*'s skiff had miraculously waited for him? Certainly, Cesare and the others would have tried to stop it leaving. Possibly they had not even gone themselves. But then, he realised that they had to have left. If they had remained ashore Hassan would have focused some of his attention on them, and some of the many calls would have involved them instead of focussing singly on him. Orsini had done as he was bade and they had left for the ship.

Still, perhaps he could get there himself.

Puffing and panting, sweat carrying white paste into the corner of his eyes, Skiouros burst out of the clutter of market stalls once more, emerging onto the riverbank almost at the dock. Though mere minutes had gone by, when he scoured the river for the Genovese skiff, he finally saw it being hauled aboard one of the carracks and no sign of his friends. Too late. Even now the Italian crew were bustling about, messing with lines and sails and all the myriad arcane tasks required to get a ship underway. With a visible effort, the anchor chain began to rise from the water.

A shout from away downriver to the left drew his attention momentarily. A corsair of the *Yarim Ay* moving along the shore path had spotted him and was calling out to his shipmates. A quick glance the other way confirmed that another had been alerted beyond the dock – the net closed all too rapidly. There was now no sign of the few officials and guards from the dock. Whether they had fled to some place of safety or fallen foul of Hassan's bloodthirsty crew, he could not guess, but whatever the case, they would be no help. Nor, clearly, would the local civilians – the myriad merchants, traders, labourers and citizens were judiciously ignoring all this fuss and the strange, white-faced man in their midst and staying out of the way of armed men, whatever their nationality.

His eyes fell upon another skiff, this one busy untying from a post a few yards from the end of the dock. The boat's top strake was painted in rich gold and green, and its crew – packed tightly within – were busy unshipping oars.

Jogging across the open riverside towards the boat, Skiouros watched more Turks arriving at the edge of the market, drawn faster by the cries of their shipmates.

He was pinned at the shore as the corsair net closed in. The guards were coming behind them, and very likely the Turks would be facing a number of charges from the local authorities. Spanish justice was infamous, though, for its venality. After decades of endless expense driving out the Moors, the new Spain of Fernando and Isabella would turn a blind eye to many things for appropriate recompense, or so Parmenio had vouchsafed more than once on their recent journey. Hassan and his fellow captains would have to pay heavily, but they would be free in the end.

None of this did Skiouros any good, of course. Skiouros, who would be dead of two dozen sword blows before ever a Spanish pike was levelled at the corsairs.

With a last look up and down, Skiouros tried to find another way out. Perhaps the Genovese ship had other skiffs heading back from shore.

No.

The day was drawing to a close as the sun lowered, turning the world to molten gold and as the light waned, so did all activity in the port. The ships would want their boats back aboard before dark, and the merchants would pack up their stalls any time now – many were already doing so.

There were now only three ship's boats left on the shore line. Two were half loaded and would still be here for at least a quarter of an hour. The other – the brightly painted one with a full crew – was already a few feet out, two oars being utilised to heave it away from the gravel and out into the current. The fishing boats were coming ashore, but they would be of no use. He had to go now and put his trust in a God that had, frankly, been a bit of a let-down so far.

'Look after them, Lord,' he muttered under his breath, his gaze falling on the Genovese carrack that was clearly using the last of the light to navigate its way out to the open sea, the busy river becoming less cluttered with every passing minute.

His eyes drifted back to the colourful boat. It was now out in the river and the men were lowering the oars, ready to take her back to the ship.

Sheathing his sword, Skiouros took three steps to his right and five back, to the edge of the market, where a man was packing away boxes.

'I must be insane.'

With a burst of speed, the young Greek exploded from the edge of the market, streaking across the narrow open stretch, and then leaping out from the gravel bank, his legs cycling as if to propel him as he arced relatively gracefully through the clear evening air.

Would that his landing was half as graceful as the jump!

Skiouros hit the skiff hard, the sternpost driving the breath from his lungs and his head glancing off the sheer strake, almost knocking the sense from him. All but unaware of his situation as his mind flashed and swam with pain, Skiouros felt little, and it was only as his wits started slowly to return to focus that he realised that he was being hauled aboard the ten-man boat by two of the sailors. Even before his vision properly returned, he recognised the pain in his chest and realised that he had broken at least one rib, if not two or more. His eyes flickered and he realised that what he had thought was sensory blindness was in fact caused by the sheet of blood through which he

238

looked, combined with the gluey wet flour. His head had taken a hefty cut as he landed and the flow had gone into his eyes.

One of the men yelled something at him, angrily, but it was in either Spanish or Portuguese, and he simply shrugged, wincing at the pain the move brought.

Rapidly, now, his wits were coming back to him.

He realised that the skiff was shaking and rocking and it took him a moment to come to the conclusion that it was his own unbalanced movements that were causing it. Clearly the angry sailor was trying to stop him capsizing the boat.

Skiouros steadied himself as best he could, though his mind was still whirling. Reaching up gingerly and slowly to put the least strain possible on his ribs, he wiped the blood from his eye, causing the boat to rock a little again.

It was a ten-man boat, judging by the seats, and already contained twelve. There was no seat for him – not even a space to crouch – and he would have to remain standing and maintain his balance.

Now he was almost fully compos mentis once again. His mind seemed to be linking things in the right order and performing the calculations asked of it. His body was more or less under control once again, too, though he constantly had to shift his balance to prevent himself falling overboard.

'Shit,' was all he could think of to say.

Gritting his teeth against the rising tide of pain in his chest and trying to keep enough equilibrium to prevent himself capsizing the boat, Skiouros turned to look ashore. The skiff was already halfway out across the river, between the bank and the great caravels sitting in the deepest water.

Turks were closing on the point opposite him from both sides, but two men in particular held his attention.

Mehmi stood, squat and square, watching him and fiddling with something, while Hassan next to him…

'Shit!' he said again as he watched the Butcher retrieve the ramrod from his musket and slam home the wadding and the ball in the barrel. In that horrible moment, Skiouros realised that he was standing perfectly still in a slow moving boat, with no hope of cover and easily in range of the weapon.

As Skiouros watched with rising panic, Hassan turned to Mehmi and held out his hand. The Greek could not hear the conversation, but it looked very much as though Mehmi was arguing with his captain. After a short, angry discussion, Mehmi capitulated and with steel and bloodstone struck sparks until the slow-match he was holding took light, smouldering and giving off a tendril of smoke.

Skiouros looked around at the faces of the sailors as they pulled on the oars. To a man they glowered at him in a most unfriendly manner, and a few of them muttered to one another in Spanish. Skiouros had the distinct feeling they were debating whether simply to throw him back in the river like an unwanted catch of the day, and he knew enough about swimming to recognise the danger inherent in attempting that swift current. Most likely he would drown long before reaching shore or before anyone else helped. He turned back to the river bank, aware that his safety aboard this small boat was precarious at best and rested on the whim of a number of unfriendly sailors with whom he could not exchange even the simplest of words. His hand went to his waist where he had a small pouch that he now remembered contained not a single coin. No buying their friendship, then. Next to the pouch, his hand fell upon the prayer rope. For some reason he had not relinquished it alongside the rest of his priestly garb. All he could do now was place his fate firmly in God's hands and hope for the best. He began to work around the rope with his fingers, casting up prayers to any God who might be listening.

On the shoreline, Mehmi handed the smouldering match to Hassan, who took it and pinned it in the jaws of the 'serpent' on his weapon before lifting the musket and settling it into position. Everything about the movements of Hassan suggested that he was a master at the weapon. Skiouros felt his heart skip a beat and he slowed his breath.

Closing his eyes, he listened out for the bang and wondered just how much he had offended God these past months.

Etci Hassan Reis settled the weapon against his shoulder and took aim. A musket was not a weapon for sailors and his ship only carried a few for the occasional land-based raids, but Hassan was a thorough man. He knew how to use half a dozen different blades, as well as pole arms and daggers. He could throw a knife with a reasonable level of accuracy and was better than many with a bow. He had also, though he rarely found cause to fire one, practiced with a matchlock musket until he was happy that he could hit even a difficult target three times in four.

240

The fake priest son of an infidel dog-woman who stood on the boat out on those waves was *not* a difficult target. Even Mehmi could hit him from here.

Hassan's attention wandered from his target just for a moment and his eye flashed to the diminutive officer by his side. He feared that Mehmi's time was coming to an end. He had been a faithful servant of both Hassan and of God and the Prophet for many, many years, but these past months the short, ugly man had seemed almost wilfully disobedient, often questioning or even gainsaying Hassan's orders. Well, no more. Once the bane of his recent life out on that boat was dying, clutching at the red-pink hole in his own face, Hassan would return to the *Yarim Ay*, sever his ties to the old man and put to sea, seeking plunder before returning to the praise and glory of the Sultan in Istanbul. No more fawning around an old greybeard who had less pride and mettle than a harem-bitch. Hassan would become the greatest captain of the Imperial Navy. A scourge of Christianity such as the world had never seen.

Again, he squinted down the barrel, his sight settling on that strangely mottled white pasty face which even now made his blood surge with fury.

Oh how he would like to take a musket ball to the face of every one of these jumped up djinn who thought so highly of themselves as they rabidly destroyed a Muslim nation that had stood proud for six centuries. Or better still, he would just wound them and bind them to the seats in their infidel church and then fire the building, crisping, cleansing and purifying everything within.

Hassan felt a sense of calm settle over him at the thought of such a glorious conflagration. Perhaps he might even sack this town before he left. Allah would preserve him until he was away from Spanish waters, he felt sure.

The tip of the barrel dropped and Hassan momentarily considered shooting the fake priest through the gut, giving him a few days or even weeks of agony to consider his sins before death took him. But no. There was always the faint possibility he might survive, as he had when Hassan had driven a blade through his side. And there was no small chance that Hassan would allow that to happen. The boy must die.

Again, the barrel came up so that the ball would be discharged directly at his face.

The slowmatch hissed in the serpent as it hovered above the pan full of black powder.

With a malicious smile, Hassan contracted his finger to squeeze the trigger.

His death took him so much by surprise that he stood, watching the Greek and waiting for that smug white face to explode in meat, blood and gristle, until he realised his musket barrel had dipped at that very last moment and the shot had gone horribly awry, the ball plunging into the Rio Tinto and disappearing into the deep.

Something had caused him to drop his shot. What was it again?

Etci Hassan turned to his faithful Mehmi.

Or at least, he tried to...

His body seemed not to work properly. He paused and listened to the symphony of his body. His heart was erratic, hammering out beats with no sense of time or rhythm. As he listened, the beating stopped altogether and he felt sure that had to be a good thing after the strange erratic hammering.

He looked down at Mehmi, standing squat and grim, as ugly and sour as ever, but with a look of profound regret and sadness on that wicked face. Hassan's cold grey eyes fell to the beautiful ornate silver dagger in Mehmi's hand that ran with crimson, droplets of blood falling to the dusty ground.

Blood?

And no heartbeat.

'I am most profoundly sorry, my Reis,' said Mehmi quietly, 'but this had to end.'

Hassan opened his mouth to rebuke the little homunculus, but all that came out was a gobbet of blood.

The riverfront erupted into activity as the crew of the *Yarim Ay* rushed to their two officers, stunned. Hassan wondered for a moment whether they would kill Mehmi for what he had done. He wondered why Mehmi had done such a thing. And he wondered why in this final moment, Allah and the Prophet – all blessings be upon him – had abandoned him?

It was the last thing he ever wondered, as his face hit the dirt and the light of jihad faded in his strange grey gaze to be replaced with the peace of the dead.

Mehmi shook his head.

All this over one priest...

Epilogos

Evening, August 3rd 1492. Rio Tinto, Spain

Cesare Orsini returned to the stern rail of the *Orgoglio Genovese*, rubbing his hands in a business-like fashion.

'The captain's satisfied, then?' Parmenio sighed as he leaned on the rail with folded arms.

'I don't know about satisfied, but he *has* agreed to take us as far as their first stop at Malaga in two days' time. If I cannot withdraw funds from a Medici banking house there, we may find ourselves at the short end of Genoese justice, but that should not be a problem. From there, I suggest you two accompany me to Genoa.'

'Strange the paths down which life takes you,' Parmenio mused.

The three men stood at the rail and watched the town of Palos – all twinkling lights in the indigo evening – slip away upriver. The vague shapes of the other ships in the channel were still visible, slowly making their own way back out to sea. All three of them had watched from the deck of the *Genoese Pride*, their hearts in their mouths, as Skiouros leapt across to the boat, as Hassan took aim and died there on the shore at the hand of his own man. They had watched Skiouros, standing in strange, slightly concussed shock as the skiff took him across to the smallest of three vessels moored close together – the *San Teodoro* according to the man who'd been standing nearby, though nicknamed '*The Painted*' by the locals for its elaborate green and gold decoration.

Parmenio cleared his throat and gestured to a sailor a few yards away who was busy tightening a rope in its cleat. 'Where are they bound?' he

243

asked, pointing at the trio of vessels. The sailor looked around at the last minute passengers aboard ship and shrugged.

'For the Islas Canarias, around the coast of Africa. Then on to the Indies, or so I hear.'

'Long trip.'

'Too long for any sensible sailor. Genoa's just fine with me.'

The man finished with his rope and moved on about his work, leaving the three men alone.

'Do you think there's a chance of getting him back aboard this ship?' Parmenio sighed.

'We're bound through the Pillars of Hercules and back towards Italia,' Nicolo answered quietly. 'He's heading south and west into the ocean. Not much chance of that.'

'Do you think he'll be alright?' Parmenio found that he already felt guilty having left the boy on the dock. He had voiced his opposition to leaving, but Orsini had pointed out that Skiouros had put himself in dreadful danger in order to keep them safe and to turn his noble gesture into a futile one was unworthy. Nicolo had hustled them aboard the boat with his usual casual expediency. Skiouros knew what he was doing, Orsini felt sure. Parmenio was less convinced. It felt as though he had betrayed a boy who had become something akin to a favoured nephew over the past two years.

He sighed.

Cesare peered out into the purple evening as the *Orgoglio Genovese* swung slowly to the east, watching the two caravels and the leading carrack, resplendent in their red and white sails with the cross of Saint George, as they manoeuvred from the river out towards the Gulf of Cadiz.

'I am almost positive Skiouros will be fine. I don't think he was ready yet for what he has to do, and God watches over him. Possibly more than *one* God.'

Parmenio glanced guiltily about to make sure they were not being listened to. Phrases like that were dangerous in the rabid Catholic world of Spain.

'Will we ever see him again?'

Cesare turned to his friends, a wide grin on his face. 'Of that I am certain... at the Palazzo Visconti in Genoa, I suspect. Something looms in our friend's future and I think we are a part of it now. But we have a few months' grace, I think, to try and piece together what we know of Skiouros, son of Nikos, and determine whose bitter fate it is that drives our friend.'

The other two turned frowns of incomprehension on their companion, and Cesare Orsini smiled.

'I play games with observation, and I have observed a number of things about our young friend. We have a fortnight and more of journey ahead of us before we make landfall in Genoa, and that gives us plenty of time to talk and plan. Let us find a friendly crewman who knows the way to the wine stores and I will tell you of my conversation at Tugga and what I know so far of a pair of Greek brothers who fell foul of an Ottoman conspiracy. It's a long tale, but we seem to have the time on our hands.'

END

Author's Historical Note

While writing *The Thief's Tale*, which was originally intended as a one-off novel, it quickly became apparent that there would be more to the story of Skiouros than fit in the scope of that book. By the time I had written the word 'END' on *The Thief's Tale*, I already had the very bare bones of the other two books in the series planned out in my head. By the time the first novel hit the e-shelves, I even had the titles for them.

The simple fact was that it was clear the story was not over. Lykaion's head rested in exile in Crete, his disembodied ghost plaguing Skiouros. The man who was at the very centre of the plot that killed him remained alive, in captivity certainly, but very luxurious captivity and with the potential to cause further mayhem. Skiouros would never settle until Prince Cem was gone and Lykaion returned to his rightful place.

Moreover, Skiouros had changed by the end of the first book – he had promised to renounce his thieving ways. What lay ahead for him, then? He was still very young, at the mercy of the events surrounding him. Such a young, relatively naïve, man could hardly hope to hunt down and destroy the great Ottoman usurper, and so Skiouros had to grow. He had to change and to learn. He had to become part of something rather than a solitary creature.

The result is this book, which is – to use my own comparison when reviewing others – the *Empire Strikes Back* of my Star Wars trilogy. It is about growth and change and becoming. It is still reactive, rather than proactive, in the same manner as the first book, with Skiouros plunged from one disaster to the next, but it is also a fulcrum for the overall tale. Occasionally in this story, hopefully, you have seen something of what Skiouros could be.

The scope of this novel has clearly expanded way beyond the first book, which took place over around a week and all in one city. Here, we have explored the Medieval Mediterranean, from the Greek east by the Arab south to the Spanish west. As a visitor to – and lover of – Crete, Tunisia and Spain, the opportunity to revisit them in my head in their old days was a great lure.

And, of course, certain events called me. Having left the story in Crete in 1491 and involving sailors, it was somewhat difficult to imagine a sequel that did not involve another group of sailors who set sail in 1492 from southern Spain in search of a new route to the Indies...

Oh come on! You got that, yes? *The Painted*? *The Pinta*?

With his 25 companions, Skiouros has set sail on one of the greatest adventures in the history of the later Medieval world.

A few notes on characters and religion and places may be valid here.

Parmenio and Nicolo had always been intended to carry over into this book. They had too little limelight in the first, I think, and we can see that they will likely have a role in book three when the time comes. So, Skiouros and his two Venetian sailor friends were a given. Cesare Orsini was a character in flux. In early drafts of the plan, the role was played by a female! But also, he was not originally planned to remain in the book throughout, but to leave partway through so that he could return in the third. If I have to make honest admission, the main reason he stayed 'til the end was that I really enjoyed writing Orsini. For those of you wondering why as yet there is a distinct lack of female characters in the series, it is not misogynistic leanings, but rather an attempt to recreate a more realistic world. Female characters can be strong and influential in this era, but generally not aboard ships or in the world of corsairs and merchants. The Tuareg lady was my nod in that direction, but given what you suspect will come in book three, you can see where the potential for more female characters lies.

1492 is a little early in truth for the great Ottoman pirates – or the Barbary Corsairs as they would become known. They were certainly operating on a very small scale in the eastern Med, but there were still a couple of decades to go before the heyday of the infamous Barbarossa and the Barbary Coast (the dreadful pirate himself was only 14 at this time.) Soon, though, the world would shake to the cannon of the Ottoman pirates. To the Empire they were still military personnel – they retained ranks, and Barbarossa himself was an admiral! But their sanctioned piratical activity on the enemies of the state earned them a place in the history of violence.

Here we see an early sprouting of that situation. Kemal Reis (one of few true characters in this novel) was an honourable naval man who led a doomed expedition to save Granada. Of his lesser captains little is known, and certainly Etci Hassan – the Butcher – is fictional, though I feel he is very indicative of a surprisingly large proportion of the Ottoman navy of the era. I will say little more of the characters for fear of spoilers for the next book, but suffice it to say that Kemal Reis impresses me.

In exploring characters for this book I have learned more than I ever thought I would about piracy and the 15th-century navy. I have learned much about Turkish superstitions and about religions.

The religious aspect of the book is, needless-to-say, a central thread.

With Skiouros still in his guise as an Orthodox priest from the end of the first book, the story fell together quite easily, but would require something of an exploration of the religions involved. Of course, as we all know there are vastly more similarities between Catholicism, Orthodoxy and even Islam than there are differences. If is not difficult to see how a man thrust into a mix of them all might come to understand multiple viewpoints. The fact that the Tuareg of the time still managed to mix their traditional pagan beliefs with Islam shows that such a thing is possible, and if that peculiar mix is possible (witness also the combination of Voodoo with Catholicism in Haiti) then it should not be too much to expect a man surrounded by the major religions to find a way to combine them in a similar fashion. You may find something odd in Skiouros' attitude to them, yet you must remember that he was brought up in the Orthodox Church within a predominantly Muslim nation that permitted freedom of worship at that time. An understanding of both is, I think, natural and to be expected. Plus, of course, there's a third book to go! *Touches side of nose in surreptitious manner.*

Of course, this book is not meant to glorify or vilify any religion or nation, any more than the first was. It is a tale of ordinary men and wicked men, but men nonetheless. The Islamic world is perhaps cast under a pall here due to the mind and actions of Etci Hassan, but one must remember the noble activity of Kemal Reis too, as well as the Muslim Tuareg. Equally, Cesare is clearly a Catholic, but no lover of the Pope. People are people.

As anyone who has read my books before has probably noticed, location is important to me. Location is what provides most of the atmosphere in a tale, and places I have visited and can see in my mind's eye are more likely to come across well in writing. Hopefully this shows in places such as Crete, Tunisia and Spain. The one hardship is trying to strip away half a millennium of civilisation from these places to see how they would have looked in 1492. Fortunately, I find that almost as fascinating as the history itself.

Little remains now but to thank you again for reading (I figure if you got this far, you probably enjoyed it).

Skiouros has been a Thief.

He has been a Priest.

Skiouros will return in *The Assassin's Tale*.

Simon Turney, July 2013

If you liked this book, why not try other titles by S.J.A. Turney

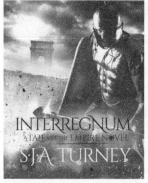

Interregnum (Tales of the Empire 1)

(2009) *

For twenty years civil war has torn the empire apart; the imperial line extinguished as the mad Emperor Quintus burned in his palace, betrayed by his greatest general. Against a background of war, decay, poverty and violence, men who once served in the proud imperial army now fight as mercenaries, hiring themselves to the greediest lords. On a hopeless battlefield that same general, now a mercenary captain tortured by the events of his past, stumbles across hope in the form of a young man begging for help. Kiva is forced to face more than his dark past as he struggles to put his life and the very empire back together. The last scion of the imperial line will change Kiva forever.

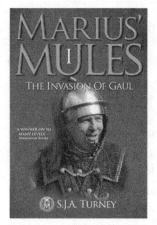

Marius' Mules I: The Invasion of Gaul

(2009) *

It is 58 BC and the mighty Tenth Legion, camped in Northern Italy, prepares for the arrival of the most notorious general in Roman history: Julius Caesar. Marcus Falerius Fronto, commander of the Tenth is a career soldier and long-time companion of Caesar's. Despite his desire for the simplicity of the military life, he cannot help but be drawn into intrigue and politics as Caesar engineers a motive to invade the lands of Gaul. Fronto is about to discover that politics can be as dangerous as battle, that old enemies can be trusted more than new friends, and that standing close to such a shining figure as Caesar, the most ethical of men risk being burned.

* Sequels in both series also available now.

Other recommended works set in the Byzantine & Medieval worlds:

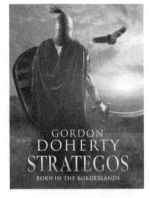

Strategos - Born in the Borderlands

by Gordon Doherty (2011)

When the falcon has flown, the mountain lion will charge from the east, and all Byzantium will quake. Only one man can save the empire . . . the Haga! 1046 AD. The Byzantine Empire teeters on full-blown war with the Seljuk Sultanate. In the borderlands of Eastern Anatolia, a land riven with bloodshed and doubt, young Apion's life is shattered in one swift and brutal Seljuk night raid. Only the benevolence of Mansur, a Seljuk farmer, offers him a second chance of happiness. Yet a hunger for revenge burns in Apion's soul, and he is drawn down a dark path that leads him right into the heart of a conflict that will echo through the ages.

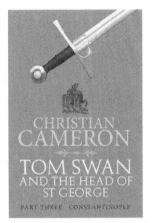

Tom Swan and the Head of St George

eBook series by Christian Cameron (2012)

1450s France. A young Englishman, Tom Swan, is kneeling in the dirt, waiting to be killed by the French who've taken him captive.

He's not a professional soldier. He's really a merchant and a scholar looking for remnants of Ancient Greece and Rome - temples, graves, pottery, fabulous animals, unicorn horns. But he also has a real talent for ending up in the midst of violence when he didn't mean to. Having used his wits to escape execution, he begins a series of adventures that take him to street duels in Italy, meetings with remarkable men - from Leonardo Da Vinci to Vlad Dracula - and from the intrigues of the War of the Roses to the fall of Constantinople.

Made in the USA
Las Vegas, NV
24 June 2024

91446527R00152